About the Author

I0594432

INGRID FRY was born and raised in Berkhamstead in the UK, but spent much of her childhood commuting with her family between England and Austria. Emigrating with her parents to Melbourne, Australia many years ago, she has called Australia home ever since.

A business development consultant, writer and minder of a husband and a beagle with superpowers, she lives in a leafy suburb on the outskirts of Melbourne. Lakes Entrance is her second home, and it was from there, much of the Crystal Sphere series was developed.

In her spare time, Ingrid enjoys pistol shooting at the local gun club, dancing her socks off at The Caravan Music Club, and is a passionate karate nerd, well on her way to a black belt in karate. Ingrid models the belief that it is never too late to achieve your dreams, and age is definitely just a number.

You can find out more information about Ingrid via her website www.ingridfry.com.au
Email: Ingrid@ingridfry.com.au

Other Books
by
Ingrid Fry

Crystal Sphere Series

Descent into Darkness
Journey to Hell
Quest for Light
Search for Truth
Battle for Blood (forthcoming)

This is a work of fiction. Names, characters and events are the products of the author's imagination. Any resemblance to actual persons, living or dead, or actual events is purely coincidental.

Content Warning: The Crystal Sphere Series is intended for mature readers and contains sexual situations, violence, and other representations that may cause some readers distress. Please prepare accordingly.

Copyright © 2020 Ingrid Fry

All rights reserved.

National Library of Australia Cataloguing-in-Publication entry:
Creator: Fry, Ingrid, author.
Title: Descent into Darkness: Crystal Sphere Book 1
/ Fry, Ingrid.

ISBN: 978-0-6486816-1-8

Tale Publishing
Melbourne, Australia

Tale

Acknowledgements

Thank you first and foremost to my parents, whose love and talent for writing inspired me to become a pen monkey too. I'm sad they can't be here to witness the outcome of their love and encouragement. Well, perhaps that's not such a bad thing — the content may have shocked them!

Then there's the Melbourne astrologer who prepared my chart all those years ago. I've forgotten her name, but not her prediction. She looked closely at my chart, and said, '... it is extremely clear, your destiny is either a nun, or a writer.' Option two was definitely the path of preference for me (although sometimes as a writer, one can feel as cloistered as a nun).

The Australian Writers Centre online courses provided me with the skills to get started whilst juggling work and ill parents, and Carl Lakeland, Author — who I met through AWC — for his generous advice and encouragement. All the folk at The Monash Writers Group for their support and inspiration, and to Writers Victoria for their resources and assistance.

To my wonderful editor, Kathryn Moore, whose attention to detail and editing skills improved my writing, and Dmetri Kakmi, whose manuscript assessment, generous editing and genuine delight in my book gave me the encouragement to keep going.

Thank you to Robert New from Tale Publishing for believing in me and my books and for giving me the opportunity to be a part of the Tale Publishing journey.

To my muse, Maggie, our beagle cross, who listens patiently and with fascination as I read aloud, and my wonderful, supportive friends, in particular Cate Hutchings, Christine Chandler and my #1 beta reader, Cheryl Hutchinson.

Finally, to Bruce, my biggest fan. Thank you. Always.

For my parents, Margaret and William,
whose own lives were an epic, action adventure,
my husband, Bruce, and our beloved Bindi the Beagle — the
inspiration for
The Crystal Sphere Series

Follow Maggie's music playlist on Spotify!

Type *all* of the following ridiculously long code
into the Spotify search bar:

spotify:user:z s 8 x y x p x z b t 1 m j c i r 5 9 q z 1 j z w

Click the Follow Button for Crystal Sphere

Chapter 1: The Encounter

'But evil shall come upon you, which you will not know how to charm away; disaster shall fall upon you, for which you will not be able to atone; and ruin shall come upon you suddenly, of which you know nothing.' — Isaiah 47:11

I knew things were seriously wrong with the world when a piece of furniture started eating my arm.

I mean, things had never been what you'd call normal in my world—given the state of my brain an' all—but when that incident occurred I knew the descent into darkness had begun.

The bombardment had always been constant. I'd tried to ignore it, shut it out, meditate, exercise, turn down my chakras, visualise, drink, take drugs. Nothing worked as well as music, computer games, counting things, and sex.

I seemed to have been born like a big antenna. A receiving station for every thought form, spiritual visitation, psychic flotsam and jetsam plus a whole pile of other scary stuff. Blocking it out used a lot of energy, but I'd got better at it over time. Animals helped to keep me sane. And Jason.

Home helped too. It was our safe haven in the 'burbs. I loved our house. We'd made it beautiful inside and out. Every window had a view of greenery and something artful to lift your spirits. Inside everything felt right. It was simple, stylish, with good feng shui. People liked being in our house; it radiated good energy. Boo, our dog, loved the surrounding parks. We could walk for hours through the bush and often did. Sometimes I could forget we were only thirty minutes from the city.

On the evening everything changed, the lights were low and Jason sat with Boo on a rug in front of the fire. They stared into the flames, a perfect picture of peace and contentment.

I pressed my hands hard against my skull and tried to shut out the world's psychic energy. 'Walk?' I asked Boo.

Boo's head flicked around so fast it was surprising her neck didn't snap. The magic word did it every time.

She was half beagle, half cocker spaniel. Perhaps more beagle, with the long soft ears and big brown eyes. Boo jumped to her feet and spun around in excited circles.

'I need to clear my head, Jason. Won't be long.'

'Want me to come?'

He knew the answer already.

'No, I'll be fine. Got my phone in case I need you.'

'See you.'

I loved the dark streets. The energy at night felt more subdued. Dad used to enjoy our 'crepuscular walks', as he called them—that special twilight time. He'd vanished Christmas Day twelve months ago after giving me a handmade wooden trunk. He took a walk after lunch and never came back.

He was an astrophysicist. Everyone affectionately called him 'The Prof' as he was always writing a paper on one thing or another. I missed his love and eccentric brilliance.

I'd tried reaching out for him with my mind. My psychic abilities were strong, but with Dad, I got nothing. It was as though he'd completely disappeared from earth and the other side. There was only silence, a vacuum where his energy had been. That scared me.

I tried again, reaching into the ether with my senses. Still nothing. A void.

My throat thickened and tears pricked my eyes.

Boo stopped and stared at me. As I shut down my senses, I sensed a lick of darkness in my mind, something strange. I physically shook my head to try and dislodge the feeling. Boo shook her head too.

'Let's go,' I said.

A sense of unease played around in my mind. Would I lose it like Mum had? I'd love to be average. I wanted everything to stop. Sixty seconds with no thoughts—how hard could it be? It would be bliss, but it was like asking for the impossible. It was never going to happen. Suck it up, kiddo—I'd be lapping up the world's thoughts until I died.

'Come on, Boo. Let's focus. Count steps. One, two, three, four...'

It was late; the night was still with a cloudless sky and a full moon so bright that inky black shadows accompanied us.

A tawny frogmouth sat atop a street lamp. Its big yellow eyes followed us as we walked by. Boo stared at it and yapped. She never missed a trick.

A fruit bat swooped low over our heads with a loud *whoosh* and we instinctively ducked. The air was rich with the scent of eucalypts and I breathed in the heady aroma.

We passed a double storey home next to a small park. I'd always liked this house. Lovely old-fashioned table lamps were visible through the downstairs windows. They sent a soft light up the staircase gently illuminating the antique style furniture and stately sitting rooms. There never seemed to be anyone home, but the lights were always on. Perhaps the owners were away and the lights were automatic.

A dark shape moved at speed past the upstairs window. It whooshed like a fruit bat. Someone must be home.

'There it is again, Boo,' I said, as the shadow made another pass by of the window.

What would make a shadow like that? It wasn't a person's silhouette; however it was kind of person shaped. But it moved so fast—a shadow on roller skates.

My paranoia kicked in when Boo growled low and

ominously. Her hackles rose. Not a good sign.

I pretended to check my phone whilst still looking from under my eyelids at the upstairs windows. No more shadows. A low-pitched hum began to reverberate through the air, as if machinery had kicked into action. The sound grew intense. My bones vibrated and my teeth chattered as if I was operating an invisible jackhammer.

A sense of dread descended on me and my head spun. I put my arms out to steady myself. I'd either developed a severe case of vertigo or was on a merry-go-round ramping up to top speed. I struggled to stay upright. My stomach lurched and I felt nauseous. The world spun around me in a blur of colour.

It stopped, violently and suddenly. I pitched into a brick wall and leant against it trying to focus. I didn't remember this brick garage being by the large house. Boo lay on her side looking at me. I rubbed my eyes. I couldn't get oriented. Nothing was familiar.

Dazed and confused, my brain pulled the pieces together— this was a totally different street, right around the block.

A molten heat burned in my cheeks as though my atoms were being shaken. Was I being blasted with microwaves? You never knew what was bouncing around the atmosphere these days.

Boo glanced about in a state of extreme alertness. The hackles on her back had risen all the way to the base of her tail. It was the most extreme hackle raise I'd ever seen. She appeared like some reptile dog with a Mohawk.

The back of my neck prickled. *Someone was watching me.*

Boo flicked her head upwards. The tawny frogmouth sat on the streetlight and observed us before it took off on silent wings and disappeared.

My hands shook, my curious nature not so curious anymore. Boo still had her Mohawk. She stared into my eyes and a voice in my mind said, 'Leave now!'

4

Jeepers. No way was I going to hang around and argue with a voice in my head.

'Let's get out of here, Boo.'

She was way ahead of me. Our pace home was brisk, almost a run. I sensed darkness—a pressure—behind me. Looking back, I expected to see a hideous demon on our tail. Nothing. A couple of lost spirits floated by and stared at me.

What the hell had happened? My face still burned hot. Maybe it was the extra wine I'd had after dinner. But why was Boo so spooked? Perhaps she'd picked up on my vibes. And the voice in my head had to be my imagination. I'd always perceived messages, never heard them. They'd never sounded like the spoken word. Taking a gasp of night air, I focused on the cracks in the footpath, the weeds poking through, a cigarette butt, a bottle top. Hold on to reality. What was reality anyway?

We arrived at our driveway thirty minutes later, and there, perched on the streetlight, was the tawny frogmouth. The same friggin' one. I recognised its energy signature. I didn't stop in case I heard a tawny frogmouth voice in my head. That's all I needed.

Home seemed even more welcoming than usual. Jason was on the couch, drinking beer and watching his favourite cooking show, *Secret Meat Business*.

He looked up. 'What's wrong with Boo?'

Her Mohawk was still set to extreme.

Jason stood and ran his hand along her back. 'What happened? I've never seen her like this before.'

'I need a cup of tea, then I'll tell you all about it,' I said, feeling like I needed something normal to be able to feel normal.

'I'll get one for you.' He went into the kitchen to put the kettle on. I followed him and sat at the kitchen table, watching him make it. Boo sat beside me, staring into space.

Jason plonked two cups down and pulled up a chair. I told him everything, voice in the head and all.

'I reckon we revisit the house tomorrow night and check things out,' he said. 'You need to face whatever it was you spooked yourself about.' He nodded sagely. 'With me there, you'll be perfectly safe.'

My paranoia gene—the one inherited from Dad— kicked into action. Dad had been like a scout master drilling it into me to 'always be prepared'.

My mind ticked over various preparedness possibilities. Grandpa's .45 caliber 'Grease Gun' M3 submachine gun sounded good. Or our potato canon. Jason had made it from a PVC pipe and powered it with an aerosol can. It could shoot a potato clear across the lake opposite our holiday shack. Both were highly illegal options.

'Maggie? Earth to Mars?'

'Sorry, I was thinking about what weaponry to take.'

Jason rolled his eyes and smiled. 'That'd be right.'

I decided on my usual kit: a triple strength ball thrower—we used this item for hurling Boo's balls across the oval. Made of heavy duty plastic, it was about twenty-four inches long. It made a handy 'whacking stick'. I also decided to include my super-duper, special edition Swiss Army knife. The items would give me a sense of security, if nothing else. We stared at Boo, who stared at us. Her extreme punk dog Mohawk wasn't going away.

'We might have to take her to the vet,' Jason said. 'It could be a permanent disfigurement.'

Boo hightailed it out of the room. The word vet did it every time.

'Let's see how she is tomorrow,' I said.

Next morning, still sporting a Mohawk, Boo blasted out through the dog flap, nearly knocking it off its hinges. A huge cockatoo bobbed up and down as it drank water from the bowl on our deck. A magnificent sulphur crest crowned its head, and its snow white chest puffed out defiantly as Boo bounded over.

It screeched raucously at her. She barked back with gusto.

When she lunged the cockatoo screeched and took off. A lone feather floated to the floor. Boo flung herself on it and rolled back and forth. She leapt to her feet, shook, and the huge hackle melted back into her body, like some terminator dog.

'Ha!' Jason said, 'I reckon old man cockatoo gave Boo the heads up. He didn't like being "out-crested".'

'Thank heavens she's back to normal.'

Boo cocked her head and locked me in a penetrating stare.

Words echoed around in my cranium.

Say goodbye to normal, Maggie. Say goodbye to normal, Maggie. Say goodbye to normal, Maggie. Goodbye normal.

'Are you feeling all right?' Jason asked. 'You're paler than normal.'

I rapped my fingers against my head, trying to stop the words. 'What's normal?' I asked.

A gust of wind collected the cockatoo's feather and carried it aloft. It floated away, and I sensed the small, slim, precious sense of normality I thought I had fly away with it.

I just knew.

Nothing would be normal again.

---

[1] *Maggie's Playlist: Happy Wasteland Day —Open Mike Eagle*

Chapter 2: The Dark Force

'Before I go - and I shall not return - to the land of darkness and deep shadow, the land of gloom like thick darkness, like deep shadow without order, where light is as thick as darkness.' — Job 10:21-22

The evening arrived in a flash.

'Come on,' Jason said, 'let's check out this mysterious house.'

Boo was excited and spun around in circles, indicating she was raring to go. I wasn't so keen.

'It's already half eight. We don't need to go.' My heart raced at the thought of returning there.

Jason gave me that look, the one not to be argued with, so I kitted up with my bum bag and off we set.

The evening was clear and beautiful, with a slight nip in the air. Maybe summer had had enough of scorching us with endless thirty-seven degree days and was allowing autumn a look in. We loved autumn. The anticipation of mellow balmy days, coloured leaves and open fires always buoyed our spirits.

The walk was lovely but uneventful, and the tawny frogmouth was nowhere to be seen. Boo marched on in front of us, her gaze fixed on something in the distance. The aging, well-to-do neighbourhood was beautiful at night. The darkness hid the fading beauty of the homes and neglected gardens—its folk either too old or too busy to keep things maintained. The area was heavily treed and the aroma of lemon scented gums filled the air. Thirty minutes of pacing it out brought us to the street.

I pointed. 'There's the house.'

It appeared exactly as it always did, except for one thing. The front door was wide open.

'Nice place,' Jason said. 'Not my style of architecture, but nice.'

'What should we do?'

'Nothing. Go home. What are we supposed to do? There are no shadows, no noise, no tawny frogmouth, no nothing.'

'How about we ring the doorbell?' I suggested. 'It's not safe to leave your front door open when it's right on the street. Anyone could walk in. Let's ring, and when they answer we can say we noticed the open door, and we were worried for safety reasons. Neighbourhood watch an' all that.'

'I don't think it's a good idea.'

'Why? Maybe the owners are away and the house has been burgled. We should check it out.'

'Trust me, you don't want to get involved. You'll just get us into trouble.'

Jason's unwillingness surprised me. I wanted to get the hell away from the house, but I was also worried for the owners.

'I think your attitude—' A sharp yap from Boo cut me off. She leapt forward, jerked the extenda lead from my hand. It clattered along behind her as she tore across the road, through the front door and up the fancy staircase.

'Bloody hell,' Jason said.

'Boo, Booo-ooh, come back!'

I unzipped my trusty bum bag and extracted Boo's favourite squeaky toy. She always came when she heard it.

Squeeeeeeeek. Squeeeeeeeek. Squeeeeeeeek.

Jason gave me a look. 'Maggie, shhh. You're disturbing the neighbourhood.' He strode across the street. 'Come on, let's ring the doorbell.'

'There's no one around to disturb,' I said as we walked up the front steps and he rang the bell.

It was your ordinary, everyday doorbell. Nothing special.

We waited. We looked expectantly into the hall. A large mirror over the antique hall table reflected back our anxious faces. Intricately designed octagon floor tiles spread out before us in a black and white mosaic. Thousands of eight sided white tiles interspersed with black diamonds were corralled by white zigzag tiles around the edges. So many tiles. They needed to be counted.

'Don't even think about counting them,' Jason said.

'Wasn't,' I lied.

Two beautiful table lamps with brass stands illuminated the gilt edge of the ornate mirror and cast pools of yellow light on the walls and floor. A carpeted staircase hugged the wall behind the hall table, its bannisters casting teeth-like shadows.

Ding Dong. Ding Dong.

Still nothing. Only silence.

I stuck my head inside the door and yelled, 'Boooo,' whilst frantically squeaking her toy.

Silence. No Boo.

'Helloooo, anyone home?' I called.

Not even an echo.

I turned to Jason. 'Now what?'

'We have a number of options,' he said, in his let's be rational, we have all the time in the world kind of way.

'One, we call the police and tell them our dilemma. We wait at the front door until they arrive, then we all go in together. I mean, Boo's in the house, so she's definitely not run away.'

'Yes, but why isn't she coming back? She never does this, never goes near strange places in the first instance, let alone inside weird houses. It's not like her. I have a bad feeling.'

'Calm down, don't panic,' he said continuing. 'Two, one of us stays here, while the other goes to a neighbour. We tell them what's happened, ask if they know anything, and get them to come in the house with us. Three, one of us stays at the front door, while the other goes into the house and gets Boo.'

'You can count out number three. That's dumb, unless you want to go into the house alone, and I wouldn't let you do that anyway. I'm calling the police.' I took out my phone and dialled the number. 'Damn. No signal. What's going on?'

I tried once more. Still no service. 'For God's sake, we're in the suburbs. Ridiculous.'

'I'll try the neighbours,' he said. 'Can you stay here and look out for Boo?'

'No worries.' I pulled out my Swiss Army knife and tucked it in my sock.

Jason grinned at me, rolled his eyes and strode off. His silhouette cut a fine figure under the street lamp. He tried the house next door, but no one was home. Nor at the next one, or the one after that, or the one after that.

He yelled from halfway along the street, 'I'll try the other side.'

Jason was soon out of sight. I stood by the front door feeling upset. It was deathly quiet. Where the hell was everyone?

Peering inside the house again, I noticed it was exceptionally clean. Utterly spotless, so pristine it didn't seem real.

'Boo?' I called, in a squeaky little voice.

The house must've been soundproofed as there was no echo; the sound was sucked away.

My heartbeat ramped up as I stepped into the hallway. I left one foot firmly on the doormat. I'd read somewhere if you have one foot outside you can't be charged with trespass, and I liked to be a law-abiding citizen.

A sound tinkled in the distance—Boo's collar?

'Boo?'

A whimper.

'Boooo?'

Perhaps her lead was caught on something and she couldn't break free. Without thinking, I stepped fully into the hallway.

11

BANG!

The door slammed shut behind me.

I jumped. Bloody hell. I was trapped. I grabbed the door handle in a panic and the door opened. It must have been the wind—yet there was no wind. Where the hell was Jason?

Tinkle. Tinkle.

There it was again. Boo was upstairs. This was ridiculous. If there was a burglar they'd be long gone by now. I had my phone. I'd video myself going into the house, collecting my dog and leaving. Jason and I would call the police when we got home. That way I'd have evidence, just in case. I'm sure Dad would give that plan the tick of approval.

I opened the front door wide and tucked the doormat over the frame to stop it closing. Then I started recording.

'Hello, is anyone home? I'm going upstairs to find my dog.'

The sound evaporated as soon as it left my mouth.

I touched the smooth wood of the staircase banister. It felt inanimate. Funny, it didn't have a vibe. Lifeless.

A few steps up the staircase now, treading on the plush, spotless carpet. My heart was beating faster with each step. At the top was the window facing the street, the one where the shadow had been.

The house felt unreal, the colours just that tiny bit brighter, the wood just that tiny bit woodier. And what was with the damn silence?

My heart pulsed in my throat. I was breathing and moving but couldn't hear anything inside myself. I'd gone deaf. I tapped the banister with a fingernail. No sound. Panic stirred in my gut.

A movement near the front door caught my eye. I whirled around.

Oh, thank God. It was Jason.

He saw me at the top of the staircase, waved and stepped inside. His lips were moving, but no sound reached me. I replied but couldn't hear myself either.

Jason ambled towards the stairs, as though someone had pressed the slow-mo function on the TV. At that speed, it would take him a day to reach me. He suddenly launched into fast-forward and was halfway up the stairs before he stopped, frozen in mid stride. His eyes locked desperately onto mine for a moment before he shifted into fast forward again and appeared right next to me.

A sound smashed through the silence—the front door had slammed shut. It was a beautiful resonating sound, which reverberated in my chest. The ominous finality of it reminded me of a castle gate closing. As the noise dissipated, a surge of colours gushed from the door. Chromesthesia—colours evoked by sounds. I was a synesthete, but I'd never experienced it as acutely as this. The look on Jason's face made me realise he saw it too. How could that be?

A thousand glistening hues of colour rose in a tidal wave of effervescence and coursed towards the ceiling. We stared speechless at the spectacular display as the wave of colour rushed along the path of least resistance: the stairs. As it hurtled towards us I gripped the banister and braced for the oncoming tsunami.

'What the hell?' I screamed, and a silent current of coloured shapes gushed from my mouth.

Jason's eyes widened. 'Stuffed if I know!' he yelled, and an equivalent stream of colours erupted from his mouth. Nothing was behaving as it should.

I held my breath and steeled myself as the wave rose over our heads and crashed down, swamping us. We were surrounded, drowning in colours and shapes. I couldn't help but breathe them in. My body tingled as the colours penetrated my skin. Jason became a shadow in the wash and whirlpool of opalescence. If it weren't so terrifying, it would've been beautiful.

A kaleidoscope of luminous colours dripped from our bodies as the wave receded. Florescent pools glittered on the floor like mirrors. My horrified face was a brief reflection before the pools evaporated, faded into nothingness.

Jason shook his head, sending out a spray of drops which sparkled like rain drops in sunlight. His mouth moved, and I recognised the shape of some choice expletives.

'Are you okay?' My voice was distorted—deep and slow.

'You sound weird!' he replied, in the same slow-mo mode.

Our movements were sluggish as though we were trapped in a permanent Tai Chi class. Something caught our attention, and we oh so slowly turned and gazed back down the staircase.

Tendrils of blackness flowed through the doorframe of a downstairs room. Smoke! The house was on fire. Jason stared at me with enormous eyes that screamed *run!*

We would've if we could've, but we couldn't. So we didn't.

The smoke filled the lower hallway. A thick tendril moved towards us, pointing like a bony finger. The cloud of black swirled and thickened, drawing its tendrils back into itself. It expanded and contracted, forming strange shapes. The vague outline of a winged creature appeared, its wings flowing and distorting like ink through water. Morphing into new forms, the smoke creature drifted across the shiny tiles towards the staircase.

The black cloud solidified into a tall, dark form, which stretched from floor to ceiling. Skeletal arms and legs formed and the arms stretched out extending long clawed fingers towards us. A head formed, pointed and skull like. Amid the inky darkness, the whiteness of a ribcage appeared, the crystal blackness of a beating heart, a collarbone, vertebrae, and eye sockets whirling with volcanic fury. It was at that point I figured the house wasn't on fire.

The powerful, muscular entity slowly ascended the staircase.

I'd watched enough nature shows to recognise its stance, crouched low, slinking, head extended, each clawed foot carefully and precisely placed—it was stalking. Us.

I tried to swallow, but my mouth was as dry as a chip. My

knees knocked uncontrollably. I'd never had that happen before. A barrage of hideous psychic images assaulted me. The thing was trying to beat me to death with them. I started to count the floor tiles in the hallway below.

'One, two, three, four, five, six...' Distract yourself, Maggie.

Jason's eyes were fixed on the darkness as it approached. I hoped his brain was coping with what he saw. I could sense his mind racing.

'... seven, eight, nine, ten, eleven ...' What harm could a shadow do? It was only a shadow. But what was making the shadow? Maybe the shadow maker was invisible but still cast a shadow? Then it wouldn't only be a shadow. The idea made me feel sick.

The creature surveyed the path before it. The blackness of the thing pulsated with energy. It was a dark force the likes of which I'd never experienced in all my supernatural encounters. A billion laser pinpricks pierced my skin and danced across my flesh. The radiation prickled in my muscles. As it progressed up the stairs the smell of stinking, charred flesh burned in my nostrils. Was it my flesh?

Shiny fragments incandesced within the creature. It was a piece of the night sky out for a stroll. The Dark Force paused; its head quivered as though sniffing the air. I sensed invisible eyes latch onto mine. Their focus burned into my brain and my heart filled with despair as an avalanche of demonic images continued to assault my mind.

A Bogong moth dropped from the ceiling light. It hit the banister generating a puff of moth dust. The dust settled for an instant before it was sucked, along with the moth, towards the creature. They swirled in a slow-motion tornado towards the thing and fluoresced in contact with it. Sparks erupted. *Fizzzttt!* Gone. The effect was similar to an electric light insect trap, except in this case, not a skerrick remained.

Jason stood frozen, hands clenched around the banister,

mouth open, eyes wide. Definitely not a confidence inspiring look. In situations like this—if you believed the movies—the guy was supposed to have the steely narrowed eyes, clenched, chiseled jaw, one muscled arm shielding his loved one, and a shiny Smith & Wesson in his other hand.

I looked at Jason again. Check none of the above.

The thought occurred to me that what had happened to the moth could, in all probability, happen to us, if we chose to stand and gawp.

The Dark Force was three quarters of the way up the stairs and faced squarely towards us. The paintwork faded as it passed, the banister pulsed and buckled under its touch and the walls flowed and rippled like water.

We attempted to move away, but our minuscule movements got us nowhere. '... twelve, thirteen, fourteen, fifteen ...' Maybe I was having a magic mushroom flashback. If so, Jason was having the exact same flashback. But Jason had never taken drugs, never got wasted, aside from getting rotten on apple cider with his mates in the back of a panel van, while listening to Neil Young, down by the surf, once upon a time. '... sixteen, seventeen, eighteen, nineteen ...'

We needed to move and move fast. I had no intention of doing the 'Fizzzttt! Gone' thing. But fast was not happening. The Dark Force was moving ever so slowly. We needed to move ever so slowly, but much faster, away.

There was a door behind us. It was more a cupboard type door, than a room type door. It was next to the big window where I'd first seen the shadow. Boo was nowhere to be seen.

We had limited options. Fling ourselves out the window, jump over the banister and land in the hallway, or hide in the cupboard. Perhaps the thing couldn't open doors. Then again, maybe it didn't need to.

My limbs were as heavy as lead, each movement like walking through mud. My jaw rattled with an agonising vibration. Great, we were dealing with an invisible dentist as well.

I grabbed Jason's arm with one hand and turned the door handle with the other. I opened it and peered in. Blackness. An inky void. *Shit.*

The Dark Force was at the top of the staircase. Decision made. I dragged Jason inside and slammed the door.

In the pitch black, it was impossible to determine the size of the area. Was it a cupboard or a room? There was nothing but Jason's ragged breath rasping in and out. I took a breath to calm myself and the sense of heaviness departed from my limbs. The unsettling vibration stopped. I tested my voice.

'You okay?'

'Who knows,' Jason said in a strangled voice I hardly recognised. 'It's dark,' he continued, stating the bleeding obvious.

'Yes, even the white bits are black.' I giggled but wanted to scream hysterically.

I took Jason's hand and shuffled two steps forward into the blackness, one arm outstretched for obstacles. My stomach gurgled—sound had definitely returned. My heart was thumping so loud it scared me.

Our footsteps sounded out as if on wooden floorboards. Nothing impeded our progress. It was a room. I let go of Jason's hand and waved both arms around. I felt my pupils straining into the darkness. A faint tinkle sounded.

'That's Boo's collar,' Jason said, his voice back to its normal deep timbre.

'Sshhhh, listen. There it is again.'

'Boo?' Jason called softly.

My eyes had grown accustomed to the dark, the blackness not so black anymore. A small pinprick of light came from somewhere. I couldn't tell if it was close or distant. We stood expectantly, eyes straining.

The pinprick of light grew larger and the blackness receded.

About twenty-five feet away there was a small night light on the floor. Next to the light was Boo. She sat and stared at us with the earnest gaze she gets when she's really focused. Like when she sees a cat.

We were in a huge bare room with floorboards and no windows. It seemed safe enough, albeit weird. What a bizarre space. The house must have been way larger than it appeared from outside. How had Boo got in here?

We moved towards her, but as we walked she receded and the further away the end of the room seemed.

'Oh, for fuck's sake!' Jason said. 'It's like Alice in bloody Wonderland.'

His language alerted me to the fact he was niggly and in no mood for recalcitrant rooms which wouldn't behave according to the agreed laws of physics.

We walked on with purpose, making some headway, although it was still like walking up a down escalator.

'Let's stop and call her,' I suggested. 'See if she can come to us.'

We enthusiastically called her and slapped our knees.

Boo sprang to life and trotted towards us, nails clicking on the wooden boards.

'Come on, girl, come on!' Jason said.

Boo picked up the pace but wasn't getting anywhere either. It was like walking on a treadmill. Curiously though, the room contracted with each of her steps. Eventually she stood right in front of us. She had brought the corner of the room, and herself, to us.

The space was now smaller by half, and the light next to her was not a night light after all. It was a spherical object made of crystal or glass and blazed a beautiful luminescence with subtle variations of the most exquisite colours. It was about six inches in diameter and gave the illusion of hovering slightly above the floor.

'Wow, it's amazing,' Jason said, reaching out to touch it.

'Don't!' I growled. So did Boo.

My teeth began to chatter. The horrible vibration was back. The door rattled and started to bubble and pulse like cheese on toast under a hot grill.

An ear-shattering screeching assaulted our ears—the sound of a million fingernails clawing on a chalkboard. Jason clapped his hands over his ears. Darkness appeared around the doorframe and flowed into the room. Its blackness oozed like Vegemite through the cracks. The Dark Force was coming for us.

The crystal sphere erupted into a blazing wall of fluorescence. The black momentarily shrank back in response, but then surged forward with renewed purpose. The humming increased, and my atoms vibrated. Fear and hopelessness clutched at my heart. Jason yelled at me, deep and slow. I couldn't understand what he said. Slo-mo mode had kicked in again.

The crystal sphere flamed out a penetrating brilliance which blasted our eyeballs and rocked our molecules. This was a war. A war between dark and light, and we were stuck in the middle.

'Jump!' I screamed at Jason and Boo, pointing to the space behind the sphere.

Jason grasped my hand, his eyes latched onto mine, and we jumped. Boo ignored me and plonked her bum on the floor. She wasn't moving.

We leapt over the sphere into the heart of light. Heat like the sun on a perfect autumn day penetrated my bones. The warmth was as thick as treacle. We hovered, held in suspension above the sphere. Jason still held my hand tightly. Thousands of celestial tones chimed through my body, while my atoms buzzed with sound and light.

The Dark Force and the light faced off. Every time the light pulsed forward, the Dark Force retaliated. Boo was caught between them.

'Boo, get back!'

Boo looked up at me with her big brown eyes and didn't seem concerned. Amazing really, she was usually scared of anything strange—ceiling fans in particular. As there wasn't a ceiling fan to be seen, she seemed quite at ease.

Boo's fur stood on end as the Dark Force approached. Hair and dust particles flew from her coat in a whirlpool-like stream and vanished, sparking and crackling into the Dark Force. The stink of burnt hair filled the room. Boo's face began to distort and her nose grew longer until she resembled a doggie greeting card. The end of her nose began to spark.

'Run, Boo, run!' I screamed.

Boo lifted her front leg. I knew that move. For Christ's sake, she was going to 'shake hands' with the Dark Force.

'No!' I screamed. 'No tricks, Boo! Don't!'

'Phffft!' Boo's trademark sneeze. She stared defiantly at the Dark Force. Its vortex sucked her beautiful long ears over her head, where they burst into flame and vanished. We screamed as Boo slammed her paw down on the sphere.

Our world disappeared in a blaze of light.

---

[2] *Maggie's Playlist: Crystal Ball — Pink*

Chapter 3: Lost Time & Dust

'But do not overlook this one fact, beloved, that with the Lord one day is as a thousand years, and a thousand years as one day.' — Peter 3:8

It was dark. A rib crushing weight pressed on my chest barely allowing me to breathe. Tired, almost drugged, a stench reached my nostrils, carried on the breath of something foul. It was close. Too close.

Frozen rigid, I strained to listen past the pounding in my ears. Lungs demanded breath, but breathing wasn't an option. The putrid odour flowed over my face. A chilling growl rumbled in my right ear. An image of the Predator came to mind. I so wanted to morph into Arnold Schwarzenegger—a seriously awful, motherfucking monster was about to rip my face off.

A bone like finger poked me in the ribs.

'Ow!'

The pain forced my heavy eyelids open, and I was confronted by—Boo! She sat on my chest, with her nose to mine. One bony paw dug into my side.

'Eeewwuh! Stinky dog breath! Get off, Boo.'

Blinking to clear my vision, I surveyed my surroundings. Bloody hell. I was in bed. At home. The predator growling into my ear was Jason, snoring, dead to the world.

'What the?'

Apparently, your mind can reel in mind-boggling situations.

I'd always wondered what that felt like. Now I knew. My mind reeled out of control, trying to make sense of ... of what?

Had I had a nightmare? Disjointed images slipped from my mind's grasp.

Maybe one too many red wines last night combined with the Chinese take away had produced a lethal combination leading to the side effect of extreme nightmares.

Maybe they should put warnings on the takeaway containers—Danger! Do not combine with Shiraz.

'Jason. Wake up!'

I pushed his shoulder. He instantly came to life and sprang out of bed.

'Run, Maggie! *Run*!' he shouted.

He caught a foot in the bedding and hit the deck with a sickening thud. It was a spectacular face plant and I feared for his safety.

'Where am I?' he groaned. His face appeared over the end of the bed, a bruise already developing in the middle of his forehead.

'It appears we're at home in bed,' I said. 'You obviously had nightmares too.'

I helped him off the floor, and we staggered out to the kitchen to make coffee.

Jason scratched his head. 'The last thing I remember is we'd come home from work, picked up Chinese, a good bottle of red, and after dinner didn't we take the dog for a walk?'

'I can't remember. It's so strange. Maybe there was something in the wine. I feel displaced.'

'What time is it?' he said, rubbing his eyes. 'Let's go out for breakfast. I'm starving.'

'Clock says eight. We're up early for a Saturday.'

'I'll duck around to the milk bar for the paper,' he said. 'You have a shower and then we'll go. A good breakfast is what we need. I feel like I've run a marathon.'

I made coffee and sat at the kitchen table, too tired to move. My brain tried in vain to find a memory that made sense.

Jason returned with the paper, his face as pale as a ghost.

'What's wrong?'

'The milk bar was about to close. I was lucky to get a paper.'

'Closing? They should be opening. Were they robbed again?'

'They were closing because it's eight o'clock, *Sunday* night.'

'No, it's Saturday.'

Jason turned on the television and *Sixty Minutes*, a Sunday night staple, was just finishing. Peter Harvey—looking like we felt—was wrapping up the mailbag.

The newspaper in Jason's hand was the Sunday paper.

My brain was tired of reeling, but it reeled some more.

We had lost two whole days.

Worse, they were weekend days, and I had to go back to work tomorrow.

That seemed to be a fact more shocking than anything else, right at the moment.

'I think,' Jason said, slumping in a chair, 'we may have been abducted by aliens.' A lock of sandy hair fell across his forehead, and he stared at me through it, his eyes wide and worried.

'Well, if we have, they could've done it during the week. Those aliens really are nasty pieces of work.'

---

3 *Maggies' Playlist: Time — Pink Floyd — The Dark Side of the Moon*

Chapter 4: The Beginning

The screen saver on my twenty-seven-inch iMac ran through the seven National Geographic images three times before I tapped the keyboard. There was programming to be done, a contract to fulfill, but I wasn't in the mood. The missing time played on my mind. What had happened to us? Why couldn't we remember? Would we ever be able to remember? Loose ends annoyed me.

I took out some old receipts from my oversized wallet and shredded them. Clicking on iTunes, I selected a playlist—*Classical Music for Exam Study*. I cranked up Bach. Nope—not doing it for me. *Time Bomb* by Beck. That was more in tune with the vibe running through my brain.

"We got a time bomb. We got a time bomb. Tick. Tick. Tick. Tick."

Boo was asleep on the couch in my office. She opened an eye.

'Yes, I know, I'm procrastinating. It's what I do.'

'Phffft!' she sneezed back.

Opening another part of my wallet, I pulled out a pile of papers from a section where I shoved anything important. A piece of pink paper caught my eye. It was the printout of the online ad I'd posted six years ago. The one which led me to Jason. I unfolded the paper and read it.

"Maggie #7345   Kind soul seeks kind soul.

Me: *I don't talk a lot. I look pretty good, I've been told. I like my own company. I'm not demanding or clingy. I have my own life but want to share it with a kindred spirit. I'm a computer geek, love animals, nature and a quiet life. I need someone who listens, and gets me. Oh, and I'm psychic, so don't even try to bullshit me. My favourite food is egg and chips.* **You:** *Honest. Truthful. Kind. That's a good start.'*

It made me cringe to read it now. But the ad worked. It brought Jason into my life. I folded and returned it to my wallet. I picked up another piece of pink paper. 'Boo, here's the ad Jason wrote!'

Boo rolled her open eyeball at me and shut it.

'Don't be like that, Boo. I'll read it to you.'

"Jason #9261   R U the one?

I'm honest, truthful and kind. I'm a plumber who hates football. Let's get that out there upfront. I'm looking for a woman who is independent and low maintenance. Someone I can share my life with. I love motorbikes, animals, landscaping, nature. I'm six foot one and people say I'm good looking."

'Phhht!' Boo opened both eyes, leaned back on the couch and stared at me fixedly.

'See, I thought you'd be interested.'

I remembered Jason telling me later on that he thought his ad was pathetic. But he liked mine, and the fact we had things in common—egg and chips being one of them. He said he liked women who didn't talk a lot too. I remembered him saying my description intrigued him and my photo stole his soul. He plucked up the courage and sent me an email.

'He's poetic for a plumber don't you think, Boo?'

He said he couldn't stop looking at my photo. He reckoned I could double for Snow White, with the long dark hair, white skin and red lips. The only difference he said was I had green eyes, rather than blue.

I told him my pale skin—he called it a snow-white tan—was

due to years of computer gaming. The fact I was at the top of my league in 'first person shooter' category impressed him.

After our first meeting, Jason wrote me a letter. The first love letter he'd ever written apparently. He wanted to prove to me he did listen, and he did "get me".

I unfolded the letter and spread it out on the desk. Boo locked on to me with a fixed stare, her big brown eyes bored into mine. She seemed interested. Boo and I had many conversations—she was a good listener.

The letter read:

Dear Maggie, when I walked into the café you were tapping away on your laptop. You looked up and our eyes connected. Green eyes met blue. Click.

That was it for me. I heard it in my head and felt it in my body—a key turning in a lock.

You jumped. I knew you felt it too.

I sat and learned more about you—the person I'd fallen for at first sight. We talked until the café closed and they had to throw us out. That's never happened to me before.

I learned we both loved coffee, food and good wine. I noticed you had a healthy appetite. I liked that in a woman. You've got curves in all the right places and you look hot.

You told me about your psychic abilities and how things could get a bit weird around you. No worries at all—my Grandmother was psychic too. I experienced supernatural events whilst staying at her house in England. She had a couple of resident ghosts and I saw them on occasion. Gran taught me how to see auras. I'm not very good at it, but when the lights are low and conditions are right, sometimes I can see them quite clearly.

You said you inherited your psychic abilities from your mother, and having too many people around feels like an assault. Your psychic sensitivity has forced you into more solo pastimes. I wanted to let you know that's okay with me. I'm not big on crowds of people.

I found out you work from home developing software, and your dog, Boo, is never far from your side. You love animals. You said they don't give off bad static like people. I agree, and I love animals too.

You play classical music when you game and I found your iPod's playlist diverse, to say the least—I loved it. I've never met anyone like you Maggie McLaine, and your eyes … I'm bewitched. The moment our eyes met—that was it for me. I'd fallen hard.

Afterwards, back at your place, it felt like all the stars had aligned to bring us together. I'm not scared to say it. I have to say it, and in writing. I reckon we're meant to be.

The depth of feeling I have for you is beyond words, so it sounds lame just to say—I love you, Maggie McLaine. But I do, and will, always. Jason.

'How romantic and beautiful is that, Boo?'

Boo cocked her head and stared at me. It was a look that said: *Are you going to stop talking anytime soon?*

I remembered the day Jason and I first met like it was yesterday. I'd hoped he wasn't going to be late. It was getting close to ten in the morning. I was never late and didn't like to be kept waiting. We'd be off to a very bad start if that happened. So, with five minutes to go I was nervous. I started counting the people in the café. What the hell was I thinking with this online dating thing? I didn't get out much. I was always on a computer. But at the time, it had seemed like the logical thing to do.

I'd flicked through the online photos with my eyes closed, tuning into the energy of the images. A pulse of energy spiked into my body. My fingers tingled and my heart raced. I opened my eyes to see which photo had caused such a reaction. It was Jason.

I liked the look of him. He had beautiful eyes, intense like a hawk. A shock of sandy blond hair fell across his forehead. He had high cheekbones, a serious look about him, and was handsome in an interesting way. In another photo he sported a wide, crazy grin which made me smile just looking at it.

At four minutes to ten, I sensed his presence in the café. I looked up straight into his blue eyes. The sight of him made my heart pound. And the energy from him—I could barely speak or breathe. In the end we talked for hours, an easy ebb and flow. He didn't make my head hurt like so many others. He seemed uncomplicated. Uncomplicated was good.

It was late when the café owner closed the door behind us. Jason took my hand and I felt my knees go weak from his touch. I'd never believed in beating around the bush so I said, 'I'd like you to come back to my place for coffee, and coffee doesn't have to mean coffee, but of course, if you want coffee, you can have some. I have a machine. A coffee machine, I mean, but if you didn't want coffee, we could keep talking and—'

He stopped my nervous babble with a passionate and intoxicating kiss. He held me as my knees gave way.

That evening our minds and bodies merged in sexual bliss beyond anything I'd ever experienced.

'You remember the first night don't you, Boo, when I put you out of the room?'

In response to my question, Boo shoved her head under a cushion.

I laughed. 'Don't be like that. There's nothing to be embarrassed about. You know Jason and I are made for each other.'

I remembered how at home he was in my kitchen. He made me egg and chips for breakfast, just for fun, and because he knew it was my favourite. It didn't get any better than that. I was in love.

'We were never apart from then on were we, Boo?' Boo sat up from behind the cushion and seemed to nod in agreement.

Jason introduced me to all his friends, except for his best mate, Ashley, who was on deployment in Iraq. In a strange twist, it was only later I found out I'd been dating the exact same Ashley. We'd met when I was living in Sydney, working on a one year contract. Ashley had broken it off when he had to go fight in Iraq. I was crushed. He said he didn't want me to wait, and I should move on with my life. And the funny thing is, I did—

with Jason.

I only found out they were best mates when Ashley showed up at Jason's front door eighteen months later on return from his deployment. Talk about awkward. Ashley still laughs remembering the look on my face when I answered the door. The expression on his face was priceless too—a mixture of shock, confusion and joy. Anyways, Ashley was pretty screwed up after his deployment. He went off the rails with booze, drugs and women. We saved his life twice, helped him back from the abyss. It was awkward for a while, but now the three of us are closer than family.

I found it liberating Jason accepted my psychic nature and eccentricities. He'd even got used to all the visiting spirits and strange occurrences in our house. On occasion, he would see spirits too.

'He was like you, Boo. It freaked him out at first, but now he's used to it.'

Boo nodded at me and cocked her head. She could see entities and would alert me with a high-pitched yap.

I jumped as Boo let rip with that exact same special yap. She leapt off the couch and barked frantically at the window. On the railing of the deck was a large black blob with baleful yellow eyes.

What the hell was that?

I moved to the window to have a closer look. It was a cat. But it was the blackest of black cats I'd ever seen. It was so black it sucked in the light, making it hard to fathom any detail. Boo was frantic and scratched at the glass door, wanting to get out and see the thing off. Neither of us were cat fans. For me it was because they decimated the wildlife, for Boo—well, she just hated them.

'There's no way I'm letting you out, Boo. That cat's like a baby panther. It'll scratch your eyes out.'

I banged on the glass. 'Shoo! Bugger off!'

In response, the cat flattened its body and ears, and black almond shaped pupils grew larger as it fixed me with its lantern eyes.

A loud rumble issued from the neighbour's motorbike … um, wait, no … it was the cat!

Whaa Oooh Whaa Oooh Snort Whaa Oooh Whaa Oooh Snort Grrrrr.

The ominous guttural growl rose and fell in pitch, reaching a crescendo of a scream like yowl. The cat drew back and opened its mouth to reveal large white fangs and a pink tongue which curled between its teeth as it hissed at us like a mad snake.

Boo barked hysterically in response.

The cat rose to its feet, arched its back and expanded to three times its size. It launched itself at Boo like a scud missile, and smashed into the shatterproof glass door. The glass cracked under the impact of its skull. The cat retreated a few steps and then threw itself against the glass again, and again. Blood and fur stained the glass and it began to give way under the frenzied assault.

'Come on, Boo, out! We need to evacuate the office.' Boo didn't want to go; she wanted to face off with the cat, but she wouldn't have a face left, if that thing got to her. I dragged Boo from the room and shut the door. If the cat got in, it couldn't break through a wooden door, surely?

A cacophony of screeching, hissing and shrieking came from outside. We dashed around to another window to see a maelstrom of black and white birds flying around the cat. Feathers and fur flew as a flock of magpies attacked the cat, dive bombing it, pecking it relentlessly, until the cat gave in and raced away, thumping up and over the fence.

The deck was littered with feathers, fur and blood.

The cat was so vicious, it had to be feral. The cracked glass of the shatterproof door filled me with horror. If it came back, Boo wouldn't stand a chance.

---

4 *Maggie's Playlist: Time Bomb — Beck*

Chapter 5: Too Clean

'All go to one place. All are from the dust, and to dust all return.' — *Ecclesiastes 3:20*

Jason's face appeared in front of me as I lifted my head from the laptop. He bit his lip and looked at me from under his eyebrows.

'What?'

'It's been two weeks and we still don't know what happened. I can't shake the uneasy feeling.'

'Me too. It's always at the back of my mind. But what can we do?'

Jason did a double take as he noticed the glass door. 'Jesus, what the hell happened?'

'Cat.'

'Cat?'

I filled him in about the black cat incident.

'There's a huge black cat at the end of the street—maybe it's that one,' he said. 'But I fail to see how any cat could smash shatterproof glass.'

'Well, it did, and it was terrifying.'

'I'll organise to have the glass fixed, and in the meantime we need to keep an eye on Boo in case the bloody thing comes back. By the way, Maggie, are you turning into a clean freak?'

'What do you mean?'

'The house is immaculate. How often do you vacuum?'

'I haven't—been too busy. I was going to ask you the same thing.'

'Same deal, too busy. So, who the hell has been breaking in and cleaning our house?' He ran his hand over various surfaces and held it in front of my face. 'See? Not a speck of dust anywhere.'

I shivered as a sense of dread overcame me. Why on earth I felt that way about a dust free house, I had no idea. However, having a sense of dread was not unusual for me. In fact, it was probably a pretty normal state, given my sensitive psychic disposition. But due to a lack of dust?

'We should call the police,' Jason said.

'And report what? An exceptionally clean house?'

We laughed.

'I've an idea,' I said. 'Come with me to the bedroom.'

He checked his watch. 'Really? Now? It's three o'clock in the afternoon. You're insatiable.'

'Not that, silly.' I took him by the hand and led him out of my office, along the hall and to the bedroom.

He gripped me around the waist. 'We could you know.'

'No, we have other pressing matters. We need to get a blanket from the bed box and give it a good shake.'

He gave me a quizzical look. 'Hokay, then.' Jason handed me an old wool blanket. 'Here, shake this out.' He paused. 'Why are we doing this?'

'To make dust. We don't have any, and I think we need some.'

He stared at me like I'd gone mad.

'You grab one end, and I'll grab the other,' I said. 'We'll shake it over there where the sun's coming in through the window.'

We shook the blanket vigorously. Then we shook it some more. Not one single solitary particle floated in the air. No lint, hair, fluff, or dust.

'Impossible,' Jason said.

'Hmmm, we have no dust. What do we do?'

He folded the blanket and threw in on the couch. 'I still think we should go to the police. No, wait. We'll notify one of the universities.'

'To do and say what?'

'We have a dustless house and they need to come and investigate. You know, set up scientific experiments, cameras and stuff.'

'You get right on to that then.'

'I will.'

'Look, why don't we just enjoy the clean house for the time being,' I said. 'We can conduct and film our own experiments— then people won't think we're whacko.' I could sense Jason's mind ticking over.

'We'll go with your plan then,' he said, 'and I'll make us coffee to celebrate our self-cleaning house.'

By the time Jason plonked a coffee in front of me, my sense of dread had vanished and I was chuffed with the idea of a self-cleaning house.

Floorboards shone, glass tops sparkled, ornaments held not a smidgeon of dust, no hair in the bath, spotless cupboards, immaculate bookshelves. I marvelled at our pristine environment. This wasn't something to be worried about. I was being silly. Having no dust was a good thing, wasn't it?

---

[5] *Maggie's Playlist: Dust — Anthony & Cleopatra*

Chapter 6: House of Shadows

The morning light shone on Jason's naked torso highlighting his muscular physique. He stood next to our bed and stared down at me.

'The house is looking cleaner than ever. Way too clean, I reckon. It's almost sterile,' he said, zipping up his jeans.

He looked so handsome that I wanted to rip his pants off and drag him back to bed. I arose, wrapped my arms around him, and ran my hands over his body. 'The camera didn't reveal anything untoward other than some weird static,' I said, closing my eyes as Jason kissed my neck. 'What bothers me more than the lack of dust is the shadows in the house. They're black. Shadows are generally grey, dark grey, all sorts of shades of grey. Seldom pure black. It's creeping me out—'

Jason kissed away my words. He was good at doing that, and I liked it.

'You need to pull up the blinds, Mags,' he said, laughing. 'As much as I'd like to stay, I've got to go. I'll take Boo out before my first plumbing job, if you like.' He grabbed my bum and hoisted me up for another kiss.

'No worries. See you later chip potato,' I said, trying to remember what it was I was concerned about.

Once he'd left and I entered the lounge, I remembered. The shadows. There was an inky black one blanketed around the hall cabinet.

The venetian blind rattled as I tilted the slats to let in more light. No difference. Yanking the string, I pulled the blind right up to the top. The shadow stayed put. It moved, very slightly—in and out, in and out, like breathing. I rubbed my eyes.

Racing from window to window I opened all the blinds, glad Jason wasn't around to lecture me about pulling them up too fast and ruining the cords. My efforts proved fruitless. Black, ominous shadows clutched limpet like to walls and furniture. Perhaps it was the angle of the sun.

The floorboards hurt my knees as I knelt on all fours staring at the shadow under the cabinet. A patch of yellow flared in the gloom—Boo's tennis ball! That was where it was. She'd be happy to have it back.

The gap under the cabinet was barely arm width in height, so extracting her lost treasure would be awkward. Lying flat on my face alongside the cabinet, I twisted my shoulder forward, and inserted my arm into a world of excruciating pain.

What the hell?

Pain shot down from the tips of my fingers to my shoulder joint.

I pulled back. The pain intensified to fifty out of ten. My brain initiated immediate shut down.

It was a dream ... a nightmare ... A psychotic butcher was feeding my arm into a mincer and the humerus crunched like a branch in a chipper chopper. Knives slashed. Needles stabbed.

A high-pitched screaming wrenched me from the dream. My ear drums vibrated with the cacophony, adding to the pain.

It was me.

My shrieking continued, wavering in intensity, tone and pitch. I wished I'd shut up.

'HELP!' One word. One word only.

The only word I could summon. The pain owned me, controlled every action, and erased every thought.

Bands of steel tightened their grip on my chest and my heart strained against the pressure. Heart muscles prepared to explode.

Unbearable agony. A new, distinctive torture—branding irons, red hot, molten, sinking into my bones.

The stench of roasting flesh. Vision fading.

Oblivion …

A ceiling light. Eye to eye with it.

That was my body down there.

Pain gone. Freedom. Death?

I must have been.

Dead.

A lamp glowed softly, illuminating the wood of the cabinet my body was spread-eagled next to. Wine bottles on the wrought iron rack glinted rich reds and soft pinks. My wingback chair sat next to a rug on the oak floorboards. A mirror reflected a reading lamp, candles flickered in the stone hearth. Lush plants in fine china pots, walls adorned with books and art. A photo of Mum, Dad, Jason, Boo and me.

How strange it was to see my body on the floor below me.

Slam! Back into my body.

The taste of iron. The stink of old pennies. Blood. My blood.

No! No more. Flip out of the physical shell. Come on. You could do it, Maggie. Flip out.

A red mist filled the air, rendering the room a blur of ghostly shapes. Blood vapourising. How much had I left? Dizzy, weak. Not much.

Red volcanic eyes stared out from the blackness as my face drew closer to the gap. The eyes fixed onto mine and crinkled with laughter.

I knew you. From somewhere. How did I know you?

Pain burned in my bicep.

I couldn't have much arm left. I had to break free. Rip the

rest of my arm off if I must. It was my last chance. I could do this. I could do this. I could do this.

My shoulder joint made a sound like a pistol shot as I jerked away as hard as I could. The thing pulled back, harder. The edge of the cabinet sliced into my body as it increased the pressure. It wanted more of me.

You couldn't have more, motherfucker. I would fight you till my last breath.

Using my legs, I pushed away from the cabinet.

Smash! It snapped me back.

Oomph! The breath left my lungs as I kissed wood.

Bang! Bang! Bang!

The thing ratcheted up the speed. The cabinet rocked. Dad's crystal wine glasses tinkled, then smashed. What if it tipped over? I'd be screwed.

The pace was frenetic. It pounded out a rhythm and I was the drum.

I'm going to get you! Bang!

Get you! Crash!

Get. Crash. You. Smash!

Twenty rounds with a cabinet, and the crowd roared. *Was that me?*

The side of my cheek stretched out towards the gap. A sound like Velcro ripping as the skin and muscle on my face pulled away.

Sharp as chlorine, a whiff of clean air tingled in my nose. *Ozone? A thunderstorm?* My nostril dissolved. A sense of it being there, and then, not being there—cool air on raw tissue.

Blackness descended, and I welcomed it with open arms.

Dear Nellie-No-Nose sat on a chair outside the lifts of the aged care centre. Cancer had eaten her nose, and in its place was a plastic one.

Poor Nellie couldn't get her plastic nose to sit right. It was either too high, too low, or way off to one side. Sometimes, she'd forget to put her nose on at all. Today was one of those days.

Nellie smiled at me, and the gaping red hole in the middle of her face expanded, so I could see right into her sinuses.

Would I be able to get my plastic nose to sit right?

'Jason … Jason … Jason.'

The ceaseless murmuration of his name whispered mantra like on my breath as senses returned. A heavy weight crushed my chest, making each inhalation a challenge. My eyelids were glued shut by congealed blood. I forced them apart and blinked. The weight was Jason. His head lay heavily between my breasts, his face a mask of death. The stench of vomit filled my nostrils.

The pain ebbed and flowed, consciousness came and went. Blood congealed around me and a fresh trickle flowed into it from somewhere. Hope drained away with the blood from my body.

That was it. Life was over. Eaten by a hallway cabinet. They'd find our remains, and no one would be able to work out what happened. Maybe the thing under the cabinet would get them too.

The dog door squeaked and clattered. Boo flew into the room holding a muddy ball in her mouth. It matched the rest of her; she was coated in mud from the pond outside. She wanted to play.

Damn all the mud she'd brought into the house. *I'm dying, Boo. Delirious. Go away. Can't play. Never. Ever.*

Boo flicked the ball with her nose and it rolled across the floor leaving behind a trail of mud. Everything was in slow motion. Mud particles blew off the ball in a halo of dust.

Dust! I hadn't seen dust for ages.

The ball rolled into my hand and transformed into an incandescent crystal sphere. It was icy hot against my skin. Déjà vu.

Jason groaned, raised himself to his knees, and swayed unsteadily above me. *Oh, thank God. He was alive.*

We must've appeared equally horrified as we surveyed the

carnage of each other. Involuntary sobs escaped my lips as I took in the damage to his body.

Jason's right arm was missing. His chest cavity was open, exposing layers of skin, bone and muscle, along with a moosh of bloody innards. Bits and pieces of flesh decorated the remains of his jumper. A fine mist of blood had painted his face red, and the whites of his eyes stood out eerily in the half light.

Judging by his expression, I must've looked worse.

'Ich you vomit again, pleesh get bucket,' I whispered, finding speech difficult with half my face missing. The cold air hurt my teeth. Sensodyne toothpaste would be number one on my shopping list.

'Where's the bucket?' he croaked.

'Itch on top of the laundry cupboard'.

My body was a bloody, ruined mess, but the blood flow from my wounds had ceased, and the pain had gone. Given our inane conversation about the laundry bucket, Jason must've felt better too.

'This is weird,' he said.

'Sure is,' a voice agreed.

Jason and I started. There was no one else around. Only Boo.

'Don't worry!' a voice in our heads said. 'Quick, hold Jason's hand. The crystal's reaching critical mass.'

I normally questioned everything. So did Jason. This time, we didn't.

We automatically put our right shoulders forward before realising we had no arms, and definitely, no hands to hold.

Take two.

We reached out with our left arms.

The crystal blazed in my hand, and it was so damn bright I wished for sunglasses. Light flamed out, irradiating the house so not a single shadow survived. Not a one.

'I'll have to drop the ball if we're going to hold hands,' I muttered. I opened my hand, but the ball stayed put. The thing was superglued to my flesh.

'Bloody hell!' I'd been half consumed by a hall cabinet, and now I had a glowing snow cone melded to my only good hand.

'Take her hand!' the voice commanded.

Holding my hand, and the crystal, Jason looked into my eyes. He had such beautiful eyes, and I was immensely grateful he still had two of them. For a moment—if I ignored the missing body parts—I was in a Mills & Boon novel, lost in the depths of those gorgeous blue eyes.

I still had two eyes, but they were set in a half-chewed face. I was envious of Nellie-No-Nose. Who'd have ever thought?

Sadly, this wouldn't be a Mills & Boon moment for Jason. More like an extract from a Stephen King novel.

'I love you,' he whispered, as we disintegrated into an inferno of incandescent light.

---

6 *Maggie's Playlist —Bits and Pieces, The Dave Clark Five*

Chapter 7: Resurrection

'Your dead shall live; their bodies shall rise. You who dwell in the dust, awake and sing for joy! For your dew is a dew of light, and the earth will give birth to the dead.' — *Isaiah 26:19*

I floated in a world of light, soft, yet so powerful. I breathed light. I was light.

A golden radiance permeated everything within and without. It was— bliss.

My broken body was a shadow, a faint watercolour outline over which lay a structure of pulsing light. I stretched out my missing arm—it was a see through grid of radiant energy. Atoms and molecules shimmered in a breathtaking aurora borealis, weaving structure from a loom of light.

Who was I?

I couldn't think.

Thought was—so far away—the sound of a raindrop on the far side of the universe.

I was gone.

I was—Everything. Everywhere. Everyone.

***** *

Awakening, I found myself sitting on the lawn in the back garden, unsure of how long I'd been there. Ants crawled over my legs and a dragonfly rested on my knee, its wings phosphorescent rainbows in the sun. I hated ants. Well, I used to. Now, they felt part of me. Everything was a part of me.

The world was bathed in a golden radiance. I couldn't fathom right or wrong. Everything simply was. All I felt was Love.

Unlimited. Unconditional. Glorious.

I had everything. I had nothing.

I was everyone. I was no one.

I was everything. I was nothing.

I sat there in wonder.

Jason was in the garden too, sitting on an old wooden bench. He watched Boo, who was on her back in the grass, legs spread-eagled, long ears flopping back as she gazed at the clouds.

I stood, with legs so stiff I could hardly walk, and made my way towards Jason in a manner reminiscent of Frankenstein's monster.

We gazed wordlessly at each other, and registered, without surprise, our bodies had returned to their former wholeness.

I couldn't say the same about our clothes, however. They hung from our bodies in dirty shreds. Jason's hair appeared as though it hadn't been washed for a year. His eyes were rimmed with black mud and set in a dirt-streaked face. He resembled a camouflaged commando ready to do battle. A bare muscular arm extended from his tattered thin knit. The arm was perfect.

He stood and took a step towards me, as stiff as a rusty rifle. Those two beautiful arms reached out, and we literally fell into each other's embrace. Well, staggered awkwardly, but I wanted another Mills & Boon moment, so 'fell' it was. We hugged for much longer than the twenty seconds required for bonding. We hugged for an eternity—at least that's what it felt like.

An angry growl from my stomach made me realise I was starving.

'Egg and chips?' I suggested.

'You bet.'

The word chips broke Boo's relaxed trance. She sprang to her feet, full of beans. 'Me three!' a voice proclaimed.

A disembodied voice that sounded like Prince Charles sounded out in our heads. Judging by Boo's intense eye contact, it appeared to emanate from her. This didn't register as a strange phenomenon, given what we'd been through an' all. In fact, nothing was strange; everything was beautifully perfect.

Our priority was egg and chips and a nice cup of tea. It was a sensible priority too, considering we'd been sitting out in the garden for quite a while. Judging by the newspapers we found scattered along our front driveway, we'd been out of action for three days.

Egg and chips—a meal we'd loved before what we now called 'The Event'—sent us into paroxysms of heavenly delight.

One of the reasons I liked Jason so much was that he shared my love of food. I wasn't an agreeable person to be around when I was hungry, so we lived by the quote "First we eat, then we do everything else."

'Oh God. Mmmm. Mmmm. Yum!' Three voices hummed in unison, until all the food was gone.

Replete, we sat in silence savouring our cups of tea. Jason's face was glowing underneath all the dirt.

'You look like you've swallowed a light bulb.'

'So do you!' he said. 'A five hundred watter. Check out Boo! How can a dog glow through fur?'

After the food, a tiredness as deep as space settled over our shoulders.

We staggered off to bed, two dirt streaked, glowing humans, and a dog that spoke like Prince Charles. Surrounded by softness and warmth, I spooned Boo, and Jason spooned me.

'It doesn't get much better than this,' I said as slumber took us. We slept like that for eighteen hours straight.

* * * * *

I floated near the ceiling admiring Jason's handiwork. He'd recently painted our bedroom and the quality of his workmanship was extraordinary. Not a drip or errant brush mark was to be seen, even up here.

My ability to astral travel never ceased to amaze me, and I felt a peculiar thrill as I viewed my body below. The three of us hadn't stirred. We breathed in sync, Boo's two breaths to our one.

A large wood-framed mirror hung in the bedroom and reflected the soft green of the bamboo outside. The last rays of autumn light gave way to dusk, and the currawongs' call echoed eerily through the air.

A tawny frogmouth alighted silently on the windowsill, its yellow eyes fixed on a ghostly face peering from the mirror. The face stared intently at our three sleeping bodies. A translucent finger traced patterns on the glass.

The ghostly face remained watching for most of the night. The tawny frogmouth's eyes never wavered. When the face disappeared, the bird left on silent wings.

* * * * *

I awoke refreshed, enjoying the softness and warmth of flannelette sheets on my skin. Who, or what, was the ghostly face in the mirror? It didn't have any features and I couldn't get a sense of who it was. The ghost didn't have a 'vibe' to it. That concerned me. It was an unknown entity. Don't tell me I had another worry to add to my list.

Jason was still sleeping soundly. Boo was snoring and had managed to take over most of the bed, leaving us squashed to one side.

Still feeling somewhat disembodied, I headed to the bathroom for a hot shower.

It scared me to look in the mirror in case the reflection had bits missing. Thankfully, I seemed to be intact, but my image left a lot to be desired.

My skin—so pale it was almost translucent— was streaked with dirt. Jason called it my 'snow white tan', a line from his favourite Bowie song. Black hair, stiff and matted, stuck out at all angles. Lips needed an urgent application of lip balm, and my eyes seemed bigger and greener than usual. Well, that part wasn't so bad.

I forced a big smile—yep, all teeth present and accounted for. Opening my mouth wide, I stuck out my tongue, half expecting to see some nasty alien maggoty thing smiling back at me, but no, all clear.

Removing my shredded clothes, I stood naked in front of the mirror. All good. Everything seemed to be there. I tentatively examined my reinstated arm and it seemed fine. I compared it to the other arm and noticed the skin seemed smoother on the reinstated one. Hmmm. If Boo had waited a little bit longer before coming in with the crystal sphere, I could've had a complete makeover.

I stood in the shower feeling the hot water run over my body. It was divine, like a gift from heaven. The aroma of lemongrass and sandalwood body wash filled the cubicle. I closed my eyes and was transported to celestial realms by the power of its scent. Nearly dying sure heightened one's appreciation of the simple things in life.

I tried not to think about what happened. My brain was having trouble processing the whole thing, so I focused on what to make us for breakfast—or lunch. I wasn't sure what time it was. When in doubt, eat. After danger, eat. I laughed to myself. With all the bad things happening, I was going to end up like Ten-Ton Tessie.

Jason wandered into the bathroom looking like an extra from a zombie movie. He leant against the basin and stared keenly at his reflection, carrying out a similar routine. He stripped off his tattered clothes and checked himself out in the full-length mirror.

One handsome head, two eyes, sandy hair, two muscular arms and legs and other important accoutrements. He didn't have a six-pack, but he looked pretty darn good to me. 'All bits present and accounted for?' I asked.

'All good. What about you?'

'Fine, 'cept I think the new bits actually look in better condition.'

He held out both arms and examined them carefully.

'Huh, you're right. My new arm looks newer.'

'Do you feel okay?' I asked.

'Yep. Do you?'

'Sort of. We need to debrief. I'm used to weird stuff, but not this weird … everything that happened, and Boo, talking? You did hear her—in your head? I didn't dream it?'

'I heard her all right. My brain's in overload. Hearing a voice in my head, well, I thought I'd lost the plot. We definitely need to debrief.'

'Have a shower, and I'll make breakfast. We can talk then.'

He gave me a peck on the cheek. 'Thanks, Mags.'

Jason's thoughts whirred in my mind as he desperately tried to process what happened. My mind was in overload too. Nothing that bacon and eggs wouldn't fix. I raced off to the kitchen to get breakfast underway. One of Virginia Woolf's quotes buzzed around in my brain—"One cannot think well, love well, sleep well, if one has not dined well." Now there was a woman after my own heart.

Moderating and controlling my psychic brain used massive amounts of energy. I required more food than the average Joe to enable me to function efficiently. For me, food worked better than any drug—except for sex. Food and sex kept me sane, enabling me to function like a 'normal' person. Sort of. Even the process of preparing food kept me centered, and I was completely in the present moment as I cooked up a storm in the kitchen.

Jason sauntered in, stopped and inhaled deeply. Eyes closed, he seemed transported to another world. Aromas can do that to you, and Jason was in Bacon World.

A smile exploded across his face. 'God that smells good!' His gorgeous dimples appeared, so he must've been happy.

I loved his smile. It filled me with joy at each appearance. I knew Jason was self-conscious about his imperfect teeth in today's world of the Hollywood smile. His front two pearly whites were ever so slightly angled backwards, and the teeth next to them sat slightly forward and caught the light when he smiled. It made him look unique—and gorgeous. His eyes had a hawk like appearance, and his well-shaped nose and high cheekbones gave him a European look. When his smile was turned off he had a thoughtful, serious look about him.

His imperfections made him strikingly beautiful, and at this moment I wanted to eat him more than my bacon and eggs.

Warm autumn sunlight shone through the glass sliding doors in the kitchen and warmed our backs as we sipped our coffee.

Jason drew his lower lip between his teeth and stared at me. 'I can't believe we're still alive.'

'If you hadn't come back when you did, I probably wouldn't be alive.'

'Boo brought me back,' he said. 'I was walking along the street, steeling myself for cat corner. Boo's nemesis the cat was there, ready and waiting to razz her up. Boo tugged hard on the lead to get to the cat, then suddenly, she froze, dropped a u-ey and pulled in the other direction. Boo barked like I've never heard her bark before. It was desperate. Hysterical. Howling. She tugged harder than a sled dog. I could barely hold her. I tried to reel her in but she yanked free of the collar and hightailed down the street.

I set off in hot pursuit, worried she'd run in front of a car. I knew you'd never forgive me if anything happened to her. In the distance, I saw her turn into our driveway—then I knew something was wrong.

Boo was at the front door, scratching at it, barking and spinning around in anxious circles. The door was locked, of course, your security consciousness and paranoia at work!'

'Better a thousand times careful than once dead,' I said.

'But Jesus Christ! All the friggin' locks. It took me forever to get in, fumbling for keys, the security door and two main door locks. I could hear noises coming from inside; I was freaking out. When I opened the door, you were on the floor next to the cabinet. I could smell the stink of burnt flesh, and the room was filled with a red mist. Boo pushed past, saw you on the floor, then blasted straight out the dog door into the back yard.'

Jason paused and took a sip of coffee. He tapped his fingernails against the tabletop and his foot pumped anxiously.

'Stop with the foot, Jace.'

It twitched even more.

'You'd morphed into the cabinet,' he said, ignoring my request. 'I shifted into paramedic mode when I rolled you over. But, bloody hell, even my experience didn't prepare me. Half your face was gone.'

He paused and took a ragged breath. 'Your skin was stripped off leaving bones and teeth exposed. You only had half a nose. The top of your head had lost flesh and bone too, and your brain was visible, for fuck's sake. Your right arm was gone, most of your shoulder, and chunks all along the right side of your body were exposed raw flesh, muscle and bone.

I gotta tell you, paramedic mode left as quickly as it came. I went straight into shock.'

Jason's mouth was tight, and his Adam's apple moved in his throat as he tried to swallow. He fixed his eyes on the ceiling.

'You don't need to talk about this,' I said.

'Yes, I do,' he said, meeting my gaze again. 'Seeing you like that, well … my stomach lurched into my throat and brought my breakfast with it. The blood ran away from my brain, my legs gave out, and I pitched forward on top of you. What a joke. Then the thing latched onto me and tried to drag me in as well. My arm was too big, but the damn creature was determined to make it fit.

The edge of the cabinet razored the flesh off my arm as the thing yanked me under. I blacked out watching the skin and muscle fold along my humerus like a bloody concertina. I'm sorry, Maggie. I shouldn't have left you alone.' He pressed the heel of his hand into his forehead. 'I can't get those images out of my mind.'

I stood and wrapped my arms around him. 'You weren't to know. It's not your fault, for Christ's sake. And we're fine now.'

His body was hard and rigid like steel, and an image of ice shattering filled my mind. I held him until his tension released.

Jason met my eyes, and said tentatively, 'Before we talk about the thing under the cabinet, I have to tell you that I know what happened to us the first time— at the other house. It's come back. Boo running into the house, the dark entity on the stairs, the distortions, the weird room, the crystal? Do you remember? Or am I crazy?'

'Yes, the memories came back for me too.'

Jason took a deep breath and let out a sigh.

'Yep, you're not crazy,' I said. 'I remember all that and waking up back home in bed. But I can't remember where we were in-between jumping over the crystal and waking up at home. I'm still missing a few days. Have you got the missing bit?'

'Nope. I was hoping you had.'

'Damn. I wonder where we went then? Maybe another dimension?'

'I wouldn't like to speculate,' Jason said.

Over numerous cups of tea, we compared memories until we

felt in sync.

'So, do you reckon the thing under the cabinet was the Dark Force? Not some other entity?' Jason asked.

'It's the same creature. It followed us home. We should've been alerted by the lack of dust, but we had no memory of what happened the first time.'

'What the hell is it?'

'I'm not sure, but it feels human.'

'You're kidding?'

'Nope. It has a human energy to it. I could sense it. And what's more, as it was consuming me, I sensed it enjoyed eating my fear and pain more than my flesh and bone.'

Jason scratched his head. 'I don't even know where to go with that theory. And the crystal sphere? Can you enlighten me?'

'The crystal!' I jumped from the chair, and nearly sent my fifth cup of tea flying.

'What's wrong?' Jason asked.

'The crystal! Where is it? Did you put it somewhere?'

'Definitely not. I haven't seen it. Maybe it rolled under the cabinet?'

I dashed up the hallway and bent over to have a look. Chills ran down my spine. 'Oh Jesus, yes, I can see something under there. Can you get it?'

'Yeah, right,' he said. 'There's not a snowball's hope in hell I'm sticking my arm back there.'

'Me neither. I'll get the long-handled tongs.'

'Good plan,' he said.

I handed him the tongs. He held them against the side of the cabinet. 'No good, not enough safety margin. What about a broom handle?'

'No worries.' I ran to get the broom.

'Here 'tis,' I said, handing it to him.

'Much better, thanks.' He slowly inserted the wooden broom handle under the cabinet. I held my breath.

'Wait!' I said.

He started in fright. '*What?*'

'Shouldn't we have a plan? I mean what if you stick the broom handle under the cabinet, and some kind of residual energy shoots along the handle and gets you?'

Jason gave me a look. The sort he gives to people he thinks are severely lacking in intelligence.

'Don't give me that look!'

'The shadow thing's gone. Haven't you noticed the dust and dog hair everywhere? It's only the crystal sphere under there, nothing else.'

'Explain to me why we're using a long stick then?'

'Just in case. I don't know.'

This time I gave Jason a look. 'Oh, give it here!' I took the broomstick. 'Stand clear!' I poked it in the general direction of the object and gave the broom handle a hefty flick. The handle caught on something and wouldn't budge. 'Something's got it,' I said in a little Minnie Mouse voice.

Jason took the broom, pressed his face to the floor and peered under the cabinet.

God, he was brave. Or stupid.

'Nope, not caught on anything. The handle's behind the crystal ball, but nothing's happening.'

Jason pushed on the handle and strained with effort.

'It won't budge!' he huffed. 'Either stuck or weighs a bloody ton. It's like trying to move an elephant with a matchstick. This isn't going to cut it.' He stood and brushed dust and dog hair off his pants. 'Don't touch anything! Put the kettle on for a cup of tea. I'm going to get some stuff from the shed.'

'Please?'

The hawk eyes shot me a withering look.

'There's no excuse for rudeness or bad manners, even in the most trying of circumstances,' I said, as he disappeared out the back door. I put the kettle on and pondered our tea addiction. It was another of our passions. Having a brew up always settled the nerves. Dad loved his cuppa too—I'm sure my DNA had a tea gene.

Jason returned with a very long crowbar, an old blanket, and a large block of wood. He had a crazy grin on his face and an air about him that said, *I'm a man with a damn good plan!*

'Tea's on!' I said.

'What sort?'

'English Breakfast for me and Japanese Green for you.'

'Perfect! I'll do this first.'

Jason spread the blanket on the floor near the cabinet and placed the large wooden block on it. He slid the blanket and block under the cabinet. It fitted under by a hair (or a 'bees dick' as Jason would say). Once the wooden block was in place, Jason had some leverage. He inserted the crowbar behind the crystal and pushed against it with all his strength.

Judging by the look of his bulging biceps he was still experiencing resistance.

'The thing weighs a bloody ton,' he said. 'But it can't be that heavy.' He jammed his feet against the wall and pushed.

I moved to one side. 'Careful, it might fly out and hit something!'

Slowly the crowbar did its job and out slid the crystal. Except it didn't look like the crystal anymore, just a lump of rock—white-grey, dull and pock marked. I couldn't see any light—all the iridescence had vanished.

'Is it the same thing?'

'I think so,' he said. 'It's the same size.'

I gingerly extended a finger to touch it.

'Careful!'

My finger hovered millimetres away from contact when the doorbell rang.

We jumped out of our skin.

Ding Dong! Ding Dong! Ding Dong!

'Who the hell's that?' Jason asked.

'It can't be the Dark Force; it wouldn't bother knocking.'
What other danger lurked at our doorway?

---

[7] *Maggie's Playlist: Who Can It Be Now? — Colin Hay — Men at Work*

Chapter 8: An Unexpected Visitor

I recognised the familiar silhouette through the stained-glass panels on the front door.

'It's Ashley,' I whispered. 'What do we do? Let him in?'

Even though Ashley was one of our best friends, I wasn't sure I was ready to speak to another human just yet.

'We have to,' Jason said. 'He would've come all the way from the bush, probably Alice Springs.'

'Do we say anything?'

Again the look. 'Of course not!'

Struggling up from my knees, with one foot well and truly asleep, I shouted, 'Cover the stuff with the blanket. I'll get the door. Coming! Hang on!'

I opened the door, and familiar brown eyes stared out from a rugged tanned face and met my gaze. Brown hair fell across Ashley's lined forehead, and a short beard and mustache set off his strong jaw. He was six foot three of solid muscle.

A smile split his larrikin face and revealed teeth in urgent need of dental attention. 'Hey! Magster! Long time no see!' he said, his voice deep and raspy.

Ashley looked like he'd encountered more paranormal events than us. However, his were purely terrestrial in origin, events such as an overdose of sun, smoking, booze and drugs. He stepped inside and enfolded me in warm, welcoming arms.

I loved a full body hug, and Ashley could give one of the best. It was pure, innocent affection from a not so innocent man.

'Jace! Good to see ya, man!' he said. 'Can I smell coffee?'

'No. But I'll make you some,' Jason said.

They gave each other a bear hug punctuated with slaps on the back.

'What's with the crowbar?' Ashley asked, looking over Jason's shoulder.

'Testing for termites.'

'With a crowbar?'

'I'm only tapping lightly.'

'Oh.'

Ashley seemed satisfied with the most ridiculous explanation I'd ever heard. We made our way to the kitchen and Jason fired up the coffee machine.

Ashley pulled out a chair and sat at our refectory table, running his hands over the weathered timber. 'I love this wood,' he said, caressing the grain. His strong, tanned hands moved rhythmically across the tabletop, mesmerising me with their action. The sensual movements took me back to the time when we were together, and an unexpected flush of heat bloomed in my body.

'Wake up, Maggie!' I jumped visibly as Jason plonked a mug of coffee in front of Ashley.

I gasped. 'You startled me!'

'Talk about jumpy,' Jason said. 'It's been ages, Ash. Hope you like the coffee.'

'Black, extra strong, extra hot?'

'Yep. Exactly how you like it, and how any self-respecting coffee drinker wouldn't,' Jason said with a grin.

'Bloody coffee snobs.'

'What brings you here?' I asked.

'Gold.'

'Gold?'

'Yep. Thought I'd dust off the detector and poke around the Golden Triangle a bit. I've gotta feeling. Reckon I could find a bit of colour.'

Jason and I knew a bit about prospecting through my dad. It was one of his favourite hobbies. We'd shared many a weekend at the Lerderderg Gorge panning for gold.

I glanced across at the small glass bottle glinting in the sunlight on a shelf nearby. It was filled with gold flakes, a nugget the size of a shotgun pellet, and a pinhead sized ruby. Our entire Lerderderg Gorge bounty.

Ashley followed my gaze. 'Any news about your dad?'

'No, not a thing.'

He leant across and took my hand. Tears pricked in my eyes. I blinked them back and quickly brushed an escapee tear from my cheek. Damn it. A simple gesture of concern was enough to set me off. I'd thought I was doing fine. I squeezed Ashley's hand and withdrew from his rough warm grasp. The wall holding back my emotions started to crumble—random acts of kindness could seriously undermine its foundations.

Don't cry! I pinched my leg hard. If the wall gave way, it would be an avalanche of epic proportions. I wasn't ready. Not now.

'Maggie? *Magster?*

'Huh? Oh, sorry, Ashley. Off with the fairies. I'm back now.'

Jason's mouth was in thin serious mode. I looked away from his gaze.

'So, Ash, will you be around for a bit, or are you heading off?' Jason asked.

'Gonna head off. Got the truck outside loaded with everything I need for a few weeks out bush. Wanted to stop by and say hi before I left.'

Booze hound and stoner aside, Ashley had turned his hand to many pursuits over the years. A motor mechanic who loved to race cars and dirt bikes, a soldier in Iraq, a landscape gardener, sheep shearer, cook, miner, postman and also a paramedic with Jason for a while—until he ended up more stoned out than the people he was trying to save.

Half of me wished he'd stay. I knew he would, if we asked, but I also knew we couldn't afford to have a dam buster around right now.

Ashley stood, stretched, and gazed down at me with soft eyes. He knew something was up. His pickled boozehound brain still managed to run a perfectly working, finely tuned, bullshit detector.

'Thanks for the coffee. I can always count on you two for a good brew.'

He ambled towards the front door, but paused by the crowbar and blanket. Jason and I exchanged glances.

'Funny way to termite hunt, you guys.' He nudged the lump under the blanket with the toe of his Blundstone boot. 'What's that?'

'A rock to keep the blanket in place,' Jason said.

Don't say *rock*! I screamed in my mind at Jason. Ashley loved rocks.

'What sort?' He flipped the blanket back with his boot.

Oh hell. We were screwed. He was screwed.

Before we could move, he'd bent over and scooped up the 'rock.' We winced in anticipation as he tossed it in the air a couple of times.

'Hmmm, this ain't no rock.' He peered closely at its pock marked surface.

'It … it isn't?' Jason stammered.

'What is it then?' I said, feeling somewhat more relaxed now Ashley hadn't vaporised or shown any other obvious signs of paranormal weirdness.

'It's a meteor.'

'A meteor?' Jason and I echoed.

'Yep. Got one exactly like it in the truck. I mean *exactly* like it. Same shape, colour, weight an' all. Too weird!' His big hand rubbed circles in his hair.

'Found it near Big Bell Ghost Town in Western Australia. I've collected a pile of meteors, but I thought my Big Bell find was unique. Huh. Now it's got a sister. Amazing! Whereja find this?'

'Um, Boo brought it in from the back yard,' I said. It wasn't a lie.

Jason seemed relieved.

'Dead set?' Ashley said. 'It's a big 'un to pick up and carry in. Must be five kilos I reckon.'

Boo had a number of hobbies, one of which was rock collecting. In our back yard was a creek fringed with river pebbles. Every week or so she'd select a rock and bring it into the house. She'd flip onto her back, legs in the air, and roll the rock around in her mouth. The expression on her face was always one of pure joy. Boo would then drop the rock at our feet and wait for us to ceremoniously add it to her collection, contained in a wooden bowl on the coffee table.

Ashley glanced at the bowl. 'This is the doozey of the lot,' he said.

'Yep, we're always worried she'll crack a tooth or get a rock stuck in her throat, but no problems so far,' I said.

'That rock has to be way heavier than five kilos,' Jason said, obviously concerned the after-effects of 'The Event' had turned him into a ninety-pound weakling.

'Nah. I'm a human digital scale. Definitely five. Here, catch!'

Ashley tossed the rock to Jason and a number of things occurred in rapid succession.

Jason's face turned white, his hands shot forward in 'catch' mode and he bent his knees, bracing his legs like a weight lifter ready to hoist 150 kilos.

The meteor flew through the air. Boo burst in through the

dog flap. Jason caught the rock with muscles primed to receive 150 kilos. Instead he only got five. His primed muscles propelled the meteor skywards at speed, and it smashed through the skylight and onto the roof where it thunked along the tiles like a crazy possum.

Ashley stood opened mouthed and wide eyed.

I guess the description fitted us all, Boo included. She'd reverted to silent mode, by the way. That was a good thing.

'What the *hell*?' Ashley said.

'Oh bollocks!' Jason said. 'I've trashed the skylight!'

'What the hell?' Ashley said again, staring at Jason like he'd gone mad.

'I thought it was heavier than it was, is all,' Jason said, by way of explanation.

Ashley rolled his eyes. 'No kidding. I'll give you a hand to clean up.'

'Nah, it's all right. What a *stupid*, stupid idiot!' Jason said, looking at the hole and rubbing his forehead.

The three of us surveyed the scene in silence, before we all fell about laughing.

Ashley convulsed silently, holding his stomach as tears ran down his face. I had a serious case of the snorts, which turned into a cough, and Jason's glorious smile was in face splitting mode. Deep laughter roared from his belly. Boo ran anxiously from one of us to the other, obviously concerned for our wellbeing. This made us laugh all the more.

Still red in the face and wiping tears from our eyes, we ambled out to Ashley's truck. He fished around in the back and pulled out his meteor.

'Here it is. Told ya it was identical.' He held it out to Jason. '*Careful* Jace!' he said, which set everyone off again.

Composure regained, we examined his meteor, and it was indeed identical.

'If you ever lose yours, you can have this one,' Ashley said, giving me a farewell hug. Joyous from the after-effects of all the laughter, I surrendered into the warmth of his embrace. My sadness was once again locked safely away.

You would think, as a psychic, I could have anticipated what was coming. However, seeing my own future was off limits.

Who knew how short lived my joy would be.

Chapter 9: Contact

After Ashley left, the weather turned nasty and Jason hurried to tape up the hole in the skylight. It was too risky to climb on the roof to retrieve the crystal. I hoped it would be safe up there until the weather cleared.

Our sleep that night was restless—we were still in a state of high alert. When early morning came, I sat at the kitchen table watching the rain streaming over the glass roof of the deck outside.

There was a sense something could happen at any minute if we dropped our guard: something that involved a Dark Force entity that didn't like dust or much else for that matter. Maybe if we could harness the dust destroying part, we could happily coincide, and make a fortune in the process.

On the other hand, we had the meteor—the crystal sphere which had now saved our bacon on two occasions, and appeared to have sacrificed itself in the process. It was completely dull and lifeless when Jason retrieved it from under the cabinet.

Between the dark thing and the light thing was—*us*. The question was why?

Where was the Dark Force? Could we go back to our normal lives? Should we be forever scared of dark shadows and always hire cleaners to clean under our cabinets? Who could we even tell about any of this? No one would believe us.

Well, actually, one person would. My dad.

Unfortunately, the Prof was no longer around and I still missed him. I wished I could get a sense of him.

Mum had strong psychic powers, but she couldn't handle them. In the end, they drove her mad. She was gifted with all the 'clairs' as she used to call them— clairvoyance, clairsentience, clairaudience, clairolfactance, claircognisance and clairgustance. This meant she could acquire information through extra sensory perception, feelings, paranormal hearing, smell, intrinsic knowledge—she knew things without knowing how she knew them—and she could taste essences and substances from the ethereal realms.

I'd inherited all the 'clairs' too. It made my life a misery. When Mum committed suicide, I made the decision to stop using my abilities and to actively disengage from them. My efforts bore fruit, as some of them were now dormant.

At least I'd been able to grieve Mum's death, but Dad was missing, so I had no closure.

'Where the hell are you, Prof?'

I opened a drawer and took out the yellowing pages of a newspaper cutting headlined: "Leading Astrophysics Professor Vanishes".

It'd been a year since he'd disappeared, and months since I'd tried to reach out to him. I stood and moved to the side of the table. I unfolded my mind like a flower reaching out to the sun. Opening my perception wide, I searched for a trace of his unique vibration.

I'd contacted many souls using my skills, and never was afraid in doing so. My energy was always in sync with the higher levels of vibration, and as such I attracted only positive energy.

My senses opened fully and I sifted through the energetic worlds surrounding us. As fast and lethal as a shark hurtling towards its prey, darkness struck my mind. Gasping, I rocked back on my feet as it slammed into me. It gained easy purchase on the open tendrils of my mind, its tentacles feeling robotic, mechanical, as it sliced, diced and dissected my brain, probing ever deeper into my atomic structure. It savoured the essence of my atoms and molecules. I sensed it found them delicious.

Boo barked somewhere in the distance. My mind burned, disintegrating with a pain worse than a million migraines. Caught in a spider's web of psychic energy, it was impossible to break free.

A gunshot exploded in my head, atoms shook with internal vibrations, heart jolted and I slipped out of my body and away from the agony. Floating to the ceiling, I had a bird's eye view of myself standing catatonic in the middle of the room. Eyes wide, mouth stretched open, I clutched frantically at my head.

Boo blasted through the dog door and launched herself at me with an ear-splitting howl. Flying through the air, with teeth bared and fangs gleaming, she knocked me to the ground.

* * * * *

'Maggie! What happened? Jeez, I leave the room for one minute. Boo, get *off* her!' Jason pushed Boo from my chest and helped me stand.

His face was a mix of horror and concern. 'Fuck! You've got blood running from your eyes and nose. And your ears! What happened?'

'My brain's on fire.'

It was as if all the nerves had been stripped bare and each thought generated took an excruciating journey along them.

'I'm taking you to hospital.'

Collapsing back to the floor, I curled into a fetal position. 'They can't help me.' I held my head. I was going to die.

Rocking back and forth trying to cope with the pain, I made

a weak attempt to call angels. I couldn't take one more second of it—not one.

A soft vibration tickled my ears. An indescribably beautiful sound echoed through my body, soothing it with celestial tones. A soft blue light, calming, iridescent and divine enfolded my body. The light spoke to me beyond my senses, beyond pain. It was my guardian angel and it wanted to use Jason as a conduit to the physical realm.

'Jason, hold my head.'

Without question or hesitation, he took my head in his hands and closed his eyes. He jolted as the healing energy flooded through him into me, restoring my mind with its radiance.

The energy faded and the pain vanished. I opened my eyes to find Jason knelt on the floor behind me, his hands still on my head. Surrounding him was an angel. Powerful, sublime, shining with blue and gold light, its outstretched dazzling silver wings encompassed the room. The feathers shone in radiant glory as the wings retracted, the energy receded, and it rose like an eagle and disappeared.

Jason opened his eyes. His face was peaceful; it was as though he'd just stepped out of a sixty-hour float tank session.

'Incredible,' he said softly. 'Are you okay now, Maggie?'

'Yes.' Tears of relief flowed over my face, mingled with the blood, and dripped rose coloured drops onto the floor.

'What happened?' he asked.

'I'm not sure. I … I can't remember.'

Boo trotted over and licked me. Her big brown eyes were almost black, and she stared at me with an unsettling intensity.

I staggered to my feet. 'What, Boo? Jason, is she saying something? Can you hear anything?'

'Nup. Nothing. Sure looks like she's trying to say something though.'

Boo jumped up and pushed against me with her front legs. Then she did it again and again.

A surge of annoyance flared. 'Stop it, Boo!'

She kept at it, jumping against me, pushing me.

A tiny black seed, smaller than an atom, quivered in the deepest recesses of my mind.

'Stop it, Boo! Get down. What's got into you? Stupid animal! Knocking me over. You could've killed me!'

Pure anger, fuelled by a distilled essence of hate, arose inside me. My arms and legs began to shake—stiff, rapid, jerking movements. Jason's mouth moved but I couldn't hear the words. Sound was muffled. Every tiny thing was in exquisite detail. My chest heaved as I panted like a rabid dog. An image of old leather bellows flashed into my brain as the air sucked in and out of my lungs. In, out, in out, in out, faster and faster. My heart beat was so rapid I felt the blood pulse in my neck.

Jason was in my face yelling at me. I couldn't hear him, only the hurricane in my ears. The room narrowed, closing in. The pressure in my head was intense. I could feel my cranium expanding. My brain was about to break out of my skull.

No fear. No pain. No consequences.

Through a haze of rose red, all I could see was Boo.

This. Was. The. Last. Straw.

I wanted to slap that dog to kingdom come. I snatched the iron off the table and lunged. I needed to smash her head into oblivion, grind it into the floor, pulverise and mash it.

I was death. I was destruction.

'*Maggie!* Stop!'

Jason gripped my wrist so hard it hurt. He wrenched the iron from my hand. His face was white, and on it was an expression I'd never seen.

He yelled at me. 'Are you insane? What the hell's gotten into you?'

I don't know what he saw in my face, but he slapped it so hard I saw stars. With the slap, I awoke. My head throbbed, my face stung, and I cried. I cried because I didn't know what was going on. I cried because I'd wanted to kill my dog. I cried for Mum and Dad and because Jason hit me. I cried because I was scared, no, make that terrified, and because of all the bad things that ever happened to me and to those I loved.

I'd experienced hell, heaven, and gone back to hell in the space of a few moments. I knew then that I had no idea of what was to come, and the realisation made me cry some more. Everything I knew about life had been thrown into a blender and blitzed on high. The result? Mayhem. Danger. Terror. The stuff of your worst nightmares. Our lives would never be the same, and neither would anyone else's. Every man, woman and child was at risk. What scared me witless was that no one knew it yet, but it wouldn't be long. The descent into darkness had begun.

Jason took me in his arms and held me until I had not a single tear left. Then, as I put one leaden foot in front of the other, he slowly steered me towards the bedroom. He drew back the covers on our California King, sat me on the bed and said, 'Skin a rabbit.'

I held up my arms and he pulled off my jumper and gently removed the rest of my clothes, as I sat zombie like. Covering me in the bedclothes, he disappeared into the ensuite and returned with a glass of water and two pills cupped in his hand.

'Take these.'

'And they are?'

'Sleeping pills,' he said. 'I've got The Magic Blankie too.' He draped me with a bright orange alpaca throw.

'Thank you,' I murmured. 'That'll fix me.'

When feeling poorly, having Jason wrap me in our orange 'Magic Blankie' always revived me. Tucking it around my body, he transformed me into a bright orange mummy. Encompassed in orange warmth, I surrendered to the embrace of benzodiazepine.

Sounds reached my groggy brain—I struggled to interpret them, they seemed far away.

Tic-tic-tic-tic-tic — Boo's nails on floorboards.

Squeak, squeakady, squeak — Jason's runners.

BANG! — Front door, slamming shut.

Despite being drugged, the ferocity of the sound made me flinch. It was an ominous exclamation mark to the day's events. Jason and Boo had left. Given my insane behaviour, I doubted they would return. Ever.

* * * * *

A surge of relief flowed through me as I awoke hours later to find myself in bed with Jason and Boo. Jason lay beside me, staring into my eyes.

'I'm glad you're here,' I whispered. 'I thought you might have run away.'

Jason's face was in serious mode. 'I did think about it.'

I immediately felt sick to my stomach. My face must've reflected that, as Jason grabbed me and held me tight. His wool knit was soft against my cheek, and I could smell a faint aroma of garlic and mushrooms. Perhaps a touch of cinnamon?

'Are you making breakfast?' I asked hopefully.

'Your weakness has always been food and men—in that order,' he teased, tickling me in the ribs.

I gave him a whack. 'Very funny. I believe the quote relates to Dolly Parton, not me.'

He stroked my cheek. 'I am indeed making you breakfast, my love. Sautéed mushrooms with garlic and herbs, sour dough toast, followed by cinnamon pancakes with butter and maple syrup.'

I knew then all was right with the world. Well, fingers crossed, for the next couple of hours anyway.

---

[9] *Maggie's Playlist: Her Diamonds — Rob Thomas*

Chapter 10: The Voice

'A person finds joy in giving an apt reply - and how good is a timely word!' — *Proverbs 15:23*

Lately, it seemed we were always debriefing. I hoped we'd get through this next debrief without anything else happening because I really wanted to finish my pancake.

'So, what happened?' Jason asked, slipping another pancake onto my plate.

'I don't know. All I remember is standing there minding my own business and then bang, I'm on the floor with Boo sitting on my chest.'

A sudden recollection hit me. I gasped.

'*What?*' Jason asked.

'A memory came back. It was Boo sitting on my chest after she saved us from the Dark Force. 'Boo, I'm sorry,' I said, stroking her. 'You've been through a lot too. We're all going to behave a bit crazy. Given what's been happening, it's only normal to be crazy.'

'Do you realise what you said?' Jason asked, with what I hoped was the start of a smile.

'Yep, crazy is the new normal.'

The smile wasn't a happening thing. His eyes were filled with worry, his mouth a thin line. He brushed back a lock of hair, took a breath and said, 'You weren't you. You were … were …

psycho. Your face was not your face. You were strong. Scary strong. I thought you were going to brain me with the iron. Your face, your whole persona—it was pure evil.'

Jason paused, raked his hands through his hair and then took me by the shoulders. 'Seriously, if I hadn't stopped you, you would have killed Boo,' he said softly, 'and maybe me. That's not normal. It's *crazy*.'

A mirror on a nearby wall rattled and we started at the noise. The newspaper clipping I'd tucked under the side of it, dislodged and floated towards us like a yellow autumn leaf. Mesmerised, we watched as it finally came to rest on my plate. The headline read: "Leading Astrophysics Professor Vanishes".

I shuddered as a white-hot chill ran down my spine, along both arms and then dropped a u-ey back to my brain. My head burned, like the first time I visited a Japanese restaurant and swallowed a small ball of wasabi, thinking it was marzipan. I remembered feeling every sinus right to the back of my cranium. It hurt a lot. This felt like that.

'Ow! Jason, I remember!' I rubbed my head frantically to ease the sensation. 'Before I tried to kill Boo, I was attempting to contact Dad and something terrible latched onto me. I couldn't control it, couldn't block it out. Bloody hell! I've gotta stop thinking or it might come back.'

I jumped up, raced into the bedroom, and yanked open a dresser drawer.

'Where is it?'

I rummaged around assorted underwear and socks until I felt the coolness of the necklace.

'Got it!'

I dropped it over my head and an immediate shroud of protection enveloped me. It was so heavy it was as if I'd put on a real cloak.

I returned to the table. 'I'll be fine now.'

Jason eyed my green crystal necklace.

70

'Ash gave that to you, didn't he?'

'Yes. Moldavite. Protects against psychic attack. He came across it in a new age shop and figured it might be useful for me.'

'You might want to think about stocking up on a few more then,' he said dryly, doing a first-rate impersonation of Mr. Spock's raised cynical eyebrow.

I'm a big fan of the one eyebrow lift; it speaks volumes without a single word. I've tried numerous times to gain sole control of one brow, but can only manage a crumpled worried look rather than sardonic splendour.

'Whatever it was, it took me over,' I said, recollecting my thoughts. 'I had no control. It was hunting me. It changed me. I was it. I was homicidal rage. I was like a … a … *Dalek*! That's it! All I wanted to do was exterminate. Destroy. Kill. Kill everything.'

There it was. Jason's face found his smile and it was a thing of pure joy.

'Yes! You were a goddamn Dalek! Dead set, we're in a real-life episode of *Doctor Who*. I always thought that would be cool!' His smile wavered. 'Now I'm not so sure. Do you remember the blue light, when you asked me to hold your head?'

'Yes, everything's coming back.'

'That was the most beautiful thing I've ever experienced. What was it?'

'A guardian angel. It saved my life, through you. Boo, the angel and you saved my life. Everyone has a guardian angel.'

Jason's face reverted to serious mode. 'Good to know. Ours are going to be working overtime, I reckon.'

I held Boo's face and gazed into her beautiful eyes.

'Oh, you gorgeous girl. You fair dinkum legend. Thank you, Boo!'

'It's my pleasure,' a disembodied voice in my mind said. Judging by Jason's expression, he'd heard the voice too.

Prince Charles was back!

'I wasn't particularly enamored about being brained by an iron, but it wasn't you, dear Maggie. It was the Dark Force.'

'What? You mean the shadow creature?'

'Indeed,' Prince Charles—I mean Boo, said.

'Oh hell,' Jason said. 'It's not dead.'

'Indeed,' Boo confirmed.

'Fuck,' Jason said.

'Jason! Language. You've been hanging around Ashley for too long.'

'Indeed,' Boo said.

Jason had a smug look on his face. 'I beg to disagree. Current scientific studies indicate creative swearing makes you smarter and, "a voluminous taboo lexicon may be considered an indicator of healthy verbal abilities rather than a cover for deficiencies."'

'You've been practicing that for months, haven't you? Just waiting for the right moment.'

'Fuck, yeah!' His wrap around smile was back in full force.

'Humph,' Boo said. 'I'm reminded of a joke your father used to tell. Prince Charles arrived in outback Tinnambanooba, and was collected by the Mayor en route to open a civic building. "I don't wish to be rude," the Mayor said to Prince Charles, "but I'm curious as to why you're wearing a big fur hat when the temperature is a blistering 140 degrees in the water bag?"

"Well," Prince Charles said, "I consulted with Mummy as to the appropriate apparel I should wear in Tinnambanooba, and she said, 'Tinnambanooba? Wear the fox hat!'"

We laughed and I said, 'Boo, you couldn't be a more perfect person ... er, I mean dog, to tell that joke, with your accent and all.'

'What accent?' Boo asked.

'English. You sound exactly like Prince Charles,' I said.

'You're kidding?'

'No.'

'But I'm a girl dog.'

'I know. That's what makes it so weird.'

'Indeed. I was watching the *Antiques Roadshow* when Prince Charles was being interviewed. He had me spellbound. Perhaps my accent is an imprint from then?'

We shrugged our shoulders.

'Who knows?' Jason said.

'And what's with this communication thing?' I asked. 'Your lips aren't moving, but we can hear you crystal clear.' I turned to Jason for confirmation, and he nodded in agreement. 'And why haven't we been able to hear you all the time? And how come we can hear you at all?'

'If you would let me get a word in, I will endeavour to explain what I know before we lose the wavelength.'

I went to ask another question, but Boo looked down her nose at me, as if over imaginary spectacles, so I shut up.

'Firstly, our communication is precious, so only important things must be said. The joke was a waste of a precious resource. Please accept my sincere apologies.

'I have something important to say,' I interrupted.

'Do proceed.'

'I love you, Boo.'

I'm not sure if a dog can blush, but if they could I'm sure Boo was as red as my mum's strawberry jam.

'You're most kind. Shall we continue?'

Jason and I nodded in agreement, and I think we were a little red in the face too, from trying to suppress our mirth.

'The frequency on which we are able to communicate seems to wax and wane and I am uncertain as to the reason why this is the case. The reason we are able to communicate was caused by our contact with the crystal sphere. I believe contact with this artifact results in changes on many levels, most of which have not yet become apparent to us. Telepathic communication is one obvious modification. Maggie, I believe your psychic abilities have been enhanced. Jason, you are physically stronger than before.'

'Yes, you nearly broke my arm getting the iron off me,' I said, touching the ring of blue bruises around my wrist.

'Sorry 'bout that. I broke a couple of glasses yesterday, smashed them in my hand picking them up to take a drink. And look at this,' he said as he crushed a paper cup with one hand. 'Brute strength, or what?'

Jason was having fun and relishing the idea of being a superman.

'Want me to rub some arnica on your wrist?' he said, with a genuine hangdog look of remorse on his face.

'No, she'll be right. Thanks, but. Looks like we're going to have to invest in some cheap glassware. And whatever you do, don't touch what's left of Dad's crystal glasses.'

'No worries.'

'Before I forget, we have to go on the roof and find the dead meteor you launched up there.'

'Yes! See, another example of my strength,' Jason said.

'We are digressing,' Boo said.

Jason nodded. 'Yes, we're good at digressing. We like to digress. Good word that. Please continue, Boo.'

'I am unsure why, but the crystal sphere drew me to the house,' Boo said. It was calling to me, and you sensed the call too, Maggie.'

'You mean the weird, high frequency noise that vibrated my bones?'

'Yes, I believe so.'

'Now, dear Maggie, I wanted to tell you this many times, but of course I didn't have the ability. All I could do was stare at you, trying to will you my message. The only effect this had was to freak you out as you say, and lead you to compare me to Eddie, the dog in the television series, *Frasier*. Eddie is a marvellous dog,

74

and I quite enjoyed watching his antics, but for me, I most enjoy the *Dog Whisperer*. Cesar Millan and his pack are an inspiration. Mister Millan's education program for humans has saved many dogs from insanity. For example, teaching humans how to properly meet and greet a dog. I mean, going to greet a dog, crouched over like an orangutan, waving your hands and saying in a high-pitched voice, "Here, Doggie, Doggie, Doggie!" is uncouth and the height of rudeness. It's not good etiquette and all dogs hate it. No touch, no talk, no eye contact, now *that* is how you greet a dog. Stand close and ignore them. If a dog wants to interact with you, the dog will let you know. Mister Millan has saved countless dogs from the unwitting cruelty and stupidity of humans and I—'

Jason and I stared at each other with wide eyes, and I knew exactly what he was thinking. This dog is on a roll, has a lot to get off her chest, and what if she never shuts up? We enjoyed the silent company of dogs and often wondered if they could talk, if they would be little chatterboxes that never quit—a sort of stream of consciousness type of communication.

Jason rolled his eyes. 'Oh my God. It's come true!'

I nodded.

'What's come true?' Boo asked.

'Nothing,' Jason said.

'I was digressing, wasn't I?'

'Yes,' we said.

'You were about to tell Maggie something important.'

'Indeed. Now, where was I? Oh, yes. It's about your father and what he did before he disappeared.'

My breath caught in my throat. *'What?'*

Jason took my hand.

Boo continued. 'As you know, he was working on a project utilising the Large Hadron Collider in Geneva, and then on his return to Australia he did some additional work using The Australian Synchrotron facilities. It was around that time I saw him—'

'Yes, yes? Go on!' I said.

Silence. And there it was: the Eddie stare.

I thumped my fist on the table. 'Oh, damn it!'

'Don't worry,' Jason said, 'the comms will come back. Boo said so. We have to wait.'

'God! It's frustrating. It's like getting to the end of a drama and seeing the deadly words, To Be Continued.'

Poor Boo was sad, making raised eyebrows and scrunchy, folded ears.

'How long will we have to wait? Jason, this is important! What a bloody—' A surge of rage hit me. I stopped mid-sentence, frightened by the force of the feeling.

'What?' Jason asked.

'Um, nothing.'

Damn those hawk eyes. They always burned the truth out of me.

'I was angry,' I said, sheepishly.

'Like before?'

'It had potential.'

'I saw it flash across your face. Your expression was evil. What the hell is it—a demon?'

'Nope. It's human.'

'That's nuts. How can it be?'

'Because it feels like it. The energy resonates similar to human pain and rage, but concentrated, and not from a single human either, millions of them. I feel negative vibes from humans all the time, but this is distilled, dense. It feels like the essence of every negative emotion generated by humankind. It feels like the Dark Force.'

Jason sat back in his chair, alarmed. 'Hell, so what? It's manifesting in you?'

'I hope not, but it's left a residue. I'm contaminated. It could ignite at any time. The slightest annoyance could trigger it.

Christ, you might have to lock me away because how can I be trusted? My bottom lip quivered and tears pricked in my eyes as the ramifications hit me.

Jason stood, pulled me to him and wrapped his arms around me.

'Ouch! Careful Mister Muscles. I hope your new super strength won't impact on the integrity of our hugs.'

My fears were allayed—if anything, the quality had improved. The hug was like being held in the arms of … Sly Stallone? Jason Statham? No, just my new and improved Jason.

He kissed my forehead. 'Don't you worry, Magster. We'll get this sorted. Everything will be okay.'

I knew it wouldn't, but his words were exactly what I needed to hear.

---

10 *Maggie's Playlist: You're the Voice — John Farnham*

Chapter 11: Creation of a Creature

'The fear of you and the dread of you shall be upon every beast of the earth and upon every bird of the heavens, upon everything that creeps on the ground and all the fish of the sea. Into your hand they are delivered.' — Genesis 9:2

Jason stared up at me, eyes wide with horror. His mouth hung open; it wasn't a good look.

I must've been astral travelling again, but I couldn't remember what happened, or where I went.

Hang on, how could he see me? He couldn't possibly. Where was my body? I wasn't on the bed. Where the hell was I?

Jason leapt out of bed and pressed himself against the bedroom wall. 'Jesus Christ, what the fuck!'

'What? What's the matter? How can you see me?'

'I can see you because you're crawling around on the ceiling like a fucking cockroach!'

Twisting my head, I instinctively scuttled sideways across the ceiling. The movement brought it all back—the nightmare. I screamed. The power which transformed me departed, and I plummeted to the bed.

'I had nothing to fear anymore. I had nothing to fear anymore. I had nothing to fear anymore. I had nothing to fear anymore.'

The sound of the Jason's slap brought me back more than the pain of it.

He rubbed his hand and then my cheek. 'I'm sorry. I didn't

know what else to do. You were babbling … possessed. You kept saying you had nothing to fear anymore. Are you back? Are you with me?'

I nodded. 'I was dreaming, but it was more than a dream, more than a vision. I was a cockroach. I was a roach for God's sake! Well, it wasn't me, but I was seeing through its eyes. I lived in a white room in a huge facility. There was always food on the floor and I wasn't hurting anyone. I just wanted to eat. I was hungry. There was a human male in a white coat, and it hated me, it was after me. It tried to kill me day after day after day. It was relentless. It sprayed me with stuff that burnt; it tried to step on me, smash me, crush me. It left out little black boxes of delicious smelling food, which made me sick. I quickly learned to leave them alone. I sensed that human's hatred, its rage, its evil energy, every day, and the energy of those hateful emotions was worse than all the things it tried to do to me. Its energy penetrated me, contaminated me. I couldn't take it anymore. I had to leave. I didn't know where to go. I would probably starve and die, but it was better than being hunted, fearing for my life for a few crumbs. So, I left, looking for a peaceful place.

I travelled far along the underground pipes of the laboratory and squeezed into a gap so tiny and dark, it was like heaven. Then ice came, colder than space, and I was entombed. In the ice, I became warm—my body absorbing radiation from the beginning of time, the energy from experiments being conducted there. After a while, I don't know how long, the energy of microscopic black holes and dark matter stablised in my body. I could taste an evil residue from that damn human and I was hungry for more of it. It was dark energy and I needed it. But more than anything, I wanted revenge.

The ice melted and I was free, free to return home. I skittered back along the pipes returning to my source of food and water, intensely aware I had nothing to fear anymore. Nothing could stand in my way. I was filled with the infinite power of the universe. I had nothing to fear anymore, Jason. Nothing to fear, nothing to fear anymore ...'

A slap on my other cheek brought me back, and I cried out with the shock of it. Jason sat next to me on the bed and stared into my eyes. He held my hands and kept staring, searching my face, my eyes, for something.

A feeling of exhaustion flooded my body. 'Let's go back to sleep and pretend it didn't happen.' I couldn't think of what else to say.

Jason didn't say a thing. He drew back the bed clothes, and we clambered in. I held him tight, his head resting against my breast. I stroked his hair until he fell asleep in my arms.

---

[11] *Maggie's Playlist: Revenge (Feat. Eminem) — Pink*

Chapter 12: The Trunk

Lying in bed, I listened to the rain and wind tug fiercely at the roof tiles.

Jason's breath was soft and deep except for an occasional puff, a sharp exhalation of breath. If I didn't know it was him, I could've been in bed with a small whale or other seafaring mammal.

Boo had snuck in and lay between us, eyes open, staring into space.

'Any comms yet, Boo?'

She continued with the stare.

Damn. Still nothing.

I felt a hand on the top of my head.

'Morning Mags.' Jason's eyes were sleepy, and his hair tousled.

I leant over and gave him a kiss. 'Morning, sweet cheeks.'

Jason stared at my face and seemed pleased with what he saw. Obviously, no sign of demon-like features. He pulled me on top of him with such ease I appeared to weigh next to nothing, which was definitely not the case.

'Watch out for Boo!'

'Got it.'

Jason made like a koala and encircled me with his arms and legs. He smothered my face in kisses, which always made me laugh.

'Satdee today. We're going to try and have an ordinary day,' he said. 'What would you like to do, Mags? Maybe stay in bed all day?'

'We have a very important task to take care of.'

He groaned. 'What?'

'We, actually, you, have to get the meteor off the roof, or from wherever it may have landed.'

'It's not going to go anywhere.'

'We can't be sure. I would rest easier with it in our hot little hands, rather than in someone else's. Or something else's.'

'All right then. S'okay if I wait 'til the storm stops, or do you want it done right now?'

'Now! I command you, superman!'

He lifted me in the air by my hips.

'Wow! Incredible,' I said. 'We could do the *Dirty Dancing* thing.'

'What thing?'

'You know, the dance scene where Patrick Swayze lifts what's-her-name over his head and holds her there.' I stretched my arms out in front of me, my legs out straight behind, in a perfect plank.

Jason sang, *'I've had the time of my li-i-ife, no, I never felt this way before.'*

He had a beautiful voice, and despite all his years in Australia, he still carried a tinge of his East London accent. I'd tried to convince him to join me at our local a cappella choir, but he said he could think of nothing worse.

'We've got to try this with the running jump,' I said.

'You wouldn't be able to jump high enough.'

'I would too. I could have developed superpowers of my own.'

82

'Nope. I'm guessing yours will be mind-based powers.'

'You're probably right. Never was much good at sport.'

My shaking arms, legs and stomach muscles were already proving his point.

He grinned. 'Best stick with computer programming. Mmmm, I like what I see up there. My superpowers are giving me wicked thoughts, and there's nothing you can do to stop me.' He lowered me and cut off my words with a kiss.

It was quite some time before we left the confines of our California King, and as I stumbled to the shower, I figured the delight in my mind and body would stay with me for at least a week—maybe forever.

Making love was one of the activities that stopped all thought for me, and our delightful distraction took my mind off the roach. Not for long though. As I opened the shower door a chill ran down my spine, and I sensed the roach's energy in my mind. Its spikey legs skittered around and plucked at wires in my brain.

✳ ✳ ✳ ✳ ✳

Jason clattered around outside as I made lunch. He'd taken a ladder from the shed to climb onto the roof. I didn't want to watch. People on ladders always made me nervous.

Jason told me when he was a paramedic, they received more call-outs for ladder accidents than car crashes. Go figure. Most were men over fifty years of age.

Roof tiles creaked as Jason's footsteps crunched on the edge of them.

'Got it!' he yelled.

'Be careful!' I yelled back.

He came into the kitchen holding the crystal meteor.

'Still in one piece? Nothing untoward?'

He placed the meteor on the kitchen table. 'Everything's A-Okay. We could use it as a paper weight.'

'I think it's over qualified for a paperweight.'

'It wouldn't be happy,' he agreed. 'I'll stick it on the shelf, next to your gold booty. It'll catch the sun there, maybe get a bit of its ole spark back.'

'I'd prefer to put it somewhere safe and out of sight. It might have saved us, but it reminds me of the bad stuff too.'

'You're right again, Magster. Where do you want to put it?'

'Dad's trunk! It can live in there. It's an exotic home for an exotic artifact.' I hurried to the wardrobe to retrieve the trunk dad had given me for Christmas. I dragged it out from under a pile of shoes and other wardrobe flotsam and jetsam.

When Dad had given it to me, I'd thought it beautiful, but in all the hustle and bustle of the day, and then with his disappearance, I hadn't studied it properly. I'd shoved it away in the wardrobe as I found looking at things connected with him too painful.

The trunk had leather handles, each fixed with ornate brass clips. I used them to carry it to the kitchen table.

'Wow! It's a thing of beauty,' Jason said. 'How come you haven't put it on display before?'

I gave him a look.

'Sorry. Of course. Sorry.'

'I will now. You're right. It's gorgeous.'

The trunk was curved and covered in black leather embossed with a lizard skin design. Five evenly spaced, curved wooden ribs, wrapped around the outside. It stood on round oak legs.

Jason touched the smooth wooden ribs. 'These are what you call steam bent wood bows. All handmade. Stunning!' It amazed me how Jason always knew how everything was made.

An ornate brass lock, with Aztec inspired embossing, and brass edgings on the upper and lower side of each corner of the lid, gave the trunk an elegant appearance.

I clicked the two latches open and pushed the lid back. A fragrance of oak and leather filled our nostrils, and the lid creaked slightly as it sat back on its hinges.

Jason peered inside it. 'Oh my, check it out!'

Two curved oak boxes nestled at each end of the trunk, taking half the total space. Jason gently removed them from the trunk, and set them down on the kitchen table. The bottom of the trunk was lined with rows of small oak panels.

'It's so intricately finished,' I said. 'I've never seen anything like it.'

The underside of the lid was covered in luxurious black fabric with a continuous pattern of diamond shapes traced in fine gold. The tips of each diamond were adorned with a tiny gold flower made of six dots and one in the middle. Five oak ribs divided the fabric, mirroring those on the exterior.

'Is there anything in the tray boxes?' I asked.

Jason opened their hinged lids to reveal … nothing, just a finely finished timber interior. He pressed and poked various sections of the trunk. 'This has to have secret compartments. It's way too cool not to. Can't seem to find any though.'

'Let me have a go,' I said, pulling the chest towards me.

I had a feeling, and following it, I pushed and tugged at the ribs on the underside of the lid, then pushed the second and forth ribs toward the hinges. They seemed fixed solid, but suddenly clicked and slid down an inch, which released something else with another click, and the whole underside of the lid came free.

'Bingo!' I said, as a cascade of items clattered over the kitchen table and onto the floor.

'Strewth!' Jason stared open mouthed at his bare foot.

A murderous black knife had narrowly missed it; the tip of the knife was firmly embedded in the wooden floorboards right alongside the edge of his foot. A nasty looking cigar shaped spike was lodged between his big toe and its neighbour.

'Blimey!' I said, as Jason carefully extricated his foot from the offending articles and pulled the knife from the floorboards.

'Boy were you lucky!' I said. 'Who would've thought having a quiet cuppa at the kitchen table could be so dangerous?'

Jason flashed me a look with an added eye roll. 'Fair dinkum unbelievable!' He held up his lucky foot and wiggled his toes. 'We'd better put on protective clothing. Who knows what other dangers lurk in this trunk. Beaut present! Thanks, Prof,' he said dryly.

While I made us a fresh cup of tea, Jason collected all the scattered items from the floor and set them out on the table.

'Here you go.' I put a steaming mug of green tea on the table. Jason was busy writing a list, cataloging the items. Both of us were big list makers. We had lists for everything. This list went as follows:

- 2 x brown 'Field Notes' note books
- 1 x Mont Blanc Pen
- 1 x engraved silver ring
- 1 x map of Victoria
- 1 x map of South Australia
- 1 x map of Northern Territory
- 1 x copy of the Table of Elements
- 1 x 12" Mollard Lancio Conducting Baton – black handle with pearlescent white carbon fiber shaft engraved with the word *The Maestro*.
- 1 x Smith & Wesson Carbon Steel Pocket Baton
- 1 x UZI Tactical Defender Pen with DNA catcher and built-in handcuff key (made from lightweight aircraft aluminum)
- 1 x Cold Steel Torpedo fifteen inch throwing knife
- 3 x Cold Steel Sure Balance nine inch throwing knives

We had to undertake a bit of Googling before we could identify exactly what some of the items were.

'What's with all the weaponry?' Jason asked. 'He's a professor for Christ's sake. Was he in fear of his life at some point and forgot these things were in the trunk when he gave it to you? Or maybe he meant you should have them, or needed them?'

'None of those things could have defended us against the Dark Force. It would have inhaled them for horses duvers.'

'What?'

'Sorry, *hors d'oeuvres*. Ashley calls them horses duvers.'

'Yeah, whatever.'

'Grandpa was in the war and he had a secret stockpile of weapons,' I said. 'Dad and I were interested in all that sort of stuff; it's a genetic thing I reckon. Maybe his notebooks will tell us more.'

The notebooks were numbered thirty-seven and thirty-eight. I remembered Dad always scribbling in these little brown notebooks. He filed them in chronological order in a wooden box with a sliding lid.

I opened number thirty-seven to see his familiar handwriting. My eyes filled with tears making it difficult to read. Blinking them away, I read the first line.

'And God saw the light, that it was good: and God divided the light from the darkness.' Gen 1:4

'The Prof wasn't religious. What's with the Bible quote?' Jason asked.

'He was interested in all things metaphysical, particularly given Mum's and my psychic abilities.'

Jason took the notebook and flicked through the pages.

'Why has he written the number 137 on the top of every page?'

'Beats me.'

The notebook was filled with notes, mind maps and diagrams. It would take some time to work our way through it.

'Why is there a music baton in all this weaponry stuff?' Jason asked. 'Who's the Maestro anyway?'

'I have no idea. Dad loved all music, including classical.

Maybe it's a souvenir? It seems like all we have is a pile of questions and no answers.'

I could feel my impatience and anxiety growing. Patience was never one of my strong points. I wanted answers. Now. 'Do you think it has more secret compartments?'

'I would bet my life on it. Want me to look?'

'Go for it.'

I straightened the mirror near the sideboard for what seemed like the umpteenth time. 'What the hell is it with the mirrors in this house? They seem to have a life of their own—foggy, crooked, rattling. This one's crooked again.'

Ding Dong.

The sound of the doorbell made us jump. Boo flew in from outside and barked her head off.

'No comms yet?' I asked.

She gave me a penetrating stare, followed by her *Phhht!* faux sneeze.

'I guess that's a no then,' Jason said.

'Oh, bloody hell, who is it?'

'I don't know, you're the psychic,' Jason said, creeping up to the side window to check. 'It's someone in a cape.'

'A cape? Who the hell wears a cape?'

'Maybe we should answer the door and find out.'

I could tell from his tone he was impatient with me, but I hated 'pop-ins'. It wasn't like the old days when everyone seemed to have endless time on their hands. These days, no one had time for the pop-in.

'Are you going to answer the door?'

I sighed, pushed Boo out of the way, and opened the door.

---

12 *Maggie's Playlist: Strange Things—Tom Jones*

Chapter 13: The Conductor

She filled the doorway with her Amazonian height. Her violet eyes glowed, highlighted by a dark violet cape. Exquisite gold embroidery buried in the cape's velvet depths caught the afternoon light. Black hair was drawn back tight, framing a pale face with high cheekbones.

She smiled, revealing perfect teeth. 'Good afternoon. I apologise for disturbing you, and calling unannounced. I know how annoying it can be. I am looking for Maggie, the daughter of Professor McLaine. I'm an old friend of his.'

She took out a photograph from the depths of her cape, and held it in front of me. 'This is us in my dressing room after a concert.'

My psychic radar was on high alert. 'Danger, Will Robinson, danger!' *The Lost in Space* robot inside my head was waving its arms.

Her features were powerful—strong jaw, black eyebrows, and an expression that was knowing, proud and haughty. Her body, from what I could tell, seemed slim but muscular. Androgynous, I reckoned.

'You're Maggie,' she stated.

'Ah, um, yes. And you are?'

'I,' she said, pausing for effect, 'am The Maestro.'

'The Maestro!' I said loudly. 'You're the *Maestro*.'

Jason scrabbled around in the background clearing the table.

'Yes, indeed,' she said, looking at me oddly. 'Do you know who I am?'

'Ah, no, sorry I don't. I've never heard the Prof, I mean Dad, mention your name.'

'May I come in?'

'Sorry, of course,' I said, meaning exactly the opposite.

I opened the door and she swooshed in, black shiny high heel boots clicking on the floorboards. I hoped her heels wouldn't mark them.

She reached out to pat Boo. 'What a lovely dog.'

Boo growled and drew back.

'Sorry, she takes a while to feel comfortable with people.' Especially Amazonian sized folk wearing swishing capes.

She swept up to Jason and grasped his hand. 'And who have we here?'

'Jason, my partner.'

'Mmmm, so handsome and such a powerful handshake! I adore that in a man.'

I rolled my eyes behind her, and she wheeled around. I pretended to be looking at something on the ceiling.

'How can we help?' I asked. 'Would you like a cup of tea or coffee?'

'Green tea would be lovely. Gyokuro if you have some.'

Jeez, she didn't want much. It was one of the most expensive teas in the world—one of Dad's favourites—and, yes, I did happen to have some.

'Sorry, only got Japanese Sencha.'

She raised an eyebrow. 'Fine.'

Oh, beaut. Now I had two people who could raise their eyebrows at me. I glanced across at Jason, and, as expected, he raised one too. I couldn't help but giggle.

'So, Maestro, how did you know the professor?' Jason asked, as I clattered around in the kitchen.

'He was, as I'm sure you know, a patron of the arts. He had a particular affection for classical music. We met at an after-concert soirée. I was the conductor at the concert, but wasn't keen on attending the after party. They can be frightfully boring, depending on who's there. And indeed, it was frightfully boring, until Maggie's father and I gravitated to each other. We clicked instantly and remained firm friends from then on.'

'Did you know the prof was musical and played electric guitar?' Jason asked.

'My word, yes, he was marvelous! I remember him quite drunk one night and he played me *Love You till Tuesday*, an absolutely silly ditty written by David Bowie back in the late sixties. I can still see him bobbing around the room singing 'Daa daa da dum, Daa daa da dum.''

I listened from the kitchen and felt like I wanted to be sick. I couldn't get my head around Dad being with this woman. She was entirely different to Mum. And Dad's behaviour—drunk, playing her songs—it seemed out of character. He obviously met The Maestro after Mum died, and I knew Mum would want him to be happy and move on, but it shocked me, and really, I was shocked at myself for being shocked. I guess I'd never imagined Dad with someone else.

The Maestro tilted her head and scrutinised me. 'Do you have his guitar, Maggie?'

'Sure do. It's a Gibson Les Paul Custom, absolutely gorgeous.'

I served the tea and we sipped it in awkward silence. The Maestro drifted off into a world of her own, gazing with unfocused eyes at the nearby mirror. She made us all jump when she abruptly banged the table. 'There are no more developments regarding the whereabouts of your father?'

This was said more as a statement than a question.

'No, nothing,' I said.

'Dear Maggie, I have deliberated long and hard as to whether I should share this information with you. Time has passed, and as it appears your father is lost to us, I think it is only right I enlighten you. I would always keep his confidences, but in this situation, I think it's appropriate to share, which is why I came here today.'

My heart was beating in my throat, and my throat constricted to strangle my heart. Who was this woman and why didn't Dad ever mention her to me? It sounded like they were pretty cosy, with him playing guitar to her an' all. Mum would be spinning in her grave.

I realised I'd been tearing the edge of a magazine into tiny strips. The Maestro watched me with a kindly face and soft eyes.

'Maggie, it's difficult for you. I understand. We can do this another time perhaps?'

'It's fine. Go ahead.'

Jason leant across the table and rubbed the back of my neck. 'I'll make us all a fresh cup of tea. Wait, better still, it's getting close to the cocktail hour. How about a drink of something?'

His suggestion was the best idea I'd heard all day. 'A glass of bubbles please.'

'Same for me, please,' the Maestro said.

Jason grinned, doing his best to lighten the mood. 'And one VB for me, coming right up. Mags, where are the champagne glasses?'

Jason knew full well where everything was kept. 'Use Dad's crystal ones. I'll show you where they are.'

We buried our heads in the glass cabinet, and Jason whispered, 'Do we tell her about the baton?'

'No, not yet. There's something dodgy about her.'

'The cape's dodgy, and she's eccentric for sure, but she seems okay to me. I can see why the Prof and her would get on.'

'Yeah, whatever,' I whispered, making my way back to the

92

table.

'Okay,' the Maestro said, 'there is no easy way to say this, so I'll tell you what the Professor told me. He was in CERN for a while, as you probably know, assisting on a special project, plus observing and advising on other projects.'

'Yes, he kept us in the loop about that,' I said.

'It's a long story, but I'll be as succinct as I can. The Professor rang late one night, sometime after his return to Australia, asking if he could visit me. He seemed anxious, not his usual jolly self. Of course, come around, I said.

'When the Professor arrived at my door, he stank of petrol, was streaked with blood, and was pale and visibly upset.'

'Blood streaked!' I said.

'Wait. I'll explain from the beginning. He told me that during an inspection of the Large Hadron Collider at CERN, he'd spotted a cockroach near one of the detectors.'

Jason and I locked eyes. There was a strange tingling all over my body and I knew I'd turned white. *She's telling me my goddamn vision.*

'Are you all right, Maggie? You don't look so well.'

'I'm fine, thanks. Keep going.'

'Anyway, he caught the cockroach, and his colleague gave him a cigarette packet to put it in. They didn't like to kill things and planned to release it later. He thought it was an unusual specimen, and wondered how it could have survived in the harsh environment.

'Being slightly absent minded, he completely forgot about the cigarette packet, and the cockroach, which he'd tucked away on the inside of his jacket.

'When he returned to Australia, he attended the Australian Synchrotron to complete some work. Whilst taking a break in the tearoom, he searched for a handkerchief in his jacket, and discovered the cigarette packet, and the cockroach, which seemed alive and well. He put the packet on the table, made a cup of coffee, and was then called away to take a phone call.'

The Maestro paused to take a sip of champagne.

'In the meantime, a young lab assistant came in to take a break. When the Professor returned to the tearoom and opened the door, he saw the lab assistant sitting on the chair with the cigarette packet in his hand. The assistant, and this is how he described it to me, "Imploded before my eyes, vapourised in a silent whorl of blackness that sucked out all the dust and debris in the room".'

Jason gave me a knowing look. 'Crikey.'

'In a split-second, the assistant vanished, and the only thing remaining was an extraordinarily clean tearoom, and a large black cockroach sitting on the chair where the assistant had been.'

Jason and I locked eyes again. I felt unsteady, as if all the air had been sucked out of the room.

Cockroach. The word filled me with dread. My waking dream must have been a premonition, but it was much more. I still sensed the insect in my brain, scurrying around in my skull, plucking at neurons for the fun of it. And the dust eating blackness she talked about. Was that the Dark Force? I squeezed my skull between the heels of my hands (it helped to abate the scurrying sensation) and turned my attention back to the Maestro.

'The Professor was in absolute shock of course. What was he to do? Who was he to tell? There were no security cameras in the room, so who would even believe him? They'd think he was mad, or worse, had murdered the poor assistant.

'The Professor wrapped the cockroach in a paper towel, cleaned the room of his fingerprints, and left. All the while he hoped he wouldn't disappear into a black hole as well.'

I felt sick. Jason must have noticed. 'Are you all right?'

I nodded feebly.

'Shall I continue?' the Maestro asked.

'Yes, please.'

'Now, where was I? Oh, yes. On the way to my apartment, in need of a stiff drink, he stopped at a bottle shop to buy some brandy. Two customers in the shop became upset and aggressive, and pushed him into a rack of bottles. Luckily the proprietor intervened.

'By this point, he hadn't eaten for hours, so he stopped at a supermarket. There, he noticed a man breaking off expensive vine tomatoes from the vine and substituting them as ordinary tomatoes. He challenged the man's behaviour. The man lunged at him, dug his fingernails into the Professor's face, and raked them all the way to his chin. Apparently, the man's face was so twisted with rage he didn't look human. The man fled, chased by one of the supermarket attendants who had witnessed what happened. The Professor was in shock and bleeding profusely. Luckily, the perpetrator was caught and arrested. Police at the local station cleaned up the Professor's face before he headed on his way.'

'Poor Dad.'

'That's unbelievable,' Jason said.

'Shall I keep going?' the Maestro asked, with a concerned look. 'You've turned pale.'

'It's normal for me. Keep going.'

'The Professor stopped for petrol at a convenience store. A group of young people were hanging around in the shop. They became violent towards him, dragged him outside, bound him in a bowser hose and soaked him with petrol. One of the youths was searching for a cigarette lighter when the police happened by and rescued him in the nick of time.

'The Professor said at the police station that the offenders were upset and dazed. They insisted it was totally out of their character to behave in such a way. The Professor believed them and didn't want to press any charges, much to the disbelief of the police.

'Your dad continued to my apartment, and in the course of

the relatively short trip, he was subjected to five episodes of road rage.

'The worst occurred when stationary at a red light. A smartly dressed woman in a black Maserati screeched to a halt in the lane next to him. She opened her car door, extended two well-turned legs garnished with black, shiny high heels, and walked to the back of her car to retrieve something from the boot. The Professor, who admitted he'd been rather fixated on her shapely legs, thought she'd retrieved an umbrella. The illusion was violently shattered as his windscreen imploded. The woman had a crowbar, which she used to smash in every window of the Professors car, in record time, despite the constraints of a tight skirt and high heels.'

'Impossible,' Jason said. 'A friend and I tried to smash in the windows of a car with a crowbar, and it's not that easy. The crowbar kept bouncing off, and when the window did shatter, my friend cut his hand from all the glass.'

I looked at Jason with wide eyes. 'You smashed a car window with a crowbar?'

'Yeah, relax, Max. It was an old wreck at Ash's place. Maestro, there's no way a woman like the one you described, could've done so much damage in such a short time, if at all.'

Go, Jace. I knew he was looking for loopholes, and this one seemed big enough to jump through.

'My dear, I would beg to differ. It's exactly what the Professor told me. The woman had superhuman strength; it was as though she was possessed. Her face was ugly with rage, and she did indeed cut herself, but it didn't slow her one iota.

'Anyway, continuing on,' she said, dismissing Jason's assertion, 'it was three in the morning when he finally arrived at my apartment. At that stage, he said he wouldn't have been surprised if I had turned on him with a meat cleaver.'

'Oh, poor Dad,' I said, and burst into tears.

Jason appeared to be about to laugh.

'*Jason!*'

'Sorry, Mags, sorry, totally wrong. But the story sounds so insane it's funny, really.'

He turned to the Maestro in an attempt to divert my furious attention away from him and his insensitivity. 'You've got to be making this up.'

'There you have it!' the Maestro said. 'It's exactly the dilemma the Professor found himself in. Who was going to believe such a story? The Professor knew the cockroach was involved with the assistant's disappearance. He discussed numerous theories, his preferred, being the cockroach had absorbed radiation and microscopic black holes from the Hadron Collider. This didn't kill it, but transformed it into an entity which triggers and magnifies the negative psychic energy of human beings, specifically, anger and rage. He thought its food was the negative emotional energy generated by humans.'

'So why didn't you kill the Prof with a meat cleaver?' Jason asked.

She smiled. 'Probably because I don't own a meat cleaver. But seriously, I don't know. Maybe because I loved him? I do know wherever we went with the roach we were subjected to unprovoked human rage.'

'Where's the roach now? Did you kill it?' Jason asked.

'I wish. We were out for dinner one night, and left it at my apartment, sealed in a Tupperware container. On our return, the container, the cockroach and my two dogs had vanished. I haven't seen them since.'

Boo sat up startled and gave a loud '*Phhht!*'

'That's awful,' Jason said, his face in serious mode.

The Maestro's eyes filled with tears. I went over and put my arms around her. She smelt of lavender.

'Oh, I'm so sorry,' I said.

'Since then, the crime rate in my area has tripled, and a woman was stabbed and killed right outside, simply over a parking space dispute. Plus, there's no dust in my apartment anymore, not a fluff, dust bunny or dog hair.'

'Nasty,' Jason said. 'You've got to have dust. I'd be getting the hell out of your apartment.'

Suddenly, the Maestro didn't look so Maestro'ish or powerful anymore. In fact, she appeared crumpled and sad.

'So, this entity's primary purpose, other than absorbing people and small creatures, is to trigger and magnify people's inherent anger and pain, which then generates more anger and pain, literally a vicious circle, which keeps it fed with what it likes,' Jason said. 'Hmmm, things are starting to add up.'

The Maestro glanced sharply at him. 'What things?'

I flashed Jason a look. 'The things Jason said, in response to the things you said.'

A raised eyebrow on each side of me was an apt response to that bit of stupidity.

'You don't trust me, do you?' the Maestro said.

'No, sorry, I don't. I don't know you well enough to trust you. I take a while to trust people.'

'Fair enough, I understand. Where do you want to go from here?'

'Another drink would be good. And pizza. Would you like to stay for pizza, Maestro? It would give us an opportunity to get to know each other better.'

'Lovely, thank you.'

Jason ordered the pizzas and we amused ourselves looking at the pizza app on the iPad.

'The app says the doorbell's going to ring in three seconds,' Jason said.

We all counted, 'One, two, three…'

Ding. Dong. Right on cue.

We settled ourselves around the table and began hoeing into the pizzas. Well, Jason and I did the hoeing, the Maestro ate in a more refined manner.

'You know, your dad has a similar rock,' the Maestro said, munching a piece of thin-crust gourmet pizza, and pointing in the direction of the sideboard.

'Rock?' Jason asked.

She pointed. 'Yes, the one on the middle shelf there.'

Jason and I turned to look, and there was the crystal sphere. Jason had forgotten to put it away with the rest of the things. Good one.

'It's exactly the same as his, except yours has lost its luster. The cockroach hated his rock, you know. When the professor put the roach near it, the roach went ballistic. As soon as he moved the roach away, it settled down. Where did you get it?'

I pointed to the bowl on the coffee table. 'Boo collects rocks. She brings in choice specimens from the backyard as gifts for us. She brought that in too. It's the largest in her collection.'

'And what about the feather in the bowl?' the Maestro asked.

'Another of Boo's obsessions,' I said. 'She normally doesn't collect them though; she just rolls on them. She's quite particular about the types of feathers she chooses. We believe the one over there is an eagle feather. Boo rolled on it, picked it up carefully by the quill, and carried it all the way home to add to her collection.'

'Amazing!' the Maestro said. 'However, I'm sure rocks like that one aren't a dime a dozen. Are you sure it's not the Professor's?'

'Pretty sure,' I said. 'I've never seen anything like it in his rock, or should I say, *mineral*, collection.' Dad hated people calling them rocks.

'But Ash has got one,' Jason said. 'Maybe they're a dime a dozen.'

The Maestro sat up straight. 'Who's got one?'

I glared at Jason.

'A friend of ours who collects rocks, but his is not exactly the same, really,' Jason mumbled.

'The Professor told me his crystal was given to him some years ago by an Aboriginal in the outback. During an exploration of the Bungle Bungles, a man came out of nowhere and handed him a ball of red clay, within which was the crystal. The Aboriginal gave the Professor a message, which he wrote in one of his notebooks. Do you happen to have the Professor's notebooks? It would be interesting to know what the message was.'

'They're under lock and key at the university,' I said.

'Is that right?'

'Yes,' I said, knowing she knew I was lying. Damn it. I had to get better at lying.

'You don't happen to have any more of those crystals hanging around, do you? I'm a collector you know.'

'No, sorry we don't,' Jason said.

'It appears Boo and I have something in common,' the Maestro said, changing the subject.

Boo cocked her head and listened raptly.

'I love feathers. And birds. Particularly raptors, birds of prey.'

'Another shared interest with the Professor then,' Jason said.

'Yes, in fact I carry this one around with me for luck.' She fished around inside her cape.

I was betting her cape had a few secret compartments.

'Here it is,' she said, taking out a long feather with black and grey stripes. 'A harpy eagle feather.'

What happened next was not to be expected. Actually, that statement was more suited to my old life. Now, I expected the unexpected.

Using turbo-powered haunches, Boo launched herself through the air, whipped the feather out of the Maestro's hand, and captured it delicately in between her front teeth. Her momentum was such she continued in a belly slide across the kitchen table, her front and back legs extended like some super dog in a western bar scene, sending cups, glasses, pizza boxes,

100

plates and cutlery flying in all directions.

Jason yelled and resembled a frantic soccer goalie valiantly trying to save the airborne items. A pizza box found its way onto the Maestro's lap, closely followed by a glass of champagne. I ducked out of the way of torpedo Boo. She flew off the end of the table, hit the wall, and knocked the mirror off the wall. The mirror sent the lamp flying, a vase, our gold bounty, and two picture frames, one of which Frisbeed across the room taking out the four crystal glasses good old Jason had neglected to put back in the cupboard. Arrgh!

Boo skidded across the floorboards, legs extended, and came to a gradual halt near a rug at the end of the room. She carefully placed the harpy eagle feather on the rug and flipped over onto her back, where she proceeded to roll methodically back and forth on the feather, legs moving rhythmically in the air.

Seated amongst the debris, watching this performance, were three silent, open-mouthed humans. Well, two anyway. I wasn't sure about the Maestro yet.

Boo leapt to her feet, gingerly picked up the feather, which still seemed in remarkable condition given its treatment, and trotted over to her collection bowl. She placed it alongside her other feather, then turned and stared intently at us for a moment, her eyes dark and insistent. With a flick of her head she gave a loud *Phffft!* and rocketed out through the dog door leaving it swinging in her wake.

We stared speechless, mesmerised by the to and fro motion of the door flap as it squeak, squeak, squeaked slowly back and forth. Simultaneously shaking our heads to awaken from our door flap induced trance, we surveyed the devastation around us.

'Bloody hell!' we said together.

Jason brushed pieces of broken glass into a pizza box. 'I didn't realise she liked feathers *that* much.'

'Oh, Maestro, I'm so sorry,' I said. 'Look at you. You're covered in pizza toppings and champagne. Here, let me take your cloak.' It pleased me to have an excuse to take the damn thing off and see exactly what was underneath it, and possibly inside it.

The Maestro didn't protest as I unclipped the gold clasp securing the cape around her neck. She stood so I could pull it free of her. It weighed an absolute ton, with endless yards of heavy, velvet fabric.

'The gold embroidery is exquisite,' I said. 'I've never seen anything like it. The way it catches the light is almost magical.'

'It is magical. It's sea silk, byssus, priceless. It was a gift.'

'Where can you buy it?' Jason asked, always interested in marine related topics.

'It can't be bought.'

Jason was going to reply, but then thought better of it.

'Luckily your cape seems to have avoided being soiled, but your pants and shirt came off second best,' I said.

'No matter,' she said offhandedly. 'I'll clean up in the bathroom.'

'It's through there, third door on the right. Plenty of towels in the cupboard. Let me know if you need anything.'

Jason stared as she strode away, apparently transfixed by her super tight black leather hipster pants, threaded with a black leather belt and large gold buckle. They were slung so low on her hips she just needed a holster and a gun to finish the look. She probably had those items tucked inside her cape. Ultra-tight, over the knee patent leather stiletto boots embraced the black pants, and on top she wore an extremely tight, perfectly fitted white shirt, under which I could glean a hint of expensive lace lingerie. All the leather and lace covered a lithe body which exuded grace, sexuality and sheer animal magnetism.

'You right there?' I said to Jason. 'Put your eyes back in your head.'

'Don't have a go at me. You should've seen your face. You looked like you wanted to eat her.'

'Not so, that look's reserved only for you. It's amazing she doesn't squeak when she walks, with all the leather.'

'She's one hot mama. Probably got a whip and cuffs in her cape somewhere.'

'*Yes!* Yes! Quick. Let's look!' I hooked the cape on the coat rack and patted it down.

'You *want* cuffs and a whip?' Jason said, sounding hopeful.

I found something and turned the cape over to try and retrieve it. 'There's definitely stuff in there.' I examined the stitching. 'Jeepers, there's hundreds of quilted pockets, but I can't work out how they open to get to anything. It's like the trunk, but made of fabric.'

Jason glanced anxiously along the hallway. 'You're running out of time.'

'Damn! I'll have to leave it, don't want to get sprung.' I let go of the cape as the bathroom door opened.

The Maestro strode into the kitchen, sans shirt.

I was right—she was wearing expensive lingerie. A satin, ivory bra. An underwired little number, quarter cup style with strips of filmy, intricate lace across the bust, provocatively displaying flashes of skin in between. The bra was obviously chosen for its structural ability to create maximum definition and uplift, not that she needed it.

Jason also seemed to share my interest in the structural integrity of this flimsy, yet perfectly engineered piece of cloth. He seemed more than interested actually, but who could blame him faced with this rampant exhibitionism.

'My shirt is too stained,' she said, holding it between thumb and forefinger. 'Would you have a T-shirt or something I could borrow?'

'Nice bra,' I said.

'I enjoy beautiful lingerie. *Honey Birdette.*' She ran her thumbs under the lacy straps and let them go with a snap. Jason visibly started, as though a spell had been broken. He flushed red realising he must have been staring unashamedly.

'I've got a new white T-shirt you can have, still in the packet,' he said, probably relieved to be able to beat a hasty exit from the room.

'Bless him,' the Maestro said. 'He's so sweet.'

'Ah, yup. I'll help him find that tee.' I hurried to the bedroom. Jason was standing at the open window, fanning himself with the T-shirt packet.

'Oh, for God's sake, you've got to be kidding me. It's like you haven't seen a pair of breasts in lingerie before. You're like a school boy!'

'Well, holy shit Maggie; I was kind of taken by surprise. There I am minding my own business, and hey presto, a Salma Hayek lookalike appears in my kitchen.'

'Did you think you'd died and gone to heaven, in a scene from Desperado?' I giggled, pulled up my top, and thrust out my chest.

Jason's arms were around me, holding me tight against his body. He grasped the back of my head and brought my face forward to his for a deep, passionate kiss. My knees went weak. I clung to his shoulders as his right hand found my breast, and his left hand slid inside the front of my jeans.

'You make me hot. I love you, Magster,' he whispered in my ear, pushing me against the wall. I yanked his T-shirt out from his jeans, and ran my hands over his taut muscles, over the body I loved. His hot breath was on my throat.

'How are we going with the T-shirt?' The Maestro stood in the doorway.

We jumped to attention, clothes awry.

She entered further into the room. 'Don't mind me. I'm getting a bit chilly is all.' Her violet eyes scanned us picking up every detail. 'Is that it on the bed?'

'Yes. Yes!' Jason said. Grabbing it, he threw it at her like a Frisbee. It landed between her feet, and she performed a straight leg bend to pick it up, ensuring we received maximum exposure to her voluptuous cleavage. Rising slowly, she turned on her heel to walk out of the room. Before she left, she said, 'Thanks Jason. Let me know if you need a hand.'

We listened to the click, clack, click, clack of her heels moving back along the hall.

'She's *unreal!*' Jason said. 'What's with her? Seriously?'

'I didn't hear her,' I whispered. She must've tip toed up—an exhibitionist *and* a voyeur.'

Jason cradled my face in his hands and gave me another kiss. 'To be continued. Let's get rid of the broad.'

'That was an interesting diversion,' the Maestro said when Jason and I returned to the dining room. She was collecting broken crockery from the floor.

It pleased me—though not so sure about Jason—to see she was fully covered in his new, white T-shirt, complete with nice, sharp packet creases.

'Never a dull moment around this house,' I said. 'It seems your harpy eagle feather is still in one piece.'

'Good. Do you think Boo will let me take it?'

'I'm sure she will,' I said, not having a clue as to Boo's intentions.

The Maestro lifted our big mirror and hung it back on the wall.

'Amazing this survived Boo's onslaught,' she said, standing back to see if it was correctly aligned. 'It's still in one piece.'

Picking up some broken glass we'd missed, I went into the kitchen to put it in the bin. When I came back, the Maestro was still standing in front of the mirror. She'd removed the clip from her 'do' and was shaking out her long black tresses, pushing her fingers into her hair to create body and form after the severe restrictions of her French Knot.

Oh, for God's sake, she looked even more like Salma Hayek, and I felt even more like a frump. She must've been sixty something, and still her natural beauty outshone everyone's. I felt a severe decline in my self-esteem.

Jason stood partially hidden behind a cabinet, watching her. Transfixed, he stared with an intensity I'd never witnessed before. My self-esteem plummeted to new depths of fifty fathoms below.

Dragging herself away from her reflection, she turned and tossed her head, flicking lustrous locks over her shoulder.

'It's awfully late. I think I'll take my leave. A car will collect me in fifteen minutes.'

Boo was nowhere to be seen, so I said, 'I'll get your feather.' Of course, as soon as I said the words, Boo trotted in.

'Would you like some tea while you wait?' My politeness and hospitality amazed me.

'Lovely, thank you,' she said taking a seat at the table.

'Oh, and here's your feather back,' I said, handing it to her.

I ambled into the kitchen to make the tea, leaving Jason and the Maestro to chat about the weather.

As I returned with the tea, the Maestro had moved to sit next to Jason in *my* chair. Cozied up to him, she chatted softly, and he seemed enthralled. I plonked the tray on the table clattering the cups and saucers, and they both jumped.

I didn't know why I'd bothered to dust off the fancy tea cups for this floozy.

'Here's your tea, Maestro.' I gave her the stink eye and placed the cup on the opposite side of the table. Her violet eyes latched onto mine and her mouth twitched. She was going to say something, but perhaps thought better of it. Standing, she ran her hands along her body and smoothed out the T-shirt, before moving to the other side of the table.

We sat quietly sipping our tea in awkward silence. Boo was on the rug behind the Maestro. She brushed the feather backwards and forwards against her cheek. Boo didn't seem concerned about her repossessing the feather.

106

Jason flicked on the sound system, and after a couple of minutes the Maestro seemed to relax. Triggered by the music, she chatted softly about her love of Mozart and David Bowie.

Behind her, Boo rose slowly off the rug, floating upwards, still in a lying position. Boo continued her levitation until she reached a point slightly above and behind the Maestro's head. There she hovered, looking straight at us, grinning, as dogs do when they're particularly happy with themselves.

Jason was staring into his tea, so I pinched him to get his attention. Boo began a slow, clockwise barrel roll, pausing to hover upside down, legs stretched up straight, ears and tail dangling, pink tongue out to one side, and cheeks relaxed into a silly puffy grin.

Jason, who'd taken a mouthful of tea, coughed and spluttered it all over the table.

'Oh, dear,' the Maestro said. 'Are you all right?'

'Fine,' he wheezed, wiping the spillage.

'You two look rather shell-shocked,' the Maestro said, as behind her Boo continued her rotation, and then slowly floated back to the rug, landing just as the Maestro turned around.

Boo cocked her head, and chose her most innocent and endearing expression.

'Such a sweet, darling dog,' she said to Boo. She stood and held Boo's head in her hands. 'You are a clever girl, aren't you?'

Boo looked smitten, unless it was just another selected expression.

'I will leave you to digest my incredible story,' the Maestro said. 'Here's my phone number. I'd very much like to keep in touch. I loved your father, and I hope perhaps we can solve the mystery of his disappearance together. I do have considerable resources at my disposal, if you need my assistance. Perhaps we can meet again next week? At my place?'

Despite her 'out there' eccentricities, and my insecurities, I suddenly experienced a surge of warmth and affection towards this strange woman.

'Yes, it's a mind-boggling lot to think about,' I said. 'Thank you so much for sharing your story, we appreciate it. And I'm sorry for the havoc Boo caused. Let me get your cape.'

I lifted the god-awful heavy cape from the coat rack and stood on my tiptoes to place it over her shoulders. She turned around, and I gently moved her shining tresses aside, fastening the cape around her neck with the gold clasp. She resembled a goddess from centuries past. No wonder Dad fell for her.

'Au revoir, dear Maggie.' She enfolded me in her arms and held me tight against her body in the warm velvet depths of the cape. My cheek rested on her generous chest, and she kissed me softly on the top of my head. My knees became instantly weak. This woman radiated a powerful sexual energy. It was heavenly, and wanted to stay in her embrace forever.

Ding Dong! Ding Dong!

That damn doorbell. Boo barked madly.

'It's my driver,' she said, releasing me and striding to the door.

'Goodbye, dear Maggie. Goodbye, Jason. Bye, Boo.' And in a whirl of velvet, she was gone.

---

13 *Maggie's Playlist: I'm Too Sexy—Right Said Fred*

Chapter 14: The Attack

'For we do not wrestle against flesh and blood, but against principalities, against powers, against the rulers of the darkness of this age, against spiritual hosts of wickedness in the heavenly places.' — Ephesians 6:12

'We need to debrief,' Jason said. 'What was that about?'

'What was what about? At this rate, we may as well debrief on a daily basis, or minute by minute. Jason, I'm too bone weary to think now, let alone speak. I can't do it.' I rubbed my eyes. 'I need to go to bed.'

'You seemed pretty cozy with the Maestro just then. What was going on there?'

'What do you mean what was going on there? You're kidding, right? *You* should talk! I saw you skulking behind the cabinet staring at her like you wanted to rip her clothes off and fuck her against the wall.'

'*Maggie!* No, you're wrong. It's not true! Let me explain.'

'Don't give me that crap. I saw you. Pathetic. She could be your mother. Of course, a goddamn MILF. Duh. How stupid am I? You're such a bastard!'

Rage. Jealousy. Envy. Anger. Hatred. Pain. Insecurity. Bitterness. The essential essences of those emotions melded, magnified and ignited. They erupted in my body like a volcano. A blood red haze enveloped the room. My limbs jerked and burned with the ferocity of the feelings exploding through my body. The emotions tasted bitter, like bile in my mouth. Poison and venom condensed. My heart was in rapid fire—a beat so fast and loud it was all I could hear. Thunder cracked through my skull. Blood seeped through my fingers as I crushed a Royal Albert bone china cup in my hand. He couldn't treat me so badly and get away with it.

'*Maggie!*' Jason screamed. 'Don't let it take you!'

Boo barked ferociously as I took a knife from the kitchen table. She sounded a million miles away.

* * * * *

I awoke paralysed, unable to move my arms or legs. I couldn't speak. My mouth was sewn shut. It was dark. A wave of fear and panic churned in my gut. Concentrating on my senses, I felt a rough fabric over my face, a heavy weight pressed on my torso, and sharp objects dug painfully into my ribs. It was cold and I started to shiver.

As consciousness returned more fully, my eyes perceived some colours. Through the weave of the rough fabric I could make out strobing red and blue lights. I heard the loud hee-haw, hee-haw of an approaching siren, and the crackle of police radios nearby.

Police! I tried to move. Limbs twitched. Oh, thank God, I wasn't paralysed.

My hands were bound together tightly above my head, and my arms were numb. My ankles were similarly bound. I seemed to be suspended horizontally.

I wriggled and gyrated trying to get a sense of how I was suspended. I tried to open my mouth but it was sealed tight with tape. I inhaled as best I could given the weight on my chest. It hurt to breathe, but I could smell … chocolate. Chocolate lilies. I knew where I was! We had pots of them around our alfresco area—I was in the hammock on our deck.

What the hell was going on? Why were police here? Why was

I here? I had to escape the hammock. I tried to move my arms and legs to get a swing going. My plan was to swing upside down and hope somehow, that way, I could break free. It was a bad plan because I couldn't move. It was impossible to generate any momentum with my arms and legs bound.

I tried to scream and delivered only a high-pitched mewling. In response to my efforts, I received a sharp dig in the ribs.

I froze. The weight on my body was someone sitting on top of me—with a gun.

Footsteps in the house, voices, snippets of conversation, which waxed and waned in volume.

'... knife as evidence ...'

'... statement taken ...'

'... he'll be dead, with a wound like that ...'

A flush of cold heat bloomed like an atom bomb in the pit of my stomach. I wanted to vomit, and gagged violently.

I remembered! I remembered Jason. I remembered the knife.

Oh my God, I'd killed him.

That's why I was restrained. I'd gone nuts like Mum. They were going to lock me up. Tears trickled over my cheeks and dripped onto my neck.

The sliding door rattled open. The voices moved closer.

'Nothing happened out here?' a deep masculine voice asked.

'No.'

I made a noise and received a responding violent dig in the ribs.

'Who's in the hammock?'

'Boo, my dog. She sleeps there.'

It was Jason. I froze and held my breath.

'Looks pretty comfy cozy on top of all those blankets. Lazy mutt wasn't much help in this situation,' the voice said. 'You've made her too comfortable.'

Footsteps approached the hammock. 'Who's a spoilt little doggie?'

I felt rather than heard the rumble of a low growl.

My heart pounded in my ears like a bass drum.

'Hey, Sarge! The inspector wants you.'

Footsteps retreated.

'I think you've misjudged Boo,' Jason's voice said. 'There were bite marks all over the bastards.'

The door rattled closed.

I let go of my breath.

The itchy fabric lifted away from one side of my face and a rough wet tongue gave me a big long lick—and then another lick, and one more for good measure. I smelt chicken breath. The blanket settled over my face again, and Boo removed her elbows from my ribs so I was a little more comfortable.

Noises receded and silence fell. It seemed like an eternity passed before the screen door rattled open again.

I kept quiet, not sure who was approaching. There was the flap, flap, flap of Boo's tail, so I figured it must be friend, not foe. I hoped beyond all hope I hadn't imagined Jason's voice, and he was alive, not carved into tiny pieces.

'You're a fair dinkum legend, Boo,' the voice I was hoping to hear said. 'Couldn't have done it without you. Come on girl.'

The weight lifted from my body and then the tic, tic, tic of Boo's nails on the deck. The blanket lifted from my face, and there, silhouetted against a sky painted with a blazing pink and orange sunrise, was Jason's gorgeous face.

I felt like I'd died, and he was the angel sent to take me through the pearly gates. Even if I was going to hell, I would've willingly gone with him—no big deal, we'd kind of been there already.

Super serious mode would describe Jason's expression. Concerned eyebrows knitted over worried hawk eyes, his mouth a soft thin line. He caressed my face. 'Maggie, you're back. I can tell you're okay by your eyes. 'I'm going to take the tape off your mouth. I'll do it slowly, but it may hurt a bit. Shall I start?'

I nodded.

The tape was stuck fast, and it felt like getting a slow wax as it came off.

'Oh, thank God!' I said. Words tumbled out. 'What a relief … Jason I thought you were dead … that I'd killed you … what on earth … why was I—'

My words were cut short by Jason's mouth as he tenderly kissed them away.

'Let's get you inside and get some food and coffee into you, then we'll talk.'

He removed the tape from around my wrists and brought my arms down. They were completely numb as he tried to rub life back into them. I continued to rub my wrists and arms as Jason freed my ankles.

'Duck tape,' I said.

He smiled. '*Duct* tape. Seeing you tied like this is giving me ideas.'

'Save 'em for some other time, Mister Grey. I think I may have lost the use of my arms and legs forever,' I said as he pulled me out of the hammock. 'Ow!'

My limbs were so stiff I could barely walk; hands and feet burned with pins and needles. Staggering, Jason caught me, scooped me into his arms. He slid the door open with one foot and carried me into the house. He didn't miss a beat. My superman seemed fine.

'It's like getting married,' he said, 'carrying you over the threshold.'

'Maybe one day we will.'

My arms were around his neck, my face against his chest. His heartbeat was strong and steady, and I did indeed feel as happy as a bride. A bride's happiness usually lasts longer than about sixty seconds though.

'Where shall I put you, Mags?'

'Is anyone else here?'

'No, everyone's gone. What would you like first? Food? Bath?'

'What the hell happened? Tell me.'

'We'll talk later. You're so cold. I think a hot bath, then food, and then talk, or go to bed and talk after. In fact, I've already drawn you a bath m'lady.'

'With crayons or pastels?

'Ha, ha.'

'Sounds good,' I said, as my teeth started to chatter.

'I need you to close your eyes tight now, and remember everything is going to be fine.'

'Why?'

'Do it.'

I disobeyed him. As he carried me to the bathroom, negotiating around upturned tables, chairs and books, the devastation of our home was revealed. A toppled bookshelf had disgorged its contents across the lounge room. A pool of blood three feet across congealed near the heater duct. Micro venetians hung in shreds across windows. Streaks, blobs and splashes of blood adorned the walls like a Pro Hart painting. Head shaped indentations decorated cupboards and doors.

Our beautiful things were scattered far and wide. A toy dog Dad had given me hung upside down from a light fitting, knives, forks, spoons and kitchen utensils were strewn the length and breadth of the house, a toaster hung off a battered floor lamp, and a selection of large kitchen knives were impaled into the walls.

So much for the honeymoon.

I squeezed my eyes tight shut for the rest of the journey and hoped we didn't have to move a corpse out of the way when we arrived at our destination.

Jason set me down. 'You can open your eyes now. If you did indeed actually close them.'

'I did in the end.'

The bathroom had somehow avoided the action and was in perfect condition. Thank heavens.

'Can you stand?'

'Yep.'

'Skin a rabbit,' he said.

I raised my arms and he took off my top.

'I have a strong feeling of déjà vu,' I said.

'Me too.'

He knelt on the floor, undid my jeans, and pulled them to my ankles.

'Step.' I dutifully lifted my feet clear. He slid my undies to my ankles and kissed me gently on the belly holding my hips with his hands.

'Step again. Now in you go,' he said, helping me into the bath.

'Are you coming in too?'

'Yes, but I need to make a phone call first. I'll be back.' He lit a candle and dimmed the lights.

I lowered myself into the steaming bath and the scent of lavender enveloped me. Bless him. He'd put essential oils into the water.

The scent reminded me of the Maestro.

* * * * *

Jason eventually returned, stripped off, and slid into the bath behind me. He encircled me with his arms and legs and I leaned back against his chest.

Nuzzling my ear, he said, 'You okay, Mags?'

'If I hold myself in this moment, I am so okay.'

'It's the secret to life, if only it were that easy.'

Jason moved his hands over my hair and onto my shoulders. He massaged them, and I felt the tightness in my muscles give way. My arms surrendered their pain as he worked his way downward. He entwined his hands with mine and lifted my fingers to his mouth kissing them gently.

I turned to face him, trying not to send water cascading over the side of the bath. We surveyed each other in the candlelight. Jason's body was patch worked with dark striations, blotches and shadows. A dark ridge ran from the top of his right shoulder to underneath his armpit. I reached out to touch him and he caught my wrist in his strong grip, holding my hand away from his body.

'What is that? You're injured … black and blue.'

'I'm getting better, just a bit delicate at the moment.'

'You need to go to hospital.'

'I'm fine.'

'You're not fine, I can tell, even in this dim light. I'm taking you to the hospital.'

I pushed myself back from him and held on to the sides of the bath trying to stand. He seized both my wrists.

'I'll be fine. I don't need to go.'

I felt more upset by the moment.

'But look at you,' I said, trying to break free of his grip. 'Ow! You're hurting.' He wasn't, but I needed to get free to call a doctor. 'Let go!'

'Sit back down! I. Do. Not. Need. A. Doctor,' he said, in a tone so low and forceful I acquiesced, plopping back into the water and creating a small tidal wave in the process.

Still holding my wrists, he pulled me towards him, creating more waves. His eyes were burning, and he kissed me passionately, still holding my arms away from him. He pushed me backwards, and his mouth was on my breasts.

'Let me touch you! I need to touch you,' I pleaded.

He shook his head in the negative and pushed me backwards until I was under the water again, with his body on top of me. My arms were held fast in his grip as his mouth devoured every part of my body, until finally, we were one, in a tidal wave of passion and bath water.

116

What a way to stay in the moment. Bliss coursed into every cell of my body. Every ache and pain vanished, along with most of the bath water.

I opened my eyes and stared at the bathroom floor; the water on it shimmered like a lake in moonlight.

I gazed at Jason who laid with his head on my chest. Narrowing my eyes, I attempted to clarify the impression before me. The muscles on his back gleamed with oil and water, accentuating three dark streaks running across them. The marks ran the width of his back and the edges were dissolving, flowing down into the bath. What was that? I touched the trickle pooling dark on the white porcelain and put my hand to my nose. The metallic pungency of iron filled my nostrils. *Blood!*

'Jason, you're bleeding. Get up!'

'Can't,' he murmured. 'Too tired.'

I shook him. 'Move. Get up!'

He was a dead weight and I was terrified he would be dead, if I didn't get him to hospital. I attempted to slide out from under him, pushing up and sliding my legs free. Jason flipped onto his back in the process, and his body lay rimmed in a pool of red, his face white.

I extricated myself from the bath and turned the lights to full brightness. In hindsight, it probably wasn't a good idea. The full force of the image of Jason hit me like a tram. My head spun, and I clutched at the sink to stop myself falling.

'Keep it together, keep it together!' I slapped myself hard across the face and brought me back to myself. There was blood everywhere. *Don't faint, breathe. Don't faint, breathe.* I repeated it in my mind like a mantra.

The pristine bathroom had obviously felt left out of the carnage that'd occurred in the rest of the house, and had decided to do something about it.

Jason's body was drenched in red.

Tomato passata? Maybe it was. I had a bottle in the pantry. I reckoned you'd need fifteen of them to create this scene. It was blood, you idiot. No, it was paint—Dulux Symphony Red—I had a colour swatch for that. White bath with Shiraz pooled at the bottom? We had plenty of Shiraz.

Rivulets of rosé trickled down the sides of the bath, with sections smudged into crazy finger paintings. The scene overwhelmed me, and I knew I was standing there doing nothing, and there was nothing I could do about it.

Jason groaned and extended a hand. I grasped his hand, slippery with blood and hauled him to a sitting position. He sat head slumped on his knees. The three long gashes on his back oozed a fresh flow of blood.

'Jason, who did this?'

'You did,' he murmured.

I pretended I hadn't heard those words, otherwise I would have remained there, paralysed.

'I'm calling an ambulance.' I headed towards the door, wading through pools of blood-tinged water.

Mobile phone. Where the hell was my phone? Exiting the ensuite, I faced the ruin of our house. Where was Boo? There was broken glass everywhere. I had no shoes on. Shoes, where were my shoes?

'Boo! Boo!' I screamed. Boo was always good at finding shoes. If there was a stray one anywhere, she'd parade around with it, waving it under our noses. She'd only give it back for a trade, which for her was one of her favourite biscuits.

'*Boo!* Biscuit! Find shoes, Boo. Find the phone, Boo!'

Where the hell was she when I needed her? Maybe she was dead or dying somewhere too.

A shoe was wedged under a chair; I pulled it free. It felt sticky and was covered in congealed blood, inside and out. It wasn't a shoe I recognised. It was a man's shoe. Not Jason's, but.

I couldn't be choosy, so slipped my foot into the huge black shoe feeling the gooiness between my toes. I shuffle-hopped clumsily on one shoed foot towards the kitchen, and there was the landline—in pieces on the floor.

I uttered a string of expletives, feeling the situation warranted it.

Standing balanced on one foot, I became aware of the silence in the house. It was magnified by the ticking of the clock on the wall. The ticking became louder, each tick a drumbeat, measuring out wasted seconds, each tick a drumbeat, measuring out wasted drops of Jason's blood.

Tick! Tock! Tick! Tock!

Drip! Drop! Drip! Drop!

I knew it was a countdown to death, and all I could do was stand there and listen to it pound in my brain. The sound was so loud it filled the house.

Bang! Bang! Bang!

Bang! Bang! Bang!

BANG! The front door flew open, and I screamed as a huge hulk of a man stepped into the dark hallway. He turned towards me and stared.

I would have stared too, confronted by a house that looked like a war zone, in the middle of which stood a stark naked, pale skinned, blood streaked woman standing on one leg and wearing a big black shoe.

The man moved towards me and I screamed like a banshee.

'Maggie, it's me! Ashley! His voice was barely audible over my noise.

'Ashley? Oh, *Ash*!'

His boots crunched over the glass as he raced towards me, taking off his coat on the run.

'Holy Mother of God,' he said, as he wrapped me in his coat and picked me up, the shoe still dangling from my foot. 'Bloody hell, Maggie, were you … are you … what the hell happened? You're hurt!'

'Don't worry 'bout me. It's Jason. Get an ambulance! He may

be dead already.'

The sound of crunching glass came from behind us. A force knocked Ashley off his feet, sending him sprawling face first onto the floor. He threw me out of his arms, mid fall, with such force that I landed in a tipped over couch on the other side of the room.

The attacker clutched a wooden rolling pin ready to smash down on Ashley's skull. I realised who it was. 'Jason, no! It's Ashley!'

Ashley rolled over in the nick of time and seized Jason's arm. 'Freaking hell!' he said as he gazed at the bloodied, naked figure standing above him. 'Get that thing away from me—and the rolling pin!'

Jason's knees buckled and he collapsed on top of Ashley.

'Sorry, mate ... thought ... someone ... after Mags ...' Jason mumbled, before passing out.

Ashley now fitted the scene, covered in blood and with a body on top of him. He gently rolled Jason to the side and stood.

Jason opened his eyes. 'I'm all right, Ash. I'm fine.' He sat up and brushed broken glass off his hands. 'Where's Maggie?'

They turned to see me sprawled in an unladylike position on the upturned couch, the black shoe still dangling from my foot.

I hastily covered myself with the coat. I was so glad to see Jason alive I must've had the biggest, silliest grin on my face. Jason reciprocated, flashing me a smile that ignited my heart.

I giggled, and he started to chuckle, holding his ribs and wincing as a belly laugh made its way out into the room. Our laughter sounded unreal in the oppressive atmosphere. Perhaps we'd both gone insane.

Ashley rubbed his hands through his hair, shaking his head. He kept on shaking it as he helped Jason to his feet.

'You stay put,' Ashley said to me. 'I'll come back for you.'

'Come on, Jacie Boy.' He held out his arms. 'I need to take you to a glass free zone.'

'I can walk,' Jason said.

'I'm sure you can, but you're not allowed. Let me carry you to the bedroom.'

'You've gotta be kidding, man.'

'Nup,' Ashley said. He bent and swept Jason off his feet before Jason knew what was happening.

A large, wild haired, blood smeared man crunched through the house in his biker boots, carrying a naked, wild haired, blood soaked man gently in his arms.

I heard Ashley's urgent command. 'On the bed. Stay there. Don't move. I'll be back.'

Ashley returned, gathered me in his arms, and ensuring I was well covered by his coat, made his way back to the bedroom. It was the only glass free area in the house.

'I'll wait outside while you get dressed,' he said, leaving the room.

Jason had zoned out. I covered him with a blanket and hurriedly pulled on some undies, jeans, bra and a top. I picked a piece of glass from my foot, put on socks, found a pair of R.M. Williams boots under the bed, and put them on.

'I'm decent, Ashley, you can come in.'

He entered the room and chuckled. 'I don't know if you're decent, but you're clothed.'

'Ha. Ha. Can you check out Jason while I find him some clothes. We're going to the hospital.'

Jason was awake again. 'You stay away from me, big fella. I'm fine, and I'm not going to hospital.' He sat up and pointed to his chest, 'Look, Maggie, it's not as bad. Check it out.'

I examined his chest. It did look slightly better, particularly the long slash around his right arm. Of more concern to me was his back. The three vicious gashes looked angry, but the bleeding had stopped. The regenerative powers of the crystal must be at work—our contact with it increasing our healing capacity.

'Ashley, what do you think?'

'He needs to be checked out by a doctor for internal injuries, no buts about it. And, judging by the amount of blood everywhere, he could need a transfusion.'

Ashley threw some clothes at Jason. 'Put these on. We're going.'

'Here, I'll help you,' I said.

Jason was compliant and silent as we got him dressed.

I locked the front door, wondering why I was bothering, and helped Jason into the front of Ashley's ute. I slid in after him.

Ashley drove, and we travelled to the hospital in silence. Jason sat staring straight ahead. When we reached the hospital, Jason handed me a card.

'They're going to ask questions about my injuries, and they're required to notify the police. You need to give them this number for Detective Inspector Johnston. Tell them the police have been informed, and they can verify everything with him. If you're asked any questions, say you just got back from staying with the Maestro. She'll vouch for you. You don't know anything; you got home to the mess, and to me, and thought I should get checked out. That's it. Got it?'

'The Maestro?' I said. 'She knows? How?'

'You needed an alibi, and it made sense to call her. She's fine with it.'

'Why would you do that? You told her I tried to kill you?'

'What?' Ashley said, looking horrified.

'No, I said we'd confronted burglars, and I didn't want you involved. I wanted you kept out of it.'

'Okay then,' I said in a small voice. I wasn't happy about involving the Maestro, but for Jason's sake, I'd zip it.

'Jeepers,' Ashley said.

'It's a long story,' Jason and I replied, simultaneously.

---

[14] *Maggie's Playlist: Demons — Imagine Dragons*

Chapter 15: The Hospital

Jason was admitted quickly—luckily it was a quiet night for emergencies, except that is, for our household. The medical team patched him up, took scans, and sought to keep him in overnight for observation.

'Come on, Mags, let's get you something to eat,' Ashley said.

'I want to stay with Jason. I don't want to leave him alone.'

'The doctors and nurses are close by. You need to look after yourself now.'

'We have to protect him.'

'Protect him from what?'

'From … from … things that want to kill him.'

Ashley regarded me with gentle, questioning eyes.

It dawned on me then that I was the thing. I was the murderous, unpredictable entity who posed the greatest threat to Jason's life. I'd inflicted his injuries. He was in hospital because of me.

I turned on my heel and left the room, heading for the canteen. 'I feel like shit,' I said to Ashley as he followed me along the corridor. He caught up to me, and famished, weak and dizzy, I held onto his arm.

'You don't look so good,' he said. Ashley was always the

master of understatement. That was okay with me. I didn't need to hear I looked like crap, even though I knew I did.

'We must've had a hell of a time. I need food so much, even the idea of hospital canteen food is making my mouth water,' I said.

We entered the canteen and Ashley pulled out a chair. 'Food's like sex—when you abstain, even the worst stuff begins to look good. Sit. I'll go see what they've got.'

I sniffed at him. 'You haven't changed. Everything relates back to sex with you.'

'We wouldn't be here without it,' he said with a smile, and loped off towards the counter.

He came back with a tray. 'Bingo! We're early enough for bacon and egg rolls. I also got you a large flat white coffee, with no sugar, just how you like it.'

'You're my savior.' I ripped open the sandwich bag and began devouring its contents. 'How come you came when you did?' I said through a mouthful of food. 'Thank God you did, by the way.'

'I wanted to catch up with you guys again, so thought I'd swing by. I changed my mind about the fossicking and took a quick trip to Thailand instead.' He flashed me a huge grin.

'Thailand? *Ashley!* What were you doing in Thailand?'

'It's not what you think,' he said, smiling broadly again.

'Oh, my God! You've had your teeth fixed! I can't believe I didn't notice before.'

'You were slightly preoccupied.'

He smiled wide, obviously proud of his brand new pearly white choppers. And boy, were they pearly white—perhaps more like 'appliance white'.

'Wow, they … you look fantastic. Hell, you're even more of a chick magnet now.'

'Yeah, right.'

'No seriously, you look gorgeous.'

124

It was the first time I'd seen Ashley look embarrassed.

'Honestly, I don't know what we would've done if you hadn't arrived. You're a life saver.'

'Always a pleasure to be of service.'

'You'll be wanting to know what happened, but I can't tell you much because, honestly, I don't know what happened.'

'Mags, you don't have to tell me now. You need to eat, drink and regroup. Have a freshen up.' He handed me a cosmetic bag. 'Here, I got you an overnight pack from the chemist while you were with Jason. It should have everything you need. There's a shower here you can use.'

'Oh, Ashley, thank you,' I said, tears pricking in my eyes.

He dipped a serviette in his glass of water, leaned across the table and wiped the side of my face.

'Dried blood,' he said. 'Now, if it's all right with you, I'm going to leave you to finish your coffee. I want to check on Jason. You can have a shower through there to the right. Will you be okay here for a while?'

I nodded.

'I'll stay if you want.'

'No, I'm fine. Thank you.'

He slid a phone across the table. 'Since you can't find yours, I got you a disposable for the meantime. It's got my number in it in case you need me. I'll come back and wait for you here.'

I nodded mutely, awash with emotion.

Ashley leant across the table and kissed me on the forehead. 'I'll be back!' He flashed another grin, pointing both index fingers towards his mouth. It made me laugh. You gotta love a man who makes you laugh.

He was gone in a flash, his long legs taking him along the corridor in a matter of seconds.

Unfortunately, I wasn't to know his last words to me would be a lie.

***** *

I wanted to rest my head on my arms and sleep for a million years. Tired? You don't know the meaning of the word. I put my head down on the canteen table for a tiny second. That's all.

The next moment, something prodded me in the back. A gun! I flicked up my chair and pushed it backwards. It connected. Crockery clattered and smashed as I wheeled around to face my opponent, plastic knife at the ready.

'Madam. Madam, please, please, it's fine!' It was a cleaner, arms outstretched, hands waving from side to side. 'Please, Madam. You have been here for a very long time. I was simply tapping you to see if you are dead, Madam.'

'Oh. Oh, I'm so sorry!' I attempted to right his toppled trolley.

'No Madam. You be leaving it to me. I'm sorry I frightened you.'

I stepped towards him. 'I'm sorry I frightened you.'

He backed away from me. I was still waving my plastic knife at him. What must I look like? A blood streaked madwoman with a plastic knife. I giggled. My laughter sounded slightly hysterical, maybe a lot hysterical. I needed to go before they came to take me away. Grabbing my things from the table, I apologised to the bewildered employee and beat a hasty retreat.

Judging from all the people about, it must have been around lunchtime. I checked the phone Ashley had given me. No messages. Where the hell was he? He was supposed to come back.

I reached out with my mind. Darkness. Claustrophobia. Cold. Silence. Trapped. Images flooded into my mind. Ashley was in trouble.

I ran back to Jason's room. He stood by the bed, facing the window. His hospital gown was open at the back, and I paused to enjoy the view of his muscular physique. A passing nurse did likewise. The white curtain like folds of his gown had parted to reveal the curve of a perfect pair of buttocks. The 'V' of his muscular back intersected with his bum, leading the eye to well-formed inner thighs. He was a hunk and I was a voyeur. That made it all the hotter. *Phew!*

He pulled on his jocks, took off the gown, and picked up his jeans, wobbling dangerously on one leg as he tried to put them on. I ran forward and caught him before he hit the deck.

'Great save. Thanks, Mags.' He kissed the top of my head. 'Where the hell have you been? I've been worried sick. I was coming to look for you. Ash said he was going to get you, but that was hours ago.'

'I fell asleep. I came back as soon as I woke. You're shaky on your legs. Here, sit back on the bed.'

He leant back on the pillow, and his naked chest caught the light. The wound around his right arm was now a faint scar. I traced its journey across his body with my finger. Two more scars ran across his heart. The scars reminded me of a scene from our favourite movie *Jaws*. I pointed at them. 'Bayonet, Iwo Jima?'

'No.'

'Don't tell me, Mary Ellen Moffit broke your heart?'

He smiled softly. 'No, Maggie McLaine did.'

I didn't want to know, but I had to know. I forced myself to say the words.

'What happened back at the house? You have to tell me everything. Did I do all that?'

'No, but you did a fair whack of it. You went psycho again and tried to kill me. You tried with the knife, and then with anything you could get your hands on. I'm sorry, but I was forced to knock you out. It was the only way I could subdue you.'

'Jesus. No wonder I've got a cracker of a headache.'

'I can't tell you how it felt having to do that to you.' He

turned away and focused intently on the ceiling. 'After I'd finally disarmed and bound you, three thugs came to the door. They were after the crystal ... and you. I had you secured in the back room. They forced their way in, and I took them on. Boo was there, biting and attacking them too. She took a fair blow to the head from one of the bastards.'

'Oh,' I said, feeling sick to my stomach.

Jason took my hand in his. 'I knocked two of them out, and one fell on his own knife, resulting in the big pool of blood you saw. I called the cops, so that's why I hid you in the hammock. I secured you overly well as I wasn't sure when, or if, you'd be yourself again. After I'd finished tying you up, I returned to the house and found the thugs had scarpered. The police arrived shortly after.'

'So, after battling with me, you had three more maniacs to deal with. Plus, you had to handle the police. My God, Jason, this is a nightmare.'

'What's happening, Maggie? What the hell's going on? And more importantly, what the fuck can I do to stop it?'

'Not you Jason, we. We have to stop it. As to what it is, I'm not sure, but I have a theory. I can tell you what it felt like too. Imagine all the negative emotional energy of human beings amalgamated into one creature. Everyone's hate, anger, rage, sorrow, jealousy, despair—you name it—manifested into a single entity, and the energy is so dense it begins to manifest on the physical plane.'

Jason furrowed his brow. 'It can't be.'

'Hear me out. Negative emotional energy resides in all humans, some more than others. Some intuitives call this energy the Pain Body. I'm calling it the Dark Force. This destructive energy lies dormant in all of us until something triggers it. The trigger could be as simple as an untoward comment, or someone cutting you off in traffic. In response, you feel a surge of fury, which often elicits aggressive behaviour. Road rage is a perfect example.'

'Yep, we've all been on the receiving end of that,' Jason said. 'My mate Fraser had his windows, and his head, smashed in in a road rage incident.'

'Exactly. The Dark Force needs negative emotional energy of all types to survive, so it makes people overreact. It generates uncontrollable rage and other negative emotions in order to produce its food—more negative emotional energy. People have committed murder under its influence. Once replete, it becomes dormant again, leaving the human to mop up the disaster left in its wake. Generally, the victim has no idea why they got so carried away. And that's the thing—they *were* carried away, taken over, possessed.

'Jason, there are over seven billion people on the planet generating negative emotional energy. The largest population ever. This entity is the result—it's the Dark Force. Welcome to the new age.'

'So essentially we're fucked.'

'Language.'

'Sorry, so essentially we can bend over and kiss our arses goodbye.'

His face was so serious I laughed.

'No, we have the weapon to defeat it.'

'Um, I must have missed something. What weapon?'

'The crystal!'

'Oh Jesus. We are fucked. The crystal is dead, in case you hadn't noticed. Plus, it appears this Dark Force has latched onto you in particular. We're screwed.'

'No, don't say that. You're never this negative. It's the entity talking. We'll find a way. Somehow. Something will reveal itself. Trust me.'

Jason sighed and took me into his arms.

I extracted myself from his grip. 'We have another more immediate problem. Ashley is in trouble.' I explained the images in my mind. 'He's trapped somewhere.'

'He can look after himself. You know he can.'

'Yes, but things are different. We're dealing with something supernatural.'

Jason swayed to one side, and I pulled him upright.

'Maggie, I'm beat. At this point Ash is going to have to fend for himself.'

'Yes, I'm sorry, of course.' I touched the gash on his arm. Already the injury was barely visible. 'It's incredible. Contact with the crystal has given you amazing recuperative abilities.'

'I still feel stuffed.'

'Yes, you need rest. You're right. Ashley will be fine.'

'The doctor insists I stay another night, but I'll only do so if you stay right here with me.'

'Where else would I go? Certainly not home. Oh, crap! What about Boo? I have to go home. Poor Boo. The house is a mess. She'll be hungry and confused. With her new powers of levitation, she's probably floated over the fence and disappeared.'

'She'll be right,' Jason said. 'Anyway, she can float across all the broken glass and raid the pantry.'

'S'pose you're right.'

The last thing I wanted to do was go home on my own and face all the mess, and God knew what else. Boo would just have to cope.

Jason gripped my arm. 'I'm not letting you go home alone and that's that. You look as beat as I feel. I want you right here with me, in my arms, where I can protect you.'

The only person he needed to protect was himself—from me.

The thought made me sad. 'Get back into bed, Mister. I'm going to have a shower. I'll be back.'

They were what you'd call "famous last words".

---

[15] *Maggie's Playlist: Bad Case of Loving You (Doctor, Doctor) — Robert Palmer*

Chapter 16: The Morgue

'Dark, dark! The horror of darkness, like a shroud, wraps me and bears me on through mist and cloud.' — *Sophocles*

Walking along the corridor, I anticipated a lovely hot shower. I was glad to see a toothbrush and toothpaste included in the bag Ashley had given me. My mouth felt like the bottom of a cockatoo's cage.

I opened the shower room with the key he'd given me. Good old Ashley. He must have sweet-talked one of the nurses into letting me use the staff shower room. First things first, I had to clean my teeth. Looking into the mirror, and brushing thoroughly, I enjoyed the minty freshness.

Ashley came to mind again. Those images I'd seen, and the feelings. The icy coldness, surrounded by black, claustrophobia, the stench of decay. My stomach knotted in response.

I looked at my reflection. Oh crikey, we had ourselves a mirror of death. The harsh fluorescent lights highlighted every flaw and washed away any remaining colour left in my face. Holy crap. If I got any whiter, you wouldn't be able to find me in a snowstorm. The lights sucked out the colour from my green eyes, making them look eerie under my dark lashes and eyebrows. My black hair had lost its luster and lay in matted clumps, and my blunt cut fringe had gone AWOL, curling in multiple directions.

The overhead lights flickered and my reflection was overshadowed by another face. It was blurred and shadowy, but it seemed like a man. I shrieked and dropped the toothbrush on the floor.

Almost as soon as they'd started, the lights stopped flickering and my reflection returned to normal. I rubbed my eyes. What was that? The image had been so brief, I hadn't had time to fully register it. I was way too tired. Perhaps my eyesight was playing up. Or maybe there was a ghost in the mirror.

I often saw strange things. Ghosts and stuff. We had a ghost in our house. Harmless, but she liked to muck around with the lights. We had a lot of blown lightbulbs from her efforts. I don't know who she is, but apparently, she likes being with us. She's a clean freak. She got highly upset when we were renovating and there was mess around. Cost us a fortune in lightbulbs. God knows how she's coping at the moment.

So maybe it was a ghost in the mirror. The mirrors at home seemed to have a life of their own lately. Just great. I had a ghost who played with electricity, and now one with a penchant for mirrors.

Still thinking of Ashley, I zipped the toilet bag and headed for the shower. He felt close. I held the image of his face in my mind and became aware of a soft humming in my head. Don't tell me on top of everything I've got tinnitus!

I moved towards the door and the humming increased in strength. Ashley's presence felt stronger. Deciding to forgo the shower, I exited the bathroom and raced along the corridor towards Jason's room. The humming faded. Following the sound in my brain I ran towards the lifts.

The lift arrived and I got in. When the doors closed, the automated voice suggested I select a floor. I ran my eyes over the numbered buttons, and when they hit the bottom level, B5, the whine in my head dialed up in volume. I was being led to Ashley! I'd turned into a human Geiger counter, or Ashley detector.

I pressed B5 with my finger covered in the sleeve of my jumper—those buttons would be crawling with germs. As I pressed the button, it occurred to me I should get Jason, but no, he needed to rest. I could do this.

The lift door opened and I stepped out into a long corridor. Unlike the modern hospital on the floors above, this was like stepping back in time. It reminded me of a mineshaft—a corridor stretching out to forever.

The high ceilings were lit by dim fluorescent lights, which fought a losing battle against the encroaching shadows. The Dark Force would love it here.

The place seemed deserted. I followed the hum to the left, and winced when my boots made a racket on the green linoleum floor. Too loud. I yanked them off and left them inside an open office door. Office, twenty-three. Remember that, Maggie. Don't want to lose those boots.

Now my footfalls were silent as a mouse. Mucho bettero.

I followed a blue line on the floor to who knew where. All the shiny linoleum made me want to take a run and see how far I could slide in my socks.

The place was heavy with silence and appeared deserted. This was definitely the bowels of the hospital, probably housing laundry rooms or secret labs filled with failed experiments.

I slipped along the corridor past rows of doors, all identical except for their numbers, and finally found myself at a fork in the corridor. There were three directions to choose from. Getting the hang of my new skill, the direction I needed to take came immediately—the middle corridor. I still hadn't come across a living soul, or even a dead one for that matter.

I followed this new corridor to a set of double doors with restricted access signs all over them. I peered through the window in the door and saw a little office to the right with a sign on the window: Medical Records / Mortuary. N.B. Cremation Certificate MUST be paid for at Cashier on Level 1.

It appeared no one was in attendance, so I pushed on one of the double doors, and hey presto, it opened. So much for restricted access. I hugged the wall and ducked below the office window, like I'd seen in the movies, in case someone was in the back having coffee and doughnuts.

The light was dim and the corridor radiated a peculiar greenish tinge. The ceiling was low with pipes running along the walls. Tiles were coming loose and the air smelt stale. All in all, it was a pretty spooky place, but I was starting to enjoy myself.

A sign for the mortuary pointed straight ahead. The humming increased, so I kept going. Suddenly the buzzing in my head stopped. *Now what?*

Footsteps, not the squeak, squeakady, squeak of rubber or vinyl soles, but the tap, tap, tap of leather. A second set of footsteps followed the first. Office doors opened and closed systematically.

Someone was searching for something, or someone.

I had a strong feeling it would behoove me not to be discovered by the owners of these footsteps, even though I didn't know who owned them. I tried the handle on the office door behind me. It was locked.

Bang! If I didn't know any better, that sounded like an office door being kicked in.

Bang! Yep. Their search was slow, methodical and relentless.

Bang! I assumed with all the door kicking they weren't hospital employees. Or maybe they were.

Bang! I stood, unsure what to do next; my Geiger counter seemed to have given up the ghost.

A sign indicated the mortuary was to the right, and there was a laundry to the left. Opposite me was a short unsignposted corridor.

I couldn't go back. I had to choose. Right? Left? Straight ahead? Where were my psychic powers when I bloody needed 'em?

A short, angry exchange in a foreign language echoed through the tunnel, followed immediately by the sound of running footsteps heading my way. Decision made! I took the short corridor opposite and strode along it, looking desperately for a suitable hidey-hole. I came across a large doorless room on the left. Inside, the light was dim, but I could make out rows of what looked like boilers. The equipment, whatever it was, seemed to be old and disused. If Jason were here, he'd know exactly what all this stuff was.

In the dim light, back at the T-junction where I'd come from, was the silhouette of a man moving steadily towards me. Before I could react, a hand slapped across my mouth and dragged me backwards into the boiler room.

It was one big mother of a guy who held me in his paws. My body became limp with fright. My legs and arms were useless appendages as he dragged me at speed to the back of the room. His face was next to mine. He smelt like ... death.

I felt myself disassociate from my body. Jason was going to be so angry with me for disobeying him and getting into more strife. Huh, if I died here, maybe I would end up in the mortuary around the corner. That would be weird. Handy though.

Clarity returned slightly. There was a bench, I made a restricted grab at whatever came to hand. Hmmm, it felt like metal, and heavy. Good.

I couldn't whack the bastard behind me because I didn't have full movement of my arms. Hope began to evaporate. Maybe he was a grizzly bear; he had the arms and grip of one. I'd have to bide my time.

We reached the wall at the end of the room. My mouth was tightly covered, but there was a slight loosening of his grip around my chest and upper arms. This is it, Maggie. You've got to brain him—*now!*

I went for it, but he grabbed my wrist.

I have to say, I was sick and tired of my wrists being grabbed,

136

particularly as they were still sore from their previous abuses.

A voice hissed in my ear. 'It's Ash, idiot. Shhh.'

He released my mouth, put his hands on my shoulders and pushed me into a squat between his legs, his arms wrapped around me. We were wedged behind one of the boilers at the back of the room. It was dark, but we were like two sitting ducks.

My heart hammered in my ears, and I felt a ridiculous urge to scream.

Wait! I had it! It hit me like a bolt of lightning. I had the answer. I needed to get angry. It was that easy. I needed to turn myself back into the monster who nearly killed Jason. I could have those two blokes on toast. No worries.

I screwed up my face—I'm angry; I am soooo angry. So angry, angry, *angry!* I focused my concentration on all the things which made me furious. I tried to whip myself into a frenzy, but like a woman with too much Botox, all I got was blandness. What the hell?

As footsteps made their way into the room, I had a lightbulb moment—I could be a tad slow at times—the darkness wouldn't attack its own. That must be why I couldn't get any rage going. But was it really the Dark Force? The vibe from this pursuer was different. I couldn't sense unadulterated rage. It was an energy devoid of emotion. I wasn't sure what the hell I was dealing with.

I didn't know if Ashley had a plan, but I knew exactly what I was going to do. I whipped myself out of Ashley's grasp and squeezed between the boilers, making my way to the front of the room. The man was heading towards the spot where Ashley was hidden.

I took aim and hurled the metal object I'd found earlier at a small window at the top of the wall outside the room.

Smash! A direct hit! The noise was loud enough for the man to hightail it back outside the room. He didn't notice the window and kept going, running off along the corridor.

Ashley was by my side a second later. He grasped my hand and pulled me from the room, dragging me behind him to the end of the corridor where he raised his fist and stopped. I'd seen enough action movies to know what that hand signal meant, and Ashley had seen enough action to use it automatically.

We peeked around the corner. The man was nowhere to be seen. Giving the forward motion hand signal, Ashley dragged me along the corridor towards the mortuary. Ashley was in his socks as well, and a big toe stuck out through a hole in one of them.

Blasting through more doors with Restricted Access signs, we finally arrived at the mortuary. I stopped, confronted by an awful orange linoleum floor and a big bank of stainless-steel fridge lockers.

'Come on, this bottom locker's empty,' Ashley whispered, indicating a blank identification ticket on the door. He pulled off a whiteboard pen clipped to the front of the locker and wrote something in the blank space.

'You're kidding?'

'Nup, it's the perfect hidey-hole.' He opened the door and slid out the bottom trolley. 'I put a tagged body bag in there already.'

'Not a used bag?'

'No silly, it's brand new. Come on, we have to get bagged and tagged.'

The look on my face must have said everything.

He spoke to me like I was a child. 'Just imagine … pretend it's a sleeping bag, and we're going camping.'

I rolled my eyes.

Ashley sat in the body bag on the stainless-steel body tray and swung his legs on, stretching them out in front of him. He held out his arms. 'Get in. Now!'

I lay on top of him, face to face. I figured I'd rather stare at Ashley than have my nose millimeters away from a stainless-steel plate, above which rested four dead bodies.

'Watch your noggin.' He held the steel above and rolled us into the fridge. Then he reached back and pulled the fridge door closed.

'I've been laying low in here,' he whispered. 'After I left you, I sensed I was being tailed, and I was. Three blokes. I could've taken 'em out, but I didn't want my new choppers smashed, so I lost the dudes and hid in this locker. I thought the blokes had scarpered and was making my way out when I saw you. We can wait it out in here 'til the coast is clear. I couldn't understand their language, but I did make out two words. They said Maggie a few times, and Kris-tal, which obviously means crystal.'

'So, what? They know you're associated with me so they're after you too?'

'Looks like it, kiddo.'

'Shit.'

It was pitch black. The steel was cold on my hands so I moved them to rest on Ashley's chest. I tried not to think about the men hunting us, or their soulless energy. I tried not to think about the bodies stacked above us. It felt like they'd definitely gone spirit wise, so that was something. I guess. I also tried to not think about my close proximity to Ashley. We were the best of friends now, but I had dated him before Jason.

'This is cozy,' he whispered. He stretched his jacket across me to keep me warm. 'Reminds me of the time we all went camping. Remember the storm and how my tent got trashed. We all had to huddle in your two-man tent.'

'Yeah, it was beaut,' I said, as my teeth began to chatter.

Ashley held me tight in his arms; one big paw cradled the top of my head.

'This is dumb,' I whispered. 'They'll find us. We're like sitting ducks.'

'They didn't find me before.'

I pinched his arm. 'Listen. Footsteps.'

We held our breath as rubber soles squeaked around the

room, stopped, then squeaked some more, off into the distance.

I slowly let out my breath to try and settle my pounding heart. 'What's the plan if someone opens the door? We're screwed.'

'I have a plan.'

'What's the plan?'

'We play dead,' he said.

'Oh my God, that's it? We are *so* dead.'

'Think positive.'

'Ashley?'

'Yes.'

'How do we get out?'

'Self-releasing mechanism. Red button on the inside of door.'

The tip of my nose was an ice block, and I couldn't feel my fingers and toes. Seriously, I could not stay in this refrigerated coffin. I hated going into supermarkets with open freezers, or walking into the refrigerated back room of the liquor store. This was my worst, worst nightmare. I would happily hand myself over to the bad guys rather than stay in this subzero box.

'When can we go?'

'Soon, pumpkin.'

'How soon?' I asked.

'Soon.'

'Soon soon?'

'Yep, soon.'

He was in no hurry to leave. In fact, he seemed quite relaxed. How odd. Maybe he was a vampire, and this reminded him of his coffin at home. Just my luck. He was probably going to bite me any minute, and I'd be doomed to drink blood and roam the earth for eternity. What would happen to Jason? Or Boo? I would have to bite them too.

'You're a vampire, aren't you?' I whispered. 'You love it in here.'

His belly shook with silent laughter. He moved my head to

one side exposing the soft flesh on my neck, then bent forward and bit me with his brand-new choppers, sucking in my flesh between his teeth.

'Ow! Stop, it hurts!' I jerked away and cracked my skull on the top of the fridge. It echoed like thunder and we both let rip with an expletive.

Ashley became rigid; I felt us both hold our breath. Ashley was still holding his when I had to let mine go, blowing softly into his chest.

'I think we're okay, Mags.'

'You're an idiot.'

'No, you're an idiot. A vampire indeed! Hmmm, but I like sharing my coffin with you,' he said, trying to nuzzle my neck again. Ashley was easily bored, and I knew he was trying to amuse himself at my expense.

'I'm outta here.' I wriggled upwards trying to find the door release button. I was cold—no, make that freezing— claustrophobic, and highly annoyed. It was at that moment I felt the beast stir.

Except it wasn't my beast, it was Ashley's.

'*Ashley! What?*

'Sorry,' he whispered. 'I'm only human. You wriggle too much.'

'Awkward.'

'Uh huh.'

I tried to wriggle to one side to take the pressure off.

He drew a sharp breath in through his nose. 'I wouldn't do that.'

'Sorry, only trying to help.'

'It ain't helping, sweetheart.'

I started to giggle and buried my face in his chest to muffle the sound. Convulsing with laughter, and knowing it wouldn't benefit things, made me laugh even more.

Ashley groaned underneath me.

My stomach hurt. I couldn't breathe. I gasped for air. I think I'd used up all the oxygen. At least I was warmer. I raised my head to catch a breath, and Ashley kissed me. Oh my.

The flame I thought dead burst into life.

Uh-oh.

His hand slid to the back of my head, holding me in place, as he gave me a long, deep, passionate kiss. His other hand wrapped around my bum, and he pulled me in close. I didn't think we could actually get any closer, but Ashley obviously had other ideas.

Against my will, my body responded.

What was it with my knees? I felt them go weak even though they had no weight to support.

I might as well stay here in this goddamn morgue now, because I was so dead already if Jason found out.

'Mmmm,' I said, trying to pull away and speak. I dug him sharply in the ribs.

'Ouch!' He jerked his head back. Both his hands had found their way under my top where he'd already released my bra strap with one quick flick. Oh, here was a man of remarkable know-how. Years of practice, right there.

His hands were trying to manoeuvre their way to my breasts, but were frustrated by the lack of space. He went to Plan B, sliding both hands along my body until his thumbs hooked into the back of my jeans, and then he yanked downwards. I felt a button give way.

'Ashley! You're insane. What the hell has gotten into you? *Stop it!*' I hissed, trying to wiggle my way towards his feet and away from those groping hands. I wasn't sure which was the best direction to go. I was caught between a rock and a hard place, and the thought made me giggle.

'Enough, Ashley! This is wrong. Cut it out!'

Passion. Desire. Regret. Lust. Betrayal. Love. Ashley's feelings and thoughts washed through my mind and mingled with my own. I tried to shut them out but they were identical to mine. What the hell? This couldn't be happening. We'd moved on. Hadn't we?

A noise came from outside. The creak of a door, the rustle of paper. We froze. The sound of a phone number being tapped into a mobile phone. Swearing, someone walking away. Silence.

Ashley let out his breath, and his hands continued their downward journey taking my jeans with them. When his arms could stretch no further, Bingo! He was holding my naked bum, a cheek in each hand, and more. A sharp intake of breath as he explored my body. He groaned, and whispered, 'Oh, you want me.'

'Well, *I'm* only human. Ashley stop it! We can't do this. It's not right. Have you gone mad? Think about Jason. He's your best friend. Besides, in *here*? Way too weird.'

I must have been convincing because, in an instant, the beast was vanquished.

Ashley gave a long, slow sigh and yanked my jeans back to their rightful place.

'I'm sorry, luv. So sorry. Don't know what the hell came over me. It's inexcusable,' he mumbled. 'I'm a bloody idiot.'

I nodded in agreement and he enfolded me in his arms.

We lay in a silence broken only by our breathing and the sound of approaching footsteps.

---

[16] *Maggie's Playlist: Love Me Now — John Legend*

Chapter 17: Adam

Ashley pulled the zip of the body bag over our heads to chest level.

'It's a two-day ride to get here,' a man's voice said over the rattle of a trolley.

I heard a woman say, 'Yes, it's bizarre how hidden mortuaries are. It's the same in most hospitals, as if they're trying to deny people actually die. Oh, Jesus, there it goes again.'

'What?'

'The lights flickered.'

'So?'

'I swear, every time I bring a body down here the lights flicker. Creeps me out.'

'Yeah, let's get this done. Where's Mike anyway? He should be here.'

'Got a training session, he'll be back soon. He said to put the body in bay one, locker five.'

'Hell, this place is a shop of horrors. Look at all this stuff,' the man said, jangling something metal.

'That's a hanging digital scale, used to weigh people's brains and internal organs.'

'Bloody hell! What's this then?'

'It's a vibrating saw, used to cut off the calvarium—the top of the skull —so the brain can be removed.'

'And this?'

'A skull chisel. Once the calvarium has been scored with the saw, the chisel is used to separate the top of the skull from the lower skull, exposing the brain and its coverings.'

'Blimey. These things look like pruning shears.'

'They're rib cutters, and in fact, some morgue technicians do use pruning shears. They work as well and don't cost as much.'

'Dead set?'

'Yep. Come on, let's find the locker.'

Footsteps tapped and squeaked around the room.

I was going to have a heart attack—we were in bay one, locker five. When they opened the door and found us, they'd most likely have a heart attack and die too. The only person alive would be Ashley, who, judging by his breathing, seemed so unconcerned he appeared to have fallen asleep.

I poked him in the ribs as the footsteps squeaked to a stop outside our fridge door.

'Hey Jenny, it's over here, bay one, locker five, but it's in use already.'

'Can't be.' Her footsteps tapped over.

'Woah, it says EVD Hazard. Really? Impossible. Not here.'

'What's EVD?'

'Ebola Virus Disease.'

'Woah!'

'Nah, it's a mistake. Has to be.'

'But it says so! There was a case. We shouldn't open it.'

One set of footsteps backed away, one came forward, and then the handle of the fridge locker clicked.

Our fridge door opened. There was a rush of warm air and a tugging at the top of the body bag.

'Phew! It stinks in there. It shouldn't smell. Huh, there's a Red Category Three tag on the bag.'

145

The door slammed shut, more fridge doors opened and closed.

'This is an empty one. Put her in here and make a note in the book.'

Noises of metal on metal, a hydraulic hoist, a rattle of rollers and a fridge door slamming shut.

'Done. Let's get out of here.'

I waited until the footsteps had disappeared before I said, 'Ashley, get me out of here too, or I swear, I will kill you.'

'Easy babe, that won't be necessary. Out we go.' He unzipped the bag and pressed the door release.

Nothing happened.

He pressed it again.

Nothing.

Click. Click. Click.

Nothing.

'Shit!' he said.

A rising tide of panic washed over me, and a sweat as cold as the fridge ran down my face.

I whisper screamed into Ashley's chest. 'No! No! No!'

'Chill, it's okay.'

'How. Is. It. *Okay?*' I growled. 'And I am chilled. To the bone!'

'We'll have to wait for Mike to come back. They said he wouldn't be long. We'll bang on the door and he'll let us out. All is well.'

'And then we'll say what?'

'We'll say Jenny played a practical joke on us.'

'You can't be serious.'

'Nah, we'll make a run for it.'

'Ashley?'

'Yes?'

'What if he reads the EVD label and doesn't open the door?'

'He'll have to. We'll be banging the shit out of it.'

'But what if he thinks an EVD case was brought in without his knowledge, and now, the EVD case is banging on the door trying to get out?'

'Like an EVD zombie?'

'Exactly! Didn't think of that did you? No sane person is going to open the door for an Ebola Virus zombie, ever. We're gonna die in here, and it's all your fault.'

'Well then, I couldn't think of a nicer person to kick the bucket with.'

I pounded on his chest as best I could in the limited space. The result was more a pathetic tapping.

'I know something we could do to pass the time,' he said.

'You are fair dinkum unbelievable.'

'I know.' He rubbed his hands through my hair to muss it up even more than it already was.

'Shhh, footsteps!' I said.

'See? It's Mike. What did I say?'

'Wait,' I hissed.

Footsteps entered the room, stopped, then travelled across to our locker. There was a pause, and the footsteps moved off. The sound of turning pages. The clink and clank of metal instruments. A sound of something being dragged. More clinking and clanking.

Ashley zipped closed our body bag. Here we went again.

The footsteps returned to our locker. The handle clicked; the door opened. Every muscle in my body was ready to explode, and my heart ready to join them. The door closed again. We both exhaled. The footsteps moved away, fading to nothing. We waited for a minute, ears straining for a sound. Then, there was one. Ashley farted.

As if things couldn't get any worse.

'Oops, sorry, luv.'

'Ashley, try the door again. Now!' I held my breath.

He unzipped the bag and pressed the release button. The

door clicked open. He froze, listening. I listened too, but couldn't hear anything other than my heart pounding.

'Let's go!' He pushed the body board out.

No one could have seen it coming.

The gun butt smashed into Ashley's skull. It took four blows to bring him down, before he slid bloodied and unconscious off the board.

The attacker was bigger than Ashley. Thicker, built like a tank. Standing in his socks, his silhouette blocked out the light.

Dressed all in black—the villain's fashion choice—he was young, with pale skin, a chiseled jaw and stunning blue-grey eyes, framed by perfectly plucked, arched eyebrows. An aquiline nose sat above rosy lips that curved slightly upwards. Short brown hair was swept neatly off his face to one side, in the way a mother may have combed her child's hair.

He should have been doing aftershave ads.

His neck to his jawline was decorated with a thick collar of tattoos: hideous monsters interspersed with spinning symbols like Catherine wheels. The band of ink writhed with menace and set off his face to perfection. He was evil and innocence personified. Yin and Yang.

I stared at him, mesmerised. After what seemed like forever, he leant forward, grabbed my wrist and helped me out of the locker.

'Are you all right, Maggie?'

I couldn't place his accent.

'Sort of.'

'I'm glad. My name's Adam.'

I was confused; he was exceedingly polite for a bad guy. Was he one?

'Please don't scream, or I *will* kill you.'

Ah, *that* would be a yes then. A polite psychopath.

Ashley was on the floor, his face white and still. 'My friend, is he ... did you—'

'You must give me the crystal sphere.'

'I don't know what you're talking about.'

'Don't play games. Don't make me angry; it is not good when I'm angry.'

'Yeah, I know how that feels.'

'Where is the crystal?' His voice was soft but insistent.

'Honestly, I don't know.'

His left eye twitched. 'I know you know.'

My mind was racing; surely, he would have been to our house? The crystal wouldn't be hard to find. And what about Ashley's rock? Why did he want the crystal? What would happen if I told him where it was? But in truth, I didn't know where it was anymore.

'Adam, honestly. It was at my house, but I don't know where it is anymore. You should go. Mike will be coming back any minute.'

Adam nodded towards the back of the room. I turned and saw Mike propped against the wall, sitting in a pool of his own blood.

My blood ran cold. I felt Adam catch me just before I hit the floor.

I awoke to find myself bound to an autopsy table by my wrists—yes, again—and my ankles. Fluorescent ceiling lights and peeling paint gave me something to look at. Someone needed to get a cobweb broom up there and give it a serious going over.

The situation seemed grim, but I did have one thing to be grateful for. I still had all my clothes on.

Adam bent over me and rubbed my forehead with his thumb. 'Are you well?'

'Actually, no.'

'If you tell me the location of the crystal you can go free, unharmed.'

'I told you already, I don't know.'

'There are many fine instruments here.' He caressed an

assortment of stainless-steel kitchenware. 'I'm particularly fond of this one.' He picked up what appeared to be a little hand saw.

I remembered the conversation of the previous folk. 'I believe that's a saw used to cut off the calvarium, so the brain can be removed.'

Adam tilted his head and regarded me with a raised eyebrow.

Oh, for God's sake, not another eyebrow raiser in our midst.

'You're probably wondering why you still have your clothes on.'

'No.'

'It's because I'm going to cut them off with these.' He smiled and held up a ginormous pair of stainless-steel shears, and then inserted them into the leg of my jeans.

'Please don't. They cost me a lot of money.'

He rubbed the fabric between his thumb and forefinger and examined the stitching. 'Moschino?'

I nodded.

'Nice,' he said. 'Where's the crystal?'

'I don't know, Adam.'

'You will wish you did know.' He moved to the head of the table and I tipped my head back to see him. Adam tore off a length of tape with his perfect white teeth. He placed it over my mouth, and I experienced a feeling of déjà vu.

The vibrating saw screamed next to my ear. I yanked at my bindings, but it was hopeless. I tilted my head and rolled back my eyes to look at him with the most pleading expression I could muster.

'Mmmmm. Mmmmm,' I said, willing him to stop.

Still holding the saw millimeters from my flesh, he peeled back the tape from my mouth with his free hand and held my gaze.

He was a soul in torture. I was in his mind. His eyes softened. He stroked my cheek, and then the top of his skull exploded.

Adam's blood felt warm as it cascaded over my face. His body remained upright for a second, before falling backwards onto a tray of instruments.

I raised my head and saw Jason. He stood in the doorway, legs spread, arms out, with a gun clenched in his hands.

Chapter 18: Morgue Mayhem

Adam's blood trickled over my face—his final caress. The blood pooled around me on the stainless-steel table. Closing my eyes, I lay still—shattered.

Adam's blood was in my mouth. His essence. The taste of copper and iron unfolded his life in my mind. A gentle, artistic soul thrust into circumstances of abuse and neglect, he sought solace in the arms of heroin—a lover taking him to divine realms. and then leaving him abandoned at the gates of hell.

Images of beauty—paintings created by him—flowed by, changing gradually to a filmstrip of horror, death and darkness.

Adam's calm eyes appeared before me and I could feel his touch on my face.

'Maggie, I'm free. The beauty has returned. I have my soul back. I can paint again. It is better now; don't be sad.'

Adam's touch vanished as I became aware of loud groaning noises—they were coming from Ashley.

Footsteps approached. It was Jason. 'Maggie?' His voice broke. *'Maggie!'*

Steel trolleys clanged and instruments scattered nosily as Ashley staggered towards me. His body collided with the autopsy table. 'No!' he yelled. He touched my face and whispered hoarsely, 'Maggie?'

Vibrations racked me, the sound of a jet plane in my head, and I left my body, floating up to the fluorescent lights and cobwebs. Peace.

The orange floor highlighted the strewn stainless-steel equipment. Puddles of red pooled around shiny metal devices. A roll of paper towelling had unrolled across the room, a bold white stripe, emblazoned with flashes of blood.

Adam was on his back, arms outstretched to the side, the saw still screaming in his hand. A halo of steel instruments surrounded him, appearing to have exploded from his body. Glimmering eerily, they created a holy aura against the orange and blood coloured floor.

Poor Mike had toppled over leaving a windscreen wiper streak of blood on the wall behind him.

I lay on the autopsy table, my face a mask of blood.

Ashley was a train wreck—beaten and bloodied, his face contorted with grief as he looked down at me, his tears splashing on my cheeks. Jason felt for a pulse on my wrist and neck.

'Ash, she's alive. Maggie, come back! We need you to come back. I need you to come back.' He cut the tape from my wrists and ankles. 'Help me sit her up.'

Jason knew Ashley needed something to do.

Ashley put an arm around my shoulders and raised me from the trolley. Jason held my ankles and swung my legs around so I sat on the edge of the table. My mouth fell open releasing a torrent of Adam's blood.

'Jesus,' Ashley said.

'Oh my God,' Jason said, looking horror stricken.

I felt a rush as I slammed back into my body. I gasped for air, breathed in blood. A violent coughing fit racked my body, and Jason copped a spray of blood in the face.

'Ash, get some water!'

Ashley picked up the bowl from the digital scale used for

weighing brains and body parts and filled it with water.

My coughing eased and I croaked, 'I'm back.' I smiled and they took a step back in shock.

'A blood-filled grin is so not becoming,' Ashley said, dipping a paper cup into the water and handing it to me. 'Here, rinse out with this.' He sounded like my dentist. I dutifully swished and swooshed, after which he held an empty cup in front of me.

'Now spit.'

'Ew!' I said, seeing the red soup I'd spat out.

'Again. Rinse!'

I repeated the procedure until my mouth stopped tasting like a fistful of old pennies.

'Thank you, Ashley.' I smiled a big smile.

'That's better!' they said simultaneously.

Jason soaked a paper towel in water and gently cleaned Adam's blood from my face.

I took Ashley's hand. 'I thought you were dead.'

'Nah, I'm fine. Got a cracker of a headache, but.' He gingerly rubbed his temples and winced. 'It'll take more than a whack on the noggin to do me in.'

'It was more than one whack.'

He rubbed my hand. 'I thought you were dead too. Had me right worried, you did.'

'That makes both of us,' I said. 'I need to stand.'

'Here, I'll help you.' Ashley lifted me off the table and held me upright. 'Can you stand?'

I braced my feet against the sticky floor; the strength in my legs seemed to be there. 'I'm fine. You can let go.'

I took a step and turned to where Adam lay behind me. I'd seen his body from above, but on the earth plane the scene hit hard. My knees buckled and Ashley caught me, scooping me up in his arms.

'Ash, give her to me,' Jason said. 'You look like hell.'

'I'm fine.'

'No, really.'

'I'm okay, Jason, all good.'

'No, here, let me.'

'Oh, boys.' I feared this dull conversation may go on all day, or night—I'd lost track of time down here in Mortuary World.

Adam was spread-eagled on the floor. He appeared to be wearing a red and white beanie, but it was his brain protruding from the top of his shattered skull. The rest of his head was intact from the eyes down. His rosy lips trembled and moved as though he was struggling to speak.

'Bloody hell. Look!' I said.

Ashley held me tighter. 'Holy Mother of God.'

Jason followed our gaze. 'What the?'

Two quivering antennae emerged from between Adam's perfect white teeth. Bent insectile legs took purchase on his tender lips as they pulled out a chitinous shell behind them.

We stood transfixed as a large black cockroach emerged from his mouth. It paused on Adam's chin, cleaning its face and antennae with spikey forelegs. The task absorbed its attention for a few seconds, and then, it froze, aware it had an audience.

There was not a sound, not a movement in the room as three humans locked eyes with one cockroach.

Ashley broke the silence. 'Kill it.'

'Don't, Ashley. Don't move!' I hissed.

The cockroach turned and bit Adam's face. In response, his body jerked so violently it seemed as if he were trying to stand. A loud thunder crack, the smell of ozone, and Adam's body exploded into a cloud of black dust that filled the room.

I held my breath. I'd had enough of Adam already; I didn't want to inhale him.

For a moment or two, the dust sat like a storm cloud, motionless and brooding, before abruptly contracting and spinning into a black whirlpool. It rotated slowly at first, its blackness displaying an infinite galaxy of sparkling and iridescent stars. It was beautiful.

The speed increased rapidly—the air moved, our hair flew across our faces and stainless-steel instruments hovered in the air before plummeting into the depths of the whirlpool.

'Move!' Jason said to Ashley. Ashley responded in an instant and hightailed it out of the room with me in his arms.

Looking through the window, we blocked our ears and watched a hurricane of loose morgue equipment disappear into the vortex. The black hole spun faster and faster, shrinking smaller and smaller, until it was the size of a pea, and then—pop—it was gone.

The room was stripped bare. Even the blood had been sucked off the walls. The cobwebs had gone from the ceiling, along with the paint flakes. Mike had vanished too.

Jason and Ashley stepped tentatively into the room.

'You can put me down now, Ashley,' I said.

He rubbed his head and scrutinised the room. 'Holy snapping aardvarks.'

'Blimey,' Jason said.

'That proves it,' I said.

'Proves what?' they asked.

'The Maestro was telling the truth.'

'Bloody hell.' Jason took a tissue from his pocket, spat on it, and started to wipe my neck.

I pulled away. 'Yuk! That's what mums do. Gross.'

'What's a bit of spit in the scheme of things? Hold still. I'm getting the rest of the blood off.'

My heart started to pound. 'There was another man in the hospital corridor! Where's he?'

'I took him out,' Jason replied.

'Crikey,' Ashley said.

'Oh, Jason …'

He kept dabbing at my neck. 'What *is* that?' he asked.

'What?'

'Is that a love bite on your neck?'

The blood drained from Ashley's face.

Jason tilted my head and stared at my neck. 'It is a love bite! What the hell?' Pushing me away, he looked me up and down, his laser beam eyes set to maximum. 'Your bra's up around your neck.'

Just as he said that, my jeans fell down around my ankles.

He stared at me a moment longer, then bent and hoisted them up.

He tried to zip them closed. 'Your jeans are ripped.' He earnestly searched my eyes. 'Oh, Maggie, did he ... are you?'

'No, nothing happened, other than nearly losing the top of my cranium.'

'And your *neck*? How do you explain the huge red mark?'

My mind was spinning. What to say?

'Ah, that was actually me, mate,' Ashley said. 'Accident. We were hiding in a locker.'

'In a locker? What locker?'

Ashley pointed at locker five.

Jason looked at me. 'Which one were you in, Maggie?'

I pointed vaguely at the locker bay. 'Um, that one.'

'Which?'

'Same one,' I said in a tiny little voice.

A look of fury flashed across Jason's face. He pushed Ashley roughly. 'You were supposed to look after her, you arsehole!'

'I did,' Ashley said quietly.

'Yeah, sure looks like it,' Jason said, looking at my state of disarray. My jeans had fallen down again.

I hauled them up and gripped tight. 'He did look after me! He saved me. Saved me from some other thug ... in the boiler room ... I'd be dead if not for Ashley. I'm so grateful to him.'

'So grateful you repaid him how?'

'Jason! How could you?' My eyes filled with tears.

He strode across the room and opened the locker. 'Tell me.

157

What sort of monkey business happened in here?'

I took a deep breath. 'Ashley pretended to be a vampire—because I actually thought he may be one—and he was testing out his new teeth on my neck. He was trying to distract me from my fear and claustrophobia is all.'

Jason narrowed his eyes. 'Yeah? And what else did he do to distract you?'

A tide of red rushed across my face.

Jason slammed the locker door shut. 'That says it all. The body doesn't lie.'

I needed a lawyer, as anything I was going to say would incriminate me. I think Ashley needed one too. Fast.

Jason knew Ashley was a scoundrel, but they were best friends. Ashley would never really do anything to hurt him, or me, but Jason knew we had history. This was going to end badly, and I didn't want to be here having this conversation. I marched over to that damn locker number five, pushed Jason out of the way, rolled out the trolley, lay on it and dragged myself in, slamming the door behind me. It seemed much nicer in the locker, than out there.

'Maggie, get out!' Jason said through the door.

'No.'

'Maggie.'

'I'm not getting out, until you come in here with me.'

Jason opened the door, pulled out the trolley and lay on top of me. Ashley pushed us in and closed the door.

Darkness.

'See Jason? See how it is?'

'Bloody hell, it's horrible.'

'And we had to be in here for ages.' I started to shiver.

'Come on, you've made your point, let's get out,' Jason said softly.

'No.'

We lay in silence.

Jason's breath was hot on my neck, which was enjoyable, as my teeth were chattering from the cold. Tears coursed over my cheeks.

'Please don't cry.' He held me and kissed away my tears. 'I believe you. I love you. Please, let me get you out of here.'

Knock, knock, knock.

'You guys all right in there?'

'Open the door,' Jason said.

Ashley rolled out the trolley, and Jason clambered off and helped me up.

'It's cool, mate,' Jason said. 'I'm sorry.'

'All good,' Ashley said as they slapped their arms around each other and hugged like two bears.

I had to ask the question. I had to know.

'Jason, when you said you 'took out' the other guy, the one in the hospital corridor, can you confirm you didn't merely take him out for a coffee and a chat or something, but you really… killed him. Is that what you did?'

'That's what I did.'

'Coffee?'

'No, killed him.'

'How?'

'With his own gun.'

Jason seemed reluctant to talk about it, but I persisted.

'How did it happen?'

He sighed.

'I was searching for you and I found the toilet bag and phone Ash had given you in the bathroom. The nurse at reception said she saw you at the lifts. I figured you'd probably still be in the hospital, so thought I'd start at the bottom level and work my way up.'

'Good plan,' Ashley said, nodding.

'Anyways, as I proceeded along the walkway I checked a couple of offices and noticed your boots. I'd heard some commotion as I exited the lifts, but it stopped when I started walking. I was checking out an office when someone snuck up and pistol-whipped me. Long story short, he didn't knock me out. I tackled him, we wrestled, and in the tussle for the gun, it fired and shot him in the guts.'

'Bloody hell,' I said.

'You're sure he's dead?' Ashley asked. 'It can take a while to die from a stomach shot.'

'Yup, he bled out everywhere.'

Ashley was puzzled. 'Who killed the guy that clobbered me in the morgue?'

I'd forgotten Ashley was unconsciousness for most of the time.

'I did,' Jason said.

'Crikey.' Ashley appeared impressed and worried all at the same time.

'Jason saved my life, and the top of my cranium too.'

'Oh, now I'm with it,' Ashley said, putting the pieces together.

'We haven't had time to debrief you properly,' I said.

'She loves to debrief,' Jason said.

'We're so behind with debriefing we can't catch up. It's crazy.'

Ashley turned to Jason. 'You've got a gun?'

'Yep.' Jason removed it from the back of his jeans. 'It's a Smith & Wesson .357 revolver. Wish I'd had the wherewithal to grab the morgue guy's gun.'

'His name was Adam,' I said.

'He told you his name?' Ashley said incredulously.

'Yes, he introduced himself.'

Jason raised an eyebrow. 'Now I've heard everything.'

'He was a nice guy.'

Jason and Ashley stared at each other, and then looked at me as though I'd gone mad.

'He was going to cut your skull open and scoop your brains out. How is that a nice guy?' Jason asked.

I explained what I'd perceived about Adam, and it seemed to allay their fears about my sanity.

'Talking about Adam's gun,' Ashley said, pulling a firearm from the back of his pants and waving it in the air, 'somebody did have the wherewithal.'

'Good work, man!' Jason said. 'Now we need a gun for Maggie.'

'Maybe this one will do,' a male voice behind us said.

---

18 *Maggie's Playlist: Too Much Monkey Business — Chuck Berry*

Chapter 19: Marlon

The man stood six feet tall in his socks (it seemed few people wore shoes on level B5). He had a broad square face, a trimmed mustache, Roman nose and thick eyebrows set low over dark brown eyes. Black wavy hair was swept back off his face, and his ears sat close to his head. He stood legs apart, pointing a gun directly at me.

He wore a double-breasted army style coat, high collared white shirt and black cravat. There was a small Catherine wheel tattoo under his left eye and his expression was brooding and serious—maybe because of the spreading bloodstain on the front of his shirt.

He turned his attention to Jason and said, 'We meet again.'

Jason's fists were clenched and his jaw tight. 'Is there an App I can download to make you go away?'

Ashley's mouth twitched with a smile.

I yelled at Jason in my mind. *Christ Jason, now's not the time for smart arse comeback lines. Leave that to me.*

'Has anyone ever told you, you look like a young Marlon Brando?' I said.

The man seemed surprised.

I could feel Jason and Ashley's eyes on me, and heard Jason

yelling in his head for me to '*Shut the hell up!*'

'Has anyone ever told you, you look like a young Maria Schneider?' the man said. 'Perhaps we can recreate *Last Tango in Paris.*'

His voice was deadly and he had no sense of humour. Not one I liked, anyway.

We had ourselves a classic Mexican standoff. Jason and Ashley had guns pointed at Marlon, and Marlon had his gun pointed at me. I could imagine to a 'T' where this was going. My money was on: 'Drop your guns or the girl gets it.'

'Drop your weapons, or I will shoot Maggie.'

Just as I thought. And how come everyone seemed to know my name? It was incredibly disconcerting.

I could sense everyone's minds racing, but mine was calm.

'Which scene from *Last Tango* would you like to recreate?' I asked.

Ashley did the inhaling thing with his nose, and I sensed Jason's horror. The man viewed me with amusement. I was getting to him, but was also highly aware I was playing a very dangerous game.

'Which one do you think, Maggie?'

'I'd have to say the one with the butter, of course.'

He stared at me intently. 'Right first time.'

I opened my hand, and right on cue, my jeans fell around my ankles. I made the right volume of horrified gasp, and said, 'Oh my God!' and bent down to pull them up, ensuring Marlon had a full view of my cleavage.

That moment of distraction—the one I'd carefully planned— was the moment the boys were supposed to take him out.

Nothing happened. I stood to find them all staring at me. What a bunch of numbskulls! Now things had got a zillion times worse for me, as Marlon appeared all the keener to butter me up.

All righty then. Plan B. I sure hoped some blood was left in the boy's brains to enable them to respond sometime this century.

I held out my hand and advanced towards the man. 'Okay Marlon, are you ready for me? There's a fridge in the tearoom over there,' I indicated towards it with a nod. 'Bound to have butter.'

He turned, oh so slightly, and I ducked. The boys shot him dead.

Second time lucky. Hallelujah.

My knees buckled from delayed shock, and I collapsed onto all fours watching Marlon disintegrate into a black whirlpool of dust. Leaning across, I snatched his revolver.

'Maggie's got her gun!' I said as Jason took my arm and dragged me from the room before the vacuum could get us.

* * * * *

The three of us bolted along the shiny corridors following the blue line to room number twenty-three, where we stopped to retrieve my boots. Ashley recovered his from behind a nearby vending machine. Pulling them on, he said, 'Give me the gun.'

Reluctantly, I handed it over. He engaged the safety and tucked it away in his pocket.

'I want it back.'

'I don't think so.'

'It's mine. I found it.'

'Trust me, you don't want it.'

'I do.'

'Have you ever fired a gun? Do you know how to use one?'

'I've seen enough movies, and I've seen you two.'

Jason rolled his eyes and gave me a look.

I made a face.

'You can have it back, but only after I teach you how to use it safely,' Ashley said. 'Deal?'

'Deal.'

164

As we waited at the lifts, the racket in Jason and Ashley's minds filled my head. Ticking things over, they weighed and sifted events, consequences, outcomes and what ifs. My brain added to the hullabaloo.

The roaches in Adam and Marlon—where did they go? Did they survive or die? If so, why would they commit suicide? Maybe there were so many of them they were expendable, like the humans they inhabited. I didn't like that notion at all. The roaches destroyed matter in a similar way to the Dark Force, but for me, I knew it wasn't the Dark Force. It was the roach from my vision.

Ashley's brain was spinning out of control—*What the fuck just happened? What the hell's going on? What's Maggie got herself into? Why the fuck do they want her, and what's with those roaches and the black hole vacuum thing? And what the hell happened in that damn friggin' locker? I mean, really? What the hell got into me? What have I done?*

I focused on my breathing and blocked him out. Poor Ashley, we had to bring him up to speed ASAP. He was more in the dark than us.

Jason's brain was whirling too—*What are we dealing with now? What's with the roaches? Is it Maggie's vision? What happened in that locker? Should I be worried about Maggie and Ashley? Does she still love me? Does she want Ashley back? I've killed two people; how can I live with that? What's going to happen to us now? How can I protect Maggie? How can I protect myself?*

I took a breath and hauled my senses back in. I could barely cope with my own thoughts. Poor Mike, the morgue technician. Here one minute, gone the next, and not an atom of evidence remained. Mike would be a missing person and his family and friends would remain in the dark forever. Just like me with Dad. A sob escaped my lips.

Ashley took my hand in his. 'You're thinking about Mike, aren't you?'

I brushed away my tears. 'Since when did you become a mind

reader?'

'I can read you like a book.'

Jason looked at Ashley in surprise. He went to say something then stopped.

'What?' I said.

Jason put a protective arm around my shoulder and Ashley released my hand. 'I was thinking the only redeeming feature about this entity is it cleans up after itself. There's no evidence.'

'My thoughts exactly,' Ashley said. 'There's no security cameras down here. The morgue's been cleaned out, and if it's sucked the blood off the walls, no one's going to know what the hell happened. Do you think there's anything forensics could find?'

I shook my head in the negative. 'Trust me, there's not a particle left. It's more than sterile. Exactly like our house was for a while.'

Ashley raised questioning eyebrows at me.

'We had an incident at our place—no roaches—but there was a Dark Force that dissolved matter. It attacked us. We'll fill you in later.'

Ashley took a deep breath and appeared pale under his tan. 'Crikey. I feel like I'm in *The Twilight Zone*. Life's never going to be the same.'

'You can say that again.'

He gave me a grim, thin lipped smile. 'Life's never going to be the same.'

We stood in silence staring at the illuminated numbers above the lift.

'Shit! Quick, get out of here!' I said, bolting around the corner to hide. The guys followed me, bewildered.

Ding. The lift doors opened. Silence. They closed.

'*What?*' the guys said.

'There's a camera in the lift.'

'Oh, shit yeah,' Jason said.

166

Ashley nodded. 'Ah, yup.'

'We're screwed,' I said. 'The camera would've caught us going to level B5, along with everyone else—the hoods, Mike, the other two employees.'

'Well, let's take the stairs out,' Jason suggested.

'It doesn't matter! Don't you get it? The cameras will catch us once we leave the stairwell. And it doesn't matter if we can make it out without being seen—they've got vision of us going in. The police are going to be all over us, especially after what happened at home.'

'Maybe the camera's not working,' Ashley said. 'Half the time they don't, you know.'

'So, what do we do?' Jason asked.

'Right,' I said, thinking out loud. 'They already know we're in the hospital, with you being admitted an' all. But even though the camera caught us going down in the lifts, they'll have no real evidence implicating us with Mike's disappearance. We returned, but the hoods and Mike didn't. They could've left through a back door. All we have to do is formulate a good reason as to why Ashley, then me, went to Level B5, and why you came after us.'

'Um, the locker?' Jason said. 'Would it be sterile on the inside?'

'Shit!' Ashley said. 'The body bag's in the locker and my writing's on the tag. Plus, there'll be blood in the office where Jason first shot Marlon.'

'I forgot about that,' I said. 'And, I don't think the locker would be sterile. Ashley, can you—' But he was already gone, racing along the corridor to deal with the remaining evidence.

'Let's sit in the stairwell while we wait,' Jason said.

Cupping my face in his hands, he fixed me with his laser beam gaze, dialed back to a soft level one. His thumbs brushed my lips, and he took my face to his, kissing me tenderly. Dialing up the passion, his kiss was deep, urgent and fraught.

He came up for air and whispered, 'I thought I'd lost you.'

He kissed me again, and felt all over my body, as though to make sure I was really there. He sat me on his lap facing him. I wrapped my arms and legs around his body, and I kissed him back, my heart on fire.

The stairwell was cold and dark, but we were hot and alight. Jason grabbed my jeans and underwear, pulled them down, and pushed himself hard into me. He yanked my top out of the way, and his mouth sought my breasts.

Oh, my God.

This business of narrow escapes, close shaves, and death evasion did wonders for a man's libido and a woman's love life. I surrendered to the pleasure exploding in my body. This was way better than make up sex, because we hadn't argued—just nearly lost our lives, was all.

'Whoa! *Hello!* I leave you kids alone for five minutes.'

I felt Jason waving Ashley away.

I whispered to Jason, 'Later, we've got to go.'

'I can't go anywhere yet.'

Ashley laughed. I extricated myself from Jason's grasp and stood, holding up my wayward jeans.

Jason mock glared at Ashley. 'Your timing's absolute shit, mate.'

I thought it was pretty darn spot on. Place and time, Jace, place and time.'

'You should talk, Ash. Pot kettle black, mate.'

Hot and flustered, I stood fanning myself with my free hand.

Ashley flashed me a grin. 'Want me to hold your pants so you can fan yourself with both hands?'

'Don't let him anywhere near your pants,' Jason said.

'Did you fix everything?' I asked Ashley.

'Yep. All good. Got the tag, bag, found some bleach, gave everything a wipe, and Bob's your uncle.'

'All quiet?'

'Like death. Now, you two have obviously formulated a plan

of action whilst I was away?'

'Umm …'

'Lazy bloody loafers. I actually put some thought into it, and here's how we play this. We take the bloody lift like nothing's happened. All casual like, we go and have something to eat at the café. Jason checks out of the hospital, and then we all go to a hotel for the night.'

'Terrific plan,' Jason said sarcastically. 'Mind snappingly brilliant. Must have been a real brain strain to come up with that one.'

Ashley looked hurt.

'Don't be mean,' I said. 'There's actually not much else we can do. Let's face it, we'll most likely have to deal with the cops, so let's look as innocent as we can. Ashley's right.'

Ashley nodded his head, looking vindicated. He didn't say anything, but his thoughts were in my mind: *See, Jason, huh, huh, see? Not so stupid after all.*

Ashley rubbed his chin with a weather-beaten hand. 'We do need an explanation as to why we were down here in the first place, but.'

Jason stared at Ashley, and then at me. 'I know. You're having an affair with my best friend.'

'*Jason!*' I said. He held up his hand to cut me off.

'Hear me out. I suspected something was wrong when Ashley, and then you, disappeared for a long time. I started searching and discovered both of you having it off in an office on Level B5. Ashley and I had a fight—explaining our state of dishevelment—and then we headed back up and checked out. We didn't hear or see anyone or anything else. That's it.'

Ashley nodded. 'Sounds good to me.'

To my ears, Jason's explanation sounded like an accusation, and it upset me.

Ashley seemed more than happy with the whole idea and said, 'To make it more convincing, Mags could go back with me and—' He stopped short when he saw the look on Jason's face.

'Yeah? What else would you like to do to make it more convincing, Ash?'

Ashley was upset. 'What are you saying, Jace? Do you actually think something's going on, because of the love bite? Then know it ain't so. Maggie's not my type. It's why I quit our relationship … um, sorry, no offence, Maggie.'

'None taken. I think.'

Jason looked sceptical.

'Come on, Jace, you know the type of sheila I like.'

'Tall, blonde, skinny, big boobs with legs up to here?' Jason suggested.

Ashley grinned. 'That's the one!'

My heart sank. 'The stereotypical Barbie doll.'

Ashley gave me the thumbs up.

Jason seemed satisfied and backed off. He stood and held my hand. 'Are we all good to go then?'

Ashley agreed, and so did I, though I didn't feel good. If I wasn't Ashley's type, what was it we'd had? Our feelings were deep, so I'd thought. How could I have been so wrong? Well … he had broken it off. I was a fool.

'Let's get out of here,' Jason said.

I was seriously going to die if I didn't have food in the next five seconds. 'Are we doing the café or not?'

'Yeah, stuff it,' Jason said. 'I'm famished, and at this point, even canteen food sounds appealing.'

'Should I come too?' Ashley asked.

Jason paused. 'Sure, why not. We can debrief and refine our story.' He winked at Ashley. 'Maybe we can change what happened here so we can still be friends.'

---

[19] *Maggie's Playlist: Last Tango — Jacki DePiro*

Chapter 20: Moral Dilemma

It was late in the day, and the only thing on the menu at the hospital café was toasted ham and cheese sandwiches and coffee. The coffee was delicious and the sandwiches tasted extraordinary.

Ashley munched away on his. 'How good are these? Food tastes way better when you're starving, and I could eat the arse out of a low flying duck.'

Jason winced. Ashley could be as rough as guts at times.

'Now, guys, you need to bring me up to speed with what the hell's going on,' Ashley said. 'What've you got yourselves into?'

I dug down deep and summoned the energy to talk. 'Yes, of course. I'll try, but we don't really know what's going on. And we haven't got ourselves into anything. Something's gotten into us ... or me anyway.'

'Tell me what you know.'

'It all started when I took Boo for a walk.'

Ashley nodded. 'To clear your mind?'

'Yeah, yeah, the usual, you know me. We stopped outside a house and I caught sight of a weird shadow in an upstairs window. There was a buzzing in my head, all the atoms in my body went haywire, and everything started to spin like I was on a merry-go-round. I must've blanked out for a second, but the next thing, Boo and I found ourselves a whole block away. I didn't know how we'd got there.

'My body was buzzing and my face burned like fire. Then, there was this tawny frog mouth always staring at us and ... and I ran home to Jason. Boo was freaked out the whole night with a massive hackle running along her back which wouldn't go away 'till morning—' I stopped to sip my coffee. My hands trembled so much I could barely hold the cup.

Ashley looked at me in concern. 'Crikey. Take a breather. Do you need to stop?'

'No, I'm fine.' I wanted to get it all out in one go so I could focus on eating. I so needed to eat. I took a breath, stared into my coffee cup, and went for it. 'Anyways, the next night we returned to the house to check things out. The front door of the house was open, and Boo yanked free, raced into the house and disappeared. Our mobile phones wouldn't work, and no one seemed to be home. Jason tried the neighbours with no luck, and I went into the house to find Boo.'

Ashley glared at Jason. 'You let her go in the house alone?'

Jason glared back. 'No, I was trying to find a neighbour. She entered of her own accord.'

Ashley rested his chin on his fist and gave me a look. I rolled my eyes at him.

'Inside the house, everything was out of whack. Things were distorted—sound, movement, time, space, dimensions—the laws of physics had left the building. Jason came in the house to find me. He saw it too ... it wasn't one of my ghosts or visions ... it was a shadow creature, a Dark Force, half man half demon, like a walking black hole. It came for us; we were trapped upstairs, and as it moved, things were being sucked into it, bugs and dust ... dust was the first thing to go.

'To escape, we ran and found ourselves in a weird expanding and contracting room. Boo was there with a night light, that wasn't a night light, but a floating crystal. The Dark Force creature came into the room, and we were going to be toast, but the crystal was blasting out light, fighting it off. We were trapped but Boo put her paw on the Crystal, and we disappeared from the room in a flash of light. We awoke back home, but couldn't remember anything until much later.

'In the meantime, we noticed the dust had disappeared from our house, and the shadows were inordinately black. We couldn't remember anything, so didn't twig about the danger. I tried to retrieve Boo's ball from under a cabinet, and the Dark Force was there waiting for me. It was hideous, Ashley; the pain was excruciating. My body started to disintegrate as it held me in its grip. It was eating me. I was nearly dead when Jason found me, and then it got him too. Boo saved us. She came in with the crystal. She must've found it in the back yard, maybe she hid it there. Maybe it was the one from the first house; I don't know. But the crystal saved us. It repelled the Dark Force, and healed our wounds, but I think it used all its energy in the process. It's lifeless … you saw it.'

Ashley sat there looking stunned. He turned to Jason for confirmation. He nodded.

'This is insane,' Ashley said.

I rested my head in my hands to try and cope with my pounding head. Talking about what happened had brought it all back. I had to get it out, and fast.

'It's all true, Ashley. I lost half my face, head, arm and leg. Jason lost his arm, and other bits, and then we blacked out for a few days, and awoke in our garden fully healed with all our missing limbs grown back, which was good, and then I tried to reach out to Dad with my mind to try and find him, and something horrible possessed me and made me go crazy, and I tried to kill Boo and Jason, and a bit of the thing is still inside me so I can't get angry, I mustn't get angry, if I get angry it triggers, and I become a demon, it takes me over.

'I'm a monster, a ticking fucking time bomb of a monster waiting to explode and take out anyone or anything in my way. That's when you came in. It's what happened and why Jason had to go to hospital, I tried to kill him.

'And then there was the weird woman who came to tell us about Dad ... how he accidently brought a cockroach back from CERN, and how the roach had been affected by experiments at the Hadron Collider, giving it the ability to make people crazy, how he was attacked multiple times by psycho people under the influence of the cockroach, and how it had the ability to destroy people by generating a black hole, turning them into dust, and sucking everything not tied down into it. You saw it. You saw it happen in the morgue. Our contact with the crystal has changed us. We can regenerate. Jason is stronger, my psychic abilities are better, and Boo ... it's done things to her. She seems to have the strongest connection with it.

'I think the cockroach and the Dark Force are separate entities—they feel different, but they're connected somehow, maybe working together. I don't know, but I do know they want the crystal, and the crystal is connected to me, us, Boo, so the entities are after us because we have the crystal, but now the crystal is dead, so I don't know why the hell they wouldn't sense that and leave us the hell alone, and I don't know how to get this dark matter atom out of me. I don't think I can, and I'll be forever contaminated unless I kill myself which may solve the problem. That'd do it, I reckon. I need to kill myself.' I looked up from my coffee into the stunned faces of Ashley and Jason.

No one spoke.

The whirr of a nearby vending machine filled the area. It was especially annoying. It seemed to be the only sound in the room.

Whirr. Whirr. Whirr. Buzz. Whirr. Whirr. Whirr. Buzz.

The heat rose from my gut into my face. I stood and kicked back my chair. *I was going to smash that machine to bits.*

Jason gripped my arm. 'Breathe. For fuck's sake, Maggie.

Breathe!'

Jason and Ashley took long, slow measured breaths and waved their hands in slow rhythmical movements, encouraging me to follow the pace of their breathing, like I was in labour or something. I was in labour; I was about to give birth to the monster.

Breathe.

In. Out. Slowly. In. Out. In. Out. Dolphins. Think dolphins. Calmness returned.

Ashley's eyes were wide with horror. 'Holy Hell!'

'You saw her face?' Jason asked.

Ashley was pale. 'Hell, yeah.'

I wiped the sweat from my brow with a serviette. 'All up to speed now, Ashley?'

He looked at Jason, then back at me. 'You're kidding, right? This is candid camera stuff, a set up?'

I shook my head in the negative.

'No joke. Not kidding,' Jason said. 'It's the truth, the whole truth and nothing but the whole friggin' mind blowing, horrific, unbelievable fucking truth.' He directed his laser beam gaze right into Ashley's brain.

Ashley snapped a plastic fork in half and jumped at the sound of it. 'I believe you. Fuck me.'

'Enough with the language,' I said, 'or there will be nothing to distinguish us from the bad guys.'

'Humph,' snorted Ashley. 'Everything under control now? You okay, Maggie?'

'As good as I can be for the moment, all things considered.'

Ashley had developed a permanent head shake. 'Bloody hell.'

Jason lowered his voice to a whisper and put his face into serious mode. 'Now, Ms. Maggie, what in God's name did you think you were doing with the whole Marlon Brando, femme fatale thing?'

Ashley wiped crumbs and butter off his mouth and wiggled

his eyebrows. 'Yeah! I was going to ask the same thing. You're dead set nuts, Maggie.'

'What did you think I was doing? Coming on to the guy? I was creating a well-crafted distraction. It was a Mexican standoff. Somebody had to do something. So, I did, and you guys just stood there staring, doing nothing. Fair dinkum unbelievable.'

'Fair go,' Ashley said. 'I was about to kick his legs out from under him when you dropped your strides.'

'I was going to kick the instrument trolley into him,' Jason said. 'He really did look like Marlon Brando, didn't he?'

'It was his weakness,' I said. 'He would've heard he resembled Brando over and over, and he felt like Brando. I knew it. I could perceive his fantasies, and mentioning the butter scene—his mind was captured. It totally distracted him from the job at hand. You saw his bloodied shirt. He was dying from the gunshot wound that happened in your tussle. He wanted to live out his fantasy before he died.'

'Jesus, you played a risky game,' Ashley said. 'It could easily have gone pear-shaped. He could've taken us out, dragged you to the tearoom, buttered you up, and had you squealing like a pig.'

'*Ashley!*' Jason and I said simultaneously.

'There was no tearoom, no fridge, no butter. I made it up,' I said.

'Still. No matter. Very dangerous.'

'I'm glad you guys finally came to your senses and cottoned on. I thought you were both going to stand there and watch him take me out to the imaginary tearoom.'

Ashley grinned. 'To be honest it was the long, slow bend forward that got me.'

Jason rolled his eyes at Ashley. 'You're a degenerate.'

'I'm only human.'

'I learned the move from the Maestro,' I said.

'Really? The Maestro?' Ashley said. 'That sounds about right.'

'You know her?' Jason and I said simultaneously.

176

'Yeah, why? Shouldn't I?'

'How do you know her?' I asked.

'Your dad introduced me.'

'When?'

'Probably a few months before he disappeared. The Prof and I were going prospecting together, and she was at his place.'

'Oh,' I said, not sure how I felt about that.

Ashley seemed puzzled. 'Why, what's happened?'

'We've only just met her, is all. She was the weird woman I mentioned to you before.'

'Oh really? Well, let me tell you, she and your dad were pretty darn cosy.'

Jason gave Ashley a *'you need to shut up now'* look.

'Your dad hadn't known her for long though,' he said, noting Jason's expression. 'I reckon it was the first relationship he'd had since your mum died, all those years ago.'

'It's okay, you two,' I said. 'Dad's entitled to go out with whoever he likes. I wonder why he never mentioned her, especially—'

Jason sat up straight and interrupted. 'Now, talking about the Maestro, we need, I need, to get something cleared up. Something we haven't had the opportunity to talk about.'

'What?'

'The thing that set you off, when you tried to—'

'Yes, go on.'

'When you saw me hiding, staring at the Maestro … I'd been doing it for a while.'

'And that's supposed to make me feel better, how?'

'While you were in the kitchen, she was fixing her hair, looking in the mirror. She behaved in an extremely odd way, making hand signals at the mirror, mouthing words and tracing her finger over the glass as if writing. She even kissed herself, kissed the mirror. It was too weird. I wasn't lusting after her, Maggie, I was trying to glean what the hell she was doing.'

'What were the hand signals?' Ashley asked.

'They were like army hand signals—pointing to herself, hand over her eyes, I can't remember now, a bit has happened since then. It was strange. Almost as if she was trying to communicate with someone. Anyway, that's what I was transfixed over. Not her.'

I felt terrible. There was absolutely no justification for what I did. A misunderstanding triggered a strong emotion, which opened the door to absolute chaos—to the Dark Force. It could happen again, at any time, and next time the outcome could be far worse.

My neck felt bare, and I realised I wasn't wearing my Moldavite necklace. I'd promised myself I'd never be without it again. Even so, if push came to shove, I couldn't be one hundred percent sure it would be effective. I could still end up killing everyone I loved. I couldn't put Jason through it. He shouldn't have to live with such a threat, and I couldn't live with the thought of hurting him again.

The crushing truth hit me. I had no other option. I had to leave.

Jason touched my hand. 'Maggie? What's going on in there?'

'I can't do this anymore. I can't.'

'Can't do what?'

'Can't be with you.'

Ashley sat up straight in his chair, his sandwich paused midair.

'What the hell do you mean? Was it something I said?'

'I have to leave; I can't be with you anymore.'

Jason leaned his elbows on the table and covered his face.

Ashley stared at me, mouthing, 'What the?'

I stood and headed for the door. I walked in a haze of sadness along the corridor, having no idea as to where I was going. Fresh air. I needed to go outside. Run.

As I headed towards the lifts, there was the unmistakable

sound of Ashley's biker boots clinking behind me. His hand gripped my shoulder. 'Wait,' he said, steering me into a small lounge area.

'Sit, luv, we need to talk.' He gently pushed me into a seated position on a nearby plastic couch. 'What's gotten into you? What's wrong?' His eyes searched mine for answers. 'Why are you doing this? You love Jason, don't you?'

Tears streamed down my face. He fumbled around in his jacket pockets and finally pulled out a crumpled, crusty, yellowing piece of material. He proffered it to me to wipe my nose, and I laughed in spite of myself.

Ashley scrutinised it for a second and said, 'Hmm, maybe not. Wait here, I'll be back.' He returned ten seconds later with a box of tissues. I gratefully took a handful.

My emotions overwhelmed me, and I couldn't stop sobbing. It'd been a hell of a day. Along with my emotions I was also trying to deal with a psychic avalanche of visions and perceptions, all hammering at my mind for recognition. It was as if someone had cranked up the dial on my psychic radar to the max, and I wasn't sure how long I could maintain my grip on reality.

Ashley put an arm around my shoulder and held me until the warmth and comfort stemmed the tide of my emotions. He handed me another bunch of tissues. 'Here, luv, give your nose a good blow, and I'll block my ears.' I dutifully blew, making my signature trumpet noise.

He wiped something off my nose with his thumb. 'Now, tell me, what's going on. Please?'

'It's all my fault.' Emotion rose again. I took a deep breath, pinched my legs hard, and continued. 'All this bloodshed, death and destruction is because of me, and I can't do it anymore. I can't put Jason in constant danger, or Boo, or you, or anyone else I love. It follows me for some reason, and I won't, I can't bear to hurt him again. I nearly killed him. I wanted to kill Boo as well. I let it into my mind, and part of it lives in me now. It uses my anger. I have to be so careful.'

'You can't do this alone. You need us, and we need you.'

'No, I won't allow myself to hurt Jason again. I love him too much. I've made up my mind. I can look after myself. It's better I go, and go fast, before anything else happens.'

Ashley took off his leather jacket and threw it on a chair. His white T-shirt appeared worse for wear—stained with blood, streaked with dirt, and the stitching around the armbands frayed from the pressure of his biceps. He knelt in front of me and gripped my upper arms. Veins tracked across the top of his strong, tanned hands; they could've wrapped around my arms twice.

'Listen!' he said, squeezing my arms and giving me a shake. His voice was low and hoarse. 'If you walk out on him now, you will kill him. You might as well go rip his heart out of his chest. For Christ's sake, he loves you, and after everything that's happened, he needs you. More than ever. We're a team. We can beat this together, not alone. Hell, I need you.'

'Even though I'd be the last type of girl you'd go for?'

'Sorry. I knew you'd be upset. It was for Jason's benefit.'

'It's okay, I know you love your blonde, skinny Barbies.'

'To tell you the truth, I prefer a woman who's soft, warm and gorgeous to touch—a woman like you.'

My face flushed and I looked away. He gently pushed my chin up to meet his gaze. 'To be honest, something happened to me in the locker. Now I can't get you out of my head. I know it's too late for us now, but I wish I'd never let you go. I re-bonded with you in there, through our closeness, the danger. You're like a war buddy. Truthfully, if you left, you'd rip out my heart too.'

'Oh, Ashley. I feel the same; I thought it was only me. We have bonded, haven't we? We are war buddies.'

'We are comrades in arms, and we'll beat this thing together, or die trying. If we die, we die together.'

'Like the three musketeers?'

'Like the three musketeers.'

He held his hand for a high five. 'Together?'

'Together!' I attempted to return the high five and botched the timing. I was never any good at high fives.

'Up you come.' Ashley took me in his arms for one of his bear hugs. Resting my head on his chest, I hoped I wouldn't regret my change of mind.

Ashley stroked my hair. 'I'd like to stay here and hold you, but we need to put Jason out of his misery. He's gutted, poor bloke.' His eyes met mine. His hair was parted off centre, and a lock of it fell across his forehead as he looked down at me.

'Your hair's getting long. You look like a pirate.'

He laughed. 'Arrgh!'

I rubbed my neck. 'I'm getting a stiff neck from looking up at you.'

'I can fix that.' He lifted me and stood me on a kid's chair. 'There you go, eye to eye.'

'Much better. Now I know how Boo feels when she's on the deck at home, and I'm on the path below. I go to the edge of the deck and let her look me straight in the eyes. She loves it.'

'I love it too.' He held me close and kissed me.

There went the knees. Ashley felt them buckle, and he held me tight, his hands under my arms, thumbs touching my breasts.

He groaned and pulled away. 'I've got to stop this.'

'Don't let me go,' I whispered, as I wobbled on the kiddie's chair, head back, eyes closed, lost in the moment. My brain was finally quiet. Not a thought. Bliss.

'What's going on?'

It was Jason behind us.

Ashley started and let me go as he turned towards Jason. I'd developed the death wobbles on the kiddie's chair. My outstretched arms whirled like windmills as I desperately tried to regain my balance. The chair flicked out from under me, and I went flying—destination, glass coffee table. Jason launched himself forward, trying to break my fall, and landed on top of the table.

His plan worked. I landed on top of him. There was a loud crack, and the glass table gave way beneath us. Ashley moved in like lightening. He grabbed us both, hauling us off the table just as it exploded into a myriad of deadly glass shards. Losing his balance, he staggered backwards, and we fell in a heap on the floor on top of him.

'*Oomph!*' The air left Ashley's lungs. 'Stacks on the mill!' he gasped, making strange noises as he tried to breath.

'Crouch over,' I said. 'Relaxes the diaphragm. It'll help you breathe.'

Ashley staggered to his feet and assisted me off the floor. He extended his hand to Jason, they locked arms, and he hoisted him to a standing position. Jason immediately slammed Ashley into the wall. He pushed him again, his hands thumping into Ashley's chest. There was a loud crack as the plaster gave way.

Ashley held up his hands in surrender. 'Easy, Jace.'

Jason pushed him again. 'Don't you bloody easy Jace me, mate.'

'Please stop it!' I said. He ignored me.

'You!' he said, grabbing Ashley's T-shirt at the neck and twisting it tight. 'I can't trust you with anything. Look at all the glass! She could've been killed, you idiot.' He slammed Ashley into the wall again.

'I'm sorry mate, it was an accident. Calm yourself. All's well that ends well. And, um … didn't I actually just save *both* of you from being impaled by glass and bleeding out all over the floor.'

'You are an idiot.' Jason pushed him into the wall once more before letting him go.

Turning to me, Jason appeared distressed. He examined my arms, checking for damage. 'Are you hurt?'

'I'm fine.'

Jason gave Ashley a death stare. 'Every time I leave you in his care, he cocks up.'

Ashley's mouth twitched with a smile.

'Be fair, Jason. I'd be dead if it wasn't for him.'

'Maggie, don't leave. Tell me what's wrong, that I can fix things.'

'Didn't you hear what she said?' Ashley asked.

'When?'

'In this room, before.'

No, I wasn't eavesdropping. I saw you balancing her on a chair. Like an idiot.'

'We were about to come and tell you,' Ashley said.

Jason's face turned pale. 'Tell me what?'

'Go on, Maggie, tell him.'

I must've looked perplexed, as I wasn't exactly sure of what it was Ashley wanted me to tell Jason. The 'kissing bit', the 'I can't get you out of my head bit', the 'war buddy bit' or the 'something happened in the locker' bit.

'Tell him what?' I asked.

Ashley gave me a look indicating he thought I was mentally challenged.

'What you told me about why you wanted to leave. All of it. Tell Jason,' he said, staring me down.

Jason was distraught. 'What? Maggie, for Christ's sake, put me out of my misery.'

'Alrighty, here it is as best as I can remember.' I took a breath. 'I felt I couldn't stay with you for one moment longer because at every moment, I was putting your life in danger. At every moment, I was putting Ashley in danger, Boo in danger, and everyone I loved and cared about. But especially you. I love you. You're my life. I couldn't, and still can't, bear the thought of losing you, of hurting you, of killing you with my own hands. Seeing you die or suffer. The injuries and pain I've already caused you. I couldn't do it anymore. To be honest, I still don't think I can.'

Ashley nodded for me to continue. 'And tell him what I said.'

I figured I was on the right track of what Ashley wanted me to say, so taking another breath, I tried to remember. 'Ashley said, if I walk out on you now, it would be as bad as killing you.' I paused.

Ashley motioned with his hands. 'Keep going.'

'Ashley said I might as well go rip your heart out of your chest right now, and get it over with. He said you need me even more right now, after everything that's happened, and we can only beat this thing if we stick together. We can't do it alone. We are war buddies, comrades at arms, and you don't let your mates down. We're a team and we need each other, love each other. We have to stick together. If we die, we die together. Like the three musketeers.'

I looked to Ashley for confirmation; he smiled and gave me the thumbs up. Jason shook his head in surprise and stared at Ashley. Turning back to me he asked, 'So what have you decided?'

My bottom lip began to quiver as I teared up. 'To stay. I want to stay. If you still want me.'

Jason pulled me into his arms. 'Please, don't ever put me through that again. Of course I want you. I couldn't make it without you. I love you. Promise me you won't leave.'

'Are you sure? After everything?'

'Maggie, yes! Promise. Me.'

'I promise.'

Jason breathed a sigh of relief and kissed me like a long-lost lover. I opened my eyes for a second to see Ashley grinning and giving me the okay sign.

Closing my eyes, I surrendered to the kiss. My knees went weak. Those damn knees. I'd seriously have to get them checked.

A pair of strong hands gripped my waist from behind.

It was Ashley, laughing, and holding me up.

Chapter 21: The Hotel – You Can't Measure Love

'Everything that is hidden will be made clear. Every secret thing will be made known.' — Mark 4:22

It was late by the time we left the hospital. Ashley's ute had accumulated two parking tickets. We climbed in and sat there.

'We've got nowhere to go,' I said. 'We can't go home. I can't face all the mess. I can't.'

'You've forgotten the plan,' Ashley said.

'What plan?'

'The plan I formulated before. I anticipated this and suggested we'd spend the night in a hotel. On me, by the way.'

'Really?'

'Yep, I sold a couple of decent sized nuggets and I'm all cashed up. I remember you saying how much you liked the Hyatt, so while Jason was checking out, I booked us a room. Sound good?'

'Sounds fantastic!'

'A room?' Jason asked.

'Everything was booked because of an event in town. They only had one room left—the Diplomatic Suite. Luxury, but only one bedroom and bathroom. I checked, and we can get a rollaway bed for me.'

'Giddy up!' Jason said.

'Now, kiddos, I want you to know we're going to let loose.

No expense spared. I'm talking spa, massage, dinner, drinks, you want it, you got it. Hell, Jace, if you want a hooker—'

'Ashley!' I said.

'Just kidding. About the hooker, anyway.'

Closing my eyes, I imagined the simple bliss of a hot shower. One where no tattooed psychos got in my way.

'Oh, thinking of tattoos …' I said.

'We were?' Jason asked.

'I was. Do you recall the tattoos on those two hoods? Aside from all the hideous monsters, they both had spider-like Catherine wheels.'

'Yep, I remember,' Ashley said. 'They were three overlapping 9s with arrows at the end, like little dragon's tails.'

'You're good,' I said.

'I know.'

'What's the significance of three overlapping nines?'

'Could be three overlapping sixes,' Jason said.

'Ah, the devil! Six, six, six. That sounds more like it,' Ashley said.

'I've seen a design like it before,' I said. 'For some reason, it seems familiar to me.'

'Well, you're the psychic, come on,' Jason said.

Ashley started his ute and we headed off. 'Talking about your psychic powers—you said you could read the Marlon Brando dude's fantasy. Was it deduction on your part, or could you actually see his fantasy?'

'I could see his fantasy. In fact, I'm starting to get images from nearly everyone I see. It's doing my head in. I'm working on how to turn all this junk off.' *The only time my head was quiet recently was when you kissed me.*

Ashley looked concerned. 'Um, so can you see my fantasies?'

'Don't go there, Maggie,' Jason said, tapping Ashley's head. 'It would be wall-to-wall Barbies, and God knows what else. You'd never recover.'

'You may be surprised,' Ashley said.

'I haven't gone there, and I won't go there.'

'What about me?' Jason said.

'Oh, for God's sake, you guys!'

'What about you, Mags?' Jason said, tickling me.

We laughed, and I was so grateful to Ashley. It was the nicest feeling, anticipating something lovely, something luxurious after the hell we'd been through. I must've been smiling because Jason said, 'It's wonderful to see you happy again.'

Ashley winked at me. 'Sure is.'

This was a moment with no death or destruction. This was a moment of joy, and I gave myself to it fully.

* * * * *

We must've resembled a motley crew walking into the luxurious surrounds of the Hyatt hotel. A tall, gorgeous blonde manned the check-in desk, and, as we approached, Ashley brushed back his hair and adjusted his jacket.

'Hi, Melanie,' he said, reading her name badge.

Well, I suppose he read her badge, but I wouldn't have been at all surprised if he was already acquainted, with her being tall and blonde an' all. He seemed to know someone wherever he went. I remember asking him about it once and he said it was because he 'gets around a bit.'

'We have a booking under Ashley Beringer, the Diplomatic Suite.'

Melanie tapped away on her keyboard. 'Yes, Mister Beringer. Welcome to the Hyatt. You've chosen a beautiful room. Special occasion?'

He flashed his new choppers. 'Sure is, sweetheart.'

'Would you like your luggage taken to your room, sir?'

'No thanks. I can take care of it.'

Yeah, too easy, given we didn't have any.

'By the way, would you happen to have a tape measure I could borrow?' he asked.

Jason and I exchanged glances. What the hell did he want a tape measure for?

'I can arrange for one to be sent to your room right away, sir.'

'Thanks, Melanie. You know,' he said, leaning forward and sliding his phone across the counter, 'I'm incredibly rich. Here's a new iPhone with my number in it. Call me some time.'

Melanie's jaw dropped, and Ashley chuckled. 'Just fooling with you, darling. But you do have my number, if you're so inclined.' He flashed another smile. Boy, he sure was making the most of his new dental work.

Melanie handed him his phone and the entry card to our room. 'Thank you, Mr. Beringer,' she said, laughing. 'Is there anything else I can do for you?'

'Now that you—'

'*Ashley!*' Jason said, cutting him off. 'Thank you, Melanie, we'll be heading off to our room now.' He steered Ashley away from the desk. When we were out of earshot he said, 'You are fair dinkum unbelievable!'

'Sure are giving those new choppers a work out,' I said.

'Just having a bit of fun. I've been wanting to try that line for ages.'

'Don't forget the tape measure,' he called back to Melanie.

She nodded.

'What's with the tape measure?' Jason asked.

'Can't say. Come on, kids, let's get to our room, and get settled.'

The Diplomatic Suite was on the thirty-first floor, and according to the brochure at reception, it was 141 square meters of "unparalleled luxury". Ashley swiped the card and opened the door. Yep, it was huge and luxurious all right, with beautiful views across the city.

Locating the master bedroom, I stood in awe at the size of the bed.

'Hey, Jason, check this out. It's bigger than our bed at home!'

'Bloody hell, it's massive!' He threw himself on it and dragged me with him.

There was a knock at the suite door.

'I'll get it,' Ashley called from the other room.

Fear flooded my body. 'Wait!' I yelled. 'Don't!'

Ashley stuck his head in the room. 'What's up?'

'Is there a peephole? You need to be careful.'

'Don't worry, I'll be careful. I'm an army guy, remember?'

The door opened and closed with a clunk.

'Come out here, guys,' he said a moment later.

We slid off the bed and joined him in the lounge. He was standing next to a trolley on which sat an ice bucket, champagne, crystal glasses, a large platter of assorted canapés and a tape measure.

'First things first. Champagne for the lady?'

'You bet.' I did a spontaneous happy dance. Ashley noticed and laughed as he poured me a glass.

'You sure do love your bubbles, don't you?'

'Mmm! Delicious!' I said, as the effervescence tickled my nose, bringing scents of honey, spice and citrus. The taste in my mouth was fresh and delicate. 'This champagne is nectar of the gods. I'm in heaven.'

'Glad you like it.'

The smile couldn't be wiped from my face.

Jason read the champagne label. 'Taittinger Brut Reserve.'

I nearly dropped the glass. 'Taittinger! Ashley, *really*?'

'Nothing but the best for you, my dear,' Ashley said, putting on his James Bond voice.

Jason looked up from the bottle. 'Is it expensive?'

'Only about $500 a bottle,' I said.

'What!' Jason said. 'You're nuts. You can't afford this with the room an' all.'

'Yes, I can. I told you, I'm cashed up; I've got a small fortune in gold nuggets, mate.'

'But you need to save your money for a rainy day,' Jason said.

Jason was frugal by nature. He worked tirelessly in his business and he saved hard. This extravagance would mess with his head.

Ashley slapped him on the back. 'You know that's not how I operate and I always get by. We need to snap the top off a cold one.' He opened the fridge and examined its contents. 'Crownie or VB?'

'VB please.'

Ashley handed one to Jason. 'Here you go.'

They sculled their first beer in about ten seconds flat and slammed the empties on the trolley. Ashley wiped his mouth on his sleeve. 'That went down like the first cold tinnie at a butcher's picnic. Another?'

Jason nodded.

I picked up the tape measure. 'What's this for?'

'Ah, nearly forgot!' Ashley took it from me. 'Come here, Jason. I need to measure you up.'

Jason took a step back. 'What the hell for?'

'Just come here.'

Ashley lifted the tape measure over Jason's head and brought it around to measure his waist.

'We need to get us some new clobber. We can't go out on the town looking like scumbags.'

'We're going out? I'm too tired,' Jason said. He hated going "out on the town" at the best of times.

'Relax, we're having dinner at the hotel, but we can't go in what we're wearing, they wouldn't let us in.'

I grinned. 'Want me to measure his inside leg?'

Ashley scribbled the measurements on a piece of paper. 'All done.'

'I'm going to check out the bathroom,' Jason said, disappearing into the master suite.

Ashley handed me the pen and paper. 'Can you write your measurements?'

'I wouldn't have a clue what they are, other than I'm an Australian size twelve. How are you going to get us clothes?'

'I have a clothes dude.'

'That'd be right.'

'We should get your size right. Want me to measure you?'

'No, I'll do it.'

'It's too hard to get an accurate measurement. I'll do it for you.'

Ashley put the tape measure over my head and drew it in tight around my waist, bending to see the numbers.

'Twenty-nine,' he said jotting it on a note pad.

Moving the tape to my hips, he pulled it tight, but it slipped over my bum.

'It's crooked,' I said.

He put both hands at the back of my buttocks, took the tape, straightened it and moved his hands back around to my front.

'Thirty-nine.' He grinned. 'And now for my favourite part. Hold your arms out to the side'. He slid the tape along my back and moved it back and forth to align with my bust. 'Arms down.'

I dutifully obeyed.

I shouldn't have been letting him do it. I needed to keep my distance. But the energy from him … it was more intoxicating than the champagne.

'It's a bit tricky,' he said.

'Yeah, funny how the tape keeps slipping. You seem to be having a lot of trouble.'

'The clothes dude told me how to take measurements. He said it's important to get the tape aligned with the nipples.'

'I'll bet he did.'

Stop now, Maggie. Don't let him do it.

192

Ashley fumbled around with the tape, brushing my breasts.

'That's done the trick,' he said. 'Now I can see where the tape should go.'

My face felt red hot. 'You're shameless.'

'Thirty-nine,' he said. 'You've got the perfect hourglass figure, but I didn't need a tape measure to work that out. I can measure to a millimetre by eye.'

'You can take the tape measure off now.'

'Perhaps I should double check.' He drew me in close with the tape measure and pulled it back and forth across my body. 'Jeez, I nearly forgot. I should measure the upper leg.'

'You don't need the—'

He knelt and threaded the tape measure around the top of my inner thigh. His face was against my stomach as he straightened out the tape measure and moved it slowly backwards and forwards between my legs.

'It needs to go a bit higher. It's important to get the right alignment here,' he said, hoarsely. Ashley continued to have trouble with "the alignment".

Oh my God, this was so sensual.

'Ashley,' I whispered, 'stop it; you're killing me.'

'Not more than it's killing me,' he groaned. 'You love it. I can tell. I'm seriously gonna take up dressmaking as a hobby.'

My heart was pounding and I felt even hotter.

'My knees. Stop it.'

He clutched my bum and pulled me forward. 'Christ, you turn me on.'

My whole body quivered involuntarily.

'Maggie!' Jason said.

I jumped. Ashley moved back.

'You're not letting him take your measurements, are you?' Jason pushed Ashley with his foot, and Ashley toppled over. Jason read the scribbled measurements. 'Too late, I see. Gee, your writing's a bit shaky, mate.'

Ashley jumped up and quickly moved to stand behind the drinks trolley. 'Bring me your glass, Maggie. I'll give you a refill.'

When he took my glass, he took my hand along with it, and his fingers caressed mine as he poured the champagne.

'There's a lot of effervescence,' I said.

'Way, way too much.' He met my eyes and his gaze was fervent. I couldn't look away. The champagne overflowed.

'Careful,' I said, licking my fingers. 'What a waste. At $800 a bottle you can't lose a drop!'

'Here.' Jason took my hand and put my fingers into his mouth one at a time. 'Mmmm, sure is good champagne.'

'When did you have time to organise all this, Ashley?' I asked, as Jason continued to lick my fingers. The corner of Ashley's mouth twitched as he watched Jason.

'I made a few calls when you were checking out of the hospital.'

Jason dragged me by the hand towards the master suite. 'Let's have a shower together. They've got one in there as big as a ballroom.'

Glancing back at Ashley, he had one hand over his heart, and raised the other to his temple, mimicking a gun. '*Phhht!*' he said, simulating the recoil, and shooting himself in the head. Ashley's face was solemn as he blew me a kiss, and Jason closed the bedroom door between us. Behind the door, a glass smashed on the marble floor.

'I've been dying to get you alone,' Jason said, 'I keep thinking of us in the hospital stairwell. It was so hot. I can't tell you how much I want you.'

He sat me on the edge of the bed and took off my top. Kneeling between my legs he reached around and unhooked my bra. He cupped my breasts and kissed them.

'You feel so soft,' he whispered. He pulled off my jeans and then virtually ripped off my panties.

'Shouldn't we shower first?'

'No way! I want you right here, right now, right the way you are.'

He pushed my knees apart and kissed me between my legs. I felt his whole body shiver and I held his head. We groaned simultaneously.

His voice caught. 'Jesus, you're wet already.' His hand moved between my legs. I let out a loud moan and gasped, ready to faint with pleasure. There was a sound of more breaking glass from the next room.

Jason pulled me onto the bed. 'Whatever the hell's going on in the other room, I don't care.' He straddled me and caressed my face, lips and breasts. He sucked my nipples hard while one hand made its way back between my legs.

'I love you,' he whispered. 'Remember that. No matter what happens, we stay together. No matter what.'

'No matter what,' I whispered back.

He pressed on my shoulders as he entered me and our bodies merged and dissolved into depths of sheer bliss.

'I love you, Jason,' I said, to the sound of more breaking glass.

---

[21] *Maggie's Playlist: Who's Cheatin' Who — Alan Jackson*

Chapter 22:
Hey, You! You're Looking Hot Tonight.

'Beware of the false prophets, who come to you in sheep's clothing, but inwardly are ravenous wolves.' — *Matthew 7:15*

Wrapped in a fluffy white bathrobe, I entered the lounge, wanting to know when the clothes dude was going to deliver our outfits.

The room was perfect, no broken glass anywhere. Brand new crystal glasses were on the drinks trolley, and another bottle of Taittinger sat ready and waiting. The lights were low, scented vanilla candles flickered on the coffee table, and soft sounds of chill-out jazz filled the room.

Ashley was leaning against the window frame looking out at the view, with a can of beer in his hand.

Approaching him, I stumbled on the rug, caught my robe on the edge of the coffee table, and felt my face blush. 'Um, ah … hello. When will our clothes arrive?'

'Any minute now, luv.' He pointed to the laundry bag. 'You can put your old clothes in there and they'll launder them, ready for you tomorrow. Everything okay? You seem nervous.'

'Nuh, no. I'm fine.' Pouring myself a glass of champagne, I took a breath and surveyed the room. 'All this. Thank you, Ashley. You're very generous.'

'No worries, it's my pleasure. Where's Jason?'

'Having a shower.'

Ashley put his beer on the ledge. 'You two have really quick showers.'

'Not that quick.'

'Way too quick, I reckon.' He pulled me into his arms. 'I like to take time with my showers—long, hot and slow.'

Trying to disentangle myself from his arms, I said, 'Wastes too much water. We have restrictions, you know.'

He slid his hand into my robe. 'There's no restrictions with me.'

Feeling hot and weak, I held his arm to steady myself.

What had got into him? This was so wrong. But it felt so right. He was irresistible.

His mouth found mine and we kissed. His hands were urgent and insistent as they explored my body.

'You feel so good,' he groaned. 'I—'

I pushed him away. 'Jesus, Ashley, we have to stop. I feel like I'm going to explode. We can't keep doing this; it's killing me, seriously. What are you thinking? What's got into you? More to the point, what the hell's got into me? I can't believe I kissed you. This is insane. Remember Jason?'

'I know, I know, how can I forget? I love you both. Having you close has reignited my feelings. I know you're his girl, and he loves you, and you love him, but—'

'How would Jason feel if he knew what you just did?'

'Not happy, I guess.'

'You guess? He'd be devastated.'

'Why the fuck does everyone get so hung up on monogamy? If you're up for it, he might want to share. You never know. He is a sharing, caring kinda guy, after all.'

'You are seriously insane.'

'No, just different. Tell me you don't want me. Tell me the truth.'

This trajectory was going to end in tears. 'What do *you* think?'

'I think if Jason wasn't here you'd be in the bedroom with

me, having a very long, very hot shower. Probably the *best* shower you ever had.' He gripped me around the waist. 'Wouldn't you?'

I nodded mutely.

'It's so hard to resist when you come onto me like you do,' I said. 'It sets me on fire, but I feel bad. It's wrong. I'm betraying Jason. *We're* betraying Jason. I love him with all my heart. But you make me want you. It's so confusing.'

Ashley tipped his head back and sighed. 'I knew it. How could you resist me?' He laughed and mussed up my hair. 'Your body wants me, there's no doubt about it.' He slid his hand back inside my robe. His breath caught in his throat and he swayed. I reckoned his knees just went weak too.

He yanked open my robe and pushed me against the window. 'You want me. I want you. Simple. Jason's still in the shower; I can hear it running.'

'No. Stop it!' I wrapped my robe back around me and pushed him away. 'This can't be. It has to stop. Right here, right now. It won't work. How can I love two men? It would be crazy. I'd get too tired. I'd have no time to read. I wouldn't get a decent night's sleep. I'd have to devise schedules, timetables; I'd have to look my best all the time, and anyway, who does what, with who and how and when?'

'*Whoa!* Steady on, girl, you think way too much. And you would get a good night's sleep because I need to sleep alone.'

'Really? How come?'

'It's simply the way it is now. I need to sleep on my own.'

Huh. Very odd. He didn't sleep alone when we were together.

'I can't believe I'm even having this discussion. And aside from all that, what about jealousy—all the emotional complications?'

'I'm not jealous in the least,' he said.

'Oh, so what was with all the glass smashing I could hear

before?'

Ashley looked sheepish. 'I was a bit clumsy, is all. Don't worry, it's easy. I'll be your love coach, and I won't impinge on your reading time.'

'You are mad!' I punched him hard in the arm. 'Ow!' I rubbed my hand.

He flexed his bicep. 'Guns of steel.'

I pretended to look unimpressed.

'We're going to have to toughen you up and get you fit. Teach you how to punch and shoot, give you some self-defense tactics.'

'Yes, and then I can use them to defend myself against you.'

'You're right. I'll back off. I'm sorry. I'm an idiot. I shouldn't have started this; it's my fault. We're on a highway to hell—our sexual tension is off the Richter scale, right? It's like a drug. You're like a drug. I can't help myself.'

He made a good analogy. It did feel like a drug, and like a drug, it was exhilarating and intoxicating, but ultimately, exhausting and deadly.

'Like heroin?'

'Yes,' Ashley said. 'Speaking from experience, just like heroin.'

'And you know what that does to people in the end.'

There was a loud knocking at the door. Ashley responded like lightning. He retrieved a gun from under a cushion on the couch, released the safety and wedged the gun in the back of his pants. At least he didn't stick it down the front. I always thought that was a dangerous place to put a loaded gun.

He checked the peephole and gave me the thumbs up.

'It's Jon, the clothes dude!'

He opened the door and Jon entered, beaming, pulling a wheeled clothes rack behind him. A number of suit bags hung on it, and shoe boxes were stacked neatly on the rack below, along with a couple of other smaller shopping bags.

'Don't I always deliver!' Jon said. He shook Ashley's hand. 'Even in spite of your ridiculous deadlines.' He took my hand. 'And this must be the lovely Maggie. I hope you love what I've chosen for you. If you don't, you can blame Ashley.'

Jon was an exceptionally snappy dresser. Blue pin stripe suit, a matching waistcoat, and the crispest white shirt I'd ever seen with cuffs that sat perfectly under his jacket sleeves. He was accessorised tastefully with cuff links, a silk tie and a matching pocket-handkerchief. A pair of black Oxford dress shoes completed the look.

'I've included a range of shoes in different sizes. Anything you don't want, leave on the rack, and I'll have someone collect them tomorrow.'

'Ciao bella.' He kissed me on each cheek. 'Ciao, Ashley.' He stood with hands on hips looking Ashley up and down. 'What happened? You're a mess!' He laughed. 'Send me a selfie in your new clothes so I can rest easy. Ciao!' And he was gone.

I examined the bags. 'Oooh, it feels like Christmas very exciting! Everything's labeled. So organised.'

Jason appeared wearing a white bathrobe and slippers. 'Looks like the clothes dude has been.'

'Yes! I can't wait to see what we've got,' I said.

'Hey, Ashley,' Jason said, 'where's the other bed?'

'Yep, I know. They said there'd be a rollaway. Must've forgotten. No dramas, I'll get the lovely Melanie to arrange one. Okay if I have a shower now?'

'Go for it. I'm going to kick back with a beer.'

'Want me to put your clothes in the bedroom? I asked Ashley.

'Yeah, thanks.'

Jason kissed my check. 'How good is this place?'

'Simply divine.'

He turned up the music. 'Ash is amazing. An idiot, but an extremely generous one. He's a good mate.'

Sorting the labeled items into three piles, I took Ashley's into the luxurious master suite, leaving his clothes and shoeboxes on a chaise longue near the window. The luxurious bed was extremely inviting, calling out to my bone-weary body. I would've been happy to go to sleep right then and there, except for the fact I was starving.

I lay on the bed and dimmed the lights, enjoying the feel of expensive Egyptian linen. Evening was falling, and the lights of the city twinkled outside. The artworks, lighting, the furnishings, everything was incredibly beautiful—and then my mind turned to home and the mess awaiting us. No. Don't spoil it. I forced myself to focus on something else. Then, at that moment, there was something else to focus on.

Ashley had padded out of the bathroom in bare feet, so I didn't hear a thing as he walked past me towards the chaise longue. When I opened my eyes, he was standing in front of it, stark naked, bending over to pick up the suit bag. His muscular body was silhouetted against the skyline. The soft down lights accentuated each curve and ripple of his muscles. Spellbound, I watched the fluid grace of his body as he unzipped the bags, removed garments, and laid them out neatly on the longue before him.

'Are you going to leave before I turn around?' he asked softly.

My body jerked with surprise. Oh hell. I felt my face flush.

'Oh, um, sorry, ah, you surprised me, I was having a rest, shut my eyes for a bit and then, there you were, and I didn't know … what to...'

His shoulders shook with silent laughter.

'I'm outta here,' I mumbled, jumping up. My foot caught in the bedclothes and I landed flat on my face on the carpet.

Ashley ran over to help me. 'Jesus, are you all right?'

I lifted my head from the carpet to see a buck naked Ashley extending one hand to help me, while the other covered his private bits.

I giggled. It wasn't as if I hadn't seen his bits before. 'Since when, ever, have you been worried about your modesty?'

'I didn't want to scare you,' he said, with a mock serious face. 'It's happened to girls before you know. And besides, I couldn't do it to you.'

'Do what?'

'Leave you with the feeling nothing else could compare, that everything else would be second rate, and leave you wanting what we've decided you can't have.'

'I seriously hope you're kidding, you ego maniac.'

'I'm deadly serious.' He laughed. 'Now, Miss Voyeur, are you going to leave, and let me get dressed, or are you in here because you really do want a long, slow, hot shower?'

'I'm gone,' I said, leaving the room without answering his question.

* * * * *

Jason was in the lounge looking out at the view. He turned when I entered and gestured at his body. 'What do you think?'

'You look amazing! Do you like?'

'Yeah, I like. The clothes dude did a spectacular job.'

He was dressed in smart casual pants, fashionable pointy-toed black Oxfords, and a white T-shirt under an expensive looking thin knit. It was like he'd stepped out of a men's fashion magazine.

'I like the jacket he picked as well,' he said.

This was surprising, as Jason wasn't into fashion; he liked functional, practical clothes, and only shopped once a year when his jocks reached gossamer stage.

'Yes, not over the top. It's like you'd choose for yourself, but better.' I wrapped my arms around him. 'You look hot. Hotter than hot.' I held his face and kissed him.

202

Ashley stepped into the lounge. 'Bedrooms free.'

I turned to see a stranger standing before us.

Ashley laughed. 'Pick your chin up off the floor, Maggie.'

'Oh my God, talk about a transformation! Army Biker dude to Man-About-Town!'

'Not bad, eh?' He gave me a twirl. Sporting a black suit jacket made from a stunning material, he turned, providing glimpses of a luxurious silk lining. A thin V-necked, grey-black knit hugged his body, and his dress jeans were accessorised with a leather belt and silver buckle. The whole look was finished with point toed, black, low-heeled boots.

He gathered my clothes bags together and took them to the bedroom. I followed him. 'Right, it's your turn now. Get ready. Time is ticking. Oh, hang on a minute.' He disappeared and came back with a glass of champagne. 'You may like to have something refreshing while you're getting dressed.' He handed me the glass and smiled.

'Thanks, Ashley, you're very thoughtful.'

When he left, I closed the door and unzipped the suit bag. Inside was a red, mini silk dress covered with fine, red lace. It was an elegant piece of clothing but I wasn't happy. I hated wearing dresses.

Throwing it on the bed, I rummaged around in the other bags to find something with pants. Nothing. Bloody Ashley! It seemed like I had no choice. Bugger it.

Underwear. I didn't have any underwear. Noticing a lingerie bag, I took out a thin black box with *Honey Birdette* written on the front. Oh jeepers, I knew what that was. I pictured the Maestro.

Putting on the flimsy, silken wisps of material, I was amazed at how soft, supportive and gorgeous they felt. Not wanting to go bare legged, I ferreted around in the packages looking for leggings. All I could find was a box containing stockings and suspenders. Oh puh-lease! Ashley was so dead. I could imagine him laughing his head off in there thinking about this. He was truly evil.

I put on the suspender belt, attached the bits and bobs, rolled on the stockings, and fiddled around trying to attach the stockings to the belt. The whole process was tricky and annoying. Who had time for this!

Finally, done. I caught sight of myself in the mirror. Jesus, I actually looked hot—like something out of Bras Monthly. Laughing to myself, I stepped into the dress. It fitted like a glove. The neck was low cut, with three-quarter sleeves and it sat tight above the waist, flaring out slightly to finish mid-thigh. Not my style, but surprisingly cute. I spun around in front of the mirror.

Now, shoes. Opening all four shoes boxes, I found they contained exactly the same shoe in different sizes. I took one out. It was a black, six-inch heel stiletto. It had a raised platform toe and six eyelets on the outside threaded with black ribbon which was tied in a tiny bow at the top. A bloody hooker's shoe!

'Damn you!' I hurled it at the door. I hated high-heeled shoes with a passion. They were uncomfortable; they hurt your feet, and your back, you couldn't walk far or fast in them, and you risked breaking your goddamn ankles. Basically, they made you feel hobbled, the absolute antithesis of a freethinking, independent, strong woman.

'You right in there?' Jason asked through the door.

'Yes!'

Having excellent radar ears, I heard him whisper to Ashley. 'I hope she's not getting angry in there. You wouldn't like her when she's angry.'

In response, anger rose, hot and vicious. *No! Breathe, Maggie. Breathe.*

Sitting on the bed, I closed my eyes and thought of dolphins—dolphins swimming in crystal blue waters, streams of air bubbles flowing around them catching the sunlight, rolling and spinning for the sheer joy of it.

A calmness flowed through my body, and like the waves of

my imaginary ocean, the anger receded and didn't return. I focused on the city lights until I felt calm and in control.

Phew! I'd caught it in the nick of time. I danced around the room and bounced up and down on the bed. I'd finally had a win against the rise of darkness. For the first time in a long time, I felt a sense of hope for the future.

I'd wear the goddamn silly shoes; I slipped them on. Jon had included some makeup in a little bag, so I fixed my hair and put on some eye shadow, mascara and lipstick. There was one more velvet-covered box. I flipped it open to reveal a beautiful set of matching earrings, necklace and bracelet.

I gasped. They were gorgeous! They must have been worth a fortune; though surely, they couldn't be diamonds; they had to be dress jewellery. Even so, dress jewellery could be hellishly expensive. These were definitely going back in the morning.

Putting them on, I walked, or should I say, tottered, to the full-length mirror in the bathroom. Bloody hell. Who was that woman? I turned around slowly on the ridiculously high shoes. The outfit wasn't really me, but I looked amazing. Holding onto the wall, I made my way back from the bathroom. It was like trying to walk on stilts.

Okay. Deep breath. The grand entrance. I hated being the centre of attention, and in this outfit, I knew they'd laugh at me.

'Are you ready yet?' Ashley called.

'Coming.' I opened the door and slowly stepped into the lounge.

Jason gasped as he turned and saw me. I don't think Jason had ever seen me in a dress before. Ashley stood, hands in pockets, with an expression on his face I'd never seen before. Maybe he thought he'd just accomplished a 'Mission Impossible' and was quietly reveling in his achievement.

He held up a glass of champagne in the gesture of a toast. 'I approve.'

Knowing exactly where he wanted to go with this, I asked,

'You like the wine?'

'Oh, not the wine, your frock. Tight in all the right places, not too many buttons,' he said, doing his James Bond impersonation.

'You arranged all this to use that James Bond line?'

'Of course not, but it was the perfect opportunity!'

Jason and Ashley shared similar tastes in movies, and they could quote scenes word for word. I'd been brainwashed—the line was from *The Man with the Golden Gun*.

'It was my line, but he beat me to it,' Jason said. 'I hardly recognise you! You look stunning.' He gripped me around the waist, lifted and twirled me around. My dress rode up in the process, and Jason's eyes nearly fell out of his head as he caught a glimpse of my lingerie in the mirror.

'Stockings and suspenders! Oh my God, we are so not going anywhere,' he said, steering me back towards the bedroom.

Ashley was doubled up with laughter. 'Did you happen to realise the underwear was crotchless?' he said.

'What? No way. You wait. Making me wear all this stuff. You're laughing at me. Wait till I get my hands on you,' I said, trying to break free of Jason's grip.

Ashley grinned. 'I can't wait for you to get your hands on me.'

Jason's face clouded over. 'As per usual, Ash, you've gone too far.'

Ashley's smile vanished. 'I just wanted to make you happy. Take your mind off everything by spicing things up a bit. I'm sorry, Jace. I didn't mean to upset you. Maggie, sorry. I have a spare pair of jocks you can have if you'd feel more comfortable.'

'Are they clean?'

'You could turn them inside out.'

'I'll pass, thanks.'

Jason laughed, rolled his eyes at Ashley, and took my hand. 'We don't have to go out, Mags. I know you don't like dresses and high heels, and with the knickers an' all … but you look so hot, I'd love to take you out.'

My feelings were mixed, but I made the decision to be good humoured and let Ashley have his fun at my expense. Jason kept looking at me like a love-struck schoolboy, which I found quite amusing. It's odd how much men could be affected by some high heels and a bit of lace.

It gave me an idea. To ward off any psycho killers, who generally seemed to be male, I should ensure I was wearing a short dress and high heels. Mention the words crotchless knickers and they'd collapse at my feet and explode in a puff of black dust.

With this in mind, I let Jason and Ashley help me along the marble hallway in my killer heels. Despite my sore feet, this was another moment I would treasure forever.

---

22 *Maggie's Playlist: You're Lookin' Hot Tonight — Ivo Franklin & His Orchestra*

Chapter 23: The Syringe

'Deep into that darkness peering, long I stood there, wondering, fearing, doubting, dreaming dreams no mortal ever dared to dream before.' — Edgar Allan Poe

We felt a million dollars as we strode along the corridors of the gorgeous hotel, and judging by the attention we got, I reckon we looked it too. Divine aromas wafted from the restaurant and my mouth watered. I felt like I hadn't had a decent meal in decades.

The waiter, being particularly attentive to me, showed us to our booth. The lights were low, open fires flickered, soft music played, and someone handed me a glass of champagne. It didn't get any better than that.

Sitting between Jason and Ashley, I felt safe and relaxed, mesmerised by the beautiful décor, lighting and artworks. It was such a tonic after everything we'd been through, and it made me realise what a long time it'd been since Jason and I had done anything like this.

Ashley leaned towards me. 'That guy keeps checking you out, Maggie.'

'No wonder,' Jason said. 'She looks hot.'

'That woman keeps looking at you, Jason.'

'Which one?'

'The blonde with the long legs.'

'Not interested. Why would I be when I've got you.' He kissed my cheek.

The woman was supremely attractive and kept glancing over. I waited for Ashley to make some sort of quip but he remained oddly silent. Say it ain't so. Bond had lost his edge.

We ate, drank, laughed and talked. The champagne flowed freely for me, while the guys enjoyed icy cold beers in tall frosty glasses. For entrée, we had sushi, then I had salt and pepper calamari, while the guys enjoyed South Australian Coffin Bay oysters—au naturel, on the half shell with a dressing of fresh chopped shallots, peppercorns, dry white wine and lemon juice.

Still hungry, we carbed up on pasta. Jason chose linguine with an assortment of seafood, white wine, garlic, mild chilli and rocket. Ashley chose the handmade potato gnocchi with braised lamb ragu, green peas and parmigiano reggiano. I couldn't resist the gnocchi with four cheeses— Gorgonzola, Fontina, Mozzarella and Parmesan baked in a cream sauce with zucchini ribbons and caramelised leeks. OMG. I was in cheese heaven.

It was as if we were escapees from some godawful prison, and we had to make the most of this before we were eventually recaptured and dragged back to our cells in hell.

An attentive waiter ensured my glass was never empty, and I began to feel tipsy. The complimentary Espresso Martini he gave me made my head spin. I shouldn't have had it but it was delicious. A glorious mix of coffee liquor, vodka and espresso finished off with a thick, creamy froth.

Jason watched me down the final drop and lick the froth from my lips.

'What?'

'It'll blow your head off. You know you can't handle cocktails.'

Ashley laughed. 'You're not kidding there. The drink you downed was invented in the late eighties by a London bartender. The story goes a young lady asked for something that'd "wake me up, and then fuck me up", so he created the Espresso Martini to do just that.'

'I'll be fine.' My head was spinning even more.

As I sat listening to the music, a hand touched my left knee. It rested there for a while, before sliding slowly up my inner thigh.

It appeared all hands were under the table. My intoxicated brain undertook a sluggish process of deduction. Jason was on my left, so it was probably Jason's right hand. But what if it was Ashley's left hand, on my left leg? Unlikely, but he would do something like that, the trickster.

Because I couldn't work out for sure whose hand it was, I had a brain freeze. I sat immobile feeling someone's hand working its way slowly upward.

'What's wrong?' Jason said, looking concerned.

I inhaled sharply through my nose as the hand reached its target and my body quivered involuntarily.

It had to be Ashley. Jason wouldn't do this in a public place.

'Um, yeah, I'm fine,' I said, wriggling to try and avoid the probing fingers.

Ashley regarded me with amusement. 'You look flushed. Sure you're all right?'

Jason turned my face towards his and he kissed me.

Who the hell was it? Grab the hand and then you'd know.

So, I did. It was Jason.

Ashley gave me a twitch of a smile. He lifted both hands from under the table and wrapped them around his glass.

Jason! Who knew? Wonders never ceased.

Ashley leant over and put his mouth against my ear. Taking off James Bond he whispered, 'You look hot, my dear. Can I get you a martini? Shaken, not stirred?' My body tingled with his breath and voice in my ear. 'Jason's a lucky man.'

I squeezed his hand.

'How come you're not wearing your rings?' he asked.

My hands were bare. 'Oh, I forgot! I can't remember when I last saw them. I hope they're not lost.' A surge of panic twisted my stomach. 'Can I have the room card? I need to go find them.' Jason had given me those rings, so they were precious.

'Here 'tis.' Ashley handed me the card.

'I'll escort you back,' Jason said, 'with your high heels an' all.'

'Thank you, but I'll be fine. Back in a flash.'

Ashley stood up to let me out, bowing solemnly.

Feeling hot and bothered, I welcomed the chance to stretch my legs and get a change of air. I tried to walk like I'd been wearing high heels forever and not stagger or fall. God knows how it came across. I glanced back at Jason and Ashley, and they were smiling, giving me the thumbs up.

The waiter was still giving me the eye so maybe I was doing okay.

Having left the restaurant, I whipped off the stilettos and stood on the marble floors in my stockinged feet. I wiggled my toes. The tiles were cool and soothing—bliss. Stupid shoes. I almost skipped to the lift lobby, shoes in hand.

While I waited for the lift, the waiter from the restaurant joined me. I read his name badge. 'Hello, Dylan, where are you heading?'

'Lounge on the thirty-first floor. I'm finishing my shift there.' He smiled. 'How do you know my name?'

'I'm psychic. No, just kidding.' I pointed to his name badge and he rolled his eyes.

'Of course. You're in the Diplomatic Suite.'

'How do you know?'

'The key card you're holding.'

I laughed. 'Oh, of course! I thought you were psychic.'

He was a somber looking chap, French, Arabic maybe? Dark eyebrows curved sardonically over extremely pale blue eyes. The rim of his iris was dark in comparison, appearing alien under his long dark lashes. A black, extended goatee set off his full lips.

The lift arrived, and we entered and stood watching the illuminated numbers flash by. The lift was paneled with mirrors so it was hard not look at your reflection. Dylan straightened his collar and his shirt cuffs slipped back to reveal what appeared to be a Catherine wheel tattoo on his wrist.

By the time we'd reached the thirty-first floor my heart was beating like a bass drum. The lift bell dinged and the doors slid open. A group of people waited outside. I breathed a sigh of relief.

Dylan turned to me. 'Have a lovely evening, Maggie.' He headed off towards the lounge bar. I hightailed it to our room, my heart still pounding in my ears. Hastily closing the suite door behind me, I leant against it, and took long slow breaths, trying to steady my racing heart. I needed to find my rings. Where were they? The waiter seemed pleasant, really. Maybe I was wrong about the tattoo? I was half cut after all.

Feeling groggy, I bumbled around the suite looking for likely places I could've left my rings. They were sitting behind a soap dish in the bathroom. The spa bath was full—Jason must've had a spa and left the water in. The bath was so inviting, with the view out over the town. It would be wonderful to strip off and slip into it for some peace and quiet, and gaze out at the gorgeousness of the city. No time for that—the guys would be wondering where I was. I'd better get back.

I collected my high heels and threw them in the sink while I put on my rings. Damn shoes. I'd walk back down in stockinged feet. I checked my hair in the mirror and gasped at Dylan's reflection behind me.

'Hello again, Maggie.'

Oh shit, of course. He knew my name. They all knew my name, even though I wasn't wearing a nametag.

'Time is running out for you,' he said. 'Where are the crystals?'

He spoke like a robot and then moved so rapidly it was like time fast-forwarded. He grabbed my hair and yanked me towards him.

212

'Where. Are. The. Crystals?' He jerked my hair with each word before pushing me against the towel rail. He pressed hard against me, so close I felt his breath on my face.

'Crystals? I, I ... d ... don't know. Dylan, there are cameras in the corridor. They'll catch you. Please let me go.'

'No cameras. I've made sure of it.'

'Read my lips,' I said. 'I. Don't. Know!' I spat the words at him. 'I've been through this before. Don't you idiots communicate?'

'You do know.' Dylan twisted my hair tight around his wrist and pulled my head back. He pressed the fingers of his other hand over my lips, and dragged them heavily over my mouth, pulling my bottom lip over. He shoved his fingers into my mouth, and I gagged at the bitter taste of tobacco, urine and God knew what else. He sniggered, as he continued along the front of my neck and sternum. Pausing there, he pressed his hand between my breasts. 'Left, or right? Decisions, decisions,' he muttered, leaning into me. He chose, and seized my right breast, squeezing it hard. I screamed.

'Get your hands *off* me!' I tried to knee him in the balls. Dylan was fast, turning to avoid the blow. Reaching back, he brought out a gun and cocked the trigger. He scrutinised me with his alien eyes before pointing the gun at my head.

'Old fashioned gun you got there, mister. Roach not looking after you with the latest kit? Tsk, tsk.'

'It works. That's all you need to concern yourself with.' He let go of my hair and clutched at my breast again. I shrieked and he slapped his hand over my mouth, shoving my head back against the wall.

'Don't scream or do anything stupid. I will shoot you.' He pushed the barrel of the gun into my forehead. 'Right here. Or maybe here?' He slid the gun over my eye, forcing it closed. I felt the cold steel through my eyelid. 'Or here?'

He shifted the gun to rest in between my lips and moved the

tip of the barrel up and down in my mouth so I could taste the steel.

'You have sensuous lips.' He traced their outline with the tip of the gun, tracked it over my chin following his previous path, and came to rest over my heart. 'What about here? Where are the crystals, Maggie?' He pushed the barrel hard into my chest.

Rendered mute, my body quaked in fear. I sent telepathic messages to Jason and Ashley begging for help.

'Open your eyes. Look at me!'

I did as instructed.

Dylan ran his fingers around my left ear, pushed my hair behind it. He leant forward, still holding the gun to my chest, pressed his face against my cheek and nuzzled into my hair. His breath shuddered in my ear, and then the wetness of his tongue as he shoved it in, licking and slobbering. A tide of revulsion coursed through my body. Images of his fantasies flooded my mind, tripling my terror. In his head, he was torturing me in the most horrific ways.

'Since you refuse to tell me what I need to know, this is what's going to happen.' He stepped back, reached into his shirt pocket, and pulled out a hypodermic syringe.

'Oh, please, please don't!'

He held my greatest fear in his hand. I was terrified of being drugged, rendered unconscious. It happened to me in a past life. I sensed it—I knew it, and I became weak with fear.

My heart was beating in my throat, my ears deafened by its pounding. I felt hot and cold as sweat pooled on my skin. My mouth was dry, my muscles rigid, and the room compressed into a tunnel forcing me to focus solely on the nightmare standing in front of me.

He held up the syringe and compressed it to release a few drops. They caught the light like dewdrops before falling to the floor.

'Ready?' He fixed his alien eyes on mind and smiled.

My heart hammered like a freight train as he approached, needle at the ready. He pressed the gun into my chest and raised the needle to my neck. It scratched my skin and I jumped as the cold steel punctured my flesh.

'Last chance,' he said, running his tongue along the side of my face. 'Tell me where they are.'

'Okay, okay! They're over there, hidden under the pile of towels.'

He twisted his head to look. 'Finally. Thank you, Maggie.'

I grabbed a shoe from the sink, and as he turned back, I jammed the heel of my stiletto right through his eyeball.

'My pleasure,' I said, using both hands to shove it in further. The stiletto travelled in as far as it could go. He screamed and fell backwards, smashing his head on the black and white marble floor. The gun and syringe clattered across the tiles. A trickle of blood ran from his eye and pooled on the marble. His body twitched like he'd been hit by a Taser.

My body trembled with adrenaline as a young man with a shoe in his head died violently at my feet. I promptly threw up over the bathroom floor. I was still vomiting when Jason and Ashley burst through the door.

---

23 *Maggie's Playlist: Fight Like A Girl — Kalie Shorr*

Chapter 24: Hot Chocolate

Jason and Ashley had guns in their hands. They froze, taking in the scene.

'Jesus Christ! Are you okay?' Jason asked.

I nodded in the affirmative, although I definitely wasn't okay. I was as far from okay as I could possibly be.

Ashley pocketed his gun and stooped to retrieve Dylan's. As he did, he noticed the syringe and picked it up too.

Jason stared at the man with a shoe sticking out of his eye. 'Holy shit, it's the guy from the restaurant!'

'His name's Dylan.'

'How come you always know your assailants' names?' Jason asked.

'They seem to know mine.'

Ashley held out the syringe for Jason to see. 'Check this out.'

'Bloody hell! Did he use it?'

Ashley held the syringe to the light. 'Doesn't look like it. Probably Pentothal, truth serum.'

I started to sob uncontrollably. 'I've ... ruined ... our evening.'

Ashley stepped over Dylan and hugged me. 'I hardly think it's your fault, luv.'

'Ashley, move it!' Jason shouted. 'Roach! Dylan's gonna

blow.'

A large, black, shiny cockroach wriggled out of Dylan's mouth. It paused, turned towards me and hissed.

Ashley swept me into his arms, leapt across the body, and was out the door, yelling for Jason to shut it. He slammed it behind us and Jason and Ashley ran full pelt along the corridor to put distance between the roach and us. We were running in a wind tunnel. Air rushed past us blowing back our hair and buffeting our bodies, as it was sucked through the corridor by the black hole forming in the bathroom.

We made it to the lounge and closed the master suite door. Ashley kissed my forehead and whispered, 'I wanted to hold you in my arms all night, but not like this. I will never let you out of my sight again.'

He sat me on the couch. 'Jason, wrap Maggie in a blanket and put your arms around her. I'm going to make us hot chocolate.'

'Hot chocolate?' Jason said. 'Now?'

'Yes. There's some in the kitchenette.'

Ashley pointed to the coffee table. 'Light those vanilla candles too.'

'Candles?' Jason stared at Ashley like this time he really had gone insane.

'Do it. Some soft classical music too.'

He dutifully followed Ashley's instructions and wrapped the blanket around me. It was warm and comforting, and the shivering in my body eased. He lit the candles, turned on the Bose SoundTouch, and selected my favourite classical composer. Sitting next to me, he held me close. He kissed my hair. 'I'm so sorry for what happened.' His laser beam eyes were dialed down to match the candlelight. His mouth was set in a thin, grave line.

Ashley came back with a wet tea towel. He knelt in front of me, and supporting my face in his hand, gently wiped away the mess left on my face, before heading back into the kitchen again.

He returned with three mugs of hot chocolate and set them on the coffee table. The scent reminded me of a café I used to go to in Switzerland. I went there every day to enjoy the sweet, frothy hot chocolate, served in silver jugs.

Ashley raced back to the kitchen and returned with three ginormous cookies. He handed me a mug and a cookie. 'Milk and cookies. Trust me, it never fails. This will have you feeling better in no time.'

Holding the warm mug, I inhaled the sweet fragrance of chocolate. It replaced the stink of Dylan lingering in my nostrils.

I bit into the chocolate cookie—soft and delicious. The scent of vanilla, the rich taste of chocolate, walnuts and coconut displaced the taste of cold steel remaining on my lips and tongue.

Closing my eyes, I breathed in the delicious aromas. Ashley was right; I felt better. I opened my eyes to see two concerned faces looking at me.

I took another sip of the hot chocolate. 'Who knew stilettos could serve a useful purpose after all?'

Jason rubbed my neck. 'You did good. Amazing. I'm so sorry we weren't there for you. I can't forgive myself.'

Ashley's expression was solemn. 'Me neither.'

'Don't worry about it. Who's to know? Thank God for those stilettos though.'

'That's the one sentence I would never have expected to hear you say in your lifetime,' Jason said.

I nodded. 'Maybe it's why they call them 'killer heels'. They not only kill your feet but are handy for dispatching bad guys.'

'You know a stiletto is actually a dagger?' Ashley said. 'Back in the day the stiletto was the blade of choice for Italian assassins.'

'It's like the Cold Steel Torpedo,' I said.

'The what?'

'A fifteen-inch Cold Steel Torpedo. It's like what you're talking about. I've got one at home.'

Ashley was flabbergasted. 'What the hell are you doing with one of those?'

I smiled. 'It's part of my kit. I've also got a Smith & Wesson carbon steel pocket baton, UZI tactical defender pen with DNA catcher and built-in handcuff key, and three Cold Steel nine inch throwing knives made from lightweight aircraft aluminum. I can now add two guns and a stiletto shoe to my kit.'

Jason was laughing.

'Are you kidding me?' Ashley said.

'No.'

Ashley turned to Jason for confirmation. He nodded. 'It's true.'

'There's obviously something you haven't been telling me.' He rubbed his hand through his hair. 'And what do you mean, two guns?'

'I mean two guns, Marlon and Dylan's.'

'Oh no, kiddo, you are so not playing with guns.'

'You promised you'd give them back. *Promised.*'

'Yes, after I teach you how to use them properly. It's not easy, with the recoil. It's dangerous. I don't like the idea.'

'Me neither,' Jason said.

'It's all very well for you two to sit there and say what I should and shouldn't do, and can and can't do. You're not the ones being hunted by a pack of tattooed psycho killers with hissing cockroaches inside them. I need to be able to protect myself—I can't rely on you guys.'

The boys looked chastened.

'Oh, I'm sorry, that came out wrong. I didn't mean I can't rely on you, but I need to ... I have to—'

'You're right,' Jason said. 'We let you down, you do need something.'

'No, you didn't. You couldn't know.'

The feeling in my gut was that they had let me down. It was illogical, I knew that, but it was how I felt.

'Where did you get all that stuff you mentioned from?' Ashley asked.

'It was hidden in a secret compartment in a trunk my dad gave me.'

'Really?'

'Yep, I'll show you when we get ho—' I stopped, put my head in my hands and felt sick thinking about going home to the mess. I prayed Boo wasn't injured or dead.

Jason stroked my hair. 'Don't worry about home. Ash and I will take care of everything. Try not to think about it, okay?'

'I'll try,' I said, grateful for his reassurance.

Jason slapped an arm around Ashley. 'Thanks for everything, mate, and for getting Maggie those shoes. They saved her life.'

'No worries, but she saved her own life. If the shoes weren't there she would have found something else. Probably would've shoved a toilet brush up his arse.'

I laughed. 'I'd have enjoyed that.'

Jason examined the needle scratch on my neck and the round blue bruise on my chest. He pointed to the bruise. 'What happened there?'

'Gun,' I said. 'Don't want to talk about it.'

From the corner of my eye, I saw Ashley move his hand back and forth across his neck, indicating Jason should cut it.

'Do you think the coast is clear in the bathroom yet?' I asked.

'Probably, but let's wait before we go in again,' Ashley suggested.

'The milk and cookies thing really helped. I feel so much better. What gives?'

'I thought you'd gone stark raving mad,' Jason said.

'You should know, Maggie. Smell, touch, taste, hearing, all the senses are powerful. When you go through something traumatic, it helps to replace the negative sense residue with some good stuff. Positive stimuli. Especially important for you as you absorb so much more with your extra sensory perception.'

I recalled the images of torture and abuse I'd seen in Dylan's mind. 'Ain't that the truth. How do you know this?'

'I get around. You know me. I pick up things here and there. Now come here and give me a hug. You've had a rough time.' He wrapped his arms around me. 'You need all the hugs you can get.'

'It does help,' I said, enjoying the platonic body contact.

Ashley gently disengaged from our hug and headed for the kitchen. 'I need another beer.'

Jason seemed miles away, focused on his phone.

'What are you doing?' I asked.

'Researching cockroaches. It's not good.'

'What do you mean?'

'It says "some cockroaches mature so fast that only a few weeks after hatching they're ready to make babies of their own". It goes on to say one female can be the matriarch of up to thirty-five thousand roaches.'

'Holy shit,' Ashley said, coming back from the kitchen. 'So, you're thinking it's not the same roach?'

'I don't know what I'm thinking, but possibly. The roach the Professor brought back wouldn't sit around being lonely; it would be on the lookout for some buddies. It says roaches are highly social.'

'What if the Professor's roach was a male?'

'It would still want to find a lady roach and make babies, and maybe those babies would be exactly like it.'

After Jason mentioned the number *thirty-five thousand*—that's all I could think about. 'Thirty-five thousand tattooed psycho killers. I'm going to need a bigger gun.'

'Way bigger,' Ashley said. 'We need to work out what the hell we're going to do.'

Jason's phone rang and we jumped. He checked the screen.

'It's Detective Inspector Johnston. Shit, what do I do?'

'Take it,' I said. 'You have to.'

221

He declined the call and it went to message bank.

'You're going to have to talk to him sometime,' Ashley said. 'Maybe it was important.'

'I'll see what the voicemail says first.' He pressed play.

Jason, Detective Inspector Johnston. One. You need to know we arrested the three perps re the incident at your house. Unfortunately, they have since escaped. Two. Need to chat to you, Maggie McLaine and an Ashley Beringer about an unrelated incident that took place at St. Joseph's hospital yesterday. Call me ASAP.'

'Not good,' I said. 'Three perpetrators gone missing. How could they escape? Maybe they morphed into roaches.'

Ashley looked shocked. 'Can they do that?'

'I have no idea, but it wouldn't surprise me. I'd hate to think that number has just increased to thirty-five thousand and three.'

'I'll ring him later, or in the morning. It can wait,' Jason said. 'We need some serious shuteye and that might be difficult to get here, given there could be more psycho killers with access cards waiting to let themselves in.'

The thought terrified me and it must have shown on my face. Ashley rolled his eyes at Jason.

'I think we stay here the night,' Ashley said. 'There's no point trying to find somewhere else. There's only one access door to this room and I can barricade it and set booby traps. If you agree, we should sleep in the same room, and Jason and I can take turns on watch. That way Maggie can rest easy. Tomorrow we'll fill ourselves with a big hotel breakfast, and then head over to your place to clean up. Sound all right?'

'Yep,' Jason said, 'and we need to find the crystal and work out a plan on how to tackle this—I seriously need to write a list.'

I nodded. 'What about the bathroom?'

'I'll go check it,' Jason said.

'I'll come with you,' Ashley offered.

Jason took my hand. 'Come with me. Let's stay together. Wait inside the master suite where I can see you.'

The guys stood outside the bathroom door and listened, guns at the ready. Jason slowly turned the handle and pushed the door open.

'All clear,' Jason shouted. 'Clean as a whistle.'

Ashley whispered to Jason, 'We can't let her come back in here; it would seriously do her head in. We'll have to take a shower elsewhere. I don't fancy it in here myself, to be honest.'

'What about the health club? We can stand guard on each other?' Jason said.

'Good idea. Let's do it.'

They came back along the corridor and Ashley asked, 'Maggie, rather than use the bathroom, do you want a shower in the health club, if we stand guard?'

'Yes, please. I can't wait to wash away the last of that scumbag.'

'What do you mean?' Jason asked.

'What I said.'

Jason dialed his truth extracting laser beam eyes to maximum revs. 'What did he do to you?'

'Leave it,' Ashley said quietly.

'Fuck off and stop friggin' telling me what to do!'

Ashley raised his hands in resignation.

'Tell me, Maggie.'

Jason noticed the syringe sitting on a shelf nearby. He picked it up and examined it. 'Tell me,' he said softly. 'I need to know. Please tell me what he did to you.'

When Jason touched the syringe, I got Dylan. I didn't have to go back into that bathroom to relive the horror of what he'd done to me. I was there already, and he was with me. Dylan had the syringe and was shouting, 'Tell me, Maggie! Tell me, Maggie! Tell me!' Over and over again.

Howling, I descended into the pit of Dylan's disgusting

residue.

Ashley seized the syringe from Jason. 'And you reckon I'm an idiot!' He ran from the room and there was a sound of running water and the roar of the InSinkErator. The connection shattered, and I collapsed to the carpet, gasping with relief.

Ashley returned. 'Fabulous job, Jason. You've undone all my good work.' He punched Jason hard on the arm. 'She went through all that, and you sent her right back to do it all over again.'

Ashley wasn't finished.

'You're a fucking idiot. Think about it. She's got PTSD with ESP on steroids, and you touch the syringe and … Jesus, what were you thinking, man?'

Jason's face twisted with anguish. 'I'm sorry. I was scared, worried. I needed to know. I'm sorry, Maggie.'

'Dead set, I wonder about you sometimes,' Ashley said.

'Yeah, well, ditto. You're always—'

'Stop it! This isn't helping, both of you. Please stop.' My voice trembled and my heart was pounding. I swear I didn't think my heart could take much more. Surely, I'd used most of my life's allocated heartbeats in the last few days alone.

I staggered to my feet, and when the guys moved to assist, I raised my hand to warn them off. Taking a deep breath, I centered myself. 'I'll tell you what happened.'

Ashley crossed his arms and glared at me. 'Don't!'

'No, it's—' Jason said.

'Shut it. You wanted to know, so I'm telling you.'

I took another deep breath and felt myself shift into a state of disassociation, a sense of unreality. Hands clenching into fists, my nails dug into palms, and my vision compressed into a tunnel.

I took another breath. 'He threatened me, he pushed me, he jammed my back into a towel rail and he yanked my hair, multiple times. He squeezed my breast so hard it made me scream. He stuck a gun to my head, to my eyeball, into my mouth, across my lips and over my heart.

'He ran his disgusting hands over my face, my lips, my neck, between my breasts. He put his filthy mouth, and tongue into my ear, and licked my face.

'He threatened me with a syringe. He scratched me with it, and then he stuck the needle into the side of my neck. Then, to save my life, I had to jam the heel of my stiletto through his eyeball and into his brain.' I paused. 'Yep, I think that covers it. And no, he didn't stick his dick into me, if that's what you were so worried about, so no chance of STIs. You can relax now.'

Shaking with emotion I marched out of the room and slammed the door.

Crash! The sound of breaking glass.

I'd slammed the door so hard an artwork must've hit the deck.

---

[24] *Maggie's Playlist: Tell The Truth — Eric Clapton —Live*

Chapter 25: Strip Tease

Jason and Ashley were pale and quiet when they came into the lounge. I stood and stared out the window at the twinkling city lights. The reflection in the window showed me and my little red dress looking slightly worse for wear, plus, my stocking had a huge ladder in it. I pulled off the earrings, unclipped the bracelet and necklace and placed them on the window ledge.

The window mirrored Jason ambling to the fridge and taking out some bottles. He handed Ashley a beer and returned to the kitchen, coming out with a glass of champagne.

Even though I was expecting it, I started as Jason touched me on the shoulder. He moved his hand quickly away. 'Drink?'

I took it from him. 'Thank you. I think we should add champagne to Ashley's list of Cookies & Milk remedies.'

A glass of champagne made any situation better.

Jason's voice was husky and deep, cracking with emotion as he spoke. 'I don't know what to say. Anything I say will probably be wrong. I don't know what to do either. I'm at a loss. All I can say is I love you, I'm sorry and maybe I'm the one who should leave. Ash is right; I'm a fool.'

I wanted to reach out and touch him, but I couldn't. I was still in such a hyper sensitive state I couldn't bear the slightest touch. Only champagne. Champagne was good.

Stepping away from him, I continued to look out the window. 'Just keep the champagne coming,' I mumbled.

The glass reflected Ashley jamming a chair under the door handle and moving furniture in front of it. He dashed into the kitchen, came out with the rubbish bin and scattered empty beer cans across the floor.

'Better drink up, Jace,' he said. 'We need more cans.'

'No problems there.' Jason cracked open another VB.

It was late, but I needed a shower. Water is cleansing on so many levels and I simply couldn't go to bed or feel normal in any sense of the word without a shower. Coming back to earth, to 'reality', I sensed Jason's anguish.

He was standing at the Bose SoundTouch. Going over to him, I put my arms around his waist. This time, he jumped. Turning around, he tried hard to read me; his expression was unsure, sad. I'd never seen him look like that before. He kept his hands at his side, careful not to touch.

'I'm sorry I was so harsh to you, but—'

He put a finger gently across my lips. '*Shhh.* Can I touch you?' A lock of sandy hair fell across his eyes. His mouth was in serious mode, and I wanted so much to kiss a smile back onto it.

I put my arms around his neck and kissed him tenderly.

He wrapped one hand around my waist and the other held the back of my head. He kissed me fervently until I felt what his words could not express.

'Maggie, pull down your dress will you,' Ashley said. 'I don't know where to look. Those suspenders, man!'

Jason gave him a look and tugged my dress back down.

'Ashley, I thought we were going to go to the health club, but you've barricaded the door already,' I said.

'It's late. You still want to go?'

'Could we? I need a shower. I can't go back in the ensuite after what happened there with Dylan and the roach. It would do my head in.'

'No worries, luv.' He jumped up from the couch and began to undo his good work.

We locked the door to our suite when we left and descended in the lift. It was late and the hotel was quiet. Jason and Ashley were "packing heat". I wasn't, as they still refused to give me a gun, which was still a major annoyance for me. They were both determined to be my protectors, and at this point, I didn't have the energy to protest.

Jason outlined a plan. 'I think one person should have a shower and two stand guard.'

'Sounds fine to me,' Ashley said.

'When it's my turn to stand guard, I get a gun then?'

'Nope,' Jason said.

'So, if a tattooed psycho killer comes by, what am I supposed to do? Throw a bar of soap at him?'

'She's got a point,' Ashley said.

'Of course, I've got a point! You guys are unreal. Jason hasn't had gun lessons, yet he's got one.'

'No, not true. I showed him the basics of gun safety and operation ages ago, well before you came on the scene.'

'Then do the same for me.'

'I will. But not now. Let it go, please?'

'Yeah, whatever.'

The health club was deserted so we headed straight to the ladies' shower room. I didn't want to use the men's.

'You can wait outside,' I said.

Jason's brows snapped together. 'No way! We're coming in and sitting right outside your shower door.'

'I'll be quick.'

I entered the cubicle and locked the door. There was plenty of space to hang my clothes, and I didn't have to worry about shoes as I was in my stockinged feet. My fluffy bathrobe and slippers were at the ready. I couldn't wait.

'Can you fulfill an old bloke's fantasy and drape your stockings over the door as you take them off?' Ashley said. 'You know, like they do in the old movies.'

'You poor sad bloke. I can do more than that.'

Jason chuckled as Ashley sang the tune 'Keep Your Hat On' from *The Full Monty*.

I might as well go the whole hog, just for a laugh. I pulled off my dress and draped it over the top of the cubicle door. There was a twelve-inch gap at the bottom of the door so they could only see my ankles anyway. Then came the Agent Provocateur bra. Hmmm. What next? Stockings. I rolled one down my leg and draped the stocking over the cubicle door.

There was a round of applause from outside the cubicle, which made me snort with laughter. I repeated the process with the other stocking and the suspender belt. I let my undies drop to my ankles and stepped out of them, one foot at a time. Ta-dah! My first striptease behind closed doors. I turned on the shower to thunderous applause.

The hot water felt divine. I let it flow over my head, cleansing and restoring me. I doused myself in the hotel's shampoos, conditioners and body washes. My head was leaning against the tiles, hot water running across the tense muscles in my neck, when something moved. A sudden, erratic, scuttle. I knew what it was before I knew. A roach.

Very slowly, I reached back with my hand and turned off the shower.

Now it was me, the roach, and the drip, drip, drip of the shower rose. The creature paused in front of the cubicle door and stared at me. Way too creepy. I covered my private bits.

What. To. Do?

The roach scuttled forward, and suddenly I had a plan.

I screamed.

'*What?*' Jason yelled.

Outside the cubicle it was action stations, as the boys leapt to their feet.

'There's a roach in the cubicle.'

Ashley shifted straight into army mode. 'Specify location?'

'Standing between me and the door.'

'Don't move,' Jason said.

As if, and to where?

'Get up against the back wall,' Ashley said. He sounded calm and in control. 'I'm going to kick in the door and grab her. You cover me,' he whispered to Jason.

Yeah, that'd be right. Could I reach my bathrobe before he came blasting in? Nope, it wasn't an option.

'On three,' he said. 'One. Two. *Three.*'

The door slammed open with such force it hit the side of the cubicle and slammed back shut again.

Take two. Ashley gently pushed open the door.

'Where is it?' he whispered.

'It's gone,' I whispered back. 'Went that-a-way.' I pointed to the cubicle on my right.

'I've got this!' Jason said.

He held his gun with both hands, straight armed and deadly serious.

He kicked open the next cubicle. *Bang!*

Bang! And the next.

Ashley kept an eye on Jason but looked back at me. He put on his James Bond voice and said, 'My dear, that's quite a nice little nothing you're almost wearing. I approve.'

I rolled my eyes and tried to cover myself with my hands. 'Seriously, you have a James Bond quote for every situation? I'm so not going anywhere—naked.'

He grinned. 'Sorry, luv, hadn't noticed.' He took my robe and held it out for me to step into. 'I've got you covered. Out you come.'

Bang! Another cubicle door.

As Ashley wrapped me in the robe and tied it together at the front, he whispered, 'I would've loved to see you in the lingerie.'

'You've got two chances, mate.'

'Buckley's and Nunn?'

'Yep. You'll just have to imagine. That's what fantasies are for.'

'Buckley survived, you know.'

Bang! Another cubicle door.

'I gave you your stocking fantasy. That will have to do.'

'It was sensational, the only behind closed doors striptease I've ever seen. It was better than a real one.'

'And my début.'

'You're a natural.'

Bang!

'I could give you an encore,' I whispered.

'In front of the door?'

'In your dreams.'

Bang! 'There's the sucker!' Jason hissed. 'Shit!' He jumped back as the cockroach ran out of the cubicle, straight for him.

Ashley drew his gun and moved slowly towards Jason.

It was the gunfight at the O.K. Corral, except the cockroach didn't have a gun, simply the ability to turn you to dust and suck you into a black hole.

Jason and the cockroach faced off, both frozen in anticipation. 'I've got this, I've got this,' Jason said, trying to take a bead on the roach.

It scuttled forward, making a beeline for him. Jason moved backwards, still trying to line up the roach with his gun. The roach continued to advance until Jason's back was against the wall.

Ashley strode forward, gun in hand. 'I've got this.' He brought his boot down on the cockroach's head.

I gasped and waited for something to happen.

Nothing did. I started to giggle. 'Maybe it's like a land mine. Move your foot and it'll explode.'

Ashley looked concerned. 'I hadn't thought of that.'

All attention fixed onto his boot, as he very, very slowly raised the toe from the floor.

Jason and I froze in anticipation. Ashley flashed Jason a look, stamped his foot and shouted *'BOOM!'*

I jumped even though I knew it was a joke. Poor Jason nearly flew through the roof.

'You mongrel!' Jason said, clutching his chest. 'You fair dinkum mongrel! You knew it was an ordinary roach.'

'Soon as I laid eyes on it,' Ashley said, laughing his head off.

---

[25] *Maggie's Playlist: You Can Leave Your Hat On — Tom Jones*

Chapter 26: Red Ribbons, Duck Tape & Bondage

We stood at the door to our suite, kitted out in our white robes and slippers. I held the clothes so the guys could handle their firearms.

Jason swiped the entry card. 'Stand to the side, Maggie, we need to make sure the room is safe.'

I gave him a salute. 'Aye Aye, Cap'n'.' These boys were so bossy.

Ashley opened the door and pushed it back hard. He stood in the entryway assessing the room.

'Wait here,' he said quietly. He entered, gun at the ready and disappeared around the corner. Doors opened and closed.

'Someone's been in,' he shouted. 'Looks like room service with our laundry.' He stuck his head around the corner. 'All clear! I've put the kettle on.'

I stepped into the room feeling uneasy, as though someone was going to jump out and attack us. I proceeded into the kitchen to help make the tea.

Jason sat at a desk in an alcove around the corner, and was texting on his phone like his life depended on it. Maybe work stuff. Thank heavens his business partner Fraser was looking after things. Jason didn't even look up as I put the cup of Sleepy

Time tea on the desk in front of him.

Ashley and I sat at the breakfast bar in the kitchenette, mugs in hands, looking out at the city.

'That was a mean thing you did back there, Ashley Beringer,' I said, referring to the cockroach in the showers. 'Poor Jason.'

'Nah, he took it in good fun. Besides, it's good practise for him to get used to emergency situations.'

'He got right into it, didn't he?'

'Yeah, I think he was trying to channel Jason Statham.'

'How could you be sure it was an ordinary cockroach?'

'I have an excellent memory.'

'Yes, but they may not all look the same, especially if they're offspring.

'Yeah, you're right. I took a calculated risk.'

I put my hand on his shoulder. 'Maybe don't try that again. We really don't know what we're dealing with.'

'Sure, no worries. We should try and get a couple of hours' shuteye before morning.' He stretched his arms above his head and yawned.

The pile of clothes from Jon lay on the bench, and Ashley leant across and pulled out my red dress. He rubbed the silk between his fingers. 'You looked so gorgeous in this.'

A powerful image of me blindfolded, naked, spread-eagled on a bed, with my wrists and ankles bound by red silk, slammed into my mind. I jerked my hand away from him. 'Ashley!'

'What's wrong, luv?' He touched my hand. 'You look like you've seen a ghost!'

'Agh! There it is again!' I pushed his hand away.

'What?'

'I saw—' It was as if someone had shoved a graphically illustrated page of a fetish magazine under my nose. It was Ashley's secret diary, and it shocked and disturbed me.

'What, Maggie?' He tried to touch me again and I pulled back. He saw me staring at the dress, and the penny dropped.

234

His voice was a low growl. 'You said you wouldn't go there. You promised. That's a gross invasion of privacy.' He glowered at me and crossed his arms, accentuating his biceps. I'll bet he's practiced that move in the mirror.

'I didn't look. I was sitting here minding my own business and it came and slapped me across the face. Anyway, how do you know what I saw?'

'Red silk ribbons?' he said.

'Yep.'

'Oh, Jesus. What else?'

'Black silk sheets, naked, bound, spread eagled, with you standing over me.'

'Anything else?'

'There's more?'

'No. No,' he said, clearly lying.

'I'm sorry. I feel embarrassed.'

Ashley put his head in his hands. 'You feel embarrassed!'

We sat silently, and Ashley pushed the dress away using a kitchen spatula.

What was with him? He'd never shown an inclination for that sort of thing when we were together.

'Is that what you want to do to me?'

He was silent for a while before saying, 'I reserve the right not to answer that question on the grounds I may incriminate myself.'

'That would be a yes then?'

He nodded.

'Crikey.'

'It's no big deal, Maggie. It's just a fantasy. A fantasy you shouldn't have seen, granted, but simply a bloke's fantasy. Don't look so shocked. People do that kind of thing for real, all the time, you know. You can't tell me Jason hasn't tied you up or held you down for sex or vice versa.'

'That's none of your business.'

'You're kidding?'

'What?'

'You haven't? He hasn't?'

'I reserve the right not to answer that question on the grounds I may incriminate myself.'

'That would be a no then. I can't believe it.'

I recalled the time I was tied up in the hammock by Jason, and at the morgue by Adam. 'For your information, Mr. Beringer, I've been bound on numerous occasions, but not with silk ribbons.'

'What then?'

'Duck tape.'

This time Ashley looked shocked. 'It's *duct* tape, Maggie, and Jesus, by Jason?'

'Ashley, let it go! And what's with the red silk thing anyway?' I said, trying to change the subject, sort of.

'You definitely don't want to go there with that one.'

'Tell me.'

'No.'

'*Tell* me!'

'No.'

'Tell me.'

'Fine. Red silk ribbons. Your dad was into it with the Maestro. I saw the ribbons hanging on the clotheshorse at his place. I knew they weren't ribbons for her hair. He was on fire for the woman.' He laughed at the look on my face. 'The ribbons were the least of it. I told you, you wouldn't want to go there.'

'I don't think anyone wants to hear things like that about a parent. *Ew!* How am I going to face the Maestro again? Too bizarre. I wish you hadn't told me.'

He touched my face. 'Jesus, I can't win with you. Sweet kid, you're so naïve!'

'I certainly am not, and I'm no sweet kid. You have no idea what I see, the things in people's minds. It's incredibly disturbing.'

'Yeah, sorry, that came out wrong. You have this beautiful innocence about you, is all. And it sounds to me like you've been missing out on your fair share of earthly pleasures. Duct tape indeed. I need to have to have a quiet word in Jason's ear. Tell him to lift his game.'

I pinched him hard in the side. 'Don't you dare!'

'Ow! How're you going to stop me?'

'Please don't!'

'What will you give me so I don't tell?'

'Well, I'm certainly not going to ask you what you want, given it probably involves red silk ribbons.'

'Bingo!'

'You're incorrigible!' I stood and put my mug in the dishwasher.

When I turned around, Ashley was right behind me. He grabbed my wrists, put his feet in between mine, and slid my feet apart.

'What are you do—'

'*Shhh!*' He lifted my arms over my head and held them there.

I tried to move but he was as strong as an ox. I attempted to shift my feet and legs but he had me pinned against the cupboard.

'Relax,' he whispered into my ear. 'I'm not going to hurt you. But you aren't going anywhere. You, sweetheart, are at my mercy. I can do anything I like to you, and you can't stop me.'

My knees became weak as I struggled against Ashley's grip and his deep, seductive voice in my ear.

'That's gotcha!' He chuckled and let me go. I held onto the bench to steady myself.

'A little taster of restraint—looks like it went down a real treat. Still don't want me to have a chat to Jason? How many red ribbons shall I order for you?'

'Ashley, enough already!' I said, walking away. 'It's not

funny.'

He could see I was upset, but it wasn't for the reasons he thought. Actually, it was—he'd really overstepped the mark—but mainly, it was because of how much I'd enjoyed it.

Ashley was right behind me. 'Maggie,' he whispered. 'I'm sorry. I went too far. Forgive me?'

I ignored him and called out to Jason. 'I'm going to bed. I'm beat.'

'Me too,' Jason said. 'We've only got three hours till day break anyway.'

Ashley gave me a hangdog expression. He mouthed the word *sorry* and said, 'I'll take first watch. I'll barricade the door again and set my booby traps again.'

'Don't sleep on the floor,' Jason said. 'The bed's so big you could fit three sumo wrestlers in it.'

'Thanks mate, but the floor's fine.'

It felt like heaven to finally go to bed, to stretch out my tired body and feel the softness of the Egyptian cotton against my skin. Jason slipped in beside me and wrapped me in his arms. 'How good is this bed?' He planted little kisses over my face.

'I'm worried about Boo and the house,' I said.

'Boo is fine; I know it. And don't worry about the house, just lie here in my arms. Everything's fine.' He nuzzled my ear and stroked my body. I quivered involuntarily.

'I love it when that happens,' he whispered, moving to kiss my breasts. 'There you go again. Love you, Mags.'

There was a knock at the bedroom door.

'Can I come in kids? No kinky sex acts going on?'

Jason sighed. 'Yes, come in. No chance of that with you around.'

Ashley opened the door. 'What do you mean? There's more chance of that happening with me around, mate. And don't mind me, always happy to lend a hand if you need it.'

'Shut up,' Jason said.

Ashley arranged himself on the chaise longue. 'I'll leave the bedroom door open so I can see out. I've set my watch for Jason's shift in one and a half hours.'

Jason was already asleep.

'Thanks, Ashley.'

'Sweet dreams, Maggie.'

Ashley pushed himself up against the back of the longue. Silhouetted in the half-light, he was as straight as a ramrod, knees bent, arms resting on them. He held his gun with both hands, aimed straight at the door.

No one was going to make it through there alive. Except perhaps for a roach. Ashley was trying to make sure sleep would come to us easily and sweetly, and so it did.

His alarm chimed one and a half hours later, and Jason leapt out of bed.

Ashley whispered, 'Go back to bed, Jace, I'm fine. All's quiet. I'm good 'till morning.'

'No way, mate. You need some sleep.'

'Roger that.' Ashley threw a blanket on the floor.

'I feel bad you sleeping on the floor. Use the bed. Just don't wake Maggie.'

'The floor's fine.'

'Ash, do it.'

'What if she thinks I'm you and comes on to me in the night?'

'Remember I've got a gun,' Jason said.

I couldn't believe what I was hearing. We'd all shared a bed before, when we'd travelled together and could only get one room. Plus, a few times when we were camping, we'd squeezed together in one tent. But now, it was different— given what'd been happening between Ashley and me. Talk about awkward. Jason wasn't to know. His trust in Ashley was absolute.

It was four-fifteen in the morning. The bed dipped, and the sheets rustled as Ashley slid into bed. A warm and musky scent reached my nostrils. His breathing was quiet and steady, and his heart pounded through the mattress. Or was it mine?

One and a half hours was going to feel like an eternity. One and a half hours of lying there, motionless, wide awake, feeling my body bursting with the sensations and emotions he'd awoken in me back in the kitchenette.

This had to stop. I couldn't handle being near the man. He was a drug, and I was well on the way to addiction, if not already an addict. Circumstances and fate had conspired to create this. What did destiny want of me? To withdraw or to give in to him? Renounce or submit? How much time had passed? Five minutes?

Maybe I should get up. That was it. I'd get up. I couldn't sleep anyway. But then it was so warm and beautiful in the bed. I didn't want to get up. Why hadn't Jason made him sleep on the floor, damn it. Even from over there, surely Jason could feel the waves of sexual tension emanating from the bed.

I lay still and felt my mind open. Ashley's thoughts echoed around inside my head.

I can smell her scent—it's warm, musky, with a hint of vanilla. Her breathing is quiet and steady, and I can hear her heart pounding through the mattress. Or is it mine? She must be awake. Why the hell didn't I sleep on the floor? I'm an idiot. This is dangerous. I can't let myself fall asleep. Combat nightmares. I could kill her. I won't get any sleep with her so close—that's a saving grace. I can't believe I'm in the same bed with her. What a joke. I've dreamed about this, and now I can't do anything. One and a half hours of lying here motionless, wide awake, feeling my body on fire with the sensations and emotions she's ignited in me. I thought I'd moved on, was over her. What the fuck's happening to me?

Oh dear. I hadn't meant to eavesdrop. I tried to block out his thoughts. It was the goddamn proximity of him. Calm, think of dolphins. That worked before. Dolphins ... dolphins ... swimming, spinning. Nup, not happening. Every dolphin was wearing a red silk ribbon, tied in a bow around its head.

Why was it so hot? I wanted to grab the sheets and flap them around. Stop thinking. Focus on my breath. Om. Om Mani Padme Hum. Think of nothing. Christ, I was lying next to a radiator! How far away was he? An arm's length? The heat of his body could fry an egg. He was so still. I couldn't hear his breathing. Maybe he was dead. No, he was too hot to be dead.

It was pretty dark in here with those blackout curtains. I couldn't see Jason. What was on for breakfast? I loved the Bircher muesli. Damn it. There it was again. His voice in my head …

She probably hates me now. I've ruined our friendship. It's my fault. What was I thinking? After what she's been through, I pin her down. Idiot. Ashley, King of the Idiots. I'm as stupid as Jason. She responded though, and quickly. Those knees give her away every time. This. Has. Got. To. Stop. I can't handle being near her, but I want to be near her more than anything. I want her more than anything. She's a bloody drug. I'm addicted. I'm a Maggie addict. But we're friends, the three of us … this is insane. I so want her. Why the fuck did I ever let her go?

The striptease she did behind the door was gorgeous. So sexy without seeing anything really. God it turned me on. How much time has passed? Five minutes? Ten minutes? Maybe I should get up. That's it. Get up. I can't sleep anyway. But I don't want to get up. I'll have to hack it. I should've slept on the floor. How can Jason be so trusting? Beats me. Even over there, surely, he can feel the waves of sexual energy coming from this bed. Think of something else. Jesus. Those suspenders. When Jason swung her around and her dress hiked up. Holy crap. I wanted to rip her out of his arms and do her on the couch right there. Fuck! That's not something else!

Bloody hell, Ashley. Our feelings had reignited. How could I block him out? What about sheep? I could count sheep. One, two, three, four … nup, that one had a red silk sash. The sheets felt so good, soft, yet crisp; nothing felt better than expensive linen. Oh crikey, there he was again …

Don't think of her. Think of … beer. Types of beer … VB, Carlton Draft, Budweiser, Heineken, Corona, Guinness. Nup, no good. That one had a red ribbon round it. Try guns. Smith & Wesson, Beretta, Glock, Benelli, Colt, Heckler & Koch ... which gun shall I teach her to use ... she would look stunning packing heat. God it's hot in this bed. Too bloody hot. Stop thinking. Think of nothing ... nothing. Holy hell. I'm lying next to a bloody radiator. How far away is she? An arm's length? Her body's generating heat like a friggin' Weber. She's so still. Is she dead? Too hot to be dead. It's dark in here with those curtains. I've got to go to the gym, somehow get rid of this pent-up energy, or I'm going to punch out a wall.

The bed moved. What was that?

'Move over, Maggie,' Jason whispered. 'We're safe, nothing's happening. I need some sleep.' He slid into bed and reduced my Ashley buffer zone to about fifteen inches, calculating the increased radiant heat factor.

Ashley was as still as a rock. A very hot rock.

Jason fell asleep instantly and started snoring softly. I elbowed him and he rolled over, decreasing my buffer zone even further. This was a new form of torture. Exquisite and excruciating sheer torture, and all the while, Ashley's thoughts continued to echo in my head ...

Jason's in bed! Holy shit, is he mad? He's testing me. Must be. He's decreased my buffer zone to ... sixteen inches? Shit, what's he doing? He's pushed her too close ... six inches? That's it. I'm not going to be able to stop myself. What? He's snoring already! How can he sleep with her right there? What a waste. He doesn't appreciate what he's got. This is torture. Worse than Iraq. I have to touch her. But it's wrong. I have to. With the side of my hand, that's all, like an accident. I have to feel her skin.

My arms were straight at my sides. The radiant heat was at maximum degrees. If I reached out with my little finger, it would help me judge the distance. I made a poor imitation of Mister Spock's Vulcan salute and stretched out my pinky finger. A thousand volts of electricity coursed through my body as another pinky finger brushed across the top of mine and hooked around it.

Christ! I've got her little finger. Holy hell, my body's on fire. I'm never

242

letting you go. One finger! One fucking finger can do this?

I gasped from the energy of the touch. Two little fingers gripped tight in the most erotic pinkie swear ever to take place in the history of the universe.

Chapter 27: The Three Musketeers

I could see a hint of daylight coming through a crack in the blinds, glowing with tinges of pink and orange. With a final squeeze, Ashley unhooked my little finger.

'I'm going to the gym for a workout and swim,' he whispered.

'Want me to come?' Jason mumbled.

'Nah, I'm good. You stay here with Maggie. I won't be long.'

'No worries, mate. Don't forget to take a gun.'

'Got it already.' He displayed the pistol. 'Never left my hand all night.'

Crikey! In one hand, he'd had his finger wrapped around the trigger of a gun, and with the other hand, he'd had a finger wrapped around mine. Lucky he knew his left from his right. One wrong squeeze and we could've been history.

As I lay there, my level of sexual tension had moved into the red zone. Alarm bells were sounding. Every nerve ending tingled. I needed to go to the gym too, otherwise I'd explode. Jason caressed my body and I jumped violently, feeling a rush of energy discharge.

'Wow, you're sensitive.' He nuzzled my ear.

Every sound, every touch was heightened, magnified. I

moaned with the unbearable intensity of it. He lay on his side next to me and kissed my eyelids, my nose, my lips. He whispered into my ear and squeezed my breasts, tugging at my nipples. My body contracted involuntarily and I cried out with delight.

'My God, you're on fire.' Jason gave a sharp intake of breath as he slid his hand between my legs. He moved on top of me, held my face, kissed me. 'I want you now.'

I couldn't do it. It was wrong. The feeling wasn't for Jason. It was for Ashley. It would be like cheating. It was cheating. I'd cheated with Ashley in a pinky swear, and this buildup of sexual energy was for him, not Jason. It wasn't Jason's to take, but what should I do?

My mind spun out of control. I was a basket case. This was nuts. Ashley said people got too hung up on monogamy, but monogamy was peaceful, tender, respectful, dutiful, caring— boring sometimes, sure—but not crazy making like this.

'Where've you gone? You've zoned out on me.'

'Sorry.' I kissed him gently. 'I don't feel so good. I need a shower.'

'Is it something I did?' His expression was worried.

'No, not at all. I'm out of sorts. I've lost my sorts. A shower will help. And breakfast. I'm fine to use the bathroom.'

'I don't think that's a good idea given what happened in there. I'll take you to the health club, and I'll have one as well.'

'Thanks. I'm sorry.'

'I'm sorry too. I wish I could take you away; we need time to reconnect. We need to get "us" back.'

'That would be lovely. We need to, don't we?'

'Sure do,' he said.

'But, Jason, we can't. We've got to devise a plan to tackle this nightmare.'

He sighed, and his eyes seemed to droop. His mouth was tight and turned down, his gaze unfocused. 'Yup.'

I'd never seen him look so sad.

$$* * * * *$$

We made our way to the health club. It was early and there was hardly anyone around.

Through the glass doors of the gym, I saw Ashley running on a treadmill. The speed was dialed to max, and he moved like a machine, focused straight ahead, as though chasing some distant prey. His legs pounded the belt and his arms swung like pendulums as he thundered relentlessly on. His body dripped and glistened with sweat.

'Crikey, look at him go,' Jason said. 'He's running like his life depends on it.'

We entered and headed towards the showers, not wanting to interrupt, but he slowed his speed to a walk and acknowledged us with a wave.

'Is that a gun in your pocket or are you pleased to see me?' Jason asked him.

'It's gun, mate.'

And so it was—the outline obvious through his shorts.

'Be careful it doesn't go off in there,' I said.

He laughed. 'Which apparatus are you talking about?'

I'd walked right into that one. I felt myself blush. Jason rolled his eyes.

Ashley brushed back the hair from his face. 'You guys going to work out?'

'Just shower and a big breakfast,' Jason said. 'Come on, Maggie, I'm going to stand guard.'

'You go first, you're faster than me.'

'Okay, wait here. I'll be out in a tick.' He headed off to the men's change rooms.

Ashley stopped the treadmill. 'It was one hell of a night.' He stepped off, picked up a towel and wiped the treadmill thoroughly. His muscles flexed and gleamed while he worked.

'It sure was.'

He took another towel and wiped the sweat from his face and body, looking at me all the while.

I jumped as he gently touched my face. 'I've never felt anything like last night. It was a powerful thing. What's happened to us? I can't get it out of my body. I'm still on fire.'

'Me too.'

'You and Jason, you would've—'

'No.'

'You're kidding?'

'No.'

'Why the hell not? I would've.'

'Maybe so, but for me, it would have been like cheating on you.'

'How do you figure that?'

'The feeling, the energy is for you. It was from you, caused by you and me. It didn't seem right to release it using Jason. It's complicated, and it's doing my head in. So, I have our energy and I'll hold it, store it and treasure it. It will strengthen me. I know how energy works and there are consequences to its misuse. I know you think I'm weird. You wouldn't understand.'

His eyes glistened. 'I do understand, totally. That, sweetheart, is the nicest thing you could ever say to me. And do. Really, *not* do, if you get my drift. It's a gift. You're so lovely. Weird, but lovely.' He flashed me a grin, then extended his little finger and joined it with mine.

Jason appeared. 'Shower time. What's with the pinky swear?'

'Two musketeers,' Ashley said, 'just waiting for you.'

As Jason added his little finger to the collection, he started, oh, so slightly. His mouth tightened, and a fleeting expression flickered across his face. His brow furrowed and eyes narrowed slightly.

It was an expression I couldn't put my finger on. Did he know?

'The Three Musketeers!' he said.

---

27 *Maggie's Playlist: Your Cheating Heart — Bruno Capinan*

Chapter 28: The Swimming Pool

'Where, except in uncreated light, can the darkness be drowned?' — *C.S. Lewis*

I tried to scream.

I tried again, but my lungs were full of water.

Jason was on guard outside the cubicle and I was drowning in the shower.

My lungs were filled with fire, burning, tearing to shreds. I couldn't breathe. The tiles were cold on my back as I slid to the floor. A blessed calm descended on my oxygen starved brain. I left my body and hovered above Jason.

Jason saw my feet and legs on the floor under the gap of the cubicle door. 'Christ!' He pushed the door. 'Damn your security paranoia! It's fucking locked!' He gripped the top of the door, opened it with a swift kick, and grabbed my shoulders and shook me. 'Maggie! Can you hear me?' He felt for a pulse on my neck and listened for breathing. He raked his hair—something he did during brain overload—and said, 'I'm so sorry, Maggie,' and slapped me hard across the face.

'Aggghh!' I gasped as I crashed back into my body.

'Mags, I'm so—'

'It's Ashley,' I screamed. 'He's drowning. *Go!* Go now!'

Jason didn't stop to ask how, why or where. He leapt to his feet and ran five steps, before coming back to throw a robe around me and drag me with him.

We raced through the gym and slammed through the double doors to the swimming pool, shattering the glass in the small windows. Two bodies floated face down in the blood streaked water of the pool.

Where was the pool guy when we needed him? Probably dead.

Jason took a run and shot into the pool, a perfect forward pike which brought him right next to Ashley.

He held Ashley's bicep, flipped him over and swam him back to the side of the pool.

I stood on the edge, ready to help. 'What about the other guy?'

'Leave him!' Jason said.

'We can't leave him! He could be the pool guy for all we know.' I jumped into the water and swam towards the body.

'Maggie! For Christ's sake, get out of the pool!' Jason shouted, as he struggled to lift Ashley from the water.

I reached the body and it imploded into a patch of inky black sludge, glistening like an oil slick on the water. Thin black tendrils stretched out from the black sludge, circling out and around, then folding back in, as it started to spin.

'Guess that's not the pool guy, or maybe it was,' I muttered, frantically trying to swim away. I didn't even get my basic Australian swimming certificate, so 'trying' to swim away was the optimal word. I could get by in a normal pool, but this was like swimming against jets in a spa pool. I wasn't getting anywhere.

The water gurgled as it flowed into a slow-moving whirlpool. The vortex was getting stronger, judging by the assorted towels and floatation devices making their own way to the edge of the pool. If I didn't pull my finger out, I'd be sucked in along with them.

Jason hauled Ashley's limp, bleeding body from the water and checked his pulse and breathing. There obviously wasn't any, as he started compressing Ashley's sternum, both hands on his chest, arms straight, pumping vigorously. He counted, 'One, two, three, four ...'

It was at count twenty I realised I was in deep shit.

Jason could only save one person at a time. The strength of the whirlpool was such that if he came to rescue me we would both die, and then so would Ashley. There would be zero musketeers.

'Twenty-five, twenty-six, twenty-seven ...' Jason suddenly realised I was no closer to the edge. 'Christ! You're still in there!' His face filled with horror at the dawning realisation of our predicament. 'Thirty, thirty-one, thirty-two, thirty-three ...' He pushed Ashley onto his side and I knew he was coming for me.

My plan was two musketeers, not zero, so I lifted my arms in the air and shouted, 'I love you!' and stopped swimming.

The current snatched me in its arms and spun me around in a dance of death. It was like a ride at Wet 'n' Wild, but with this outcome, you'd seriously want your money back. The towels and floatation devices had already exited this universe, and the heavier weight items, like chairs and lounges were screeching their way across the tiles towards the pool.

Where would I end up? Would I be so much dust, or transmogrify into another universe? Given the nature of this entity, I didn't hold out much hope it would be a high frequency, positive energy environment. It would probably be a dead orgone energy universe, and trust me, that wouldn't be a pleasant place to hang out. Unless of course you were a demon, or some other badass entity.

I was a kind person; maybe my energy would make some small contribution to neutralising this bastard. I'd really miss my two musketeers and Boo.

The merry-go-round vortex was crazy fast, making me giddy and sick. A pole came straight for my head.

'Grab the pole! Grab it, Maggie!' Jason stood at the edge of the pool holding out a pole. I reached and missed, tried again, missed, tried again. The whirlpool held me trapped, spinning round at speed. Each pass brought me closer to the centre of the vortex. The deafening noise shattered my ears, pieces of furniture sailed past, the room around me blurred to obscurity. Jason appeared and disappeared as he stood reaching out to me. I was so dizzy I could barely see. Tenth time around, my hand connected to something. Gripping it tightly, I prayed it wasn't a chair heading into the vortex. I was dragged sideways through the whirlpool, and the spinning stopped as Jason grabbed my arm and hauled me out of the water.

'Get back in the shower room and stay there.' He pushed me towards the door and ran back to Ashley who'd been sucked to the edge of the pool and was now teetering on the brink of it.

He dragged Ashley underneath the stainless-steel pool ladder and squatted on top of him. Jason tucked his own legs under the steel supports and recommenced CPR. He obviously thought he couldn't lose another second, so wedged himself in, right at the edge of the pool.

The water was roaring, spinning and churning into the vortex. It was like watching a gigantic bathtub empty out. Stuff was flying everywhere. A chair narrowly missed Jason's head. He was still counting.

I couldn't stand there not helping, so I collected some thick rubber exercise tubing from the gym and tied it around my waist, securing it with the clips. I found a long metal pole with a hook at each end and secured one end to a railing outside the door. Inching to the end of the pole, I hooked myself onto it.

This brought me right next to Jason, who looked up at me in horror.

I'm not sure if it was the sight of a naked woman wrapped in orange bungee flapping at the end of a long pole that upset him, or the fact I'd interrupted his counting.

He just shook his head and kept desperately pumping.

Ashley's face was pale and unresponsive. I reached out to Ashley with my mind.

'Jason, let me! I know CPR. You need a break,' I shouted over the roaring of the whirlpool. He nodded and grabbed the pole with one hand and my bungee cords with the other, as I pumped steadily and determinedly on Ashley's chest.

The room sounded like the inside of a hurricane, so it was impossible to check for breathing. I couldn't feel a pulse. I started again, one hand over the other, pumping his chest for all I was worth. The noise and the chaos receded in my mind, until it was only Ashley and me.

'Come back, you bastard.'

Come back! Come back! Come back!

I pumped out the rhythm on his chest, screaming out in my mind for him.

But it was no good. He was dead, gone.

I cried and bent over his lifeless face, pinched his nostrils closed and placed my mouth over his. My tears splashed onto his cheeks.

His lips were dry and his mouth cold. I breathed into his lungs and watched his chest rise and fall. Drawing on the energy we'd created, the energy I'd earlier stored for him, for us, I breathed it back into him.

'I love you,' I whispered, as Jason pulled me away. There was a loud *thunk* as the black hole slammed shut. The swimming pool was empty and the surrounds were bare. The room was quiet.

Jason dragged Ashley's bleeding body out from between the pool steps and started CPR again. He stopped to check Ashley's pulse and breathing. I knew by the look on Jason's face there was nothing. Jason put his mouth over Ashley's and breathed into him. Ashley's chest rose and fell. His body convulsed violently. A flood of water abruptly gushed from his mouth.

Jason quickly rolled him onto his side as the torrent continued, pooling around Ashley's body.

Ashley coughed, spluttered and wiped his mouth with the back of his hand. He glared at Jason and said, 'Crikey, I know you love me mate, but *Jesus!*'

Footsteps sounded out behind us as a pool attendant rushed in. He stood, hands on head, trying to fathom why someone was administering CPR to a half-drowned person next to an empty swimming pool.

Ashley dragged himself on all fours and vomited a flood of water. And then another. He paused for a while, head down, face dripping, before turning and sitting on the floor. He pushed wet hair off his face and glanced up at us. His body was streaked with blood, and he had flecks of foam around his mouth. He looked like a train wreck.

'Thank you,' he croaked. 'I owe you big time.'

'You're bleeding.' I searched around for something to use to stem the blood flowing from a gash on his upper arm.

Ashley appraised my stark-naked body adorned with orange bungees. 'What on earth? Cover up, for God's sake.'

The pool attendant raced away and came back with robes, towels and a first aid kit. 'Excuse me, Miss,' he said, holding out a robe and looking the other way.

'I'll do it.' Jason took the robe and draped it around me before moving us to one side for some privacy and to remove the bungee cords. He stared into my eyes wanting to say something, then simply gave a half smile and tied my robe.

The pool guy tended to Ashley's wounds, and my heart lifted as colour returned to Ashley's face.

'We need to get you to the hospital straight away,' I said.

'I'm fine.'

'No, you don't understand. You're at risk of secondary drowning. You could still die. It happens all the time. You might seem fine but you can die soon after from leftover water and chemicals in your lungs. You could also have neurological damage.'

'I'm fine. You worry too much.'

'She worries because her best friend's son died from secondary drowning,' Jason said.

Ashley raised his chin in defiance. 'I'm sorry. But I feel fine and I'm not going to hospital. End of story.'

'You are a stupid, stubborn, silly man, Ashley Beringer. I'll be keeping an eagle eye on you then.'

'Right back at you, luv.'

The pool attendant finished bandaging Ashley and helped him to his feet. Ashley examined his shoulder. 'Thanks, mate. As good as new.'

'I don't think you are,' I said.

Ashley grinned. 'Nothing that a good breakfast won't fix.'

Chapter 29: Dromeus

'We can easily forgive a child who is afraid of the dark; the real tragedy of life is when men are afraid of the light.' — *Plato*

After a quick clean up and change of clothes, we headed off for breakfast. It amazed me we even wanted to eat after the emotional and physical trauma of the morning, but our energy reserves were so depleted, we were ready to do some serious damage to the breakfast buffet.

We sat at the table and surveyed the food laden plates before us.

Jason examined my choice. 'Bacon, eggs, hash brown, fried tomatoes and toast. You are so predictable.'

I crunched away on my hash brown. 'You should be grateful I am, given everything else isn't.'

'Too true.'

'As I've said before, all this action makes me appreciate my food.'

Ashley laughed. 'Jeez, Mags, I hadn't ever noticed you not appreciating your food.'

'Oh, ha, ha.' I wrinkled my nose at him. 'You know what else I appreciate more than anything?'

'What?'

'Looking across the table and seeing you two here, with me, alive.' Tears pricked in my eyes.

'Ditto,' they said.

'At one stage, I seriously thought there would be zero musketeers.'

Jason's mouth was in stern mode. 'I need to have a word with you later, about a couple of things.'

'Ooh, sounds ominous.'

'What things?' Ashley was always the sticky beak. 'Come on, spill the beans. Don't mind me.' He flashed me a cheeky grin.

God, it was good to see his smile again.

'Ash, let me fill you in with what happened from our end,' Jason said, 'and then you can enlighten us about what happened to you.'

I stood. 'I'm going to get coffee,' I said. 'Want some?'

I received two nods in the affirmative and made a beeline for the barista.

I returned with a tray carrying two flat whites and one very hot, very strong, long black.

'Did you get it very hot?'

'Yes. As if I didn't know by now.'

'Miss Maggie, I can't believe what you did,' Ashley said. His arms were crossed and his expression was serious as he glared at me from under his eyebrows.

'Why do I get the feeling I'm in trouble? You only call me Miss Maggie when I've done something wrong, according to your weird standards anyway.'

'Suicide?'

'What do you mean?'

'That's what Jason told me. You stopped swimming, gave up, chucked in the towel, let it take you. That would be classed as suicide, even by my weird standards, Miss Maggie.'

I didn't like how he described my actions, and I was upset to think Jason perceived it that way.

What a pair of scumbags to lay this on me after all we'd been through. I couldn't believe it. I wished I was back in the morgue where I could tuck myself away in a locker, shut the door and never come out, except maybe for someone decent who had at least half a brain.

Various responses came to mind, and even though the words burned on my lips, I zipped my mouth rather than say something I'd regret.

I collected my coffee and breakfast with as much poise as I could muster. 'I won't even dignify that with a response. Excuse me.' I stomped around the corner to the next alcove. No one, but no one, was going to spoil my breakfast after everything I'd been through.

And yes, it was now '*I'd* been through', not '*we'd*' been through'. I was seriously over the whole 'we' thing; it was all too hard, too weird and too complicated. Give me the simple 'I' life. Enough already. If anyone came and interrupted my breakfast I'd stab them with my fork.

Suicide? *Really?* Huh. Maybe on some level it was. I guess technically it could be viewed as suicide, but for me it was a sacrifice, motivated by love. An action taken to save the guys. I guess self-sacrifice was suicide because you would have intentionally caused your own death to preserve the life of another.

My head started to hurt—this subject was way too heavy for breakfast time—but thinking about their point of view dispersed my outrage. I filed the thoughts away in a box labeled Self Sacrifice/Suicide.

Feeling happier, I focused on another important thing; my piece of bacon.

'Is this seat taken?' a man asked politely.

I gave him the once over for any visible signs of tattoos but couldn't see any. 'No, be my guest.' I pushed out a chair with my foot. I'd always wanted to do that. I felt like the female equivalent of Ashley.

The universe had intervened—the chap arrived a split second

before Jason and Ashley. Now they couldn't give me a hard time, and I could finish my breakfast in peace, and maybe, have a decent conversation in the process. The fellow seemed likeable and pleasing to the eye to boot. I surreptitiously checked him out. Jason and Ashley hung about wondering what to do.

The chap would have to have been nearly six-foot-tall, lanky, not much meat on his bones, short blond hair brushed back off his face. He was a cross between Tom Cruise and Richard Gere. Nice. His clothes were a kind of understated urban cool, good skin, brown eyes and a big smile. All up, pretty darn good company for breakfast.

'I'm Maggie. And you are?'

'Dromeus.' He extended his hand. 'People call me Drom for short.'

I shook his hand; his grip was warm and firm. There was an immediate sense of connection and it made me jump. It was as if I knew him from another life. His energy washed over every cell in my body.

He checked me out and said, 'It looks like you live on the edge.'

'What do you mean by that?' I said, thinking maybe he meant I looked like crap.

'You've got blood on your neck, a scratch and puncture mark, your hands are grazed, nails torn, your demeanor appears soft but you've got wildness written all over you.'

Yep, I looked like crap. I felt my face turn red.

'Say what you think, why don't you? You're very observant.'

'I know.'

Oh hell, I had another Ashley on my hands—uber confident.

'I've cultivated my powers of observation and I'm incredibly intuitive,' he said by way of explanation. 'I didn't mean to embarrass you, sorry. Sometimes I don't realise I've said things out loud.'

'That's okay. It happens to me too.'

He focused on his iPhone and his thumb flicked quickly and incessantly through pages. He seemed to have forgotten about me. This dude's behaviour was definitely eccentric. He looked up and caught me staring.

'Sorry, I didn't mean to stare. Are you actually reading?'

'I speed read. First book today, nearly finished. I usually go through a couple a day.'

Jesus, Drom was my kind of guy.

'Two books a day, that's incredible, even for speed reading. How do you find the time?'

'I read everywhere and I don't sleep much. It's a waste of time. I practise polyphasic sleep techniques.'

'Polyphasic?'

'I sleep three hours in the early morning and then three twenty minutes naps during the day. That's it.'

'What do you do with your extra time, besides read?'

'I'm a traceur.'

Crikey, this guy had me fascinated. In the space of sixty seconds he'd already introduced me to two things I hadn't heard of.

'Traceur?' I hoped I wasn't starting to sound like an echo machine.

'Like parkour.'

'Parkour?' I said, despite myself.

'Have you heard of free running?'

'Yes!' Thank God I didn't have to do the echo thing again. 'It's where people run up walls and flip and spin over obstacles?'

'Parkour and free running are similar, except parkour doesn't involve all the flips and spins; it's about moving through your environment simply and efficiently. It makes you see your world in a whole new way. It comes in handy when trying to escape from the zombie apocalypse.' He flashed me a grin.

Crikey, for a minute I'd thought he might be serious.

I smiled back and rubbed the needle mark with my finger.

'Sounds like I need to get me some parkour training.'

He seemed to want to talk and I was curious, so I said, 'What do you do to earn a living when you're not being a traceur?'

'A bit of this and that.'

Oh, he seriously could be Ashley's brother.

'Sorry, I didn't mean to be nosey.'

'I'm unorthodox when it comes to work. I play the stock market and do well at it. I prospect for gold; I'm a barista, bar tender, graphic designer, masseur, personal trainer, and I make and sell orgonite. Because I don't sleep much, I fill my time learning everything I can, hence I can turn my hand to most things.'

He'd lost me after the word orgonite. Or was it barista—no, masseur. No, really, it was orgonite. Who the hell did I have here who made and sold orgonite? I'd made a piece of orgonite myself once, out of fibreglass resin, metal shavings and some quartz crystal. It was excellent for clearing out negative energy in your body and from the environment. Maybe he wasn't kidding about the zombie apocalypse after all.

'Why do you deal with orgonite?'

'You know what it is?'

'Yes.'

'Then you know why.'

I hadn't thought about using orgonite in our battle against the Dark Force. It was pooh-poohed by the scientific community, but folks in touch with the spiritual realms swore by its ability to transmute negative energy in the environment and in our bodies. Could it help me get rid of the residue in my body? It was easy to make.

'Penny for your thoughts, Maggie.'

I jumped. 'How do you know my name?'

'Ah, you *told* me.'

'Oh, oh, sorry! Yes, of course, I uh, people ...'

'It's complicated?'

'That's probably an understatement. What brings you here, by the way?'

'I'm here for a reason.'

'Which would be?'

'I don't know yet.'

'When will you know?'

'When you tell me.'

It appeared the cryptic conversation could go all day, but it seemed the ball was now in my court.

'To help me eliminate the Dark Force?'

'I'm at your disposal.'

Hmm. I liked the sound of that. But could I trust him? I didn't know him from a bar of soap. Maybe he was working for the enemy, a dark spy trying to infiltrate our ranks. It wasn't a silly idea and I knew that's what the guys would say, for sure.

'Of course, you don't trust me. You don't know me. Your friends over there wouldn't trust me either.' He nodded his head in their direction. 'And that's fine, I totally understand. Here's my card. Call me, or think of me, if and when the time is right.'

I took his card, which simply had his name, Dromeus, and a mobile phone number.

How much did he charge for his Dark Force elimination services? What did he do exactly?

'By the way, I don't charge for Dark Force related services. I consider it voluntary work.'

'Are you telepathic?'

Drom met my eyes and I knew the answer.

He stood and took my hand. 'It's been a pleasure.'

His energy poured into me. It was pure, almost angelic in nature, and I found it mesmerising. 'By the way, what book are you reading?' I asked.

'David and Goliath: Underdogs, Misfits and the Art of Battling Giants, by Malcolm Gladwell.'

I laughed. 'Perfect!'

262

'Oh, and Maggie,' he said, still holding my hand, his soft eyes looking straight into my soul, 'it's the ultimate *sacrifice*, and they know it.'

My arm was alive with goose bumps.

He raised an eyebrow. 'Maybe it will be Four Musketeers?'

Oh Jesus.

---

[29] *Maggie's Playlist: All For Love — From 'The Three Musketeers" —* Bryan Adams, Sting, Rod Stewart

Chapter 30: Plan of Attack

After Drom left, Jason and Ashley waited a respectable time, say five seconds, before coming over to my table.

I knew I had the upper hand.

'Ashley, would you mind getting me another cup of coffee?'

'Sure, no worries,' he said, heading off to the barista.

'Jason, would you mind getting me a croissant?'

'Sure, chocolate or plain?'

'Plain is fine, perhaps some butter and jam?'

They dutifully carried out their orders and my heart burst with love for them both, despite their annoying tendencies.

Their task fulfilled, they pulled up chairs and joined me. I was laying bets as to what the first question would be.

'Who the hell was that guy?' they asked simultaneously.

Bingo.

'Drom.'

Ashley looked extremely pissed off. 'Drom? What sort of a name is that? You shouldn't be talking to strange guys; it's too frigging dangerous.'

Jason took heed of the look on my face and glared at Ashley. 'I want to say sorry about what Ashley said before. It was totally out of order.'

Ashley glared back at Jason. 'What do you mean, what I said? You're the one who said it. I was repeating the message.'

'You said ...'

I raised my hand to quiet them.

'No more. Please. No more glaring, no more of this ... this stuff. We love each other; that's all that matters. We have had to, and will have to, deal with so much. We need to be gentle with each other. The three of us have such a strong bond; we love each other more than life. We know we would sacrifice ourselves for each other. This bickering has to stop, so please, enough already.'

Jason nodded. 'Yes, I'm sorry. Of course.'

'Sure, luv. Can I say one thing?'

I nodded.

'Thank you. With all my heart, thank you.'

'Ditto,' Jason said. He held my face and kissed me.

I took a sip of my coffee. Ashley was staring at me, elbows on the table, wrists crossed, chin resting on fists linked together by a pinkie swear.

Say no more.

* * * * *

Back in the hotel room, we set about packing and cleaning up the mess we'd made. I was tidying the bedroom when Ashley came in and closed the door. 'Maggie, got a minute?'

'Sure, what's wrong?' I joined him by the door.

'I need to talk to you. I know you said you didn't want to, but things are unsaid, and they have to be said.'

'Okay, fire away.'

'I wanted to thank you for saving my life, and for wanting to sacrifice your life for me, for us. I was angry when Jason told me what you'd done, thinking how I ... we nearly lost you.'

'Thanks, but Jason saved you. He's the hero. I only mucked things up.'

'You didn't muck things up, you were concerned about the other guy, and that's what makes you light. That's what will win us the war. Both of you saved my life. But it was this,' he said, linking into a pinky swear, 'the energy you saved, breathed back into me. That's what restored me. I was gone, but you brought me back.'

'I'm glad you made it.'

'If I didn't make it, I would have come back as a ghost and haunted you forever,' he said, flashing me his trademark grin.

'So, you understand where I was coming from?' I asked.

'Of course. I would have done exactly the same, and I'm sorry for what I said. I was angry at the thought of you throwing your life away because of me. Can you forgive me?'

'I already have.'

'I shouldn't do this.' He leant forward and kissed me. One hand moved around my waist to hold me up, anticipating knee problems. Breaking his kiss, he groaned and whispered in my ear—which did set off my knees—'Thank you, oh God, I just w—'

The door jarred behind us. Jason was trying to come in, pushing against the door. Ashley kissed me again.

'Jesus!' I pulled away and ran to the bathroom. That bathroom.

Bang! The bedroom door flew open. 'What's going on? You guys had me worried. Where's Maggie?'

'In the bathroom.'

Jason came to the bathroom door. 'Everything all right?'

'All good.'

'Can I come in?'

'Yes.'

When Jason opened the door, I was brushing my hair, looking in the mirror where I last saw Dylan's face.

'Are you coping in here?'

'Yes, surprisingly. It seems telling you about Dylan actually

266

helped, as painful as it was to share.'

'Sorry about what happened before, the whole suicide thing. It's my fault. I was angry because you broke your promise. You promised you'd never leave, remember? In the hospital?'

I nodded.

He gripped my arms. 'I'd rather be dragged into the damn vortex with you, than be left here without you. What we have is precious, it's deep and profound. We have to protect it. We have to fight for each other, defend what we have. Do you understand?'

I nodded.

'Promise if we go, we'll go together?'

'Promise,' I said, not entirely sure it was a promise I could keep. 'Thank you for saving me, Jace. I put everyone at risk and you saved Ashley too, despite everything. You were amazing,' I said, gazing up into his eyes.

'Risk or no risk, it doesn't matter, because you care about people. That's a good thing. I love you for it, Maggie.' He put an arm around my shoulders and chuckled to himself. 'And, I will never, ever, forget the image of you, naked at the end of a pole, tied in orange bungee.'

I laughed. 'I won't forget the look on your face either. I love you, mister superhero. You were relentless.'

Jason indicated with his head towards the bedroom. 'I couldn't stand to lose him, even though he's a serious pain in the arse at times.'

'Aren't we all?'

Jason nodded.

* * * * *

Ashley was on the phone as we came back into the lounge. 'Sure, thanks Mel, I'll let you know.' He hung up. 'That was Mel on reception. She called to say the hotel has offered us an additional night, complimentary, with dinner and drinks on the house, plus a spa treatment of our choice. What do you reckon?'

'Why would they do that?' I said.

'Not sure. I think Mel had something to do with it. Probably hates to see me leave.'

I rolled my eyes.

'Dead set? That's fantastic!' Jason said.

'So, what do you guys want to do?' Ashley asked.

'I think Maggie wants to go home and check on Boo.'

I nodded in agreement.

'If Boo was all right, would you stay?'

'I guess so.' I did like the sound of the spa treatment and welcomed another excuse not to go home to the mess.

Ashley turned to Jason. 'What if I order a couple of wagyu beef steaks from the hotel, drive back to your place, check on Boo, give her a big feed of gourmet meat and then come back. We can go home tomorrow. Would you rest easy and enjoy yourself then?'

'Good idea, Jason said, 'but I should go, and you should rest up here.' He nodded at Ashley's arm, which was bleeding through the bandages a little.

'Ashley, you're bleeding!' I carefully unwrapped the bandage and removed it to reveal an angry looking welt running across his upper bicep. 'This needs to be redressed. It looks nasty. What happened anyway? We never got to debrief.'

'Gunshot. Dodged a bullet, but it clipped me. It'll be fine, don't fuss.'

'No, don't fob me off. What happened exactly?'

'I was about to dive into the pool when my spidey sense kicked in. Luckily, I moved in the right direction and the bullet missed. The guy was behind me, so I stepped back and kicked his legs out from under him. He hit the concrete and dropped the gun. The dude grabbed my legs and was trying to get the gun, so I whacked him and he fell into the pool dragging me with him. I think I cracked my head on the side going in. That's the last I remember until I woke with Jason kissing me.' He wiped his mouth with the back of his hand and grimaced at Jason. 'Wished we'd managed to save the gun; it had a silencer an' all.'

'Bugger,' I said.

'Shame,' Jason agreed. 'So, it appears the roach entity is not only out to get Maggie, but those associated with her as well.'

'Seems like it,' Ashley said. 'There are people out there who don't like me, but not enough to want to kill me.'

Jason clutched his phone so hard the casing creaked. His face was drawn and tight. 'What's our plan? We have to prepare a strategy. How the hell do we tackle this? We're being hunted, fighting off one thing after another, trying to survive. We can't go on like this. We're on the back foot all of the time—we've got to turn things around.'

Ashley could see Jason was anxious and frustrated. 'Yeah, Jace, go easy. We're doing the best we can. Do you think I like being on the run? But we're just finding out what we're dealing with, and we ain't got much to go on. You have to know the enemy to be able to defeat it, and we're not there yet. We've got no intel. It's early days.'

'Early days? At this rate, we'll all be dead.'

'Jason! Don't talk like that.'

'Well, you're the psychic. Come on give us something, Maggie. I can't keep going like this, lurching from one catastrophe to another, always looking over my shoulder. Step up and give me something useful for once.'

The tone and the force of his words shocked me. Jason had sunk into a pit of negativity. It wasn't like him. Is that how he thought of me—useless?

Ashley slammed his fist on the table. 'Hey! You're out of line, mate.'

Don't cry. Don't cry. I started to count the coloured metal leaves on a nearby artwork. One, two, three, four, five, six, seven … I was useless. I should've known what to do. I should've had more insight. I should've been better … eight, nine, ten … I should have left. It was all my fault. I should've been smarter. I should've been stronger. Eleven, twelve, thirteen—leaf number thirteen had words on it—"Live every moment, Laugh every day, Love beyond words."

I started, the words awakening me from the spiral of negativity. Jason and Ashley were staring at me.

Jason looked crestfallen. 'We were in its grip, weren't we?'

I nodded.

'Fuck,' Ashley whispered.

'I didn't mean what I said, Maggie. I'm sorry.'

'One thing we can do is keep bringing our awareness back to the present moment. Endeavour not to let ourselves get lost in thought. That's how it attacks and undermines us. It's subtle and deadly. We can only take things moment by moment and believe the answers will come. We have to trust in not knowing. It's hard not to have a plan, but there is one for us, we just don't know the details. We have to let go of trying to be in control. I know you, Jason. You want strategy, action steps, outcomes, guarantees and a resolution with no loose ends. Life doesn't work that way, particularly now. We do have a plan. We have to go with the flow. The flow is the plan, Jason. Trust it.'

Jason took my hand. 'I trust you, Maggie. You're right.'

Ashley added his hand to ours. 'Go with the flow—that's the plan. Suits me.'

'We need to ring Inspector Johnston back!' I said, suddenly recalling the voice message Jason received yesterday.

'Hell, I forgot.'

'Why don't you ring now? Then you or Ashley can go home to check on Boo. When you get back we can have a massage and then spend the rest of the evening relaxing and opening ourselves to any insights on how to deal with this.'

'I'll get on the blower now.'

'I'll organise the steaks,' Ashley said.

'I'll arrange the spa treatment.' I looked forward to having a relaxing and uneventful day for once.

'What's that for?' Jason said.

I'd unconsciously crossed my fingers.

---

[30] *Maggie's Playlist: Go With The Flow — Sara Niemietz —Fountain and Vine EP*

Chapter 31: Truth & Desperation

"It matters not how fast light may travel, darkness shall always be there awaiting its arrival." — Mark W. Boyer

Detective Inspector Johnston wanted to see us immediately. He was currently working at city headquarters so suggested we meet him there. The three of us headed off together. It was only a ten-minute walk from the hotel, and we conferred about the details of our hospital story.

'Are we sticking with the affair story?' Ashley asked.

'Can't think of anything else which would make sense,' Jason said. 'There shouldn't be any evidence at the hospital, other than footage of us going to the basement and back. I wonder why he really wants to see us?'

'They have a missing person. Mick the morgue guy, so they'd want to interview everyone in the vicinity at the time, and we'd be on the CCTV,' Ashley said.

'Yeah, of course.'

'It would be weird if we arrived together,' Ashley said. 'I should rock up separately. I mean, if I've supposedly been screwing your girl, we wouldn't still be best buddies, would we?'

"Kin Oath,' Jason said. 'We'll go first. I did say to the Inspector I sent you a text.'

'I'll split and go for a wander, then lob in. There's a twenty-four-hour clinic around the corner. I'll get 'em to fix my dressing.'

'We'll meet you back at the hotel for lunch,' Jason said.

Ashley gave us the thumbs up and headed off.

At police HQ, Detective Inspector Johnston showed Jason into an interview room. I was asked to wait outside.

I couldn't wait to get it over with. I sat on a plastic chair and listened to the water cooler motor humming nearby. The linoleum floors reminded me of the hospital. Why did all institutions look the same? Maybe there was some institutional master planner out there who churned out these hideous designs. If you got well in a hospital, it was nothing to do with the healing ambience of the environment or the food, that was for sure.

A young constable approached. 'Maggie, would you like a coffee while you wait?'

I jumped visibly, as I seemed to do these days, on hearing my name.

'What sort of coffee?' I asked, expecting it to come from a mega jumbo sized can of International Roast.

'Nespresso.'

'Excellent, thank you. Do you recycle the pods?'

'Of course. What blend would you like, and do you take milk?'

'Roma and milk please, only half a cup. Thanks so much.'

'No worries, I'll do my best.'

While I waited, I stared at the brown stained, watermarked ceiling panels, and then at the poor sunlight starved plant languishing on the small table next to me. How was Jason going? Was there a good cop and a bad cop giving him the once over? Were they blowing smoke in his face? Not with the OH&S regulations these days.

The young constable returned and handed me the coffee. 'Here you go.' I glimpsed the black spider legs of a tattoo peeking out from under his cuff.

He handed me a bag. 'Here's a Krispy Crème doughnut as

well.'

'Th…thanks,' I stammered, feeling the blood drain from my face.

'Do you feel sick? You look pale.'

'Nun, no. That's how I am,' I mumbled, as a surge of adrenaline coursed through my body. Scanning the environment for weapons, I fixed my eye on a pointy umbrella resting against the wall.

'I'll leave you to it then,' he said, walking away.

I exhaled. I'd been holding my breath. My body felt weak and limp.

I tipped the coffee into the plant. Would it wilt and turn to dust? Nothing happened. I threw the doughnut in the bin opposite me. Bingo! Direct hit. My aim was improving.

The second hand on the clock opposite ticked over the seconds. The tick, tick, tick got louder as any minute I expected the constable to come back and offer me a Taser instead of a coffee.

Finally, the door opened and I jumped. Jason appeared, looking as sombre as I must've looked pale.

'Maggie, can you come in now?' Inspector Johnston said. I wanted to say no, but figured it was a statement not a question.

'You look pale,' he said to me. 'Would you like me to organise a coffee for you?'

'No!' I said much too loudly. 'I mean, sorry, no, but thank you so much for asking.'

Jason gave me a look.

The interview room was as inspiring as the space outside, and it smelt stale, like polyester and old socks. I imagined how I must look sitting directly under the fluorescent lights, a vision of paleness.

'I need you to account for your movements while you were at St. Joseph's Hospital.'

I giggled at the thought of having to account for my bowel

movements.

'Something funny?'

'Sorry, no. I giggle when I'm nervous.'

'No need to be. Tell me where you went while you were at the hospital, and if you noticed anything untoward.'

I told him as simply and clearly as I could my whereabouts on the day.

'Why did you go to Level B5?'

'I was stretching my legs, having a look around.'

'Is that so? And did you see anyone or notice anything at all when you were there?'

I sat silent as the reality of what I was doing hit me. I was going to lie to an officer of the law. I stressed when I received a speeding fine, so this was going against my law-abiding nature. What if I told him the truth? But I couldn't. We had to stick to the story, he wouldn't believe me if I told the truth anyway. I'd be locked in an institution far worse than this one.

'Maggie?'

I looked down at my hands.

'You need to tell me the truth.'

I took a deep breath. 'I went to level B5 because I'm having, I mean was having, an affair with Ashley Beringer. We met there to talk about things. That's all. I didn't see anyone else. The place was creepy and deserted.'

'And then?'

'Jason found us there together; he'd suspected something and came looking for me. They argued, pushed each other around; it became intensely heated. I managed to calm them down, call a truce, and we left.'

'And then?'

'We talked in the café. I got upset and left the table. Ashley ran after me and tried to convince me to go back to Jason.'

'That's confirmed in the CCTV footage we have. I'd like to show it to you.' He turned a laptop around to face me.

I nodded mutely, feeling whatever blood I had left in my face rapidly leave.

He pressed play and there, depicted in fifty grainy shades of grey, was Ashley and I locked in a passionate kiss. Entrance Jason, the fall, the table smash, the save and the exit. I tried to look on the positive side: it would've made a fabulous movie scene.

'Any comments?'

'Only two. We'll pay for the table and did Jason see this?'

'Yes.'

Yup, that was it. The three-letter word I was dreading.

There was a knock at the door and the young constable poked his head in. My heart rate ramped up to high.

'Ashley Beringer is here for you, sir.'

'Thanks, I'll be right out. Oh, and don't bring Mr. Beringer here. Hold him in a spare room until I'm ready.'

'Yes, Sir.' The constable looked directly at me before closing the door.

'Thanks for doing that,' I said.

'Don't want any fisticuffs on my watch. How are things travelling now, with Jason?'

'Now? I'm not sure,' I said truthfully.

'And Ashley?'

'Not sure what's going to happen there either.'

'And to confirm, you didn't see or hear anything else while you were on level B5?'

'Not a thing.'

If there was a hidden camera under the table, they'd see my fingers were crossed.

'I'll need to speak with you again, but that's it for now,' he said, opening the door.

Jason sat outside, his face set to grim and serious mode. His hawk eyes latched onto mine and narrowed to maximum laser beam intensity. The side of his mouth twitched and he ran both hands through his hair.

Jesus. All signs pointed to another interrogation with a capital 'I'. Inspector Johnston's interrogation would be a cakewalk compared to what I'd be in for. Would Jason request the use of a room and some thumbscrews, or even better, some Pentothal?

'Let's go!' Jason said. He took my arm and marched me along the hallway.

'Hey, stop that!' I yanked free.

We made our way through the corridors of police HQ in silence.

I hated this. Just hated it. It'd only been a kiss! My head whirled sensing Jason's maelstrom mind. I couldn't get anything concrete, only an oppressive wall of negative energy that overwhelmed me. S.O.S. I wanted to run away, to get a ticket to anywhere and leave everything behind. Go away, Jason. Go away, Ashley. Boo. Roaches. Dark Force. Everything. Everyone. They could all fuck off. Breathe Maggie. Breathe. Think of ... dolphins. Stuff dolphins. I wanted to run.

So I did. I ran. I took off as fast as my legs could carry me. I ran through corridors so fast that doors and faces blurred into one. I ran through city streets, pushing through people. I ran, and I ran, and I ran, and I ran some more, until my lungs felt like they were exploding, until I fell, smashed, crashed, blasted into a lake, in beautiful gardens, somewhere.

I floated face down staring at weeds and fish lit by sunlight and sky. A paddle of a duck's leg, the golden flick of a fin, rhubarb red water lily stems, a snow-white bud reaching for the sky. I wanted to rid myself of the physical body, to be absorbed by the beauty of the world, transformed into energy, because that's where I belonged. Not here. Not now. Not me. Take me home. Please.

And so I died. I let myself go.

Huh. It was true. It wasn't sacrifice: it was suicide. I'd been fooling everyone else into thinking I was a hero.

My lungs burned as they filled with water. No worries, I'd experienced that before. The voices in my head whispered … don't resist Maggie, don't fight for life. Life's too hard, too wrong, too bad, too complicated. Give it up. Let go. Die already.

But what about the people who loved and counted on me? I'd devastate them, now and forever. What legacy would I leave? It was easy to die, much harder to live, to face what I needed to face, to do what I needed to do. My heart had to be burned in the fires of this world before I could feel peace in the next.

Yes. *Yes.* What had I done? Too late. It was too late.

The world slammed back into me as I vomited lake water and weed.

I clutched at mud and grass. I smelt mud and grass. I tried to focus but couldn't see.

A face, no … only eyes, kaleidoscope eyes bringing me back, eyes like swirling rainbows, galaxies, starlight and raindrops, no, soft brown eyes bringing me back. Hands touching my head. Caressing golden energy. Radiance infusing me with love, returning me, cleansing me, linking me to my source.

Click.

Reconnection.

Divine bliss and restoration.

The face came into focus.

'Dromeus?'

'Yes. Feeling better?'

'Much. You saved me. You fixed me. How did you find me?'

'It wasn't hard; your energy spike was like an atom bomb. You can run. I thought I'd lost you.'

'I can run?'

'Super fast.'

'Wow. I always came last in school races.'

'Not anymore. Let me help you.'

He held my hand and I floated to my feet. I felt light and alive.

'What did you do to me, other than save my life?'

'Helped you reconnect to your source. Your link was damaged by the Dark Force, nearly gone. That's why you felt like you did.'

'Yes ... yes, it seems obvious now. I couldn't believe I hadn't realised what was happening.'

'Hardly your fault, it's insidious, like depression, sucking away your light and life. We should go to the hospital, get you checked out. Secondary drowning is an issue.'

I took a deep breath; the air flowed in and out of my lungs easily and effortlessly. I sent my mind deep into my body sensing and scanning. My body hummed with energy, and I sensed the water, weed and debris atomise and evaporate. Crystal power pulsed through the cells of my body as if I'd had recent contact. It appeared that Drom's intervention had changed my physiology. Just how powerful was he?

'I'm fine. But could you walk me back to the hotel? I'm lightheaded.'

'Of course.' He smiled and plucked green weed out of my hair. 'You're covered in lake weed; you look like a mermaid.'

I smiled back at him. 'I don't care.'

The joy and power of love—the ultimate connection—flooded back into my soul. My body tingled with light and I involuntarily turned my face upwards. The sensation was as warm and uplifting as sunlight after a thousand dark winter days.

---

31 *Maggie's Playlist: S.O.S. —ABBA*

Chapter 32: Lies & Domination

Drom held my hand to ground me as we wended our way back through the botanical gardens. The plants, trees, flowers and grass gleamed with golden light; I could feel the energy of the universe pulsing through everything. We walked in silence our minds linked, but without thought.

'This is how it should be,' I said.

'This is how it is.'

'It is?'

'We've lost our connection to what really is. Most people are slaves to their own minds, lost in a constant stream of thoughts triggered by emotions, which trigger more thoughts, more emotions, and so it goes in an endless stream of unreality, which seems real. It's a construct of our minds. That's why so many people have a continuous sense of dis-ease and discontent running in the background of their minds. Most people are lost, unconscious of the true reality. They're searching the world for what's right in front of them, or rather inside them. Oh, and Maggie, what happened then was suicide. The other was self-sacrifice. You've now experienced the difference. It was the Dark Force driving you to despair. That's what it does. You're fine now.'

'What about the residue? Can you tell if it's still there?'

'I don't want to go looking for it, so I'm not sure. But you'll be better able to deal with it now your source connection is strong again.'

'I can't thank you enough.'

He squeezed my hand. 'My pleasure.'

The world shimmered with luminosity and beauty as we ambled along a Paris-like street towards the hotel. It was difficult to differentiate myself from anything. People, cars, concrete, birds, grass, litter—all boundaries were indistinct.

Ashley exited the hotel, saw me, and loped towards us. A hand grabbed my shoulder from behind and spun me round, breaking my connection with Drom. It was Jason.

He registered my sodden, mud and weed-covered clothes. 'Jesus, what happened?'

Ashley bounded to a stop, grabbed my shoulders and asked the same question. Jason pushed him away. 'Get off her.' He glared at Drom. 'Why are you here?'

'Maggie fell into a lake and I pulled her out.'

Drom obviously didn't want to elaborate or play the hero, but I wanted them to know. 'That's something of an understatement. I was dead. Drowned. Gone. Drom resuscitated me, brought me back. The Dark Force damaged my connection to the light. Drom healed and restored it. The Dark Force was at it again. It drove me to take my life.'

Jason looked shocked. His breathing was rapid and shallow. Ashley's hands tightened into fists. I could feel what he wanted to do, more than anything, but he held himself back. Why the hell couldn't we just have a group hug for Christ's sake? I loved them both and they loved me.

Jason wrapped his arms around my shoulders and held me. He seemed more upset than I was. Ashley banged his fist gently against a light pole, but the look on his face was far from gentle.

'Drom, I owe you big time,' Jason said. 'Thank you for saving

Maggie's life. I can never repay you.'

Drom's face was serene and lit by a gentle smile. 'No thanks necessary.'

'Ditto,' Ashley said. He gave Drom the thumbs up, but his brow was furrowed, his jaw tight. His eyes burned into mine.

'We better get you some dry clothes,' Jason said. 'Drom, why don't you come to the hotel with us, have a drink, some lunch?'

'I've a couple of things to do first. What about I meet you at 12:30 pm in the bar?'

'See you then,' Jason said. 'Thanks again.'

Jason pushed past Ashley. 'You Ms. Maggie, have some explaining to do.' He gripped my arm and steered me towards the hotel. 'I was worried sick,' he said, removing bits of slimy weed from my hair.

We headed towards the hotel lifts, with Ashley following quietly, a few steps behind. Jason's grip on my arm was intensifying with each step, and by the time we reached the lifts he was hurting me.

I tried to pull free. 'Let go, you're hurting.' His gaze was a million miles away, focused on something in his own head, and his grip intensified. The lift doors opened. 'You're *hurting!* Let go!' I jerked my arm again.

Ashley's resistance broke as the lift doors closed with us inside. He stepped forward, grabbed Jason's arm and pushed him hard against the side of the lift. 'What the fuck are you doing? Let her go. You're hurting her.'

Jason released me and swung a punch, full force, at Ashley. Ashley blocked it. Jason slammed into Ashley's chest with both hands and pushed him against the doors. The air rushed out of his lungs.

'Stop it! Stop it now!' I screamed at them.

Jason launched another ferocious punch and Ashley blocked that one too. Ashley was holding himself back. 'Mate, settle, stop!'

'Don't you friggin' mate me,' Jason growled, shaping up for another swing. 'You're no mate of mine.'

Thankfully the ding of the lift indicated our floor and not the start of the next boxing round.

The guys faced the front of the lift, brushed the hair from their eyes and straightened their clothes.

We hurried silently back to our room. Ashley opened the door and guided me in, hand on my back. Jason knocked his hand away. 'Back off.'

Ashley dashed straight for the hotel phone and spoke to Mel about getting my clothes laundered. He hung up and said, 'She said they can clean your clothes right away and have them back within the hour. She's sending someone to collect them.'

'Thanks.' I went into the bathroom and closed the door. I pulled off my sodden, weedy clothes and placed them in the laundry bag. Wrapping myself in a fluffy white robe, I returned to the lounge. The laundry guy was already there.

Jason had a cup of tea waiting for me, the guys had coffee and the atmosphere was ... awkward. Someone had to start talking about the elephant in the room.

'Jason, I ...'

'Listen Jace, I ...' Ashley said.

'I need to know ...'

We stopped to see who was going to go first.

Jason had his hands on his hips. He took a deep breath and exhaled. 'I'm sorry to raise this after everything you've been through, but I need to know what's going on with you and Ashley. I'm assuming Inspector Johnston showed you the CCTV footage?'

We both nodded.

'Well?'

I remained silent on the grounds I would incriminate myself.

'It was convincing, don't you think?' Ashley said.

Jason clenched his fists. 'Convincing?'

'Yeah, I knew there was CCTV, so I thought a pash would add some realism to our story. Worked a treat, don't you reckon?' Ashley looked pleased with himself.

Jason stared at him with narrowed eyes.

Ashley made a face like the penny just dropped. 'Hell! Don't tell me you thought it was real? Shit, so that's what all the agro was about.'

Jason fidgeted and tugged at the neck of his T-shirt. 'It seemed real to me,' he said quietly.

'It was a pretend kiss, all part of the plan.'

'Was it part of your plan too?' Jason asked me.

Before I could answer, Ashley said, 'No way, mate. She was so surprised she fell off the chair.'

Jason rubbed his forehead. 'Right. It was a good plan then. Probably helped take the heat off us. I'm sorry for my behavior and for doubting you. It was very convincing after all.'

'Yeah, no worries, mate. Maybe I should go into acting if I'm that good.'

I shook my head in disbelief. 'You've got the Hollywood smile for it.'

The smile and the guile. I worried about Ashley's easy ability to spin mistruths. But who was I to judge? I was as guilty. I felt sad and bad for Jason. We were taking him for a sucker and it wasn't right. Ashley was culpable; he'd made the first move, and persisted. But I'd been too weak to resist. I could've told him where to go, but I didn't—because I didn't want him to go. I loved him too. It was hard not to. Everyone loved him. He could be rude, inappropriate, politically incorrect but he had charisma, a heart of gold and he called a spade a spade. He was a rascal, but I'm sure neither Jason nor I could imagine our lives without him. Still, things were complicated now. Too complicated.

Jason took two beers and the champagne bottle from the fridge. He poured me a glass of champagne and handed Ashley a beer. 'Sorry, guys.' He looked crestfallen. 'Here's to the three musketeers.' He held out his bottle and we clinked. 'To the three musketeers!'

'Come with me, Maggie.' Jason took my hand and led me into the bedroom, closed the door.

'What?'

'This.' He untied my robe and slipped it off my shoulders.

'I've still got weed in my hair.'

'I don't care.'

He grasped my shoulders and then ran his hands over my breasts and around my waist. He lifted my chin and kissed me gently, then deeply, as his hands gravitated to my buttocks. He lifted me and I wrapped my legs around him as he sat me gently on the bed.

'I thought I'd lost you,' he whispered. 'Lost you to Ashley. I was devastated.'

'You haven't. I'm yours.'

'I'm going to make sure it stays that way.' He lifted his T-shirt over his head. His body was lean and his muscles rippled. He unfastened his jeans, dropped them and his jocks, to the floor and stood looking down at me in his naked splendor. Holy moly. My knees were weak and he hadn't even touched me yet.

'Do you feel up to this? Are you okay?' He moved me further back onto the bed.

'Yes. I'm fine. I love you.'

Jason straddled me, held my face and kissed me deeply, before moving to my breasts and nipples, sucking and biting them. His hands moved forcefully over every part of my body and I groaned with pleasure and anticipation. I moved to reciprocate, to give him pleasure, but he held me down. He seemed different. Forceful, powerful ... driven.

I got it. Jason was making a point. Ownership and domination. A guy thing. Go ahead and make your point. He could dominate me to his heart's content, but only for as long as I let him.

'Don't move,' he whispered. He opened my thighs with his legs and teased my body with his tongue, mouth, lips and fingers, bringing me to exquisite heights of pleasure. Then he entered me, slowly, and I wanted him so much, so, so much. 'Come on, take me, Jason. Take me now, please.'

'You don't want me,' he whispered in my ear.

'I do. Yes. *I do.*'

'Like this?' He pressed his body hard into me and then withdrew.

My body shuddered with desire. 'Stop torturing me.' I tried to pull him closer.

'He pressed in hard again, then pulled away. 'Beg.'

'*What?*'

'Beg.'

'Okay. *Please!*'

'Beg some more.'

'*Please*, Jason.'

'More. You can do better.'

Damn your friggin' stupid power games. 'Fuck you!'

'No, Maggie. Fuck *you.*'

And he did. Well and truly.

Chapter 33: The Nature of the Beasts

Our bodies lay entwined in a tangle of sheets. Melded together in gentle bliss, relaxed, enjoying finally being in each other's arms, after everything.

There was a gentle knock at the door.

'Psst! You guys? Drom rang, and he's running late. He'll be here at half one. That's fifteen minutes. Maggie, your clothes are here. I've left them outside the door.'

We dressed, and I felt so happy and relaxed, I must've had a huge smile on my face.

Jason kissed me. 'Hey, my Maggie's back!' His face split into a crazy, gorgeous grin.

'God, I love you,' I said.

'Ditto. Big time.'

Click.

There it was. I felt it again. The sense of connection and deep love for Jason came flooding back. Ashley was a distraction. The emotions he generated in me could only lead to disaster. Jason was my one true love and always would be.

We returned to the lounge, where Ashley was kicking back on the couch having another beer.

'I thought you two were never coming out. A few in depth

conversations, I guess. Looks like you've made her a happy woman. I've been coaching him, Maggie, you know that, don't you?'

The man never knew when to quit. Jason threw a cushion at him. 'Shut it, Ash.'

There was a knock and Ashley leapt up to answer it, sliding his gun in the back of his pants. 'Who is it?'

'Drom.'

'No worries.' Ashley opened the door. 'Come on in.'

I gave him a hug. I could feel his bones through his clothes. 'Welcome to the Diplomatic Suite.'

'Hi, all.' He scanned the room. 'Very swish.'

'Beer?' Ashley said, proffering him one.

'Thanks, I'm parched.'

Drom dumped a carry bag of what sounded like rocks on the floor and removed the strap of his satchel from around his neck.

I could see Ashley and Jason checking him out.

'How are you, Maggie?'

I gave him the okay sign. 'A1. I didn't realise how bad I was feeling. I'm back to my normal self ... well, as normal as I can get.'

He laughed. 'There is no such thing as normal.'

Ashley pointed to Jason and me. 'Ain't that the truth, especially around these two.'

Drom rummaged in his satchel. 'I've got something for you.'

Jason and Ashley rocketed into high alert mode. Ashley reached around to the back of his jeans.

'Relax,' Drom said, handing me something wrapped in blue velvet. I unfolded the cloth to reveal—a crystal! Not dull, but shining with brilliant translucence.

'Drom! Where'd you get it?'

'From you.'

Me?

'Yes, you were clutching it in your hand when I dragged you

out of the lake. I put it in my bag for safe keeping and forgot to give it to you. Did you forget you had it?'

'I didn't have it to start with. How weird. I must've fished it out from the lake when I was half dead. Maybe that's why I was drawn there. Wow. So, this is another crystal. I wonder how many there are?'

'The number one hundred and thirty-seven comes to mind. On this continent anyway, or maybe the planet.'

'You know about them?'

'Yes. They're meteors from the beginning of time—keepers and restorers of light, destroyers of darkness. Generally, they lay dormant and only come to light and activate when an energy imbalance threatens to destabilise or destroy any part of the energy matrix in the universes.'

'Universes?' Jason said.

'Yes, there are infinite universes out there. Technically I should say there are infinite universes right *here*. Anyway, these crystals are specifically locked in to life forms which vibrate at their own energy frequency. Any life form, even inanimate objects can be aligned to the crystal, but primarily it's attuned to the energy field of a specific human life force. In this case, it appears to be you, Maggie.'

'Lucky me.'

'You may not be the only one, but I think you are the primary.'

'Primary?'

'The primary life force the crystals use to defeat the Dark Force and restore balance.'

'Crikey, I don't like the sound of that,' Jason said.

'Me neither!' I felt suddenly tired. 'I don't want to be used by anything or anyone.'

'The crystals won't make you do anything against your will. It's like you are the crystals, and they are you. It's a symbiotic relationship. You want what the crystals want, and by the way, you have done this before—all through time.'

'Huh. No wonder I'm tired.'

'You're talking about reincarnation?' Jason asked.

'Yes.'

Ashley rubbed his chin. 'Jesus. How do you know all this?'

'I'm kind of like Maggie, an intuitive, a psychic. I just know stuff. That's why I live my life the way I do, learning as much as I can. It's about remembering what I already know and following my inner compass, following where it leads and then doing whatever it is I'm called upon to do. I'm itinerant because of it, but my life is never boring. Boring would be good once in a while though.'

'You can say that again,' I said. 'Drom earns a living playing the stock market and doing a bit of prospecting, amongst other things.'

Ashley's ears pricked at the word prospecting. 'Huh, we dabble in a bit of prospecting, me especially. We'll have to have a chat.'

I held the crystal to catch the sunlight streaming in through the windows. 'So, what should I do with this?' The sunlight refracted through the crystal and a light blasted out, so bright we felt our retinas fry.

Ashley covered his eyes. 'Jesus! Put it away!'

I was impressed. 'Hell, there wouldn't be a shadow left standing after that.' I quickly wrapped the crystal in the blue velvet. 'I have another crystal. Ashley has one too. Mine saved our lives, but now it looks dead. It doesn't seem to have any energy anymore.'

Drom nodded. 'It's gone dormant. It'll reactivate in contact with another crystal. If it doesn't come in contact with another crystal, it will eventually reactivate on its own. You can help it along by washing it in salt water and leaving it in a sunny spot, or by burying it in the ground, or by leaving it in a body of water. Those things can help.'

'What now?' Jason asked. 'How can we combat this Dark Force?'

'You wait.'

'For what?' Ashley said.

'For whatever comes.'

'Why are psychics so bloody vague?' Ashley said.

I glared at him. 'Don't be rude. We do our best, and may I remind you, you're not always the cutting edge of clarity.'

'Point taken.'

Jason sighed and looked at me. 'It's the go with the flow plan.'

I nodded in my best sage like manner. 'What I don't get is if the crystals destroy the Dark Force, why are its minions so keen on getting their hands on them, Drom? Can they destroy the crystals?'

'They can't destroy them. Their purpose is to avoid having the optimum number of crystals together in one place, as that's what will generate enough energy to destroy the Dark Force. The crystals are scattered throughout our multiverses and they keep the balance between so called positive and negative energy, the yin and yang. The crystals only come together when the dark energy starts to dominate in a particular area.'

'So, the crystals are using me because the darkness is reaching critical mass on our planet, and I'm an instrument to facilitate the destruction of the Dark Force?'

'Yes, the crystals use their keepers to restore balance. You are a primary keeper. Jason and Ashley are Crystal Keepers too, as am I. When brutality and madness dominate anywhere, you know the dark energy is at work.'

Jason sat back in his chair. 'You're kidding me? Ashley and I are Crystal Keepers too?'

'Yep. At least that's how your energy signatures read to me.'

Jason looked glum. 'Oh great, so it would behoove the Dark Force to get rid of us?'

'Yep.'

'I'm confused,' Ashley said. 'Where does the dark energy come from?'

'In this case, it's the accumulated negative emotional energy of human beings. We've created it. With global populations exploding, humans are generating more and more destructive energy. Look at what's happening around you. Watch the news. It's the Dark Force daily update. The energy has become so strong and dense, it'll soon manifest in physical form. It's nearly there now.'

Ashley's hand automatically felt behind his back to check for his gun. 'Bloody hell.'

'I don't want to be an instrument,' I said, gloomily. Jason took my hand and gave it a squeeze.

'Yeah, it's a curse and a blessing,' Drom replied. 'Oh, before I forget, I've brought you these as a gift.' He tipped the contents of the other bag onto the floor. A pile of assorted, sparkly resin balls and pyramids rolled across the floorboards. Ashley held one to the light.

'What is it?'

'I make them. They're a mixture of metal shavings, crystals and copper wire, set in resin. Simply put, they transform dead orgone energy, which makes us sick, into good energy. They're useful at repelling anything that generates bad energy. If you put them around your room or house, they help to keep you healthy, protect you from bad entities. They also help neutralise the dead energy created by microwave radiation from mobile phones and cell towers. The one you're holding is called a Holy Hand Grenade.'

Ashley tossed it up and down in his hand. 'I like the sound of that.'

Ashley seemed taken aback when Drom said, 'I know you're thinking it's a lot of new-age hooey. However, it won't do any harm to put a few around the place. Totally up to you.'

'Another bloody mind reader,' Ashley grumbled.

'Thank you, we appreciate it,' I said.

'You're going to need all the help you can get,' Drom said.

'Great,' Jason said.

'What's the optimum number of crystals we need?' Ashley asked. 'And what do we do with them, if and when we get them?'

'I'm not sure, but I know you'll find out.'

'And what about the roaches?' Jason asked.

'Roaches?'

I was surprised. 'You don't know about the cockroaches?'

Drom was puzzled. 'No. I have no idea what you're talking about. In relation to the dark energy?'

'Yes,' Jason said.

'Give me a sec.' Drom sat quietly, closed his eyes and concentrated. His eyes moved rapidly beneath his eyelids. Finally, he spoke. 'The Dark Force takes over and uses other entities for its own purpose. I'm sensing the Dark Force has linked to a particular creature. Yes ... I see it ... a cockroach, but it's not actually a roach; it's a new life form.

Drom rubbed his temples and continued. 'This insect is unique. It has its own peculiar type of rage and supernatural powers. I sense the Dark Force is feeding off its energy. Shit, I've never come across anything like it before. It's a new and totally separate entity.'

Drom was like a coiled watch spring. He stretched his neck to the side as though trying to get rid of a crick. 'I'm sorry to say this, guys, but we are facing two threats, not just the Dark Force. The two entities have a symbiotic relationship. Each is using and influencing the other for its own purpose.'

I felt myself slip into Drom's mind. I didn't mean to, it just happened. I continued, 'They are linked by pure rage, but their purposes are different. The roach wants to rid the planet of the human scourge.' A chill ran along my spine. 'It hates us. I can feel it. The Dark Force wants to create more mayhem, it needs human negative energy—that's how it survives.'

'I don't get it,' Jason said. 'Which entity is after the crystals?'

Drom gave me a look. 'Looks like they both are.'

'Sorry, Drom, I didn't mean to get in your head. I wasn't trying to snoop.'

'I know, don't worry, you're welcome anytime. We glean more info by combining minds.'

'But why do they both want the crystals?' Ashley said, sounding frustrated.

'The dark energy needs to stop the Crystal Keepers getting the crystals together in one place. That's its primary objective. The easiest way to achieve its goal is by gaining control of, or destroying the Crystal Keepers,' I said.

Drom flopped his lanky body on the couch. 'I'm sensing the roach entity wants the crystals so it can control the Dark Force. The crystal power would give the roach entity the upper hand. If the roach has control of the crystals, it would stop the Dark Force taking over the roach and using the roach for its own ends. Having the crystals would give the roach supreme power over the dark energy, and probably everything else. We're caught between two powerful entities.'

'So, it's the roach that's chasing us, more than the Dark Force?' Jason asked.

'I reckon so. The Dark Force manifests as the shadow which has the ability to deconstruct matter. It eats the negative energy we generate and us as well, if it's so inclined. Getting rid of us prevents the crystals coming together. The roach entity on the other hand, wants the crystals and needs to use us to find them.'

Ashley rolled his eyes. 'Jesus Christ. We're on Candid Camera, right? Dead set. This is a joke.'

Drom and I spoke simultaneously. 'Sorry Ashley, it ain't no joke.'

Drom's phone buzzed and he jumped. 'Excuse me, I've got to take this.' He relocated into the kitchen, returning ten seconds later. 'Something's come up and I need to go. Sorry about lunch. Maybe another time?'

'Sure, no worries,' Jason said.

'I'll see you out.' I walked him to the door. 'Take care of yourself and thanks again, for everything.' I gave him a big hug.

'Look after yourself, Maggie. You have your guardians in there and I'm around if you need me. Destiny is at work and it will unfold your path for you. Try not to stress and think about things too much. Good luck!'

That's easy for you to say, I thought, closing the door.

---

[33] *Maggie's Playlist: Nature of the Beast — The Angels*

Chapter 34: Riot

'They are like wild waves of the sea, churning up the foam of their shameful deeds. They are like wandering stars, doomed forever to blackest darkness.' — *Jude 1:13*

When I returned to the lounge, the guys were quiet. Their brooding expressions and crossed arms told me something was up.

'What?' I asked.

'Can we trust this dude?' Ashley asked.

'He saved my life and gave me the crystal back. That's a pretty good start, don't you think?'

'Even so ... I don't know, there's something not quite right about him.'

Jason smiled. 'That's because he's got a man bag, isn't it, Ash?'

'Oh, for God's sake, it's a satchel!' I said. 'And what, you're worried he might be gay?'

'No, jeez, I don't care about that; some of my best friends are gay,' Ashley said. 'Look at Jason!'

Jason threw a cushion at him.

'See! That's what gay guys do, throw cushions!' Ashley said, baiting Jason.

He took the bait.

'I'll do more than throw cushions,' Jason said. He laughed, leapt up and grabbed Ashley by the wrists and forced his arms back. He put a knee across the top of his legs, pinning him to the couch. Ashley pushed against Jason and the battle of the biceps was on.

The guys had switched into alpha mode and were battling it out like two bisons for bicep supremacy. This could only end one way and that was badly. Their adrenaline was pumping and I sensed hidden tensions coming to the fore.

Jason's strength was amazing. He could never have tackled Ashley as hard before, and Ashley didn't like it one bit. They were both so stubborn someone would have to snap a bone before anyone relinquished.

'Enough, guys. Stop it, before someone gets hurt.'

Their muscles and bodies quivered with exertion and they ignored me. Okie dokie. The only way to stop them was for me to leave, then they'd have no one to witness their stupid alpha contest.

'I'm going out for some fresh air.'

I hightailed it to the lift. The doors opened as I arrived, so I hopped in and pressed for the ground floor. My plan was to go do some window- shopping. Hopefully, my departure would have brought my "guardians" to their senses and they'd come after me.

I stepped outside and found myself in the middle of two converging crowds. A tornado of hundreds of shouting, screaming youths descended upon one another. A chair flew through the air. I ducked. Its metal leg scratched my arm on the way past. Panic ran through my veins. Don't tell me this was part of the thirty-five thousand? Could it be? Thirty-five thousand roach controlled psychos? I was so dead.

Jason ran out through the hotel door and fixed on me as he pushed forward against the tidal wave of humans. He lunged to grab my hand. The river of thugs pushed us apart. It was at least twenty men across, and they swept me from his reach.

Voices shouted in unison, chanting something I couldn't

understand. The noise was deafening. Frightening. They took coffee cups, glasses, plates, ashtrays, anything they could get their hands on from the outdoor cafes. The air was filled with the sound of smashing glass and crockery as they hurled them at opposing gangs. A glass shattered at my feet and a shard nicked my ankle. Knives and machetes glinted in the light, clutched in strong hands. Surely, I was in another world? Melbourne, Australia? It couldn't be.

The dark atom quivered inside me as more people flooded from side streets to join the throng. This was the Dark Force in action, not the roach entity. I sensed the dark atom salivating with the explosion of negative emotional energy surrounding me. Hemmed in tight amongst the chaos and madness, swept along in a flood of testosterone-fueled hate, I had no choice but to run. Run with them, trying not to fall, an outsider, a diminutive girl dwarfed by walls of tall, lithe men. In their frenzied state, I don't think they even registered I was there.

Buffeted back and forth by the stampede, my nostrils filled with the stink of sweat and aftershave. I focused on my feet and the rhythm of the pack. One misstep and I'd be crushed, ground into the concrete by hundreds of Adidas and Nike clad feet. The dark energy loved a mob mentality. I could sense it drawing on their fury and violence, whipping these young men into frenzied states of emotional insanity.

The Dark Force was using Melbourne street gangs for food. A mixture of races, the mob wanted blood and I was trapped in their midst. Step by step I tried to inch across the crowd, work my way to the edge of the pack. The pack was of one mind and my head filled with images of their mindless destruction and rage.

We'd moved three city blocks before I finally worked my way to the edge and made a break for freedom. I fell against a nearby tree and gasped for breath. My body was shaking from head to foot with fear and adrenaline. I'd had a lucky escape. They were a crazed mob bent on creating violence and carnage, but they weren't specifically after me, which made a nice change. Really nice. These days, I was grateful for small mercies.

How to get back to the hotel? I needed to avoid the mob area as everything was in chaos and police were blocking off streets. Plus, I had no phone or money.

I'd double back using a side street a couple of blocks away, and return to the hotel via the rear entrance. That seemed to make the most sense, all things considered. I had to hurry; I was worried about Jason, and they'd be worried about me.

My knees had a life of their own—shaking uncontrollably— and my legs refused to work. Come on, pull yourself together! I needed to be strong, rough and tough. I had to be. My sister was, and I wished she were here.

---

34 *Maggie's Playlist: Devil Inside — INXS*

Chapter 35: The Cathedral

'For such are false apostles, deceitful workers, transforming themselves into the apostles of Christ. And no marvel; for Satan himself is transformed into an angel of light. Therefore it is no great thing if his ministers also be transformed as the ministers of righteousness; whose end shall be according to their works.' — *Corinthians 11:13-15*

'Are you all right?' a small soft voice right next to me asked.

I jumped, but relaxed realising the speaker was a child. I wasn't much chop at judging kid's ages, but this one had to be about eight. He had straight black hair, and his mother had a lot to answer for, as it was chopped into the worst bowl cut I'd ever seen. Parted in the middle his thick hair finished under his ears and curled around his cheeks like a helmet. He reminded me of the cartoon character *Prince Planet*.

His eyes were wide set; he'd have to open binoculars to maximum width, that was for sure. Narrow shoulders slouched inwards to an alarming degree. His spindly arms seemed too long for his body, and he wore leather bands covered in bristly leather spikes on his wrists. High-defined cheekbones sat above a thin wide mouth which curled to his ears—it gave him a strange other worldly appearance. What an odd little chap.

'Are you all right?' he asked again, reaching out to touch my arm with his spindly fingers. His eyes were large and almost black. He stared into my face searchingly, blinking.

'Ah, yup, I'm fine now. Just got caught in all the drama. Thanks for asking. Where are your parents? Are you with someone?'

He pointed a finger to the cathedral behind us. 'My dad's in the church.'

'I'm Maggie. What's your name?'

'Tapakah.'

'Tapakah? That's unusual.'

'It's Russian. Tapi for short.'

'How about we go find your dad? I don't think it's safe for you out here.' I offered him my hand. He put his thin little hand in mine, and I shivered at its icy cold touch. 'You're freezing! We'd better get you inside.'

He led me up the worn steps of the cathedral. The place seemed deserted. Our footsteps clicked across the ornate marble floors. The scent of incense permeated the space. It smelt lovely, like cedar.

Tapi pointed to the confessional box. 'My dad's in there.'

I wasn't a Catholic, but I knew what those fancy wardrobe thingies were.

'I guess we'd better wait 'til he comes out then.'

'I'm going to the toilet.' Tapi scuttled off along the aisle.

Gee, this was great. How long did the average confession take? I'd no idea. What if Tapi's dad had innumerable sins to get off his chest? He could be in there for ages and I needed to get back. The guys would be off their scones with worry.

I couldn't hear anything going on in the fancy wardrobe, other than maybe a couple of creaks in the timber. Maybe some whispering. It was probably rude to hang around so I moved away.

My footsteps sounded thunderous and echoed through the church. I tried to tiptoe. Jeez, you couldn't sneak up on anyone in here. Maybe I should take my boots off? Oh dear. Just like at the morgue.

Ticking sounds came from behind me. I stopped, turned around, listened. Nothing. A door creaked somewhere, a police siren. I continued and so did the ticking noise. I stopped and so did the noise.

The holy mother gazed down at me from a huge golden mural—it wasn't uplifting. Judging by the expression on her face, she seemed miserable. A noise like thunder shook the walls of the church, and the sound vibrated through my body. 'Jesus!' I clutched my chest in fright.

It was the church organ blasting deep ominous tones out through its pipes. I'm sure it rattled the foundations of the church. A massive ceiling light above, swayed slightly on its chains. Crikey. I hoped it was well secured. I stepped to one side.

That's when I felt a touch on my shoulder. I whirled around, fists clenched. It was a priest. 'Christ! You scared me. Oh, I'm sorry, I shouldn't have said that, taking the lord's name in vain an' all. Sorry.'

He laughed. 'That's okay, Maggie.'

The blood froze in my veins.

'H ... how do you know my name?'

'Tapakah. You brought Tapi in?'

I breathed a sigh of relief. 'Oh! Oh, yes, of course.'

'My name's Luca.'

'I love that name. My uncle was called Luka. Spelt L U K A, pronounced 'Loo-kah. Is yours the same?'

'Mine's spelt with a C, but pronounced the same. It means 'light'.

'That's a wonderful name for someone doing God's work.'

Luca was dressed in the standard garb of a catholic priest; black habit buttoned at the front, raised black collar with a cut out at the front highlighting the stiff white collar underneath. It sat right under his chin. That had to get annoying.

He looked Italian, broad face, square jaw, short black hair, trendy cut, thick eyebrows over big brown eyes.

'Would you like to take confession?' he asked.

'I'm not Catholic. I just brought Tapi back.'

'Have you been in this church before?'

302

'No, I haven't. It's beautiful.'

My bones vibrated as the organ blasted out a few more notes before falling into silence.

'Amazing! So loud.'

'Practice session,' Luca said.

Footsteps sounded out behind me, and I turned to see a row of priests approaching.

'These are my colleagues. Allow me to introduce you. Here we have Roberto, Giovanni, Leon, Gaetano, Francesco and Luigi.'

I had an Italian dude convention on my hands, and seriously, since when did priests look like this? Maybe I needed to take up religion. They were hot.

'You know how they have a calendar for fire fighters?' I said.

Luca smiled. 'Yes.'

'You should seriously think about doing one for the Vatican.'

He laughed. 'It's already been done.'

'Really? I'll have to get myself a copy. Do they sell them in the shop?'

'You'll find them online.'

The sunlight streaming through the beautiful stained-glass windows suddenly ceased. It was as though someone turned off a switch. Darkness brewed outside. Shadows arose inside the church and played in the inconsequential light, running their fingers over the holy relics.

I shivered. The church didn't seem so beautiful anymore. 'Looks like we're in for a storm.'

'It's already here.' Luca nodded to his brothers and they departed wordlessly in different directions. Heavy doors slammed shut and metal creaked as bolts were latched.

'Hell, I mean, sorry, I'd better go. My friends will be worried. They're waiting outside.' I made a move toward the door.

'No hurry. Why don't you join us for a cup of tea?'

Seven stiletto shoes. I needed seven stiletto shoes. The words kept running through my mind. They would make a good song.

'*She had seven stiletto shoes and she wanted to pay her dues, thrust them deep into their eyes, whilst ignoring their pitiful cries*'— sung to the tune of "Is There Life on Mars?". There certainly wasn't going to be any life here unless I did something, and fast.

It must've been mid-afternoon, but outside, it seemed like night had fallen.

'It's been a pleasure, but I must be going.' I hurried away. A hand gripped my shoulder—Luca either had very long arms or could move like lightening.

'Why don't you come with us?' he said. 'I'll show you the gallery; it's quite high.' He pointed halfway up the cathedral. 'It's a beautiful view. You'll have to be careful not to fall, but we'll look after you.' He smiled. 'We wouldn't want an accident. Or a suicide. Like your mother.'

Jerking myself free, I bolted along a pew. As I ran, I opened my mind and reached out for Drom. I felt an instantaneous connection.

Gaetano stood at the end of the pew. I vaulted across to the next one, but I was seriously outnumbered. Giovanni, with his perfectly groomed goatee and slicked back hair, was waiting for me.

Seven to one. They closed in. I must've been channeling Drom as I leapt onto the back of the next pew and balanced there, rocking backward and forward. Surprising myself, I leapt to the next one.

The pews were long and before they could get to me I jumped to the next, and the next. It was like playing a computer game, trying to anticipate who would go where in response to my move. Fortunately, I was excellent at computer games. Unfortunately, my physical abilities were more suited to sitting in a chair in front of a computer.

By the time I reached the final pew I was surrounded. The priests advanced. I jumped onto the seat and ran along it to the opposite end. They followed. I dashed back. They followed.

The priests were closing in and I froze watching them advance. Their creepy black tunics and white collars made them appear like floating heads in the falling light.

Thoughts of Drom focused my mind as they approached ... six feet, five feet, four feet, three ... *go!*

Leaping onto the back of the pew in front of me, I sprinted across a whole congregation of pews. Flying with God's grace— no thought, perfect coordination, totally in the moment. My sights were set on the front door.

I rocketed off the last pew. Footsteps resounded through the church as the brothers raced to head me off. Focusing on the front door, I tried to see how it was bolted. Glancing back to see how much time I had, I slammed right into the arms of brother Luca.

'Impressive.' He gripped my arm and twisted it hard behind my back. 'Come, we've wasted enough time with your games. We'd like to play a few of our own.'

'I'll tell you where the crystal is, and the location of all the tanks and infantry.'

'It doesn't matter; we have you.' His voice sounded disconnected, as though it belonged to someone else. His face contorted, rippling with opposing forces. He wasn't himself. Just like the guy who attacked me in the hospital, Luca was possessed. He was roached. He had to be.

'Luca! Listen to me; you don't want to do this. You know you don't, it goes against everything you believe in. Let me go. You can fight this! Fight it!'

His head twisted violently from side to side, as though some invisible thug was beating the daylights out of him. He groaned, and muttered, 'Down. Down to the crypts.'

I didn't like the sound of that.

'What happened to the gallery?' I said, trying to make conversation, all the while surveying the area for possible weapons. 'I liked the idea of the gallery.'

'Crypts,' he said flatly.

The brothers grim were bringing up the rear, while Luigi and Leon stepped ahead to open the door to the crypts. We descended rapidly, my boots slipping on the worn marble steps as Luca shoved me forward.

Giovanni and Roberto pushed past us, racing on ahead, their faces stony and expressionless.

We reached the bottom which opened out onto an area containing various large crypts. The light was dim and the temperature cool. Giovanni and Roberto hadn't simply been counting their rosary beads. At the end of the chamber, they'd prepared a cross, an upside down one an' all. Serious stuff.

Giovanni appeared stricken and Roberto was shaking. A puddle of vomit glistened at his feet.

'Don't do this!' I screamed with all the psychic force I could muster. They rocked backwards and for a split second their beautiful faces reappeared before being swallowed again by the darkness.

Luca and Giovanni pushed me against the cross and tied rope around my wrists and ankles. They pulled my wrists above my head and secured them to the cross, ditto with my ankles. My mouth was secured with tape and a bag was placed over my head.

A hand touched my chest. I flinched. Fingers ran between my breasts and played around in little circles as though trying to decide what to do.

'Ten years it's taken me to become a priest and I've never had a woman.'

It was Luca. His fingers continued to play their circle games before finally stopping.

He ripped the bag off my head, tore the tape from my mouth, and tied the bag around my eyes as a blindfold. What the hell was he doing? One minute I was going to be a priest's plaything, then letting me go?

The priests retreated; their footsteps moved away. Then silence—just the sound of my heart thundering in my ears, my breathing, and a sound like—approaching rain?

What was that noise? It sounded like fairies gently tapping on the keyboard of my MacBook. Hundreds of them—Tic. Tic. Tic. Tic. Tic. Tic. Tic. Tic. Tic. Tic. Tic. It filled the room.

The sound of retching and the splatter of fluid hitting the floor.

'Help! Help! Fire! Fire!' I screamed my lungs out. I'd read somewhere people are more likely to respond if you yell fire rather than help, so I gave it my best shot. Something weighty clung to the bottom of my jeans. Tiny pinpricks radiated up my legs as the weight shifted upwards.

Jason! Ashley! Drom! Help! I'm down here, help!

Tic. Tic. Tic. Tic. Tic. Tic. Tic. Tic. Tic. Tic. Tic. Tic. Tic. Tic. Tic.

The sound was all around me, all over me. An erratic scuttle scratched along my bare arm and I knew what it was.

Cockroaches.

I shut my mouth tight. No more screaming for me—except in my head.

Thousands of antennae and insectile legs prickled and scratched at my face, exploring every crevice. Probing insects rustled in my ears and tickled my nose. My blindfold shifted as they crawled underneath and the pinpricks of their stick legs pried into my eyelids. I squeezed my eyes tight. Insect legs poked and prodded at my mouth. They were trying to get in and I knew roaches could squeeze into the teensy tiniest of crevices.

My body was a clicking, hissing mass of insects. It was hard to breathe with them burrowing into my nostrils. I expelled the air through my nose trying to blow them out, but I barely had time to get another breath before my nose was blocked again. Smart. They were trying to get me to open my mouth by suffocating me.

They moved as one unit making their way under my clothes. I pushed out my stomach trying to stop them going into my pants, but they were already climbing on the inside of my jeans. My mouth and nose wasn't the only passageway into my body, and the thought made me retch as they crawled up my legs.

My head whipped from side to side as I tried to shake them off. I rocked my body and pulled frantically at my bindings. Side to side, backwards and forwards I jerked and tugged with frantic mania.

Unexpectedly, the cross jolted and cracked, slipping sideways, screeching across the wall. When it came to a stop, I was face up, nearly horizontal. The roaches piled on top of me. I flicked my head to shake them off, but at this angle, it made no difference.

The gallery would've been a better way to go. I was running out of air. They'd find a way into my body—it was only a matter of time. Would I implode into a black hole or turn into a roach controlled Maggie zombie? I wasn't sure which option I preferred.

There was a different touch. A touch of hands scraping bugs from my face and working on the ropes around my wrists.

My wrists were freed!

Sitting up, I flicked my head and scrabbled at my face. Neck deep in roaches, I kept my mouth shut tight. I ripped off the blindfold as someone worked to free my feet.

It was Luca.

Wild eyed, muttering, he tore at the ropes around my ankles.

Burn all these evils in hell, that they may never again touch me or any other creature in the entire world.'

My ankles were freed. He took my hand and pulled me to my feet.

'God the Father commands you. God the Son commands you.'

He dragged me behind him, our feet flying through the crypt towards the marble staircase.

'God the Holy Ghost commands you. Christ, God's Word made flesh, commands you.'

Behind us, the sound of a tide of cockroaches turning in pursuit, and the shouts of the other brothers.

'I command and bid all the power who molest me – by the power of God all powerful, in the name of Jesus Christ our Savior'

We made it to the door at the top of the stairs and Luca unbolted it.

'... through the intercession of the Immaculate Virgin Mary – to leave me forever...'

Luca took my hands, looked into my eyes, and then shoved me out through the door, slamming it shut behind me. Bolts clanked ominously on the other side as he sealed his fate. A prayer roared out through the door.

'...and to be consigned into the everlasting hell, where they will be bound by Saint Michael the archangel, Saint Gabriel, Saint Raphael, our guardian angels, and where they will be crushed under the heel of the Immaculate Virgin Mary. Amen.

I banged frantically on the crypt door. 'Luca! No!'

Cockroaches streamed out from under it, flowing like a river of resin up my legs.

Smash! An earsplitting noise thundered through the church. The sound of wood splintering, metal shrieking and tearing, the screaming roar of an engine. A Toyota LandCruiser exploded through the door of the church. It braked hard and the car spun wildly towards me in a cloud of smoke. It stopped three inches from my body. I held the bumper bar to steady myself.

The smoke cleared to reveal the stricken faces of Jason, Ashley and Drom in the front seat. Better late than never, I guessed.

The car doors were stuck. The guys kicked at them, metal shrieked, and the doors gave way. They leapt out of the car.

Shoulder deep in roaches, my mind raced. Luca! We had to save him. And what about the others? Maybe they were dead, the crypt as clean as a whistle. But what if they weren't?

Jason jumped over the debris to get to me. 'Maggie! Jesus Christ!'

The door behind me rattled, bolts clunked. The door opened.

'Get back!' Ashley screamed.

The guys took out their guns and trained them on the door.

It was Luca.

'Don't shoot him!'

Luca staggered out, pale and bloodied. He leant against the door jamb and ripped off the remaining shreds of his clerical habit entangled around his muscular physique. He stood there naked apart from his clerical collar and a pair of tight Homer Simpson jocks. He clutched a large bloodied crucifix in his hand.

I gasped. What a tremendous shot for the Vatican calendar.

In a trance, he continued his prayers. *'Most glorious Prince of the Heavenly Armies, Saint Michael the Archangel, defend us in our battle against principalities and powers ... against the rulers of this world of darkness, against the spirits of wickedness in the high places.'*

'Luca!' I held him by the shoulders and shook him. Nothing registered. I slapped him hard across the face. Focus returned to his eyes, and he looked at me. I could tell it was the real Luca.

'Hold this!' He thrust the crucifix into my hand. His face was fixed with grim determination as he began scraping handfuls of insects off my body. The roaches clung on with tenacious resolve, my body a crawling mass of chitinous shells.

'Luca, the others?'

'Gone. I think they're all gone.' He dragged me by the arm over to a pew and plunged his arms into the mass of roaches to lift me off the floor. He stepped onto the pew, held me over the edge of the seat and shook me, dislodging clumps of roaches.

Drom scattered holy hand grenades into the midst of the cockroach stream, which seemed to disorient and scatter them. Jason and Ashley found fire extinguishers and blasted the roaches with clouds of vapour. I could barely make out the guys

310

through the haze.

Luca shook roaches off me with violent intensity—my head was going to snap off any second. I opened my eyes in time to see Giovanni standing behind Luca. He had a dagger raised and it glinted gold in the soft light of the church. I screamed.

Luca moved to one side and held me tight. I thrust my arm over Luca's shoulder and rammed the crucifix into Giovanni's eye—just as he thrust the knife blade into Luca's back.

The top of the crucifix made a handy grip, giving me extra purchase as I thrust it in, again, right to the hilt. 'An eye for an eye!'

Giovanni fell backwards and smashed onto the marble floor. I had a strong feeling of déjà vu. Again. Well, that's what déjà vu is, isn't it? Again, and again, and … again.

Luca let me go. I leapt over the back of the pew and retrieved the crucifix from Giovanni's skull. It made a slurping noise as I pulled it out. Not good.

The guys materialised out of the mist—three strapping, burly, able-bodied silhouettes—like gorillas, I reckoned. The image lifted my spirits.

'Drag him into the crypt,' I yelled. 'He's going to blow. Barricade the door!'

Most of the roaches had left my body, and now, with only a couple of hundred crawling over me, I felt a rising tide of hysteria. Many of them were inside my clothes and caught in my hair. I brushed frantically at my scalp trying to flick them off. My head was filled with a loud, frantic rustling as they lodged in my nose and ears trying to settle in.

Screaming and slapping at my head, I jumped up and down, and ran on the spot like some hysterical psycho. I tore off my top. 'Get them off me!'

Luca snatched my top from the floor and wiped the roaches from my face. He plucked them out of my hair. 'Shhh, stop. I have them.' He held my head and extracted them from my nose and ears.

'They're in my clothes! Get them *out!*'

Jason undid my jeans releasing a flood of bugs.

Luca lifted me. 'Take her jeans off! Everything, off!'

Clumps of roaches fell to the floor. Jason brushed them off my body as Luca held me. He carried me away a few steps and deposited me in a roach free zone. The only remaining item of clothing was my bra. Ashley disengaged it with one flick of his fingers and yanked it off. Luca appeared impressed and shocked all at the same time. The bra was alive with bugs.

Ashley threw it on the floor in disgust. 'Jesus!'

Drom moved forward with his orgonite power wand, which resembled a bucket with protruding copper pipes. He pressed a button on an attached power pack and a blast of blue light flamed out from the pipes and enveloped us. Roaches scattered everywhere.

Another wave of roaches poured out from under the crypt door. I tried to run but my legs wouldn't work. Luca picked me up under the armpits and walked along the aisle a safe distance, careful to avoid any unnecessary body contact. His arms trembled from the effort and blood trickled down his body.

It was definitely not the time for prudery. I wrapped my arms and legs around him like a koala and pulled myself in close. I pressed my hand across the gash on his back to stem the bleeding. In my other hand, I held the crucifix. This baby was coming home with me.

The crucifix, that was.

A statue of Jesus Christ on the cross towered over our heads. So gaunt, I could count his ribs … one, two, three, four, five six … I'd seen better looking Auschwitz survivors. The white marble torso was gashed and streaked with blood. His head listed to one side, and blood trickled over his face from a vicious looking crown of thorns. It was a horrific representation of suffering. He looked as beaten and tired as I felt. I met his agonised gaze.

What did he make of the scene below him? A bloodied, semi-naked priest embracing a bloodied, naked woman holding a crucifix as a dagger.

The sun broke through the clouds and illuminated us in a single ray of dazzling light. I wasn't sure if it was a sign of God's blessing—but it felt like it.

We would need it, and more, to cope with the terror that lay ahead.

At least I wasn't alone.

I had Jason, Ashley, Dromeus, possibly the Maestro, and maybe Luca.

Six musketeers fighting against the Dark Force and an army of thirty-five thousand roach infested humans.

This wasn't the end. It was the beginning. This was our highway to hell—the beginning of the apocalypse.

We were going to need bigger guns.

---

[35] *Maggie's Playlist: Highway to Hell — AC/DC*

Appendix — Maggie's Playlist

1. Happy Wasteland Day – Open Mike Eagle
2. Crystal Ball – Pink
3. Time – Pink Floyd
4. Timebomb – Beck
5. Dust – Antony & Cleopatra
6. Bits and Pieces – The Dave Clark Five
7. Who Can It Be Now? – Colin Hay
8. You're My Best Friend - Remastered 2011 – Queen
9. Her Diamonds – Rob Thomas
10. You're the Voice – John Farnham
11. Revenge (feat. Eminem) – Pink
12. Strange Things – Tom Jones
13. I'm Too Sexy – Right Said Fred
14. Demons – Imagine Dragons
15. Bad Case of Loving You (Doctor, Doctor) – Robert Palmer
16. Love Me Now – John Legend
17. Help! - Remastered 2015 – The Beatles
18. Too Much Monkey Business – Chuck Berry
19. Last Tango – Jacki DePiro
20. Should I Stay or Should I Go - Remastered – The Clash
21. Who's Cheatin' Who – Alan Jackson
22. You're Looking Hot Tonight – Ivo Franklin & His Orchestra
23. Fight Like a Girl – Kalie Shorr
24. Tell the Truth (Live) – Eric Clapton
25. You Can Leave Your Hat On – Tom Jones, Anne Dudley
26. Pinky Swear – Jazmen Safina, Wrist.
27. Your Cheating Heart – Bruno Capinan
28. Drowning – Ellie Drennan
29. All for Love - From "The Three Musketeers" – Bryan Adams, Sting, Rod Stewart
30. Go with the Flow – Sara Niemietz
31. S.O.S. – ABBA
32. Love Is the Sweetest Thing – Al Bowlly
33. Nature of The Beast – The Angels
34. Devil Inside – INXS
35. Highway to Hell – AC/DC

Book Two: Journey to Hell
The Crystal Sphere Series by Ingrid Fry
Book Three – Quest for Light   Book Four – Search for Truth

Accidental contact with a mysterious Crystal Sphere changes the nature of a group of humans and a dog, forcing them on a terrifying quest to save the world.

The frightening mission continues in book two of the Crystal Sphere series.

Fate conspires to bring new Musketeers into the fold, and the action ramps up as Maggie is forced to deal with horrors both in the real world and the psychic realms.

Maggie is a keyboard warrior and feels ill equipped for the battle she must fight. With no shortage of romantic opportunities amongst the action, life becomes complicated. Will Maggie betray Jason?

Can Maggie and her motley crew—comprised of a plumber, booze hound, spiritual warrior, Catholic priest, nurse, Detective Inspector, Maestro and a beagle-cross—save the world?

The strange crystals hold the key to victory and survival, but Maggie isn't the only one who wants them.

Will they survive the onslaught of evil determined to stop them?
Who is the mysterious Maestro?
The truth shocks everyone.
Where does Maggie's heart really lie?
What's behind the mystery of her father's disappearance?

Time is running out for humankind, and it's certainly running out for Maggie. Evil is hot on her heels.

www.ingramcontent.com/pod-product-compliance
Lightning Source LLC
Chambersburg PA
CBHW050133120726
47903CB00002B/335